THE LAST OF THE TEMPLARS

WILLIAM WATSON is a novelist and playwright whose themes are chaos, faith, love and death. He was born in Scotland but has done much of his writing abroad, and if he writes in any tradition it is a European one.

Also by William Watson

BETTER THAN ONE
THE KNIGHT ON THE BRIDGE

William Watson

THE LAST OF THE TEMPLARS

THE HARVILL PRESS

LONDON

First published as *Beltran in Exile* by Chatto & Windus Ltd, 1979
Paperback edition published by Harvill, an imprint of HarperCollins*Publishers* in 1992

This edition first published by The Harvill Press
2 Aztec Row, Berners Road,
London N1 0PW

www.harvill-press.com

3 5 7 9 8 6 4 2

The lines from Edwin Arlington Robinson's poem, "Mr Flood's Party", are reproduced
from his *Collected Poems* by kind permission of Macmillan Publishing Co. Inc., New York.
Copyright 1921 by Edwin Arlington Robinson, renewed 1949 by Ruth Nivison

William Watson asserts his moral right to be identified as the author of this work

A CIP catalogue record for this book
is available from the British Library.

ISBN 1 86046 411 4

Printed and bound in Great Britain by Butler & Tanner Ltd
at Selwood Printing, Burgess Hill

Alone, as if enduring to the end
A valiant armour of scarred hopes outworn,
He stood there in the middle of the road
Like Roland's ghost winding a silent horn.

Edwin Arlington Robinson

CONTENTS

PART I. 1291

1	The ship from Acre	9
2	The Pilgrims' Castle	16
3	The Death of Aimard	25
4	The Chapter Meeting	28
5	Alexander	33
6	The Council in Sidon	38
7	The Fall of Sidon	45
8	King of Cyprus	54
9	The House on the Shore	61
10	Beltran and Zazzara	69
11	The Catalans	81
12	Diego and the Pirates	94
13	Geoffrey's Messenger	106
14	The Voyage in the Pinnace	114
15	Limassol	123
16	The Death of Thibaud	129
17	The Burial of Thibaud	139
18	Corberan	143

PART II. 1303–1314

19	Anagni	145
20	Diego and the Pope	157
21	Ruad	162

CONTENTS

22　Departure from Ruad　　　　167

23　The Counting House　　　　173

24　Clement in His Garden　　　178

25　Richerenches　　　　　　179

26　Nogaret's Men　　　　　186

27　Refitting　　　　　　　189

28　The Rhône　　　　　　195

29　The Wooden Tower　　　203

30　The Keeper of the Seals　214

31　The Cave　　　　　　220

32　The Oubliette　　　　　225

33　Nightride to Richerenches　230

34　A Quiet Farm　　　　　237

35　The Break-out　　　　243

36　Master of the Temple　248

37　The Bankers　　　　　250

38　Shirin　　　　　　　261

39　The Papal Bull　　　267

40　The Burning　　　　269

41　The Green Lizard　　274

42　Alexander's Heart　　277

PART I. 1291

Chapter One

THE SHIP FROM ACRE

IT was out of a midsummer storm that Thibaud Gaudin came to the Castle of the Sea. High on the castle wall the night watch saw his galley pass, bursting from the curtain of rain as the lightning broke the dark and vanishing again towards the shore. They stood amazed for moments after it had gone, the vision of it held like a dream before their eyes. Low in the water, the long beak spearing the wave tops, a handful of foresail and only two oars out a side, which were let go into the sea even as she shot from sight questing for the harbour entrance; figures on deck staring up at the castle and one of them shouting, shouting and waving, and as the rain closed again behind her the blue flame of St. Elmo's Fire dancing on the mainmast. Then nothing but the dream, and the rolling thunder, until wood struck stone with a crack like the world breaking and the three men looked at one another out of an unknown fear.

Night poured over them again. Beneath his feet, under his fingers which clutched the rampart, Beltran felt the castle shift, the whole island on which it stood move and swing through the air, flying over the sea towards the edge of the world. That was clear, that it was going to the edge of the world; and that the edge of the world was twenty leagues away was also clear. He was in terror. "I am afraid," he said. "Saint Hilary, I am afraid." He had spent a quarter of a century in wars, in one endless and inveterate war, a war cruel and without quarter, and he had seen whole cities full of dead, massacres of women and children, twice ten thousand in a day. In twenty-five years of this he had ceased to tell the tale of his dead fellows, since it marked him, he

being still alive, as strange. Dying in such great numbers over so
many years, his friends became in death his enemies, a great army
of skulls saying to him, "It is your turn today, tonight, tomorrow." Through all this he had not been afraid; fear had
touched him, panic sometimes; but nothing that could stop him
fighting while he could pass Christ's name through his lips.
Never until now had he been in terror, for to die was one thing,
to move from earth to heaven, be it in great pain from fire or
hacking wounds, was one thing; but this huge fall through the
passage of the dark, cleft from earth but not ascending, riding on
rock and castle under no stars to the end of the world, was like
the anger of God. "Saint Hilary," he said again. "I am afraid."

Lightning broke redly through the closed lids of his eyes, and
drew his gaze outward, where he saw his two hands fumbling on
the castle wall, and beyond them the same waves on which the
ship had ridden still marked with the spume of its path. He held
onto the stonework to let his hands be still, pulled in a breath of
air as if he had been about to drown, and let the fear fall back
into the pit which had opened within him. Possessed of himself
he moved from the wall, to see his companions still staring landward, and as if he had waked them they turned. The three came
together, huddled into the corner where the pot of charcoal
gleamed pale and bright in the wind.

Aimard said: "What does it mean?"

Honfroi said: "What were they shouting?"

His eyes looked into the pure heat. It was like a forge, from
which true steel was drawn ready for the purging steam. If his
eyes could be forged again, would they be bland, or would they
show his guilt? He had not known that a revelation would bring
guilt. He had thought two things of a revelation: that it would be
exalting and that its meaning would be plain. He knew that with
the terror through which he had just passed, or which had passed
into him, a revelation had come; and yet nothing had been
revealed. In place of exultation he felt the guilt of too much
knowledge better left unknown, and despite this loss of ignorance
he knew nothing he had not known before. The ship told its own
story, scarred and scorched, overladen and wearing the banner of
the Order: he knew what that meant, and he had seen such

messages before without hiding his eyes. Just before he knew he was going to lift his head, he felt the guilt which was also the fear, settle far in the depth of his spirit, and sorrow rose to assuage it, like calm lifting through the waters of a well when a stone has been tossed down. He looked at the faces before him.

"What were they shouting, Beltran? We could not hear." No one could have heard those tiny human voices thrown from the ship like leaves into the thunder of the wind and sea, but Beltran's arms curved round the edges of the ring of light and with a hand on a shoulder of each he answered them.

"It is what we expected," he said. "Acre has fallen." From far below them a bell pealed up through the storm.

"Come now," Beltran said. "We are excused the Office, since we are on watch, but we must make our prayers."

The arms of Aimard and Honfroi imitated those of Beltran, and making a circle of faith against the darkness they trusted Heaven.

*   *   *

Acre had fallen, Thibaud Gaudin said, and Tyre. It had been after dark that the wind veered north-west and the storm broke; during the day they had sailed a south wind up the coast. They looked into Tyre at sunset, and not until they opened the harbour mouth did they see the pagans lining the city's ramparts. It was very quiet, he said. There was no clashing of cymbals and no sound of drums and trumpets. He remembered that no one spoke on the ship either. The master sheered off and they sailed away. He did not think they had fought at Tyre; the city seemed whole.

They had fought at Acre.

Thibaud Gaudin, Grand Commander of the Order of the Temple, last survivor of the great officers of the Order, stood in his mail on the white sand, against the white wall, under the white sun, and looked at the small garrison of the Castle of the Sea. His mail was broken in seven places, its scars rusted with blood. A side of his face was spoiled by Greek fire. His figure was narrowed by all the light about him, and he was a man of so slight a build that as he stood there silent it became likely that he might shimmer away to nothing in the brightness and leave them looking at the empty wall.

They had fought at Acre for six weeks. No larger army than the Sultan's had ever been seen: he put a thousand engineers to undermine each of the twelve great towers; all that spring he made fire and arrows rain on the city; a hundred catapults thundered at the walls; and new mangonels called the Black Oxen threw their shafts down every street. "Beware the Black Oxen," Thibaud said. A week ago the walls began to crumble and the towers to fall, and the Christians fell back towards the sea: the citizens; the merchants of Pisa and Venice; the soldiers who had come from Cyprus; the Knights of the Sword and of the Holy Spirit, of St. Thomas and St. Lazarus, the Teutonic Knights and those from England and Syria and Switzerland, and the Knights and Brother-Sergeants and grooms of the Hospital and the Temple. Together they fought the last fight for the Holy Land until the end; they had been 15,000 men in arms against 200,000, and the end was that the Mamelukes swallowed up the city, and with it the last of the Kingdom of Jerusalem, killing every man, woman and child. It was a massacre, Thibaud Gaudin said, that must have equalled that in which the Kingdom was founded, two hundred years ago, when the first Crusaders slaughtered the Moslems and the Jews in the Holy City.

The Order of the Temple was the last to go down, Thibaud said. The great bourg of the Temple was the last to hold out. Its quay was the last place from which people could escape to the galleys lying off shore; when the galleys were filled it was the last place of refuge. The Master of the Order, Guillaume de Beaujeu, had been killed in the fighting, and the defenders held out for another week under the Marshall de Sevrey. "Yesterday morning," Thibaud said, "the Marshall took me to the sea wall. We had one galley there; the Treasury of the Order had lain in it for a month. He sent me here in the galley. They will still be fighting."

The light went on filling the air around him, but drops of blood lay on the white sand at his feet and the white wall had taken his shadow. Still he did not move. No one moved. It would be a brave man that walked across that little place. As if the bright heat made silence deeper, Beltran heard the sand crunch under his leather boots like blows striking at his ears. After some paces he felt himself under the weight of Thibaud's eyes, and yet as he continued to approach he saw that though they looked towards him their regard stopped somewhere in the space between, and this was so even when he stood at arm's reach.

The eyes were the palest grey, and bloodshot from the fatigue, fire and smoke of battle, and for a moment as he searched for their expression it was to Beltran as if they ran all to white like a blind man's. So from this, and from the earlier sense that the eyes did not quite reach him, now when those eyes finally touched his own the recognition he exchanged with them took him unawares and set deep in his breast like a pain. Within the exhausted spirit he saw the guilt and fear of the same knowledge that had descended into him the night before, when this man's galley came out of the storm like a ship running for doom. The thing moved in him now and he saw that it had uttered itself to Gaudin.

The pale eyes loosed their hold on him and Thibaud spoke. "They will still be fighting," he said, "but by tonight it will be over."

Beltran saw that Diego Maro, the Commander of the Castle, had also crossed that impossible desert, apparently both noiseless and invisible. Diego embraced Thibaud lightly, careful for his wounds, and he and Beltran stooped to let Thibaud's arms lie on their shoulders and took him back across the castle yard to where the knights in their white mantles, and the sergeants in their black, stood still in thrall to what had been told them in that stunning heat. Diego made one of those indescribable changes to his bitter countenance that those he commanded found perfectly explicit, and the knights and sergeants awoke and let them pass in at the door.

They surrendered Thibaud to the Infirmarian and to the Alexandrian doctor, and Diego took Beltran with him to the harbour. As they sat in the boat that ferried them from the island to the quay, Beltran let the blue sky dazzle his eyes, and Diego looked into the sea. They bumped against the side of the ship which had passed across Beltran's night like a phantom, and boarded her at the waist. Honfroi came down to join them on the half-deck.

Diego asked him, "What does the carpenter say?"

"The vessel's dry," Honfroi said. "For the weight in her, she's taking little water."

"Well, she's low," Diego said. He looked at the barrels that floored the ship. "That is a deal of treasure, but still she's low." He looked at Beltran. "What do you say to that Beltran?"

"It must be gold," Beltran said. "Gold Byzantines. I did not know there were so many in the Kingdom."

Diego scowled. "Come aft," he said. They went up to the poop and Diego stood there biting his thumb and kicking chunks of burnt wood down into the water. Finally he spoke.

"Honfroi," he said, "you're a sailor. I'll put the treasure into the castle before this wreck sinks, and then you will take it, this wreck, and go up to Tortosa and to Ruad and tell them what has happened. Tell them at Ruad to expect us all inside the month and tell them at Tortosa to get everything useful ready to go to Ruad, arms, clothes and provision, everything."

He turned to Beltran. "You will take the big galley and go down to Athlit. Bring them back here. They have over a thousand sacks of flour in that castle, so bring it back here, as much as you can without sinking the ship. Best pass Acre in darkness."

Diego looked at the burnt planks under his feet and stamped until at length his foot went through and they heard the debris rattle on the deck below. He looked up at the sky between their heads.

"Besides sailors and slaves you can each take two men, knights or sergeants, I don't care. You can't have more, in case you are all killed. We need enough of us to elect a Grand Master for the Order. We are only a remnant, but while the Order is in the East, the Grand Master will be elected in the East, according to the Rule. Try not to get killed, but most of all I want those galleys back. I'll give you four days, and then we shall hold the election. Take horses; you never know. Go with God."

He began to leave but stopped with his back to them and spoke towards the sea. "This election. You are young, Honfroi, but not stupid; you are experienced, Beltran: who would you choose?"

"Thibaud Gaudin," Honfroi replied.

"The same," Beltran said.

"Good," Diego said. "None other."

Chapter Two

THE PILGRIMS' CASTLE

BELTRAN and Olivier looked across the Bay of Athlit into the thinning darkness and waited for the sun to rise. Two hours before they had laid the beak of the galley to the jetty under the south wall of the castle, and meeting no challenge had backed off again, this time towards the beach, and when the sternpost had touched sand Aimard had swum his horse ashore. The horse had been forced over the side squealing and beating its hooves on the deck and bulwarks. For some time after Aimard reached the shore they waited, but there was no response to the uproar, and when they heard horse and rider move off the galley withdrew to the safety of the open bay.

"If he is there when the sun comes up," Olivier said, "that will mean something, signal or no signal."

Beltran made no answer.

"I mean that if *they* are there, a child like Aimard will not have lasted these two hours."

"I know," Beltran said.

"And he has no armour," Olivier went on. He peered at Beltran in the light that now had started off the land.

"The better for his horse to run," Beltran said, "but you are right, Olivier: if Aimard does not appear on the ridge, it will mean the Mamelukes have him. Then I will know they are there." Beltran looked up the bay, where the mass of the castle had grown into sight.

"You sent him as a sacrifice," Olivier said.

Beltran laughed with impatience. "We are all a sacrifice here. Aimard, the Order, every Christian in the East."

"It is true," Olivier said. "We have been forgotten by God. I pray to the Virgin now."

The towers of the Pilgrims' Castle lifted a hundred feet into the sky which roofed the new day in blue and gold.

"You are a poet, Olivier, so you can make such answers."

The colours of the sky sank into the water and while the galley floated on a sea of light the slaves at the oars stretched in the fresh warmth. Beltran turned to the sun. He rubbed a hand down his face, which felt like an old saddle that had been left too often in the sun without a cloth over it; heat and iron had cracked it and dug at it.

Olivier said, "Look, there he is."

Half a mile away Aimard walked his horse onto the crest and sat there while the sky behind him blazed into morning. His shape and the horse's coiled and flickered as if consumed by flame while on the ship their eyes strained and blinked to watch.

"He does not signal," Olivier cried.

The horse began to pace and as it came out of the glare to move against the clear sky they saw Aimard draw his sword and wind it over his head. Above his white mantle and the red gleam of his hair sparkled the silver flashes of his sword. The horse passed along the height of land behind the bay, and still the sword turned and turned throwing its beams back to the sky. They watched in horror.

"I said three times," Beltran said. "Did I not say three times, and then down off the skyline?"

"Yes," Olivier said. "Come down," he bellowed to the boy up on the hill, at the far end of the bay; "they will see you for twenty miles."

Beltran smiled with vexation. "Take her into the jetty," he told the shipmaster, "while the coast is clear. Olivier, I'll have the slaves unshackled and you will govern the loading of the flour."

The shipmaster had not moved. "You will have me lie on this coast with the oars unmanned?" He looked at the castle. "You think the garrison has left. Then surely the Mamelukes will be in the castle!"

"No," Beltran said. "I don't think they are."

Olivier interrupted. "Why not?"

"Because the Mamelukes are crafty," Beltran told him. "That is another reason why Aimard is dancing around up there. If they had been in the castle, they would have hidden a troop or so over the ridge. If they are not over the ridge, they are not in the castle either."

The master began to protest again, but Beltran grabbed the man's head in both hands and spoke close into his face. "You are trembling, Master Terence. I think we must all tremble while God's Kingdom falls and yet we must do our duty. Take her to the jetty!"

As the galley pulled over to the pier Beltran looked up at the Castle of the Pilgrims. It hung over his head like a giant's stronghold. It could house two thousand men, but he knew from Diego that lately it had held but a dozen. The walls were fifteen feet thick and rose fifty feet in squared and polished stone. On the east, where the two great towers fronted the land, a moat had been cut across the promontory which could be filled with sea water in time of siege. Within were a palace and a church, and a veritable town of dwellings. Beltran had served three years there and loved it, not for its strength, but for its vineyards and orchards.

Beltran spoke to Olivier. "You and I will make sure of things. We shall go armed, and we shall ride. Shipman, you can keep the slaves to your oars until I call you."

They sat on their horses, silenced by the great wall before them. It stretched from sea to sea across their sight, and if ten men could have stood one on top of the other the highest head would have reached the parapet. Although it so diminished the men before it this tall screen of masonry might, in the fresh light of the morning, have laid on them the serenity that descends from so much weight of force shaped and made still by human hands: were it not for the two towers. They were twice the height of the wall and almost their own height in width, a dimension so gross that the senses cowered from it. It was true that the purpose of the whole structure was defence, and that the towers with their sixty arrow-slits from which archers could ply all the ground before the wall filled out this purpose to the last degree, but the hugeness of these massive salients had built into them a menace so stark that the first impulse was to turn away.

It was the radiance that prevented this. The whole work was

made of giant blocks of stone, that white stone of the country which was just touched with pink, and each stone had been squared and smoothed and finally polished, to make of this wall binding the tip of the promontory—this wall behind which stood the last great fortress of the Templars to which the little castle at Sidon would have been no more than a hut—a shining curtain that shone back to the sky the brilliance showered on it by the newly risen sun.

Beltran's first course on landing had been to patrol the far side of the ridge from which Aimard had signalled that there was no sign of the enemy; for Aimard had not returned to the shore. They found neither friend nor foe, and so came to those meadows and fields of corn opposite the stem of the peninsula where the cultivated lands of the castle began, and which opened, for the poet Olivier, on a picture of Vergilian delights.

In the fields the summer wheat was heavy and turning dark, and as they passed along the sheep-walks the animals ran from them but stood in groups to watch their passing, bleating for company. In the woods finches sang and kingfishers and bee-eaters splashed colour through the leaves, while pheasants long undisturbed capered from under the horses' feet and went on feeding like tame fowls in a farmyard. After the wood they went down the floor of a valley terraced with vines. Beltran was now saying good-bye to his estate, to the Order's estate and therefore to his estate, and had the upper slopes of the valley been lined with Mamelukes instead of grapes he would have let his horse walk on until the ambush was sprung, for all his military wits were asleep and he was awake only to the husbandry of his Order.

They wound their way up a ravine where the track shared its passage with a watercourse that came down in steps and sluices to nourish the fertility behind them, and they came out among olive trees to look on the orchards spread over the plain below. There they drank of the stream, chill from its nearby spring. Beltran found that he had made his adieux to these pastoral delights that had once been a part of his life, and he became benevolent. He spoke to Olivier in a voice unusually diffident.

"You have read the Book?"

"Ah, Beltran!" Olivier exclaimed. "Yes," and he began to recite,

> "O fortunatos nimium, sua si bona norint,
>   agricolas! quibus ipsa, procul discordibus armis,
>   fundit homo facilem victum iustissima tellus."

"No, no, Olivier," Beltran said, half serious and half laughing. "The Book of Husbandry of the Order. You must read it; indeed I think you ought to have read it. You never know when you may be appointed to run a house of the Order. It says precisely how everything is to be done, everything. Ploughing, viticulture, tree-plantings, lambing, fruit-growing." He broke into this horticultural litany and pointed through the olive grove to the fig trees which grew beyond. "See, round the trunks of the fig trees!"

"See what?" Olivier asked.

"There is a circle three paces round each trunk where the ground has been hoed. You will not find that in many orchards, but it is done according to the Book of Husbandry."

"Why?"

"Bigger fruit, and sweeter."

"Then," Olivier said, "doubtless it is in Vergil."

"Bah," Beltran said, and laughed. "You are a fool, Olivier."

"We are both fools, but I shall read your book."

"Come now," Beltran said, "and you will see something."

"Something else? What a foolish morning! Are no men living but us?"

They went down through the olive trees and across the plain of orchards, pulling from the trees as they passed figs swollen with ripeness, almonds, sultanas and oranges until their saddle-bags were filled. Beltran led them slantwise across the flat ground so that instead of climbing the rise in which it ended, they passed round the slope's northern flank along the edge of the sea.

"Look," Beltran said. "Salt-pans. Everything."

Olivier said, "I have seen salt-pans before. Is this your something?"

"Wait!"

They rounded the hill and plunged again into trees, this time of camphor and myrrh whose scent lay heavy on the air. The ground here rose and fell, folding in long waves not parallel but running on irregular courses, so that the trees did not progress in orderly rows and the view ahead was closed off by them. They were well into the trees when they became aware of the strange light that trickled through the leaves in front of them, growing into brightness as they advanced. Beltran drew back and watched Olivier. He saw him lift his face to the sky as if to be sure that overhead it was still blue. Where the trees thinned out Olivier began to canter and he went out of them at a run. Beltran followed more slowly and as he crossed the space before the gleaming wall he saw that Olivier sat on the ground with his chin in his hands gazing at the bright wonder like a child. Beside him his horse cropped the grass.

Beltran kept careful eyes on the wall, and above all on the gate that faced them across the wooden bridge, and was open. He spoke Olivier's name, and the knight climbed into the saddle and rode over the bridge with his horse's hooves beating harshly against the light and vanished into the darkness of the gateway. So they came to the Castle of the Pilgrims, and it proved to be empty of men.

*   *   *

The slaves rested in the shade of the granary. From the window of the refectory Olivier watched them and wished Beltran would finish his meal. Beltran was a stickler for the Rule. They had said their Paternoster and sat down and begun to eat, and Olivier had said, "These slaves look as if they long to be back at their oars!"

"Olivier," Beltran said, "we are at meat."

"Yes," Olivier replied.

"We must not talk," Beltran said. "It is the Rule."

"You are too strict with yourself," Olivier said. "We are on campaign."

"We are in a refectory of a house of the Order."

They stood, and said their Paternoster again, and sat down to eat in silence. Beltran had the right of it, and Olivier knew that. It was not pedantry, Beltran's observance of the Rule, but custom, and faith, and obedience to their monastic vows, all of which joined together with their duty as warriors of Christ to make the Order, and without which the Order would not be. Six months ago their little wrangle would not have taken place, since Olivier would have had no thought of talking during meat. But six months ago the Holy Land had not yet fallen, and six months ago ships had not been sent north and south from Sidon to collect one garrison out of all that remained of the Order. All that remained of the Order in the East; for the Order had castles and men all over Europe, from Castile to Scotland.

Olivier finished his meal and went to the window. He himself had been inducted into the Order at Bayle in Provence, his own country, but he had been sixteen years in the Kingdom of Jerusalem and the life of the Order in Provence did not remind him of the life which had grown round him here and which was melting these last few days like snow in the desert. He found Beltran at his shoulder.

"Beltran," he said. "My faith is in tears."

"No," Beltran said, "it is not. A poet's fancy cannot reduce faith to tears. You deceive yourself, talking like that."

"I do deceive myself," Olivier said. "I cannot help it. Suddenly my faith is not where it was. I am afraid."

Olivier went on looking at the slaves, and he heard Beltran stamp about the vast and echoing refectory.

"This floor," Beltran said, "this floor of stone is built on vaulting of stone. It holds up my feet; I stand on it. It does not hang in the air, though if you could not see what held it up you might think so. It stands on vaults because when we built our castles here we found there was no wood to spare for rafting floors and laying roofs. This floor is stouter than a floor laid on beams." Stamp! Stamp! Olivier turned to look at him. "It is stouter," Beltran said again, and almost shouted. "When you were a child, your faith was not the same as it is now. Faith moves with life. Life has moved suddenly these last ten years, and these last ten weeks still more suddenly."

"Ten days," Olivier said, "ten hours. Heraclitus. Lucretius."

"What?"

"Go on," Olivier said. "Stamp on the floor again."

"You stamp on the floor!"

Olivier stamped on the floor. He jumped in the air and stamped on it. Beltran too jumped and stamped. They moved round the refectory jumping and stamping on the floor. When they began to laugh they had to stop jumping, for want of breath.

"These," Olivier said, "will be the last Christian feet that stamp on the floor of the refectory of the Castle of the Pilgrims."

Beltran looked down at the stone flags. "Your faith will catch up," he said. "Whatever it is doing now, it will catch up." He moved to the window where Olivier had stood. "What was it you said about the slaves?"

"That they'd rather be back at their oars than heaving sacks of flour."

The slaves had formed themselves into a chain again and the flour passed along it from the door of the granary to the castle wall. There was a loading gate in the wall high over the harbour and a tackle there, manned by sailors, lowered the sacks to the quay.

Beltran came away from the window and said, "I suppose even a galley-slave has his trade." He tapped at the floor with his foot as if trying whether a well-placed toe might break it. "Our trade will not be the same. After we leave Sidon it will surely be different." Their eyes met without frankness, trying to hide the fear of what change would mean.

Beltran came back to earth. "Now I shall seek Aimard," he said. "When the flour is loaded you will have the galley moved round to the seagate, and make ready to quit here in a hurry."

"Yes," Olivier said. "Very well."

Beltran looked at him still, though he did not want to. "What's the matter?"

Olivier said, "You too are waiting for your faith to catch up."

"Oh, yes," Beltran answered, and felt his shoulders ease, and then despite himself his voice went on. "For something else, also." The ship leaped past him out of the storm under the lightning, with the figure standing at the stern.

"I will go to the chapel and pray," Oliver said. There were two oranges left on the table and he picked them up and gave them to Beltran. "You will want these."

Beltran took them but offered one back to Olivier. "Share and share alike," he said, and then, "What's wrong?" Olivier had spurned the fruit with a gesture.

"The Rule, Beltran," Olivier said, "the Rule! I cannot pray with my mouth full." It was a feeble joke, but there was some return of life to that round, olive-plump face.

Beltran laughed. "Being so generous. Olivier, pray for yourself as well as me." He took up his sword and went to the door, where he paused. "How will you pray? Tell me, and I shall think of it."

"The wicked flee where no man pursueth," Olivier answered. "I shall pray that we do not flee from our faith."

Straight to the point; right into the bone. Beltran was transfixed and hung in the doorway. You forgot that Olivier could pierce so cleanly to the heart of a thing. He went on through the door to find his horse.

Chapter Three

THE DEATH OF AIMARD

THE hollow would have made a natural amphitheatre but for the hillock in the middle. On the slopes inside the hollow the Mamelukes were making their mid-day meal, and on the hillock sat Aimard with his horse standing beside him, its head on its master's shoulder as it dozed in the heat gathered by the lifeless air of the bowl. As soon as this picture was painted on his sight Beltran bent in the saddle and slipped off his horse. He led the animal back down the hill, drove his sword a foot into the ground and looped the reins over it, lifted his Turkish mace off its hook, and tied a cloth round the horse's head.

He began to climb the hill. When he was past halfway up he went down on his belly and set himself to crawl to the top. His chain mail slipped on the baked red earth and when he brought up his right knee the knife in his boot caught on a stone. He took the knife out and left it. He struggled on. A full sweat broke out on his body so that the padded jerkin under his mail sucked and squelched on and off his skin. Again, bringing his right knee up, the shield fell from his back and turned him on his side. He got to his hands and knees and worried his way out from the strap of the shield like a terrier working backwards out of a thorn bush. He sat. He was full of temper and there was no grace in him. He was in a rage with himself and with Aimard. There was much good in the boy but he was fond of heroical gestures, and now he was going to die of them.

At the first glimpse of Aimard trapped in the hollow Beltran had known the whole tale. That the young knight, taking the blame for drawing the Mamelukes towards Athlit, had led them off in chase of him till he was brought to bay, and that it had then suited the Mamelukes' humour to withhold the coup de grâce while they sat round him and dined. Aimard could have thrown himself among the heathen at any time and ended his ordeal, but Beltran saw that he had made a little Calvary of it for the sake of his friends; he had sat there to keep the Mamelukes amused, and to keep their interest from straying to the coast. All of this, Beltran had known on the instant of seeing Aimard, and it was because he knew also what was to come that he climbed the hill again: for in that instant Aimard had seen him, and knew it was time to make an end.

Beltran undid his long dagger, its belt and sheath, laid them beside the shield and resumed the ascent. He kept his mace; a man must have some weapon. He hunched himself together and stretched, hunched and stretched, and as he stretched found that the jerkin had caught in a loose rivet of his chain-mail. He turned on his back and worried it free.

"He knew I would come—he knew it would be me. He knew I'd be quick enough to hide myself. He did not know a regiment of Mamelukes would make me old and clumsy like this. He will expect me to see the rest of it. I should not do this. My duty is to the ship."

He turned on his stomach again and drew near to the top, crawling with bitter carefulness, uncouth, stupid to the uses of his limbs, thinking slowly and in words—"Now this hand, now pull. Now this foot, now push!"—heavy with contempt for the lumbering carcase he had become. Under the rim he laid aside his flat iron cap, and pulled the mail hood off his head down onto his shoulders. His toes and fingers scrabbled in the crumbling slope as he dragged himself to the edge and looked over.

The Mamelukes were stirring, some of them on their feet, others already mounted, for Aimard had moved. Upright on his knees he still faced to the west, and with his hands clasped before him he prayed with his eyes open. Beltran's own eyes filled with sweat. He slipped his right wrist from the thong of the Turkish mace to wipe his brow, and the head of the mace ran round a little mound so that the weapon rolled down the forward hillside, where it stopped at once but pushed a fall of stones on their way to the floor of the hollow. Aimard stood up and just as the trickle of pebbles reached the heel of one of the unmounted Mamelukes and the man began to look round, the whole regiment mounted and the heathen shook the dust off his crimson leather boot and sprang onto the back of a restless Barbary stallion. Like its fellows the stallion squealed and pitched, expectant to be on the move and impatient at being still restrained, and all round the shallow crater colour flowed and danced in the robes which the Mamelukes wore over their mail, and their round shields and conical helmets sparkled in the sun.

At the centre of this tumult Aimard now sat on his warhorse like a symbol of his beleaguered faith, his only colours the red cross on his white mantle and the gilded curls on his unprotected head. The boy drew his sword and held the cross of the hilt to his lips. He lifted the sword in the air and with what Beltran took for an ironic farewell wound it three times round and sent his horse down the slope.

Once over the heads of the now silent pagans came the young voice shouting the war-cry "Beauséant," and then for a brief space Beltran saw the golden head among the risen swords and axes of the Mamelukes before it burst into blood. There was not a man below who was not intent on Aimard's martyrdom, and while they finished killing him Beltran rolled over the rim of the hollow and back again with the mace in his hand. When he looked there a last time he saw the blue eyes staring blindly at him from part of a head jumping on a spear-point, and he stumbled down the slope, gathering his accoutrements to him, dragging them after him as he went. When he reached his horse he threw them down and stood shaking.

He made himself wait until he was steady, and then hung the mace on his saddle, belted on his dagger, struck the little knife back in his boot, slung his sword at his side and his shield on his back, and settled the iron cap on top of his hood of mail. He mounted his warhorse and looked back up the slope. It was not the death of Aimard that had made him shake. It had been glorious to Aimard but not to him: to him death was commonplace. It was the journey up the slope that had made him shake. It made no sense to him. He rode towards the sea.

Chapter Four

THE CHAPTER MEETING

"WE are between the sword and the wall," Diego Maro told them. "We will not be left in peace here for long." He looked round the chapter-house at his fellow monks: eighteen knights in their white mantles, eleven sergeants in their black, and seven unmilitary brothers in brown. One old knight lay on a mattress.

"How is Alexander?" Diego bent over the old man and put a hand into his fingers, which folded round it like a feeble trap.

"He does very badly," said Evrard the Infirmarian. "He should be in the infirmary."

The faded blue eyes were bloodshot and rheumy and pain had settled there, but they spoke fiercely to the man bending over them. Diego touched the pallid brow. It was dry and hot, like the clutching fingers. "In the infirmary?" Diego said. "I don't see why." The fingers eased and lay loose in his own. "He would die of rage if you took him back there." He whispered in Alexander's ear, "Fier comme un écossais." A sarcastic smile turned down the old mouth.

The Templars of Sidon were all that remained of the Order in the Holy Land, and had they called in their detachments from the northern castles of Ruad and Tortosa they would have mustered no more than fifty men; but the Order had always elected its Master in the Holy Land, and would do so while it had a foothold left to it.

"We are now met as Chapter-General of the Order in the Holy Land," Diego said, "and our task is to elect a Master." He looked at Thibaud who nodded slightly. "Well then," Diego went on, "first of all we choose who is to be Grand Commander; the Grand Commander will stand in the place of the Master until a new Master has been elected and then he will become as he was before. This is according to the Rule."

Diego was elected Grand Commander without dissent. He was much moved and his face, for once, failed to protect him by expressing a contrary passion. He looked at them, he looked at Thibaud, and he looked down at the old knight on the bed. "I feel no different," he said, "and I have not grown wiser." He thought for a moment. "We have wisdom in this chapter," he said, "but we have also wisdom that has sat in the high councils of the Order. Thibaud Gaudin is Commander of the Land of Jerusalem, and being so is also Treasurer of the Order, and the fourth man in the Order after the Master, the Seneschal and the Marshall, all of whom are killed. I will therefore," and he stopped.

He swallowed like a man taken with nausea and pallor came over his sallow face so quickly they thought he would faint. He looked at them askance. "I go to pray," he said, and stalked out of the room, his feet falling a little askew but a visible force of spirit driving his legs on until he went safely through the door. Thibaud let some moments pass and followed him.

"Why did he look at us like that?" Honfroi asked those near him.

"Honfroi, my dear," Olivier said, "he looked at us and saw the Order. He saw a thousand dead knights, a thousand dead sergeants, the Marshall, the Commanders of Provinces, the Commanders of great castles, not little forts like this. He saw hundreds of the Order, high and low, assembling to elect a new Master, and then he saw that we were those hundreds, we, less than two score men. He saw that we were all the Order in the East, we men of Sidon.'

Beltran's memory carried him on a journey of eighteen years to the castle of Tortosa. He had come there in the train of the Commander of the Pilgrims' Castle to the election that made William of Beaujeu, he who had died at Acre, Master of the Order. Already the Christian kingdom had been driven in to the cities of the coast, but it expected to spring back again. The Templars had come in their pride to their greatest castle to choose their greatest man, and they were the greatest Order in the land; even the Hospital had but a third of their strength. Over a thousand were housed comfortably at Tortosa. Beltran prayed beside Commanders of Provinces and heard Mass beside high officers of the Order. Great magnates of the Church and the State, and rich merchants from Venice and Genoa, were to be met at every turn of a staircase.

After the first meeting of the electors a light galley of the Order was made ready in the harbour, and on the third day at dawn five men boarded the vessel and it sped into the West. Only then was William's election proclaimed. The nobles and bankers met this news with much excitement, for William of Beaujeu, it transpired, was kin to the French throne and even now in Sicily with his cousin the terrible Charles of Anjou, he who had murdered Conrad of Hohenstaufen and thus acquired a claim to the Crown of Jerusalem. A crusade might follow. All that followed was civil war, and a dark cloud obscured that mid-May of long ago: Beltran came back to the chapter-house of Sidon. Thibaud and Diego had returned.

Thibaud was saying, "We are one chapter of the Order and there are close to fifteen hundred chapters in Europe."

The men round Beltran moved uneasily, and a knight older than Beltran, Alonso de Luna, put the question. "We believe that since we are the only chapter surviving on these shores, then we become the Chapter-General of the Holy Land: seigneur, is this your own opinion?"

"Yes," Thibaud said. "I am in no doubt of it. But we shall do wrong not to feel the gulf between this little castle and this little band that we are, and the great power to which we appoint a Master. We can choose a Master from Europe, we must remember that too. He need not be here for us to choose him Master."

What had been so clear to them, this task at once proud and humble, both defiant and full of despair, now suddenly became uncertain. Beltran did not quite believe his first thought: surely the man wanted to become Master? Was he trying to avoid it? Whose voice was that?

"There is more blood of Templars in the Holy Land than there is walking in skins in Europe!" It was the Magyar.

The Chaplain rebuked him. "It is my duty, Andras, to chide those who speak intemperately in the Chapter. These are heated words."

"I am not heated," Andras said furiously.

"It may be that you are not, but such a way of talking will heat us, and our meeting will no longer be peaceable and mannerly, as the Rule demands."

The Magyar set his teeth together and then breathed out. "You are right," he said. He settled himself to start again. "The power of the Order is in Europe, but there is power in the spirit. Ten thousand of the best swords in Europe will not win back Jerusalem, if they abide in Europe. The sword and the spirit of the Order are in the Holy Land. They are here in Sidon, and with our brothers in Ruad and Tortosa. They still hang above Acre. He whom we choose for our Master will be a hand to hold that sword."

Thibaud Gaudin held himself with his head forward, quick-faced and listening, as if each moment had a heart and he could hear it beat. As on the day Beltran had crossed to him in the courtyard outside, the point of his gaze stopped in the air and did not reach the men opposite. What Beltran saw was a face, that side of it that had not been burned at Acre, smooth and hardly touched by age and yet of that full experience which men mostly wore upon their skins like armour, closed and scarred. He is as much older than I, as I was to Aimard, Beltran thought. He is what we call wise, a man of state, but he carries himself among us freely enough. I think he is true. He is more subtle than I understand, but he is true. I will have him for my Master.

Beltran said, "Andras has spoken for us. We are plain brothers of the Order and there is no rank or fame among us, but since the Rule allows us to elect a Master then it also means us to do so. We will at least be electing a Master for the Holy Land." He nibbled at his lip, consulting himself. "It seems to me that now we have elected a Grand Commander to run the affairs of the Order for the time being, we must next elect a Commander of the Election, to run the election."

He looked to Thibaud for confirmation, and saw the pale eyes were making a study of him. "Yes," Thibaud said, "a Commander of the Election must be chosen. Quite right."

Beltran proposed that Diego should be Commander of the Election.

"Ha!" Diego exclaimed, "Must I do everything? I am already elected Grand Commander."

"That is no obstacle," Thibaud corrected him. "At the election of William of Beaujeu at Tortosa the same man filled both places. I do not remember why, but it is an arrangement that would serve us well now, when we are so few in numbers."

"Very well," Diego said. He looked at Beltran, tapping his foot impatiently. "You know your Rule, don't you?"

So they elected Diego to be Commander of the Election, and since no more could be done in that direction until Diego had studied what he must do, the meeting of the Chapter-General was adjourned. As they dispersed, Beltran found Thibaud at his side.

Thibaud said, scanning his face, "I have seen you before, but I regret I do not recall your name."

"I am Beltran," Beltran said simply, "and I am poulain." Although this last was an opprobrious word used of those born in the Holy Land, it was as if he had said, "I am Charlemagne, and I am Emperor."

Thibaud put a hand to his own face, where it was scorched. "I remember. It was out there in the courtyard." The regard of the grey eyes was intense. "You set store by the Rule."

"As must we all," Beltran answered shortly, wishing and wondering why he wished it, that he had not marked himself out for Thibaud's interest.

"Aye," Thibaud said, "as must we all, but some maybe more than others?" Thibaud waited, but Beltran did not answer. Thibaud waited long, so that Beltran found the answer come from him as of its own will.

"It may be," he said, "that some of us feel the need of it more than others."

"I believe this to be so," Thibaud said, and left him there.

Chapter Five

ALEXANDER

BELTRAN helped Brother Evrard carry Alexander back to the infirmary. They laid the bed on the stone floor and Beltran saw that Alexander was asleep. The ancient ravages that life had put on his face were smoothing away and being overspread by peace.

"I wonder what his griefs have been," he said.

"He will not have them long," the Infirmarian replied.

"I will sit with him."

Evrard moved up the room to the shadowed end, where a member of the Order was being ministered to by the Alexandrian doctor. The man was in a delirium and cried out and groaned, and often laughed in a low, chuckling way. He was a knight who had come in while Beltran was down at Athlit: he had been taken alive at Acre, and manacled, and had cut through his wrist to free himself and ridden a hundred miles to the gates of Sidon. With Evrard's help the Arabian poured one of his Saracenic opiates into the raving mouth and when the patient was calm the two men went away. Quiet filled the room. The evening sun came in the door and lit the white walls; cool airs came off the sea. I wish it were my spirit, Beltran thought, cool and clear and light.

I wish it were my spirit. Darkness coiled in his head. Outside him everything was light; he could see that; but the light was held in darkness. I will not flee from my faith. God has not forsaken us; but man is evil. God is light. Rejoice and give praise together, O ye deserts of Jerusalem. Have I not laid aside the passions of the world? Have I not? The sun struck at his hands, which were clasped on his knees, and he turned them open to its heat.

They were calloused with a quarter century of killing. Did not Saint Bernard say the Templar was the soldier of Christ? He

2

profits himself when he dies, Saint Bernard said, and he profits Christ when he kills. For he beareth the sword not in vain. For he is God's minister; and an avenger to execute wrath on him that doth evil.

It was Saint Bernard made the Rule for us.

Have I not been obedient to the Rule? The Rule is the bones of my body, it runs from my feet to my head and it is in my arms; these fingers. The half and more of my life. These fingers which tap this brainpan. The Rule is my marrow. Am I not also garbed in the Rule, for it tells me what I wear? The Rule is within me and about me. It is in my hand when I fight and tells me what my weapons are. Within and without. When I went up that hill to see Aimard die, the weapons of the Rule discomfited me and I laid them aside. No matter, for I gathered them about me when I came away. He should not have made a glory of his death as if it was his to give. Our death is God's. Yet he was but a halfling in the Rule and God will not keep him long from Heaven.

I am not in Heaven. Darkness coils in my spirit like blood in a fair river. If I forsake not God He will not forsake me. We are driven from Your Kingdom, Christ my Redeemer. When they come to this castle take me from this land to Heaven. Mary Mother of Jesus intercede for my sins. From this land to Heaven.

Where else would I go?

How old these eyes are, that will soon see God. I will fast and pray, and let the shadow go from my own eyes.

"You have a burden on you."

It is true. I have a burden on me. I shall fast and pray and the burden will be lifted off.

"God is good to me. I shall die in the Order."

I also, each of us dies in the Order, that has not been cast out. Yet if the Order be cast out?

"Mary look down from Heaven," Beltran said aloud, "and let me die in the Order."

"Well, Beltran," Alexander was saying. "Well, well. You have been a long way off."

"You are awake then," Beltran said. "Why, your health has

come back." The old knight's eyes were clear and the flush gone from his skin. He looked so frail that it was a wonder the blankets did not break him into dust.

"I am content," Alexander said. "Tonight you will close my eyes for me."

"I will then, Alexander."

"Aye," Alexander said. Looking at Alexander in his peace, Beltran found he could not contain the storm within him, and it issued from him in a groan.

"Do you sorrow for me or for yourself?" Alexander asked him.

"For myself," Beltran answered.

"I am pleased to hear it is not for me," Alexander said. "So much torment on my account would set me before my Maker with a bad taste in my mouth. I have lived past my three score years and ten. I have been near fifty years in the Order and for more than forty of that I have been set in this horrid land."

"Horrid land!" Beltran was astounded. "The Holy Land!"

"It's not my kind of country," Alexander said, showing remarkable vivacity and to Beltran's mind, temerity, for one who intended to die that night. "It's hot and dirty and full of worthless people. The only pleasure I have ever found in it was in my work, sending heathen souls to Hell. Where did your father come from?"

The transfigured face bewildered Beltran; its bright eyes expected death cheerfully, even with a measure of saintly zeal, and yet it chose to utter forthright abuse of the Holy Land and to ask idle questions, all in a manner which quite failed to suggest that its owner was approaching the culmination of half a century spent in the service of Christ.

"My father came from Foix," Beltran said.

"That's hot country, you see. It will run in your family, being used to hot country, so it suits you. It doesn't suit me, and it never has. I have thought of it as a purging of my sins, that I spent my life here. So I am glad that your sorrow is for yourself; had it been for me, I might be in some doubts about the purging." He regarded Beltran with a kindness oddly unblent with sympathy. "What is your sorrow? Tell me what it is, and then I will ask you to do something for me."

"Sorrow is a small word for it, Alexander. To myself I have been calling it fear."

"Tut-tut, Brother," Alexander said tartly, "will you be so particular with a dying man? I've not the time to make my words the right bigness or weeness to suit you. What's up with you?"

"Alexander!" He was desperate to put home the point of his troubles to this surprising soul, who from being merely ancient had suddenly become venerable. "There is a shadow between me and God."

"Well, well! A shadow between you and God! It is called sin, Beltran."

Beltran's hope of enlightenment turned towards vexation. "Have I been thirty years in the Order, not to have been taught what sin is? This thing is new. It is an affliction."

Alexander showed a sudden exhaustion that drew in his face and loosened his whole body, and took the light out of his eyes.

"It is sin, Beltran. Sin has come home to you at last. The Order has been your shelter, but now you feel the shadow of the world upon your head. It is not an affliction, it is a favour from God." He smiled as little as a man might. "I would be shriven."

Beltran stood up. "Wait!" Alexander said. "I'll ask you to do something for me. When I am dead, have them take the heart out of my body, and carry it for me to Balantrodoch."

"Alexander, I will try, but the infidel is everywhere now. Is this place far?"

Alexander wheezed; it was a laugh. "Balantrodoch is in Scotland, Beltran, in Scotland. It is where I came into the Order. It is a small house, in a bend of the River Esk. You can fish trouts there. Will you carry my heart there?"

"I may not live, Alexander!"

"I am telling you, you will. At least, you will not die here. Thibaud will see to that."

"Thibaud?"

"Thibaud. He has his eye on you for something. I know Thibaud."

The place from which the faded eyes saw him sped further and further back as if the living part of him was drawing off into the distance. "Will you take the heart?"

Beltran took each of Alexander's hands in his own; they were quite weightless. "Yes, I will take it there. God's mercy on you, Alexander." He kissed the white brow and went to find the Chaplain.

Chapter Six

THE COUNCIL IN SIDON

DIEGO went into the city of Sidon to talk with the chief men among the citizens and merchants, and took Beltran with him. They met in the little fortress built by the crusader King Louis forty years before. It stood on the shore opposite the Castle of the Sea, and as they crossed in the pinnace Diego looked at the Italian trading galleys that thronged the harbour and laughed. "Now we shall see something," he said.

The council room glowed. The rugs that clothed it were crimson and rust and scarlet; fruit stood in bowls of gold and confections in flowered porcelain; wine passed from silver flasks into silver cups; the men in the room wore samite, silk of all colours, purple zendado from Tyre and the pure linen of Nablus. In the hearth a low fire of chipped sandalwood and aloe glowed with a heady perfume, assisted by a Kipchak slave who cast on it flakes of galingale and cinnamon from an ivory basket. The only simple note in the chamber was struck by a Knight of the Hospital who stood alone at a window. "Get beside Bartholomew," Beltran felt Diego's breath in his ear. "The Orders must stand together."

The Hospitaller made room at the window for Beltran. He was tall, lóng in the leg, lean and hardy. "You and I are not used to these stenches," he said. "Come and share my fresh air. Well met, Beltran." "Well met, Bartholomew," Beltran said. "This does not look like a council of war." Bartholomew laughed softly. They looked down at the ships lying under the fort. The Venetians were quiet and sat low in the water, but round the Genoese all was stir, with lighters plying to and fro.

Diego began to speak. He told them that when the Mamelukes came he would be able to do little to defend the city, and that when the defence became hopeless, as it would, he meant to withdraw to the Castle of the Sea. "You must empty the city while there is time. It is doomed. They could be here in a week, and certainly they will be here in a month. Sidon will be destroyed and its people massacred."

The doyen of the merchant fraternities, a Marseillais, a man with dark eyes far in under a tranquil brow, tall of face and subtle-mouthed, held a golden bowl chased with silver to his nose and marvelled at such rare art.

"Why do you talk like this?" He looked across the bowl at Diego. "Sidon belongs to the Temple. The last Christian port on the seaboard? You will not let it go."

The old man nibbled slices of sweet-lemon from the bowl and strode masterful across the room to throw the rinds on the scented coals; it was as if he said aloud, "See, I am a man of my hands." Long strides took him back to the buffet where he laid down the bowl and dabbled his fingers in rose water, couched in Egyptian glass. He put aside an offered napkin and walked the circle inside the gathering, his white shoes kicking out stylishly against the red carpets, shaking his hands dry before him.

"If I believed you to be right, Don Diego, I should say it was a pity that the Temple foreclosed on Sidon when it did, since the Temple cannot defend it. Our Lord John, before you distrained on him, kept soldiers."

He stopped for a moment before Diego, and gave his fingers a last shake, rubbed his hands together and waited.

"History," Diego said. "John's soldiers went down at Acre."

On Diego's face two expressions met and fought briefly together, but the habit of portraying other emotions than those at work in him was overcome by the dire certainty that the pampered inhabitants of this luxurious saloon would listen, not to him, but to the Marseillais their archetype: the knowledge that because he, Diego, could not prevail upon their minds, all that lived in Sidon must soon die. He said afterwards that when that mountebank began skittering about like a dressed-up monkey in a mirage winning the approval of his fellows, he knew the outcome at once; the struggle for expression, therefore, that revealed itself on Diego's face, was won by a look of despair.

Upon Diego's dismal mask the virtuosic ancient sent down a

various little shower of smiles and crinkles, all alert with poise and whimsy, and clapped his hands together and stepped three times back unerringly, to where he might pick up an orange to toss up and down in his hand, so that it was clear to those for whom he spoke how cool was the head on which they bestowed their confidence.

"History? Perhaps so, to you. But I was here, it is my history too. Had the Temple been not so greedy, we merchants might have redeemed the pledge." He consulted the orange like a crystal ball. "We would have seen Sidon in a state of defence, I assure you. Nay," and he bent forward kindly, "do not be offended. We should not be merchants if we were not greedy too, a merchant can be as acquisitive as a banker, is it not so?" He held the orange out before him clasped in both hands, his half-bow, quizzical and coaxing, and his fellow-merchants rose from smiles to pleasant laughter.

"Anyway," he stood up fine and straight. "I do not believe that the Temple will let Sidon go. Cyprus is full of soldiery now, nothing for them to do: Templars, Hospitallers, Teutonic Knights, Knights of the Sword and valiant men not in orders. We know they will want to revenge Acre; keep one foot fast by Jerusalem; keep one harbour open for the crusade which cannot fail to come now. Europe must open its eyes now. We have," he discovered the orange and laid it down, an unfitting consort to these devout expectations "sent word to Cyprus and to the West. Therefore, Don Diego, why do you talk in this despairing way?"

He succeeded these words with a display of gentle nods, reproachful, sympathetic and ironic, which were imitated by his compeers, so that to Beltran in the window it appeared that Diego was ringed by a colourful flock of parakeets all preening themselves together.

Four men who had stood unnoticed in the doorway came into the room. One of them stepped within the circle. "You delude yourself, Nicholas," this man told the eloquent doyen. He turned to the Assembly. "Some of you know me, Zazzara of Venice, banker and worse. Bankers know what goes on in the world, or they cease to be bankers. Don Diego gives you good advice.

Sidon is finished. Christian cities on this littoral are finished. You will get no help from Cyprus or from the West. The Western princes are fighting over Sicily, or with their neighbours. There will be no Crusade. You can count the steps that have brought Christendom to the seacoast by counting the Crusades. This land has returned to the Sultan, and the Mongols may take it from him, but we shall not be here to see it happen." He paused before the bitter stroke. "As for Sidon as a trading outpost: we Venetians do not need it, nor does Genoa or Pisa," he nodded to the smallest of his companions who nodded back for Pisa. "We are treating with the Sultan, we have treaties with the Mongols. We can trade into Alexandria and Cilicia. It is no profit to us to shore you up."

He stood still while he talked and he stood still now that he had finished, a mature round-headed greying man, sharp-nosed and unchinned, nondescript in everything but his own clear assumption that he was gifted with sure judgment.

Nicholas fought back. "Come now, Zazzara, you of Venice can hardly speak for Genoa."

"Look out of the window," Zazzara said, "and you will see Genoa speaking for itself." Beltran looked down at the lighters bustling round the Genoese galleys. "My friends of Genoa are packing up." The Venetian meant, his enemies of Genoa. He smiled, becoming a man of simple jollities. "Genoa will sail tomorrow; we sail in three hours. Now to my point. We must come to realities. Your danger is real and unalterable; this gathering of sweet-tasters is not. Sidon is not, it is not real any more. It is hard for you to see that, since it is what you are used to, but see it you must."

He let the indignation mount up until it found a voice. "It is all very well, Zazzara, for you to tell us we are ghosts, but if we leave here we shall be ruined. This is our home. Your home is the sea, and no one can steal it from you."

Zazzara found the speaker. "Kind of you to say so, Adlard. It makes no difference. Your sugar factory will be burning in a month, whether you are here to burn with it or not. Your dye-works besides, Nicholas. I have certain intelligence of this. The Mamelukes are now destroying everything that might remind

them of us: they are burning crops, vineyards, forests, even
olive and fruit trees where they are ours, I should say have
been ours; or yours. They will leave no shadow of Christian
rule to vex them. When it comes to Sidon, I tell you that the
Emir Shujai left Acre ten days ago with thirty thousand men
and is marching north." He looked at the window and took the
angle of the sun. "I must be getting on, so listen. Venice has
enough ships in Cyprus ports to clear this city; Pisa would help
too, I daresay." Pisa nodded. "Charter them. We'll make a fair
price."

Outrage. Zazzara was treating with the enemy and was a spy;
he was being paid to leave Sidon open to Shujai; he was making
it all up to get a charter for idle ships, which would have to be
chartered again when the Sultan offered Sidon back to its fugitive
citizens; he was jealous of their prosperity. Beltran watched
Zazzara curiously: he simply stood still and looked once again at
the sun slanting in the window.

"It will cost us a fortune," Nicholas said. He leaned back his
head for stiffness; it had begun to tremble.

"The Temple will pay," Diego said.

Nicholas made a smile, "You can hardly commit your O_der
to such a contract."

Zazzara laid down his temper. "You are so blind; such fools.
Do you know nobody's business but your own? Don Diego is
Grand Commander of his Order; they'll elect a Master tomorrow
but today he can commit his Order to anything. In any case,
his bond will be with Venice, not with Sidon. It is not your
concern. I sail in three hours. If you want ships, send two ot you
on board with us to Cyprus, two level heads if you have them.
In three hours. You'll have your ships here in four days "

He finished. Nicholas did not answer. Silence swept into the
room like a herald. Zazzara's teeth worried his lip, Diego's chin
dug at his breastbone, and Nicholas was tilted in an unlikely
curve, a ribbon hung on the air. A gust of voices came through
the window and a lighter passed below; its sweeps creaked and
splashed and faded down the harbour. The silence in the room
had not been disturbed by the noise from outside; it was im-
perturbable, since its meaning was plain to everyone in the room

and each man acknowledged it by standing in his own silence.
All of them heard the same voice, saying: you have different
fates and they are deaf to one another, talking will not bind
them together; accept this and go, each to his own fate.

Zazzara, still chewing his lip, put his eyes to those of Nicholas
and nodded, and turned to the door. The silence ended in a
whisper.

"No," Nicholas said.

Zazzara turned to hear. Nicholas stood straight again but his
height was less, his arms hung loose. He had stopped conjuring
with attitudes, and his face was honest. "Something should be
said!" His voice lifted in enquiry to make an appeal, not a statement, and Zazzara turned a hand over as if to say he had time,
he could sail next week and Devil take the Genoese.

"We trust you, Signor Zazzara," Nicholas said, "and you,
Don Diego. We trust your word but not your judgment, forgive
me, since we cannot trust Venice or the Order. You will have
to forgive that. You see, it may be today is different, but Venice
and the Order have played politics all my forty years here. We
do too," he said in hurried earnest, "but in a smaller way; we
are citizens only of Sidon and you are of the world." He tasted
the thought with envy. "Citizens of the world. So we must trust
ourselves; we must believe what we hope. We must hope because
we are fixed here. Why, I don't know; I can't tell why, but we
are fixed here. By whom?" He wondered, and was forlorn. "By
what?" He looked ready to fall into a trance, but recovered and
was brisk. "I suppose someone must live at the edge of the world.
Perhaps it is a habit to grow used to. We will stay."

Shame flitted like an uneasy stranger into Zazzara's bland
face, and Nicholas took a step towards him. "No, Signor," he
said, "you do not desert us. We stay for no good reason. We are
grateful for your offers and your advice. You have done what
you could for us."

He turned mountebank again and tossed his hands up laughing.
"You will be back before the weather breaks in September and
we shall be still in business, I assure you!"

*   *   *

The Venetians sailed leaving long shadows behind them and the night came and passed. The Genoese galleys sat down in the water and only one lighter moved among them, back and forth, doling out the last of their wealth in spoonfuls, like an assiduous host filling his guests beyond repletion.

Three merchants of Sidon left the city's east gate, nobly horsed and trailing a mule laden with gifts. They were arrayed in brilliance and each wore fear as an undergarment, for Sidon was sending ambassadors to Shujai.

In the Castle of the Sea Beltran and Diego sat together. Diego had chosen Beltran to join him in electing a Master. They two chose Andras the Hungarian and Pico the Florentine to join them; they four chose two more to join them, and they went on in this way until twelve were assembled, eight knights and four sergeants, and the twelve called the Chaplain, Brother Marsilio, to join them. It was explained in the Rule that the twelve were for the twelve Apostles, and the Chaplain was for Jesus Christ. Marsilio prayed, imploring Christ to guide them.

"Now," Diego said, "we shall not speak until the sun comes in that window and touches the table. When the table is warm, any man may name any knight of the Order. Meanwhile we shall be alone together, with God, and the Son of God, and the Holy Mother."

Chapter Seven

THE FALL OF SIDON

THE city was under the sword.

The Emir Shujai had ridden up three days ago and yesterday the last of his army had marched into camp. The first-comers of the Mamelukes had made boldly for the walls and finding no spears or arrows or Greek fire thrown at them (since there were none to throw) began to make a pleasure ground of the fields and gardens there. They sauntered about or exercised their horses, and made game of the citizens on the ramparts. They mimed disembowelment and castration, beheading and rape, and what other calamities they meant to visit on the unhappy Christians; and this third day, in the morning, they had performed some of these acts on the three ambassadors Sidon had sent off with presents to Shujai.

The last of these screamed on and on like a slaughtered pig while his guts on the ground before him smoked in the sun. Beltran stood beside the one-handed man who had been raving in the infirmary the day Alexander died, and who was called Geoffrey, and from the east gate they had watched the torment of the three emissaries. Over that miniature shambles the two Templars looked out on thirty thousand men of Shujai's army. The Mamelukes were drawn up in regiments but keeping no silence in their ranks, so that you had to shout to be heard above the din.

A captain walked twenty paces from the regiment that stood opposite the gate and cut the head off the shrieking man. He did not look at the city at all, did not give so much as a glance at those on the walls. He swung his sword once, a masterstroke, and pushed the corpse with his foot so that the gouting neck spurted over the torturers and left his own clothes and person unblemished. He tore cloth from the least wounded of the other bodies and walked up again to the head of his men, wiping his blade clean as he went.

The sounds made by that great mass of men had begun to grow less. In the lanes between the regiments Beltran saw separate contingents making their way to the front. He could not make out what they were.

Geoffrey was fresh from the siege of Acre. "Shujai's engineers," he said, "bringing up the ladders. They are ready to make the onfall."

"Then," Beltran said, "it is time for us to run away."

"Perhaps I will stay," Geoffrey said.

"No, you will not," Beltran said. The engineers were now deploying in front of the army with the short ladders that would scale the walls of Sidon. "We know what we are to do. We will get off the wall and go down to the harbour." For the Templars were to leave before the fighting.

Behind them the street ran through the city to the quay where the barge waited. He would go down the street while its stones were still dry of blood; and his sword would keep its sheath, since the wars were done. He would step a last time off his native soil, and then in the Castle of the Sea would look back upon the sack of Sidon. Now he had only to turn on his heel and depart from the faces of those who had shared the wall with him, these three nights.

On the far side of the city rose a sorrowful cry. Round the northern wall a cavalcade came into sight and passed before the gate at a hand-gallop. The first of them was a prince of the Mamelukes. He rode hawk on wrist and wore no gear of war. He was robed in all pale colours and sat a little cream-haired mare, and held converse with his falconer as if he saw no army on the one side of him and no city on the other. The prince and his companion wore serious faces and were intent upon their talk, but the group that followed laughed and chattered, bright of eye to be on holiday. For all that, no eye of theirs met Beltran's, and they were as blindfold as their lord both to the city and the army that beset it. Chirping at the hooded birds and keeping their horses to the rein they swept along the skirts of the city, and passed from view.

"That was the war-lord himself," Geoffrey said. His voice creaked and he worked wet into his mouth before he spoke again. "Shujai has gone hawking. He has opened the city to his men."

The dismal cry from far off had followed Shujai's progress and now filled Beltran's ears. It was the lament of the city for its fate. Men who, three days past, hardly armed or armoured, had gone onto the walls grimly to fight this hopeless fight; who had over these days, sustained the mockery of the host that swarmed safely about their walls, now yielded to the Emir's perfectly displayed belief that no true battle faced his army: that the Mamelukes had only to walk over the walls and start killing. For himself, he would ride into the hills with his hawks. What he had done was to insult the coming deaths of the men on the ramparts, and of their families behind them, and it thinned their blood to water.

When, therefore, Beltran at last found the courage to face the men he was commanded to desert, he saw a scatter of weapons and the stair already empty.

He looked in on the city. Figures sped down the edges of the streets or stood, more rarely, still as statues in the unshadowed noon. Other than that you would have said Sidon was asleep: had it not been for the noise. From the shuttered windows and barred doors of the houses still rose, and still increased, the lamentation with which the city had answered the ride of the Emir's hawking-party.

The sun stood at its zenith over the town and to see the white roofs tremble in the shaking light, and at the same time hear the death-song of the multitude that cowered beneath, invisible, put Beltran in a great wish to be quit of the place and the day.

"At Acre they thronged to the sea," Geoffrey said.

"They should do that here," Beltran said foolishly.

He leaned off the rampart's inward side so that his whole body frowned across the rooftops and in a lurch for balance turned down the stair. Geoffrey followed.

"Well?" Beltran said to Geoffrey.

"Well?" Geoffrey said.

Beltran said, "You spoke of staying."

"They have released me," Geoffrey said. "To stay on the wall with them is one thing, to play Roland by myself is another."

When they were down and off the stair, and stood dwarfed by the high leaves of the now unguarded gate, Geoffrey said, "They have released you too. It is all over with them, and you and I only make a pretence of being here."

He set off down the street and Beltran went after him and caught up. The road they walked on was stoned and their iron feet clanged and rasped along its empty length. They walked in silence. The houses at their side hymned the pain in which the day would end. A child, a babe, walked out of a door a little way ahead and winked in the sun, its baby fists sheltering its eyes. They passed around it, nervous to give it room, and while their passing shapes lifted above its knee-high crown the child stumped back from them and tripped onto its back, and yelled. A woman came up into the doorway and stood on the steps that descended into the house. She peered towards the child, and perhaps seeing only the black outline of sworded men against the light, folded down with her head bent to her knees. The child howled with its back on the road, and the woman knelt for her death and the child's. Beltran looked at Geoffrey and past him up the street to the gate where death waited. He was almost mastered by the need to kill mother and child himself. His fingers wiped soaking sweat along his brow. His back and the back of his neck felt like a strung bow, trapped and fixed by some cord he could not see.

He heard Geoffrey's words as if they had travelled miles to reach him. "Give him to her!" He saw Geoffrey's handless wrist under his nose. "I can't do it. Give her the child!"

It takes two hands to lift a child, then? Why must they pass like gods through Sidon? The child was still and the woman's face showed in the doorway. Beltran made three steps and lifted the small, soft life between his mail-gloved hands and since to hold this condemned boy was as to hold a sucking pig or lamb for the butcher, he nearly dropped it and to recover it nearly fell, so not to fall he ran and pushed it to the mother and ran alongside the house, and round the corner vomited.

Geoffrey's long face stooped white and lifeless into his. "She said thank-you," Geoffrey told him.

The wailing of the city had dwindled and now behind shutters, as they walked the last part of the street, movement had begun. Here and there on rooftops figures stood, and here and there only heads showed and bobbed down again, as if to steal glimpses of approaching doom would make it easier to meet. Where a street crossed ahead of the two Templars dogs ran by in a pack and when they reached there people were walking about almost as if the day were ordinary, and from there to the harbour gate their own street now was thinly crowded; roofs inhabited and windows unshuttered. Households which had bolted themselves in the isolation of their homes put forth members into the town, as if they had been cringing in the shadows from no more than the heat of noon. For a bubble of time Sidon performed an illusion of living.

A voice spoke from a rooftop. "The Mamelukes are in," it said. Everyone looked back up the street, and where the two knights had begun their walk they saw tiny men make the familiar gestures of the sword.

The Templars, having stopped, turned and seen, with one accord resumed their walk to the harbour. Beltran hoped they went neither faster nor slower than before. At each footstep of this journey through the city he had been ready for riot to surround their passage. He had feared, in his mind's eye, women kneeling at his feet and fathers that held children to his face; cripples leaning wordlessly on sticks to watch him pass; whole families that called shame down on his head, and old men sneering to see him fly from their dying day. He was as worn as if the forenoon had been spent in battle, and as if lifting that child to its mother had been one of those hazards that tire out courage. Now at last there must be riot, and now surely they would drown him in their grief and fear, now that the Mamelukes were in the city! His legs drifted and missed their step and he stopped. Geoffrey turned to him and Beltran drew himself together.

"Wait," he said to Geoffrey. "Wait a moment, and then we will go on, but slower."

The street in front had not emptied, after that hail from the roof, but the people that were in it held to the walls. Geoffrey looked past Beltran's shoulder so that Beltran faced about. They had been coming down the street after him and Geoffrey, and now were stopped and waiting: the parents that held children; the beautiful girls and the young men who were too late to become soldiers; and the cripples on their sticks and the aged, the shawled women and white-bearded men. In the instant of turning from them Beltran stayed and looked longer. What they were doing, other than attach themselves to him and Geoffrey he could not see. He shunned the young faces that wrapped fear in a hopeless hope, and rested on old age, whose cynicism hung like a curtain against his gaze.

"Where are the priests?" He had not meant to speak to them at all.

"In the churches," an old woman answered him.

He looked then into some of the younger faces, and at two or three mothers holding babes in arms, and he knew this would be worse than before, when he had lifted the child back to the woman. Nevertheless he said it, owing it to God, as well as to this people in their martyrdom, to let them abandon earthly hope.

"You should go to the churches," he said.

There was a great sigh that came chiefly from the youthful in the crowd, and their heads sloped sadly on their shoulders. A mother that clutched a child started to weep and sobs and groans broke out; and as if he had held these despairing people in his hands and wrenched the sounds out of their throats, Beltran said inwardly, now it will come, now they will throw themselves about me, and in front of me, and I will wade knee-deep in tears.

Instead the old woman spoke again. "We will come to the church at the harbour," she said. "We will come that far with you." She did not look at him, but at an empty wall, as if to copy its expression.

He took a step back, and they began to follow and he turned and walked on again, his footing secure enough now, it seemed, and Geoffrey silent at his side. They came to the space where the street ended. In the church by the city wall the high door opened and a priest summoned with an urgent hand the people of the street.

Sea-birds perched mewing on the harbour-gate. Through its

arch the ocean lifted to a wind that had not touched the city. On top of the fort which Saint Louis had built by the quay a splash of colour moved back and forward on the small space like a fish in a bowl, and Beltran recognized in this vacillating dance some leaders of Sidon. There was no one else to be seen.

A pelican ran grunting through the gateway from the harbour. Beltran stared at it. Thin voices stretched at them from the fort, signals of alarm.

"Now what is this?" Geoffrey said, and drew his sword into his left hand.

Beltran slid the long shield off his back and took it on his arm. A handful of Mamelukes ran lightly in below the arch and putting his sword into his hand he threw himself forward and shouted, so that his throat scraped, "I thank thee, God! Oh, God! I thank thee!"

They were a ragged line, five or six. The man at the end took the edge of Beltran's sword clean through his neck and the head jumped off, eyes, hair and teeth still in the air when Beltran stopped the neighbour on his shield and at once, again with the shield, beat in his face and when he fell stamped on the throat and with this forward step he shortened his sword and put the razored, rounded point into a third man's mouth and dropped his hand and thrust up into the brainpan; and looking to see that he was safe even as he got the weapon from the dropping body, he made sure of the man choking on the ground by cutting his windpipe.

The fight was over. An opponent of Geoffrey's sat with the top of his head fallen in and jerked occasionally like a fish, and the other was on his way out of the gate again, life gouting from a severed thigh. In the wreckage of the affray, along with this man's leg, an arm lying in a round shield like meat on a dish, and a head astonished in the midst of its last smile, the pelican lay mysteriously dead. Here and there blood still pumped from Mameluke flesh and the air was sweet with it, so that the flies came feasting.

The Templars wiped their swords and looking all about them went quickly through the gate to the quay. The barge lay off less than a spear's throw and it began to move to the landing. There

was no one on the harbourside, neither of the Mamelukes nor
of Sidon, but from the far side of the city rose at last the clamour
of drums and war-shouts that meant the gates were open and
the walls over-run. Beltran walked to his embarkation across the
empty paving of the sunlit harbour like a man in a spell, half-
deaf and half-blind. In the corner of his eye he saw come towards
them from the right a tall man robed in red, not quite running,
and a small figure at his side. Beltran looked into the barge and
saw that the others had returned more timely from their posts
than he and Geoffrey: Olivier and Andras, Honfroi and old
Alonso sat two in the bow and two at the stern. The din from
across the city grew louder and within it there now climbed the
call of the dying, a single voice that flew to Heaven.

The boat knocked against the foot of the steps set in the
quayside and Geoffrey went down first, stepping carefully on the
worn stones with his mailed feet.

"The loss of a hand puts me out of balance," he said.

Olivier looked up at Beltran. "You are late," he said, "and
bloody. Oh, paragon, you have been disobedient!"

He put a hand to steady Geoffrey and helped him into the
barge, and looked up again. "Come on, Beltran! Here, reach me
your shield!" Beltran let down the shield and stood up again.

"Take the child!" The voice came along the edge of the quay
from the man in the red coat. It was Nicholas, the chief of the
city's merchants, come to his day of reckoning. His hand was on
the shoulder of a dark-skinned girl-child. His mouth was shaking
and slobbered and his head moved constantly from side to side;
his eyes were shut to slits.

A huge Mameluke ran suddenly from nowhere into the space
between them with a heavy black axe in his two hands. Nicholas
pushed the slight figure in the back so that it ran at Beltran and
the axe split him in two from the top of his handsome head to the
breastbone.

"What is it?" Geoffrey had appeared again, his head level
with Beltran's feet. Beltran swept the infant at Geoffrey with his
left hand and tugged out his sword, a little sticky, while the
infidel wrenched his axe from Nicholas. The huge man came
straight at him. Beltran's sword broke to the axe and his arm

rang with the pain and then the axe hit his leg, just over the
knee, and he fell. His leg was still there and he took in that the
axe had turned when it met the sword, so that he had escaped
the stroke of the edge. The axe was in the air again with the big
man standing astride him, and with the little knife from his
boot Beltran reached up behind the Mameluke's thigh and cut
in deep and across, and as the axe fell the man howled with rage
and went on out of Beltran's sight, axe-first over the edge of the
harbour, and into the water with a splash.

Geoffrey laughed and Beltran turned on his side and looked
at him, his face stiff from the pain in his bruised leg. There was
a sudden concerted cry from behind the city wall, of fear and
anguish, and Beltran thought the Mamelukes had broken in the
doors of the church. Geoffrey tossed the child in the air and said,
"We have saved one, at any rate." He put her on the stairs and
sent her down to the boat. "What was she to Nicholas?"

Beltran got himself to the top step. "What do you mean?"
he asked, and then said, "See, my leg hurts!" He went down
clinging to the chain in the wall. Geoffrey kept watch on the
quay till he was in the barge, and followed quickly after, and they
were rowed across the harbour to the Castle of the Sea.

They did not trouble to tell Diego about the child, but took
her to the Egyptian physician, who told her that she now belonged to him. The physician in return, as it were, presented to
Beltran the heart of Alexander, the Scottish knight. It was in a
sandalwood casket, wherein it lay wrapped in lead.

The Templars were safe, for the time, on their island castle.
The massacre of the city's people took place mostly behind the
walls; a few ran as far as the harbour or the seashore, but those
that did were hardly seen for the number of their executioners.
The blood from the city begin to drain into the sea and the
harbour turned pink long before sunset.

By nightfall, while still the noise of the sack of Sidon rang in
the air, Thibaud Gaudin had finished making his tally of the
gold, and those who were going with him said good-bye to their
friends. They sailed for Cyprus with the Treasury of the Order
for ballast.

Chapter Eight

KING OF CYPRUS

THE king sat sideways in hish all, and would have no lamps nor candles. His right hand caressed the cool jasper of his throne, and his left held the weight of his bereaved brow.

King Henry was pleased with this arrangement. The obliqueness of his throne suggested one of those biblical expressions of grief proper to a king of Jerusalem who has seen the Holy Land fall into the hands of the infidel, and the banishment of light allowed him, in the steep and shadowy hall of Famagusta, a sense of privacy during the many audiences to which he was obliged to admit survivors of the lost kingdom. Besides, Henry was not quite twenty-one, but he had been king of Cyprus and Jerusalem for six years, and he felt keenly the advantage of presenting himself in such unusual state to the refugees who had fled from the latter kingdom to the former.

"You have lost everything," he told his petitioners kindly. "I have lost only a kingdom."

The great men came to him in person, and the humble joined together to send representatives, each reciting the same tale of hardships bravely borne, inconsolable personal affliction and (most deadly to Henry's ears) utter material destitution. None of these unhappy beings had told this tale as well as he might, for it was hard to plead what suddenly became their small misfortunes to a king who proclaimed his own sorrow in a style that spoke, and with so eloquent a reticence, of matters at once royal, personal, sacred and metaphysical.

"You have lost your home," Henry would say, "and your family, and your soap-factory,"—or it might be dye-works, or tannery, or spice-magazine—"and I have lost my kingdom. God helping, we shall win them back."

Standing in that high and tenebrous chamber, looking across some yards of space to the obscure figure of the king and the dim profile masked by the hand on which it rested, the suppliant would wait hopelessly for more until the hand, still united with the face, suggested that it was time to leave. As he walked down the hall past silent courtiers his burdens would gather again upon his shoulders, and he would seek his impermanent refuge and variously weep, or curse, or pray. Sometimes they killed themselves.

A man came in at the door, outlined for a moment against the brightness of day, and walked from the light into the darkness without pause. Henry took the hand from his face. The man came to the throne and bent his head, more than a nod and less than a bow.

"Lord King," he said.

"Grand Master," the king said. "My dear Thibaud." He called for a light and when it was brought sent his people from the hall. He took a taper and went from one lamp to the next and they sat on cushions in the soft glow of burning oil. Henry was royal, sprawling out to well over six feet. Strong brown fingers played with an Indian dagger jewel-hilted in Damascus, and over samite he wore purple zendado. Henry looked on the slight body starkly upright in its white mantle, at the burnt half of the face and the fingers pinching at the remaining eyebrow, and his regard was witty and kind. Then the pale eyes turned up to hunt his own and they were frantic. The king's expression went blank.

"You are all passion, Thibaud," he said. "What do you want?"

"Will you call a Crusade?" The words jumped from the thin lips like a command and Henry found that he had bitten the inside of his cheek.

"Thibaud," he said, "when I was twelve you taught me politics. My father stopped it. He said the Temple had done enough harm to the family of Lusignan. Still, I seem to have learned something." He is as stiff as a fox, he thought: am I the prey or the hunter? He made Thibaud move. "There is wine on that buffet. Pour us some wine. And try not to look at me so wild or I'll put the lights out and get back on my throne."

The Grand Master came up like a spring and poured the wine.

"I shall move about," he said. "My sinews are too tight." Handing the cup he said, "You know the Templars in Cyprus plot against you?"

The king took the cup. "Oh, certainly," he said. "Certainly."

Henry rolled the wine over the sore place in his mouth and swallowed. "Where were we?" Thibaud walked up and down on the edge of the lamplight, thinking it was true, he was all passion, guilt, fear and love of God, and fear of the new place where he stood: not the Grand Magistracy, that brought him no fear, but of the new place where his Order stood, exiled from its duty. He had asked his question and knew the answer, his passion was grown quiet under the king's indulgence, and he would be temperate and let his mind grow broad, and hear what there was to hear, and be careful not again to fall into the sin of despair.

"You had said," he told Henry, "that once I taught you politics." He had counted five different woods in the floor of the hall. Then too, he was reckoned a subtle man, and he thought Henry was young to be as wise as he seemed. Something might be won.

The king's voice was in his ear. "Your breath all but stopped, do you know that? You might have died of—nothing. You looked at me with that thing in your eyes and might have died." Thibaud did not look up, and let the voice settle on his head. "Passion, you said to me when I was a child, is no part of politics; it comes first, and then is baled up and stored out of sight. Politics is the merchant's work, not the cargo he works with."

Henry turned mercurial, and sat on his throne swinging out a leg, and laid his face on his hand. "What do you think of this, sideways, in the dark?"

Thibaud looked, and said, "Disconcerting, but to what end?"

Henry laughed, "It wonderfully disconcerts the unfortunate." His face became grim. "I do not have livelihoods to give to those who have lost them, or lives for those they have lost. They have lost their whole kingdom and must start again, or stop forever. This kingdom has enough burdens as it is." He laughed again. "I saw that many die at Acre I never thought to see so many come from there alive." He bit his thumb. "They say I am a coward to have left Acre before the end. What do you think?"

"Not that. You fought hardily, you lost half a regiment, the thing was as good as done; you had a kingdom to see to here. I left before the end."

"I heard. Peter de Sevrey pushed you into the sea, is what I heard."

"Who tells you these things, about yourself and me?"

Henry stood and stretched himself. He stamped a few steps to behind the throne and leaned his arms on the back of it. "Spies. There are spies everywhere on this island."

"I know. Six or seven follow me."

"Not all mine, I promise you."

"Whose are they?"

Henry counted them off on his fingers. "Well, Charles Angevin of Naples senses he has a claim to the throne of Byzantium, and he will want to know what moves here; His Holiness is entitled to news; and since he will not live long, the cardinals have a claim to be informed; all these Italians have to lay new plans for their trade now—by the way, your friend Zazzara is here—and will have wet fingers to the wind; I suppose Philip of France may have ears here; and then there are all the military Orders."

Thibaud smiled dourly, "I have been here two days. They have not run to report to me yet."

Henry was very still, his chin in his hands. "Have they not, Thibaud, have they not? I wonder where they report."

Thibaud came back with irritation. "There is no need to be significant, Henry." The king smiled; Thibaud had forgotten himself. The Grand Master went on impatiently, "They had a vessel in St. Hillarion yesterday that's gone today. They are reporting to Paris." Thibaud looked up at the long face behind the throne and considered the advantages of frankness; Henry probably knew anyway. "There is a faction of the Temple in Paris that wants the Order to behave reasonably; for the most part they are our bankers, and to bankers reasonable conduct means accepting the inevitable and putting your money where the return is."

Henry said, "There would not be much return for a banker in a Crusade."

"Not short-term, no. I'm a banker too. They don't know which way I'll jump; not for certain."

Henry nodded slowly. "You are right to want a Crusade," he said. "Without its place in the Holy Land, your Order will not be what it has been."

"Nor will the Holy Land!"

"There will not be a Crusade, Thibaud. The European princes will not look at it. Charles of Naples is fighting Aragon for Sicily; England is fighting Scotland; France has just got out of the war in Sicily and has troubles of its own; the Pope is dying and the German Emperor has his hands full at home." He waited for Thibaud to speak but had to fill the space that was left. "I," he said, "shall not raise a Crusade because it will be too little supported to succeed, and I do not want to bring the Sultan's fleet down on this island."

He met the pale eyes steadily, seeing the fanatic gleam rise in them and then die down again, making a furtive, spoiling glow behind the intelligent gaze. One of the lamps flickered and went out, and a thread of smoke drifted across the space between them.

Henry came round from behind his throne. "Philip of France," he said, "is interesting. They call him the Fair, for his looks, you know. He has just expelled the Lombards."

"I did not know that!"

"Yes. He borrowed from them to the hilt. Wars are expensive. When he could not meet payment he confiscated their French properties and turned them out. He is making friends with the Jews now. I think he will have to fight England, which will certainly be expensive."

He watched Thibaud stiffen his back, but went on remorseless. "Any banker in Paris worth his salt will know that the Jews are next, and when Philip has run through the Jews, and killed them or turned them out, why, what business there will be at hand as banker for France."

Thibaud's mouth flickered in an odd smile. It laid onto a face charged with devotion, with hope against hope, with sorrow and faith, a perplexing glint of cynicism. "That too would be short-term banking," he said. "It seems then that I am not yet master in my own house, except in name."

"That, dear Thibaud," said Henry, "is what it seems."

"Nor like to be," Thibaud said.

"Go to Europe, Thibaud. You can command obedience if you're there."

Thibaud shook himself. "I might go to Europe," he said. "I doubt it. There is not much I can do here for the Holy Land, but if I go to France, that will be the end of it."

The king moved towards him. "Then do not trust your own brethren too much. Do not go out alone."

Thibaud laughed, and his face awoke as if danger were a friend he understood. "I was a soldier before I became a banker," he said. "Go out alone? I have two men scout the street for me before, and two that cover my rear, and two that watch the doorways at my side while I walk up the middle of the street." He fell into a silence and at last looked at Henry, and his eyes were not clear. "I must ask your leave to go, in a moment. Thank you for friendship. Our interests are opposite but you treat me as a friend."

Henry smiled, kind and no longer witty. Another lamp went out and the darkness moved closer in. The two men of state clasped each other's arms in an impulsive hold.

"There are Templars and Templars, Thibaud," the king said, "but God knows I wish you well."

Thibaud looked at him. "There are kings and kings, Sire."

He bent his head a long moment, and the king ached to touch it, for where was comfort for such a man?

"Come," he said. "I shall open the door for you myself." They walked in silence down the darkness of the hall and Henry opened the door. It was as dark outside now, for the short twilight was ending and stars shone in the moonless sky.

"Thibaud," said Henry, "I meant to ask you. There is a gigantic Venetian galley under your flag working offshore. What is it doing?"

"Your spies don't tell you?"

Henry laughed. "No, my spies are at a loss."

"It is doing nothing against you or your state, Lord King."

The king laughed again. "Then don't tell me," he said.

"I will tell you," Thibaud said. "It is working, Henry. Working."

The king laughed again and watched Thibaud out of the palace courtyard, and saw six men come to their appointed places in his escort.

The Master of the Temple vanished under the arch into the street and the king went back into his hall and called for more light, and company, and supper, and that evening was by turns sour and generous in his temper. The next day he had his throne face down the hall again.

Chapter Nine

THE HOUSE ON THE SHORE

BELTRAN stood among the barrels of silver and watched
the two Venetians meet. Venice rejoiced in secrecy as if it
were an element invented for her to move in, and under a sky
lit only by stars, in an empty bay off a lonely shore, the two ships
met and kissed and lay there, bow to bow, like lovers who had
learned together all the tricks of swimming.

In "The Lion of St. Mark" lay Thibaud's gold, Alexander's
heart and the infant blackamoor, and the smaller ship held something worth all this silver. It would be long before he could
carry Alexander's heart to Scotland, and very likely it would be
longer than Beltran had to live. It could take two years to raise
a Crusade, two years or more for the armies to reach the Holy
Land, and how many years of fighting after that, with all the
Kingdom to be won again. I should like at least to live until the
fighting begins, he thought, to see the Holy Land turning
Christian again. To die before that would be a kind of evil: to
be in Heaven with the Holy Land profaned would feel unsafe,
as if there were no floor. He had said this to Olivier on the night
they left Sidon. Olivier had not laughed as he expected, but
said the conceit was adequate, although not satisfactory altogether
since it did not reach down to the ears of ordinary men. Ordinary
men? Men unprivileged with our vocation, Olivier said: for them
you should say, To be in Heaven with the world profaned, or
even gone, Yes, gone! Olivier had shouted, To be in Heaven
with the world gone, vanished, taken away would feel unsafe,
as if there were no floor. But the Holy Land, Beltran had explained. Yes, yes, Olivier had answered, but God made the
whole world, and He can take it away. From ordinary men?
Yes, and from you and me in the by-going, Beltran. Our world
is the Holy Land, Beltran had come back at him. Our world is
the same world as everybody else's world, Olivier had said,

growing deeply serious, and we have been thrown out of the Holy Land. For the love I bear you, Olivier had said, open your eyes and ears when we fetch Cyprus, and your nose, and smell what the world is, which God made for us to live on.

Where was Olivier? There was a sound on the water, which should be Diego's boat, but might not be.

He called softly towards the house, "Olivier! Olivier!" Olivier, however, was already on the beach.

"I was in the rose garden," he said.

"A boat," Beltran said.

Olivier listened. "See," he said. "You can see where their oars turn the water. I shall go off to this side." They moved away from each other and down to the water, well spaced from where the boat would come in, for Olivier was as good a soldier as he was a poet. The boat only just touched and then lay there, waiting, and Beltran tossed two pebbles into the sea beside it, one splash after the other, and Diego called, "It is I, Diego." Two men jumped out of the boat and pulled it up onto the beach and Beltran and Oliver advanced to meet it.

"Good," Diego said, as they approached him from either side. "This is all very mysterious. What have you here?" He walked them up the sand a little leaving the seamen by the boat.

"Barrels of silver," Beltran answered, and showed him, "and an empty house, large, a nobleman's house, and no other house within call. We were here in daylight and proved the ground."

Diego sat down on one of the barrels. "Is the house being used?"

"Oh, yes," Olivier said. "It is a kind of palace. Empty no more than a day, it seems. I suppose men with such houses have others to move to when the whim takes them."

Diego rubbed his face. "Thibaud Gaudin has some friends, anyway," he said. "I don't know where he's taking us, but at least he has some useful friends."

There was a silence and Olivier said. "When I was in the rose garden I dreamed of an emperor whose palace was so large, that when it rained at one end he went to the other and sat in the sun."

"Be kind," Diego said, "and return to your rose garden. Have you seen anyone?"

"Yes," Olivier said. "We sat in a lemon grove and watched the house, and men came with mules, took this silver from the house to here, and went away again. When it was dark we came down and took watch."

Diego whistled and made half a laugh. "I don't know," he said. "I'd better sit down too," he said. "There's nothing to do now but wait." So they sat down on the silver and waited. From the orchards behind them the night rang with insects, and a small wind made the sea lap on the sand and the stars dance on the water.

"Much more of this," Olivier said, "and I shall not care if no more Moslems offer me their faces to cut in two."

A beetle droned by and an owl swam out from the land to the sea and back again, shrieking twice as it passed over their heads.

"For my part," Diego said, "I had rather deal with Moslems. Why do we lurk like this in seashores? I do not know. Who are our enemies? I do not know that, either." He wrung the fingers of one hand in the other until they cracked. "Unless it be everyone in Cyprus is our enemy, which could well be. The Temple is not liked here. We used to own this island, you know; before my time."

"I heard that," Beltran said.

"I didn't," Olivier said. "I wish we had kept it. Why didn't we?" Diego cracked the other fingers and looked out for a long time over the sea, and sighed. "The truth is," he said, "that in hard fighting against the infidel the Temple does very well, but in other things, well, in other things, I suppose we are like everybody else."

"That is not a reason for losing Cyprus," Olivier said softly.

"Then in some things we are worse," Diego said crossly. "The people rebelled, but that was long ago. We have much to be proud of since then."

The breeze had gone and on the sea the stars moved more slowly, and by the boat the sailors slept on the sand.

"I hope we get back the Holy Land," Beltran said, hoping to ease Diego's spirit.

"Do you?" said Diego in a trimmed and impersonal voice. "I no longer know what I think."

"Ah—"

"Hush, Beltran," Olivier said. "It is time you accepted doubt into yourself. If you seek to walk on certainty all your life you will meet quicksand."

A mile up the coast a light showed twice and was answered from the small galley in the bay. "Now we shall see," Diego said, and stood up.

"See what?" Beltran asked him.

"If you are to have the Holy Land again. Here comes Thibaud, fresh from King Henry at Famagusta."

Just once they heard the sound of hooves, and then nothing, until horses came at them across the sand. The six men who rode behind Thibaud broke off into a fan and made for the landward reaches of the bay. Olivier held Thibaud's stirrup and the Grand Master stretched himself out of the saddle and came to the ground, putting his weight on Olivier's shoulder. Beltran gave him water and he sat reclining on the beach and let his bones start to ache. Diego went to look at the horses' feet and came back.

"Muffled," he said to the place in general, as if accusing somebody.

"Will you tell me," Thibaud asked pleasantly, "what has passed?"

Olivier laughed and told him about the house, and the men with mules, and the barrels of silver, and of how the two ships had come into the bay and Diego had come off in the boat, by which the sailors still slept.

"Nothing untoward?" Thibaud lifted his voice towards Diego.

"Nothing," Diego answered, "except that here we all are, wearing sergeants' cloaks because they are black, even yourself, hiding from nothing in the middle of nowhere and starting at moonbeams."

"There is no moon tonight," Thibaud said.

"I admit it," Diego said.

"After all, Diego, our mantles are white."

"I admit that too!"

"Well then. The gold is in the 'Lion'?"

"It is," Silence grew and they heard the sound of oars over the water.

"Here comes Zazzara," Thibaud said.

Diego took Olivier by the arm and walked him along the beach. "I must cool my head," he said. "I am not safe. I shall go mad. 'Here comes Zazzara' he says. Why did he not tell me Zazzara was in that ship? Zazzara is as much my friend as his. Am I not to be trusted to know Zazzara is in that ship? Black mantles, muffled hooves, secret meetings, hired escorts—where from, we may ask—I cannot abide all this. Who is this enemy I cannot see? I am not told. I am told nothing."

He thought, what am I doing, babbling like this? Am I a child, or too old perhaps? I am too old for all this. Olivier has not spoken, he knows me too well. He is lucky, his pride is on different things from mine. Even this exile does not hurt his pride. It wounds Beltran's pride. How he hurts, my poor Beltran, he wears it on his sleeve. So do I then, so do I. Why, there is a star running across the sky, and another.

They watched the stars fly under the black night and turned to walk down the sand on the edge of the sea. "Everything is splitting," Olivier said, "and takes new shapes."

Diego made nothing of this. "It is not the secrecy itself that vexes me," he discovered, "it is that because of the secrecy, things make no sense."

"That is what I said," Olivier told him.

They joined Thibaud and Beltran as Zazzara's barge pulled in broadside to the shore. The Venetian jumped into the shallow water and ran up the beach. "Well met," he said. "That went off well. Stay a moment," and he left them until his men had put a ramp down from the barge and had begun to roll the barrels up it. "Now then," he said, "I am at your service."

Thibaud led them towards the house. "Zazzara!" Diego said. "Is that you, Diego?" Surprise and pleasure were in Zazzara's voice. "I thought you were still at Sidon." The two men embraced and moved on more slowly than the others; Thibaud was setting an eager pace.

"Well," Diego said, getting to grips once again with the

3

amazements of working for Thibaud. "You did not know I was on the 'Lion'?"

"I thought you were at Sidon. I have seen you in my mind's eye, paddling in blood and smiling like a child."

"Ah, that is not fair, Zazzara. I cannot help it if my face works the wrong way round."

"I did not know you knew of it," Zazzara exclaimed, who thought he knew as much of physiognomy as any man in the market-place.

"It is an affliction," Diego said. "It is ridiculous."

"Hardly that," Zazzara said. "When you are furious your expression is delightful, when you are delighted you look furious; in my business I should make an asset of it."

"Good," Diego said, "for it may come to that yet." At this they kept on in silence for some moments, which was broken by Zazzara.

"Still," he said, "this is better. I am glad you are with us."

"No offence to you, but I am not glad about it at all," Diego said, his voice turning low and confidential. "I had rather be on the walls of my castle, where I belong, and where I know why I am living or dying. I find this hole and corner work quite beyond me. It does not suit me; it is not becoming to men of our Order," he said with a burst of resentment in his voice.

"Is it not?" Irony and amusement flavoured Zazzara's words. "You have been long sequestered at Sidon."

"I know the Temple are bankers and politicians besides being soldiers," Diego said irritably, "but this is none of these, all these mysteries and secrets."

Zazzara laughed. "My dear Diego," he said. "This is exactly banking and politics. It is my meat and drink."

"Not mine," Diego said. "Not mine." Gripping the Venetian by the arm so suddenly that Zazzara stopped, Diego spoke close into his face. "He is behaving very strangely."

"Then tell me."

"We do not sleep in the commandery at Limassol. He has hired a house."

"Well?"

"Well? Well, and he has hired an escort of ruffians as if he feared for his life."

"And?"

"And? Well then, he tells me nothing. He did not say you would be in that galley, and he did not tell you I was in the 'Lion'."

Zazzara thought about this and decided there was not much to it. "He has only been here two days, Diego and has had a great deal to see to. At such times great men reckon their own people only as afterthoughts."

"I do not mind being an afterthought," Diego said untruthfully, "but what of these mysteries?"

Zazzara lifted Diego's hand off his arm. "The house and the escort?" It is absurd that he does not see it for himself, he thought. What a gulf there is between those who know and those who do not. "First," he said, "your commandery at Limmasol was emptied to help defend Acre, and he does not trust the new men who have come from France." Diego at once became restless and Zazzara hushed him. "Second, because he wants a Crusade and others do not, his life is in danger. Third, I found the house for him and the escort are mine, and they will be paid twice what they were paid the day before, each morning that he wakes in this world and not the next. They are Catalans, and their word is as good as yours or mine. Possibly better," he amended, and went on as Diego drew breath to speak, "and you should reflect, Diego, that he trusts you with the richest galley on the sea— which is why you were brought from Sidon—before you set too much store by the secrets that you have not yet shared!"

Oliviers's voice came to them through the lemon trees. "Zazzara! Diego!"

"We are coming," Zazzara called back, and persuading forward the reluctant Diego, who was sufficiently silenced but anxious to fit all this news into an intelligible framework, the Venetian ended on a lighter note as they stepped into the rose garden.

"As to why you did not see me on my galley. I was not, in the exact sense, hiding. My shipmaster handled the ship; my clerk tallied the gold; as for me, I have a woman with me I am fond of."

"A woman! Party to my business!" Even across the darkness, they felt the change come to Thibaud as to a man who has been bitten by a snake.

"Party to mine only," Zazzara said mildly. "But why should you think, who know nothing of them, that women may not be trusted?"

"It must be secret! It must all be secret!" His voice was out of his bidding and flickered here and there as meaningless as the darting of a lizard on a wall, but it ended, with horrible effect upon its hearers, in the forlorn wail of a child. His three knights drew together like fox cubs surprised in their earth, and only Zazzara took this revelation of frailty in the Grand Master in his stride, as something to be negotiated at the instant and measured later.

"A secret is not something that nobody knows, Thibaud. It is something that nobody tells." He felt for the Grand Master in the darkness and found that he had his face huddled into his hands. What the devil, the Venetian thought, has he turned infant altogether? "Everything has gone well tonight, Thibaud. Why, there is enough good gold in that galley now to buy Rome."

The hands came slowly from the face and he found one of them being held in his own. "Good gold," Thibaud said seriously, "Good gold." Like that, hand in hand, he went with Zazzara into the house.

Chapter Ten

BELTRAN AND ZAZZARA

THE sun woke Beltran, and the wild-haired man on whom his eyes opened said, "Hist!" with a finger to his lips, and then pointed across the room to where Thibaud lay sleeping. The night before came back to Beltran. He nodded at the Catalan and the man jerked his head and settled back against the wall. Beltran stretched and got up from the divan and found his way out of the house, going down a wide passage and across a yard into the orchards. He passed through the lemon trees to the grassland above the bay, where the scent of thyme was already lifting in the new warmth, and found another Catalan there leaning on his spear and watching the sea. They smiled and Beltran said, "The road?" The Catalan held up his arm and on the hill above the house a spear waved in reply. Beltran found himself in good humour; as he left him, he gave the man a friendly smack on the shoulder which was at once returned.

He began to laugh at this new world he was in and went on to one of the points edging the bay and looked south. He hoped the galley had cleared the horizon before daybreak. Diego had not been clear in his mind whether to stay with the Grand Master or go with the "Lion", but the ship was in his care, and since she was to hide in Crete under the Venetian flag until Thibaud sent word, Diego took Olivier and sailed in her. The Grand Master was to be Beltran's care.

He turned towards the house, and then stopped: he felt light and full of activity. He had not felt like this since the night he watched the ship from Acre run under the walls of Sidon. He walked on a little way and stopped again. That was not true about Sidon; the truth was he had not felt like this since he was a boy. He looked about him at the sea, the sky and the wild flowers on the grass. He put remembrance away and continued up the slope, raising a hand to the guard as he passed. For a while, however, the feeling stayed with him.

He found Zazzara sitting in a huge bed eating an orange and as soon as Beltran came in the Venetian asked him, "Well, what are you going to do?" The question came like a demand but there was no time to answer it. "Thibaud must have no business and he must be gentled and comforted. I have seen this sickness before. If he will talk business, mention nothing that does not occur from him, and in all things be reassuring. What are you going to do? If he is pushed back into press of business he will grow worse. As it is he will be no good to you for a month or more." He jumped up from his bed and began to rub himself all over with a towel. He was skinny and his legs were like sticks; black hairs grew thick on his front and ran up the throat to mix with his beard. As he twisted and panted in his brisk toilet Beltran became aware that the black eyes and the hooked nose pointed always in his direction. The towel stopped and Zazzara said again, "What are you going to do?"

Beltran stared at a painted chest against the wall; the blue on it was singularly sweet. "I shall look after the Grand Master," he said, and looked up again, and saw the vivacious face fall into a sneer. Zazzara's head vanished inside the towel and he set about rubbing his scalp. Cracking noises came from the fireplace and an object skittered shining across the room; another jumped into the air and landed in the ashes and began to burn. Zazzara dropped his towel and scampered to the hearth and took out a shovel. "Chestnuts," he said. "See how I pamper myself, fires, towels, chestnuts. We all pamper ourselves, we men of the world." He opened the painted chest and rummaged in it, and came out with a handkerchief and peeled the husks off the hot nuts, offering one to the knight, who declined it. "No," Zazzara said, "you will not eat before noon." He chewed chestnuts and stood there looking at Beltran as if breaking fast so early were a sign of grace.

"What will you do in the world?" He took a great bundle of clothes from the chest and threw them on the bed, and from a corner cupboard took a little pot and rubbed some ointment into his hair and beard, considering the pile of garments. Beltran went over to the chest and looked at it, laying the lid down gently. "Thirty florins," Zazzara said, and took up a shirt. When his head came out of it he saw Beltran sitting on the chest and cried, "Not there, not there!" Beltran moved to a stone bench in the window and looked down into the courtyard where three of the Catalans sat in the sun.

"They look like good soldiers," he said. Zazzara came over and looked down, hopping from one foot to the other as he pulled on his hose, pale blue with leather soles. "Good soldiers!" he said. "They took Sicily from Anjou and kept it from the Pope. They call themselves Almugavars. When you buy them they are as loyal as kin." He went back to the bed and picked up two doublets, rejected the vermilion and put on the plain linen. "You do not answer my questions," he said, and took up a cloak of black cloth lined with green. "The island is in mourning," he said. "This would do well?" Beltran looked at it as if it were not there and Zazzara shrugged and put it on.

"What will I do in the world?" Beltran's eyes were either empty or private, Zazzara could not tell. "What I have always done. When I am not soldiering I shall be in cloisters."

"But your cloisters have been knocked flat; you are naked to the world!" The knight's eyes glimmered for a moment; amusement, had it been? "I do not know you, Beltran, I met you once at Sidon and again last night."

Beltran stood up, and they faced each other, two arms'-length apart. "Very well," Beltran said. "I know what you want. You want me to be one of those Templars who handle affairs, who manage estates or money, who can traffic in your world." His brow was curiously straight across, and tilted back with the eyes half closed as if they looked into the sun, or into the dust where a breach had just opened, the whole face took a stony and abstracted cast. "I am not one of those. I am a monk and a soldier." He then said with an acumen Zazzara found perversely irritating, "There is nothing here for you to respect, even in worldly terms. My grandfather was a bastard, my father made himself a knight by fighting and was killed thirty years ago by Christian Mongols. My mother was a shopkeeper's daughter from Qara, and went back there and the Mamelukes sacked it.

I am a native, a colonist, what they call 'poulain', and being born in the Holy Land does not make one a citizen of the world."

To Zazzara, who was a man of heart, the voice came as from a forest of isolation but his impulse to be in some way kind was stopped by the Templar's next words. "You do not need to know me, Zazzara," Beltran said, and when the Venetian looked up he found the blue eyes peaceful and still, withholding as it were their touch.

"I know!" Zazzara said. "You will look after the Grand Master!" He nodded a sarcastic metre into the words. He had met Templars who might have been Doge of Venice, and see— see!—what had been given him to work with! Indeed what had been given him? He still did not know. An enigmatic mule? A brainless mystic? Not, at any rate, a Doge of Venice.

"I have a great deal to do this morning," he said to Beltran. "It will not interest you, but now that the Sultan rules the Holy Land, I am going to bring the Syrian trade down to Cyprus from under the noses of the Genoese."

"It interests me enough. Genoa has a monopoly on the Golden Horn, but if you bring the Syrian trade south it benefits Venice and the Sultan at the expense of Genoa and Byzantium."

"Quite so," Zazzara said. "Where was I? Ah, yes!"

"That means," Beltran said, "that peace between the Christian and the Infidel suits you."

"Yes," Zazzara said. "Well, not exactly. What it means is that when a situation changes, there is always an advantage to be had from it."

"If you are in trade," Beltran said.

"If you are in anything," Zazzara said smartly. "Trade, politics or banking: the circumstances turn round, and the man who turns round the quickest has the main chance." But this was not what he had meant to talk about. Now then!

"I do not see," Beltran said, "why you are helping Thibaud, since he wants a Crusade and you do not."

When Zazzara had sat up in bed an hour ago he had felt full of vigour. He had done the business with Thibaud, and while that had taken an evil turn with Thibaud's collapse, it was not his business to look after the Order of the Temple. He had done his duty by Thibaud, and he would illuminate this Beltran's mind so far as was necessary or possible, leave them this house as a hospital and be off to Famagusta. A quick meeting with his fellow-Venetians, an audience with the king and all would be in train, and then off to his little lady! He almost shouted: what is happening to my fine day? This creature, who had begun by wearing the demeanour of a dead tree, was beginning to flicker into life like a burning bush. Zazzara thought of going back to bed. "I shall eat my cap if I do any such thing," he exhorted himself.

"My cap! I have forgot my cap!" He hoisted up the lid of the chest with such force that it banged against the wall and a chip of paint flew off it. "Hell and devils," he whispered. Not to be able to swear, since this nuisance was a monk! He threw things out of the chest. He found a black cap and put it on. He faced Beltran squarely.

"I have an office here. Come on, this room is full of rubbish," and he waved his hands at the orange peel on the bed-clothes and the floor, the litter of ash and chestnut skins, and the garments that hung off the bed and poured from the chest. He hustled his visitor out with his hands still making figures in the air, as if they were not sure where the rubbish ended and Beltran began.

In the office, plain as a kennel, Zazzara felt businesslike again and started as soon as he was past the door. "I have been helping Thibaud because once he helped me. My policy, which will be Venetian policy, is opposed to his policy, but it is a rule of business to know that such divergences need make no difference to the final issue, or at least, none that cannot be turned to advantage. You need not understand that. All I say is that I owed Thibaud a favour and now he has called it in. What he wanted—." He brought a coin out of his purse and put it on Beltran's palm. "Have you seen these before?"

On one side a saint was handing a staff to a kneeling man, and on the other Christ stood in a nimbus and looked at Beltran. There were nine stars about Him and light shone round His head, and He held out His hand to bless. Beltran held the image light and firm on his fingertips. You are my sweet Saviour, Beltran told Christ. You have been long from my sight. My faith is drawn into a knot and hides from me and the parts of my being do not see each other; they stumble like men blinded and put in the desert, and being alone and separate they have no use of themselves and no way to go. When my faith lets me take pleasure of it I am whole of soul and body, but now it hides from me and I am in many parts, and each calls to me day by day from farther off. As he heard it spoken the anguish rose and he cried out, it has been a bitter trial Oh Christ my Saviour. The image in the shining cloud grew larger. The knight looked up at the Saviour and adored Him and between them lay tears, for Christ wept for the sins and sorrows of men. By Your love I am redeemed, Beltran said. The golden face reproached him with the Holy Land: who honours My Calvary? The knot in Beltran came loose and he knew Christ had untied it.

In the plain room dust fell from the rafters and the Venetian watched some of it pass through sunrays and settle on the coin. If I had a coin like that, he said to himself, for every bit of dust that's floated in this little office since that man went into his contemplation, then I could retire tomorrow. How the man worshipped!

"It's marvellously yellow." Other than that his tongue was dry, there was nothing to tell you that anything had happened to him in his silence.

"It is the soundest coin there is, the only coin you can be sure is not debased." He turned it in Beltran's fingers. "St. Mark giving his standard to the Doge, and on the reverse Our Lord, as you have seen. First minted seven years ago. That's what Thibaud bought from me, Venetian ducats." He stood up and walked the floor, three steps there and three back. "Thibaud is the only man I know who sees the same distance ahead as I do. The afterpart of that great galley is full of gold Byzantines. Now the Byzantine is a coin much debased, but so is most other coinage these days. Thibaud's been ringing gold and not so gold Byzantines in his Treasury at Acre for the last three years, and it was three years ago I conceived of capturing the Egyptian trade when the time came. So there you are: Thibaud found he was running out of good Byzantines, and the Treasury in Nicosia being mostly silver, he sought good gold coin to buy with it.

No harm to me, they are short of silver in Egypt and I'll use it to buy my way in. Good gold, you see, that's what he kept saying last night."

"Good gold." The coin lay on the table.

"What's it for?"

"For the Holy Land."

"You are in his confidence?"

"No one is."

"Then why do you say, it's for the Holy Land?"

"I saw him when he came into Sidon from Acre."

"This Crusade of his!"

"This Crusade of Christendom's!"

Zazzara sat down again. So much for meetings with his fellow-businessmen. He would try for the king this afternoon, and then in the evening, partridge and the fair Ginevra! Meanwhile, he must free his conscience of these Templars, whose Grand Master was out of his wits and whose treasure was cruising aimlessly between Cyprus and Crete.

"I must disabuse you about this Crusade. There will be no serious talk of one for twenty years; it is not possible. The princes of Europe are over-spent and either tied to their own wars or their own ends. Trade prospers exceedingly and the princes tax exceedingly, a combination too delightful to be interrupted simply to re-establish uncertain markets in the Holy Land. Yes," he forestalled interruption, "Markets, markets, markets! That is the world today. Money as well, and they are short of money. Listen! Last year Edward threw out the Jews; this year Philip is making friends with the Jews, and when he has run through them they will be out of France as well."

"Don't they know that?"

"Of course they know that! They discount it, this way and that way. Jews are not safe, ever, all they can do is last out where they can. Where was I? Yes, when Philip turns the Jews out, who will he turn to?" He looked at Beltran savagely. "You don't know! Thibaud knows! The Temple in Paris knows!"

"He will turn to the Temple?"

"He will certainly turn to the Temple. They are half his bankers already. They are bankers to most of royal Europe already, but now they would be, they would be the whole Treasury of the Kingdom of France! Think of it!"

"I cannot." It seemed to Zazzara that there were several inflections the Templar might have brought to this comment and that he had used them all. He came crossly down to earth again.

"Well, try to think of it, because if there are two things the bankers at the Temple in Paris, and the king himself for that matter, don't want, they are these." One finger. "They do not want their funds poured out on a forlorn Crusade; to them it would be a wild goose chase." Second finger. "They do not want the Treasury of the Order in the East sculling about in a galley ruddered by this or that whim or divine inspiration of Thibaud Gaudin!" He came down the straight triumphantly. "They are short of gold in Europe; they will want Thibaud's gold now that it is freed from the Holy Land! And there is another side to all these things." He stopped listening to the noise of his own thunders and began to be interested in what he was saying.

"The princes have to watch the people behind their heads. Last year the great Monteferrato ruled a dozen cities in Lombardy —Pavia, Asti, Novara, Vercelli, many more—and this year, where is he? Their communes have deposed him. Is it a sign?" He wondered cheerfully. Quite an interesting morning after all. "From these things therefore, you will see that you must not think of Crusades. Europe is not what it was two hundred years ago when it Crusaded its way over the Holy Land; everything is different, as I hope I have described. As for the Holy Land, it is extinguished. You must think of it," he sought for an image that would be easily grasped, "as out of date, like iron weapons. You must think of it as of Europe two hundred years ago. Nobody wants it back."

When the Templar answered cold ashes filled Zazzara's skull. What Beltran said was: "You are wrong. I must think of the Holy Land as it was 1300 years ago less nine, and I must think that God wants it back."

Had someone presented Zazzara with a cantata, calling it a Bill of Exchange and expecting it to be honoured, the Venetian's confusion would have been of the same kind that now overtook him: Yet the example could have been engendered by nothing but the dire transaction between himself and this mortifying knight, of which the one thing that had finally become clear to him was that one of them was merely a spectator.

It had come to Zazzara that all morning he had been in the presence of something that refused to be deciphered: something that inhabited the Templar of which in his mind the man was hardly yet aware, but to which the instincts of his body already listened and had begun to answer. From this had grown, in spite of Beltran's inattention, Zazzara's feeling of being watched, and from this the unclouded but undisclosing eye. Now Zazzara saw a shape to the paradoxes which had tripped him, to the incongruous mixture of stolid faith and sceptical acumen, the plain soldier sitting in a trance over the coin, and—what had most struck the Venetian—Beltran's stale description of himself as a nobody whose own history was cold to him, with its curt but oddly eloquent ending: You do not need to know me.

To all this Zazzara could ascribe the sense that Beltran was both there and absent, the passive calm of his regard; to this and to something more. For whereas, by Zazzara's way of it, what the man had needed was a simple lesson on how to take his first steps into the world, it now turned out that Beltran was already embarked on a journey in which his meeting with the Venetian was no more than a momentary and unimportant pause.

Zazzara, though always eager to add to his experience of men, could not quite make out what it was he was saying to himself, and he did not esteem propositions which, however well they might stand up within their own clothes, admitted of no external accountability. What is all this? he asked himself. Have I been as long in my abstraction as he was over that Venetian ducat? He looked at it glinting on the table, and heard a sound in his simple question that made him repeat it to himself: he had found the alternative proposition, that the man was after the gold.

Even then he did not believe it. It was true that the simple-seeming Beltran about whom such an evil would not occur to anybody had now been replaced by this mystery, but two things stood against it: the first, Zazzara's belief that whatever it was that moved in the man opposite, Beltran himself could not name it; the second, that the lust for gold was a shallow but perpetual thing, like a running fever, and that what lay in Beltran had not lain there long, but lay in him deep. Yet he would test it, for had he not undertaken, even as he burnt his fingers on the chestnuts, to see that before he made his adieux to this business with the Order of the Temple, he would make it as sure as might be that their Grand Master was in good hands? He opened a Levantine face upon the Templar.

Beltran smiled at him and the look in his blue eyes put an uneasy remembrance of something into Zazzara's mind. He had once been kidnapped by bandits in Albania and the ransom from Corfu had been long in coming. He recalled now the unseemly candour with which the chief of these desperadoes had regarded him each evening across the supper table, and the feeling it had raised in him (utterly contrary to justice) that he was the simple animal, and the Albanian the subtle creature built in God's image. He shifted his gaze from Beltran's.

"Have you heard of Roger Flor?"

"Yes," Beltran said. "He is a sergeant in the Order. Why?"

"He made his fortune at Acre. He seized a galley and made those who wanted a place in her leave all their jewels and money at his feet."

Beltran studied this. "Geoffrey will be sorry," he said.

"Geoffrey?"

"The man at Thibaud's house in Famagusta. Geoffrey was captured by the Mamelukes at Acre, he was manacled to a wall and cut his hand off to escape; now he calls himself Gauchemain." He smiled for a moment and then frowned. "He said Roger Flor fought manfully at Acre."

Zazzara was learning nothing. "However that may be, now Roger Flor is rich," he said.

Beltran looked at him. "No," he said. "He is foresworn. He will burn in Hellfire."

Zazzara was ashamed but persisted. "Do you know what Thibaud means to do with the gold?"

"That is plain. He hopes to support a Crusade."

"And now that there is to be no Crusade, what will he do with it?"

"You say there will be no Crusade."

"Then if there is no Crusade?"

"Then he means to keep the money safe, for the Holy Land."

The eyes of the Albanian bandit looked at him again, and he could not tell if he was being played with, or if this man was really content with the belief that enlightenment would come to him piecemeal, as it was needed, over affairs that would have made Cardinals scratch their heads. He came suddenly to the point.

"What would you do with the money if Thibaud stayed mad?"

Beltran looked at him close "I would obey Diego." Then he smiled. "Ah," he said. "Roger Flor! You think I'm going to steal the gold.

"The money belongs to the Order," Beltran said, finding his reply as he spoke, "and the Order belongs to the Holy Land, and yet you tell me the Order no longer wants to belong to the Holy Land. You say that the Order in Europe is so rich it can no longer afford a Crusade, which it would call a wild-goose chase." On the last phrase his lips seemed hardly to touch the words for distaste. He stood up. "For my part I cannot understand it; if that is how they think, then I cannot understand how they believe. Are there two Orders?" A bewildered look came up in his eyes and gave place again to that inflexible calm. "Still, I am not a young man and I can see you may be right. More than that I have no answer to your question." Then, apparently inconsequent, "I have not prayed to Saint Hilary this morning," he said, and he left Zazzara staring at the wall.

The Venetian rounded his shoulders and hunched himself together and rocked back and forward on his stool. He thought: I do not envy him, he conducts himself like a man who knows dragon's teeth have been sown in his soul. He thought also: He is like a man who has been bitten by a rabid dog, and waits. Then he grew still and looked at the wall for a long time and pictured the knight praying to his Saint.

The ashes that had earlier filled his skull now sat in his mouth, and from a corner cupboard he took a flask of spirit and drank from it. He washed the spirit round his teeth and spat out the window, and then drank again and swallowed. He looked out at the sea and the sky and the lemon trees and the roses in his garden.

Chapter Eleven

THE CATALANS

IN his dealings with Saint Hilary Beltran was plain and soldierly, for Hilary was the Saint of the Order and the two of them were on an easy footing. He knelt in the room off the courtyard where his baggage and saddlery had been put, and with his knees hurting on the stone floor and the unplastered walls about him, felt at home for the first time since he had left Sidon.

He asked Hilary to intercede with Heaven for Thibaud Gaudin, since the Order was in sore straits with Thibaud out of his wits. He asked that Diego might be strengthened in wisdom during his guardianship of the "Lion" and "that which is in her", and that he himself might be guided in his actions "for to have the Grand Master in my care is not a light matter, Blessed Hilary, and one in which I have no experience." He commended to the Saintly vigilance the whole affairs of the Temple, in case there might be any spirit in the Order in need of correction and not holding as fast as he and the blessed Hilary to the need to win back the Holy Land for the Saviour. Lastly he asked the Saint, if he found the services of the Venetian merchant acceptable, to turn Zazzara's soul towards the Order for that "he seems a man of good heart and knows the world, which I do not."

He said thirteen Our Fathers and thirteen Hail Marys and returned to Saint Hilary to point out that so long as he was in this secular house with Thibaud Gaudin to look after, he saw no way in which he might attend Mass or hear the Office, and asked to be exempt from these and other duties inhibited by this predicament, as if he were on campaign, and according to the Rule.

So his prayers ended, and he stood up. He had said nothing to Saint Hilary of his encounter with Christ, and he had made no choice to speak or not to speak of it, it was just that it had not come to him to do so.

He picked up two of the bags from the floor, and also his sword, and going out into the yard settled down in a sunny corner a little way from the chattering Catalans.

If a knight had no other task given him he should see to his harness, said the Rule. Beltran had been given, or given himself, no other task. The Alexandrian doctor, who had been brought off the ship when Diego went on board, tended Thibaud and would not have him disturbed. There were four of the Catalans in the courtyard so two of them were doubtless keeping their watch. These people were about their business and he would let them be. Perhaps Thibaud would grow well, but if he did not there would be courses to be determined, and Beltran wanted to settle into himself before he determined anything.

Three days ago they had left the Castle of the Sea, and Beltran had taken this sword fresh from the armoury, his other having been broken by that huge Mameluke. It would be his seventh sword. Being from store it was good with oil, but it must be edged. Every commandery had a brother whose skill this was, and there would be one at Limassol; but when might he get there? He would whet it himself. If Thibaud stayed ill, then what was to be done? The gold would be sitting at Crete, the Order would be waiting in Europe to hear from its Grand Master, and the houses of the Temple in Cyprus would ask themselves where he was. They were not many, as the Order of St. John now owned half the island, but they had a right to news of Thibaud. Yet these matters of the Order had to be settled in the same space of the mind that held thought of Thibaud's Crusade, his intention for the gold, and the pictures of the western world that Zazzara had painted for him.

He leaned over his sword with his whetstone and whispered to it, "If I am to answer these questions, then they shall be answered by me." The sword begun to lose its dull edge.

What he meant was that if it fell to him to answer them, it would be for the one reason: that he was a knight of the Temple. It was true that the Holy Land was lost, Thibaud prostrate, the Treasure of the Temple at sea, a Crusade in doubt, his Order perhaps divided, and the affairs of Europe intricated with many policies, but none of these things in itself, and not all of these things together, had any force that could oblige him to their service. It was only as Thibaud's watch-dog (and if Thibaud's wits continued to sleep) that he could be called on to bark or bite.

He touched his finger on the blade, harder, and got no blood, "You are blunt, sword, blunt," he said, and whetted on.

He was Thibaud's watch-dog because he was a knight of the Temple. It was from the Temple he should look out upon these questions and see them with a Templar's eyes. That was the dilemma: he was not this morning as much a Templar as he had been a month ago before Acre had fallen, or three days ago before they had left Sidon, or twelve hours ago before Thibaud had turned child. He longed to be in a commandery, with the brothers about him, knights and sergeants, to watch the armourer put the edge on this new sword, to hear the bell sound and the Offices sung by the chaplains. All things, however, had their season, and this was the season for exile from the blessings of the Order: yet they were within him and would support him in due time.

Meantime he would stay close, the watch-dog in his hutch, who lets what footsteps pass that may, in the world outside. He laid the sword down and took his harness from his bags and spread it about him, the arms and armour of the Temple in which his strength lay: Turkish mace, his long dagger, the little knife he kept in his boot and the mailed breeches, and the mailed hood and its iron cap. He took the dagger into his hand and slapped it on his cheek and held it there, and looked at the objects of iron, steel and leather among which he sat. "We knew your fathers," he said, and laughed aloud. "He and I," and he slapped the dagger on his skin again, "we knew your fathers." Only the dagger had shared his twenty and more years in the Order, everything else had been replaced here and there. He hefted the dagger in his hand, one piece of steel which had stayed true from point to pommel, the blade a foot long; the wooden pieces of the hilt were fresh two years ago and still deeply scored.

He did not see what a Templar might be expected to do about a demented Grand Master and, if it came to it, a galley filled with gold: the life of a brother of the Temple was to fight the

Infidel, pray eight times a day, obey lawful commands and among other things, keep his harness clean, and these were not practices that brought a man naturally onto the roads that had begun to lay themselves before him, but there was no question that the way would be made clear.

He took the little tub of oil from its bag and began to furbish his hauberk. It had taken some hurt on the walls of Sidon but his breeches—he stirred them with his foot to see the bent and broken rings of mail—had taken more. One sword at Sidon, but where had he broken the others, six was it, or five? He thought he was remembering but in fact his mind had stopped, and he sat there with the turn of a smile at one side of his lips and rubbed away at the dour metal.

When the voice woke him the hauberk was neatly piled at his side and he was working on the mail of his breeches, so he must have been at it for some time. He looked up and saw one of the Catalans looking down at him. The man had a frank smile touched by shyness and from his dark, almost black, brown eyes intense curiosity looked out. His hair was black and hung raggedly round his face. Beltran put him at about forty, his own age. He stopped the work and greeted the man, who nodded at an astonishing rate with his tongue in the side of his mouth for so long that after a while this seemed like a reply, but then he shifted his position, feet, and arms, and moved the leaning of his body from one side to the other, and spoke.

"Your weapons?"

"Yes," Beltran said.

"Can I look?"

"Yes."

The man came down onto his toes, squatting at Beltran's level and picked up the sword. At its weight he whistled.

"There is no point, the end is rounded," he said.

"It goes in," Beltran said, "if it is kept sharp, and it cuts across without stopping."

"It is not sharp."

"No, it is not. I lost a sword at Sidon. This is fresh from the armoury."

The man seemed pleased with that. "You lost it?"

"It was broken for me by a Mameluke."

He had large teeth and most of them became visible to Beltran, as if they waited to see the Mameluke meet his deserts. "Why did he not kill you?"

Beltran pointed to the little knife. "I cut his hamstring with that and he fell off the wall."

The man felt the knife. "It is sharp." He fingered the hauberk, nodded at the mace as if they had met before, admired the dagger and picked up the little bread-knife. He threw it up and caught it and laughed.

"I eat with that," Beltran said. The man drew his thumb across the edge and whistled. "It cuts where you put it," Beltran said, and they both laughed, and sat back and looked at each other.

"I am Corberan i Lluch," the Catalan told him.

"I'm Beltran," The Catalan looked at him. "Roche, my father's name was Roche," the knight said carefully, since his grandfather owned no patronymic. It was clear that the man understood this, and Beltran wondered at this gift of hearing what was not spoken and of speaking in return without speech.

"You are a seigneur," Corberan told Beltran.

"I am a knight."

"Then you are a seigneur." He bounced a little on his toes, suddenly at a loss like a child who suspects his presence has outlasted its worth, and then his face broke brightly open. "I will edge your sword for you?"

Beltran nodded slowly. "Let me see."

The Catalan turned, rose and moved off in one agile leap and ran across the yard to where his friends sat and returned. He sat with his back to the wall beside Beltran and held up his hand, which had a whetstone in it. He took the sword and laid the stone to it as if in six months or so there might be a use for the weapon, and stroked it as lightly as if he were thinning a spider's web. "First they must kiss each other," he explained. The stone warmed to the blade and they hissed at each other.

"You are a monk?"

"Yes," Beltran said.

"Are you a good monk?"

"Sometimes I feel I am a good monk, and sometimes I know I am not."

"No." The hissing stopped. "I mean, are you a good monk with women." Beltran looked at him, astonished. It was not a subject on which it was right for him to talk. The Catalan may have noticed that in his own terms the question was ambiguous, and came at it directly.

"Do you have women?"

"No!"

"How do you manage?"

Beltran had never before met a Christian who would ask such a question, though he had been asked by an Infidel if it would not be wiser to be eunuched. The Templar looked very hard at the Catalan but could not find, after scrutinizing the friendly and innocent face, which he must now also regard as both savage and depraved, that Corberan was seriously put out.

He spoke very distinctly. "We mortify the flesh," and he kept his eyes on the other man and his lips a little parted so that when Corberan drew breath to chase on after this forbidden hare, Beltran moved his head down a little just once, as if he had the upper hand of an opponent and his knife at the throat, and the Catalan subsided.

"We Almugavars, we need women all the time," he said, and it sounded as if the Almugavars had been bred to compensate for the celibacy of monks. Corberan's whetstone hissed and Beltran worked on at his mail.

Corberan spoke. "That was your Mameluke?"

Beltran was working round the broken mail in his breeches. "Yes," he said. "He had an axe. It turned on my sword and struck me with the back of the axehead."

The Catalan clicked his tongue in his mouth with pleasure. "He had his strength, that one. Lucky you cut his hamstring. Lucky your leg did not break. Much hurt?"

"It hurt inside; not so much now."

Another of the Catalans crossed the courtyard and sat on his toes as Corberan had first done. He and Beltran regarded each other and nodded and the man settled down to watch them work.

After a while something occurred to Beltran and he asked, "Why are you called Almugavars? It sounds like Saracen."

"Saracen? No," Corberan said. He whistled through his teeth as if he had left something at home a thousand miles away and only just remembered it. "Why are we called Almugavars? Almugavars! I don't know." He pointed his whetstone at the newcomer. "You tell him, Berenguer. He is our leader," he explained to Beltran.

"My name is Berenguer de Bellarbe," the man said.

"And his is Beltran Roche," Corberan said. "Why are we called Almugavars?"

"I am a man of family, seigneur," Berenguer de Bellarbe said.

"It was evident, seigneur," Beltran said.

Corberan i Lluch whistled once again through his teeth and spoke as if he were singing. "Two farms, one stolen from a cousin in the courts, a castle that size," and he mimed an object the size of a lemon, "that fell down two hundred years ago when the Saracens breathed on it, and he is a man of family!"

Afterwards Beltran was sure that the other was in the air while Corberan was still speaking. Berenguer had his fellow by the hair and with that hand pulled the throat taut and drove it down onto Beltran's sword which the other hand forced against the neck. His face bulged with rage, and the eyes which at peace were the same colour as his victim's had actually turned darker, and blood had run into the whites of them. In the face of this extraordinary passion Corberan gave out nothing more than a giggle, and stared with intensity but no emotion into the eyes of the avenger. After some moments of this Corberan winked at Berenguer and said, "Hey, Berenguer. Where my neck is, that sword is blunt, eh?" Berenguer thought about this and took his hands away and slapped Corberan lightly on the place where the sword had been.

"The sword is blunt, my Corberan." He went back where he had been and looked at Beltran. "How do we call you?"

With such a gift for rage, Beltran thought, and such a habit of saying whatever comes into their heads, it is surprising any of them are still alive. "Beltran," he said, "or Brother Beltran."

"He is a monk," Corberan said, "no women."

"He has no breeding," Berenguer said to Beltran. "I have thought about it," he said, "and I do not know why we are called Almugavars." He turned to Corberan, who had taken to his whetstone again. "That sword should be put on the wheel."

"We can put it on the wheel later," Corberan said, "but he may need it in the meantime." Then he laid the sword in his lap and stretched, "Still, I am tired of this. I will do more tomorrow."

Beltran was astonished: to lay down the task before it was finished.

"It is odd, I think, for so great a lord as you to clean his own armour," Corberan said.

"I am not a great lord, and it is in the Rule."

"What is the Rule?" Corberan asked.

Beltran told him that the Rule ordained how his days should be spent, from waking to sleeping; and what they should eat; and what they must do and must not do; and how they must not mix more than was needful with the world. He frowned suddenly and bent over his mail.

"What are you thinking?" Corberan asked him. What a question for such a fiery people to ask! Beltran shifted between humour and awkwardness.

"I am thinking of the Rule," he said, but the Almugavar could sustain that look of ingenuous interrogation all day, and he was driven to answer with what was exercising him.

"It says in the Rule, that on campaign we must seek permission before entering a part of the camp not occupied by troops of the Religious Orders," he said.

"Ah," Berenguer said softly, and a sneer curved through his voice as if the one were the natural element for the other. "He means he is too grand to talk to us!" This imagined slight began to raise in him another murderous fit of rage.

Beltran looked for his dagger, but Corberan chucked his whetstone at Berenguer's face so that he had to catch it, and said to his leader, "It is you has no breeding. If a man lives by a Rule, he must think about it. Look at him, he will clean all that harness until there is no spot or stiffness in it, because of his Rule. This Rule must be a pretty serious thing for him."

Berenguer was much struck by this. "Pretty serious; yes, it must be. Are the rewards great?"

"Yes," Beltran said. "They are great."

"How much?" Corberan's eyes shone with anticipation.

"In earthly things we are provided for, clothes, harness, food and roofs over our heads. We are allowed no possessions; nothing belongs to us of our own."

"Hey?" Corberan said.

"I see," Berenguer explained it to Corberan. "He expects his reward in Heaven." Beltran rubbed away and said nothing. "Is it not so?" Berenguer insisted. Corberan looked at his leader, alive to the new animosity in his voice. Beltran looked at him too, and nodded.

Berenguer brought his head round so that his eyes moved over Beltran's and then went on to look at nothing in particular. He asked, "Do you expect to sit in a higher place in Heaven than I shall?"

Corberan smiled hurriedly as if he had played enough with Berenguer's pride for the time being. This made Beltran more sure that he was right in what the question held; Berenguer was tender on the point of station, but there was a deep wound in him if he was ready to quarrel on earth over his seat in Heaven. Beltran forgot this, however, in the discovery that he found his answer a little surprising.

He waited until Berenguer would face him again, and said, "No."

"Well then!" Corberan said.

"Shush!" Berenguer told him, seeming deeply pleased, "These things are beyond you." He had been taut and now settled into himself. "See!" He pulled from its sheath the extraordinarily long knife that lay there, and put it across Corberan's thighs beside Beltran's sword. It was little more then half as long as the sword, but it was more than a knife, the blade stout and broad and coming to a point.

"It is your sword?" Beltran was pleased to ask, instead of answer, for a change.

"Yes. Here, take it," and he put it in Beltran's hand. It was heavy towards the hilt and at first felt unbalanced. "You hold

it low, and push. It is a stabbing sword," and he handled it.
How did it work in practice?

Berenguer took up Beltran's sword and held it up with the
crosspiece between his face and the Templar's, "Heavy." He
moved it up and down. "Do you have a war-cry?"

"Yes. We cry 'Beauséant!'"

"'Beauséant!' That's good, eh, Corberan?" Corberan nodded,
and asked, "What does it mean?"

"It is the name of our standard, which is black and white.
Beauséant means parti-coloured, pied."

There was some disappointment at this tame ascription, and
the two Almugavars looked a little vague.

"What is your war-cry?" Beltran asked them.

They came alive at once and Corberan leaned back and began
to howl at the top of his voice, "Aur! Aur!" Berenguer dived
forward and slapped his hand over the other man's mouth, and
the two men on the other side of the courtyard were already
on their feet. "Fool and henwit!" Berenguer spoke over his
hand. "You will bring in the sentries!" Corberan lifted his eyebrows and nodded, and Berenguer took his hand off and sat
back.

"How if I shout it quietly?" Corberan suggested, his eyes
flashing and all his teeth showing happily, shamed neither by the
forceful rebuke nor the cause of it, and Berenguer nodded.

"It goes like this," Corberan said to Beltran, and he tilted
back his face and looked down his nose—"That is not part of it,"
his leader said—and filled his face with a glowing stare through
which he smiled horribly. "Like this," he said, and passed through
his mouth from the back of his throat a sound like a dog protest-
ing against being slowly strangled. "Aur! Aur! Desperta ferre!"
Berenguer regarded the performance coldly and the two Almugavars who had walked over looked at Corberan in surprise, but
he was unchastened as ever and said to Beltran, "Not bad, eh?
Chill your blood, eh?"

"Desperta ferre!" Beltran repeated it softly to himself. "Desperta ferre!" Something in him moved and the top of his back
grew stiff. "It means iron, awake?"

Corberan glanced at the others and fixed his brown eyes

fondly on Beltran. "See!" He was triumphant. "He understands me, even though I have to whisper it in case I start a battle!"

"It sounds very old," Beltran said, still as if to himself.

He found Berenguer looking at him, and the Almugavar spoke. "Why does it make you sad?" He smiled as if that itself would do for an answer. "Yes," he said, "it means 'iron awake'! It is very old, at least to me it has always seemed very old.

"We are a very old race," Corberan said swiftly, sensing that he was being left out from something. "We have lived in the same place for a thousand years, my family, at any rate. All fighters," he ended. His voice had become lame before the indifference of his fellows. "I will fight you," he said suddenly to Beltran, and fetched their interest back to him, "We will have a trial, your sword against mine!"

Beltran did not want to fight anybody, but it was not left to him. "I shall fight him," Berenguer declared. "He is a seigneur and you are of no account."

Corberan took the insult with contentment. "He will choose," he said. "But he should fight me, because I met him first."

Beltran looked at Berenguer and said. "I shall fight Corberan, then. Because I met him first." Berenguer smiled, and apparently his pride was safe.

"Very well," Berenguer said tremendously. "Since it is only play, Corberan will be enough."

There was, all at once, a great deal of sound and movement about Beltran and it occurred to him that if they spent less time doing nothing, they would not be so excited about a little sword-play. He stood and stretched, and put on his iron cap, and took off his mantle to stand in his jerkin and trousers, to a display of eager attentiveness from Berenguer, who having folded the Templar's mantle and laid it on his armour where much of it was not in the dust, clapped his hands as if he himself were to take part in the exercise and was impatient to begin, and repeated this all the while he kept up his close regard on Beltran's (surely simple?) preparations. Corberan dashed to the other side of the court to return with his sword and a headpiece of barred iron and stood a little way off as if he had chosen the ground and had begun, for he struck hardily at an imaginary foe and, indeed, vanquished him with a succession of unseemly oaths as much as by anything else. The other two kept up a curious din and dance together, striking one another about the upper body to draw attention to Corberan's pantomine, stamping their feet on the ground as they gripped air with their own fists and made some remembered stroke of their own, and turning from time to time to exclaim at some aspect of Beltran as if they looked forward to having him for dinner, but were not certain whether he should be roasted over a fire or boiled in a pot. Beltran pulled tight the linen belt round his waist and received his sword, handed to him with a vague suggestion of ceremony by Berenguer,

As he did this Berenguer said into his ear, "Watch that one, he is cunning and will cheat," so that as Beltran reached the spot where he meant to stand (to one side of Corberan, for that worthy was dancing about with his back to the sun), he thought that these simple soldiers were growing curiously warm about an exercise bout. He looked into Corberan's face, which was full of happy good nature, if still showing signs of the ferocity with which he had dispatched his late victim; and at the expressions on the faces of the shaggy-haired watchers and was surprised to recognize their eyes. "Blood lust, or I have never seen it," he told himself, and smiled at the paradoxical notion. He made ready to face Corberan and as he did so his foot stumbled on a stone so that a twinge ran from the place where his leg had been hit at Sidon, and he limped a step.

Corberan pointed to the place with his sword. "The Mameluke?" he said, with a friendly smile, and Beltran nodded, smiling. Corberan stepped back a pace and Beltran lifted his sword, his hands level with his breast and the flat of the blade arched where Corberan must come under it if he was to reach his opponent. The rest was like an unusually fast dream. Corberan ran straight at him with his sword pointed at Beltran's throat and, yes, a dagger in his other hand held low, and then threw both his arms wide and jumping as if he had been shot from a mangonel landed with both feet on the damaged place in Beltran's leg.

Pain swelled through and out, out beyond the leg as if it were being boiled. Beltran's breath vanished in a whoop and he fell so that the agony burst through his head and he shouted against it, and his eyes showed him the exulting, fiendishly laughing face of his enemy come down at him and there in his hand—the sword had gone?—was his little friend, the little knife in his boot, the boot on that leg, and as he fell back splashing about in the hurt of it, he cut across the air above him and knew he had struck a blow and that was the last he could do except for one roll over the pain, over the ruined leg. When the end came the way of it surprised him, for even as he said to himself, "I have his blood on my face," a great blow on the head shook him through all his body, vomit tore through his mouth and his life left him.

Chapter Twelve

DIEGO AND THE PIRATES

DIEGO looked at the pirate's corpse lying below him on the iron ram. The lower part of the rib-cage was broken in to make a hollow, a kind of well from which blood had flowed to stain the ram with corruption, so that it was as if the body and the metal had rusted themselves into one: they had held together for two days. This morning, the man had died, and the eyes which had communed with Diego's during the daylight hours of those days gave nothing back.

It was a dying by which Diego was more bereft than if he had known the man in life. For a time the face of the corpse had worn signs of unfinished thought, marks of posthumous intelligence that smoothed off into the waxy secret that any ghostless being kept, and taking with them as they vanished the answer for which Diego hungered, and for which he had matched his look to that now dead for hour upon hour. Diego watched the corpse and men watched Diego, who had behaved oddly ever since the fight.

The "Lion" had worked down the Cilician coast making fifty miles a day under oars, a voyage which all except the slaves found monotonous but pleasant, enjoying the cool airs that sometimes played along that edge of the sea. Then they had turned south and an hour after noon, as the galleyslaves were finishing their dinner opposite the southern tip of Rhodes, the pirate ship came towards them out of the Karpathos Strait. To Olivier it made a charming picture. The ocean was deeply blue, and under a cheerful wind the wave-tops turned without breaking so that you saw the sunlight within them, paling their colour to the joyful flash that feathers the jaybird, and onward over this exhilarating surface came the pirate, foam ruffling under its forefoot and the oarbanks lifting and falling like wings as they sped the ship to its doom. The master of the "Lion", a man called Raspail, chose to wait for the pirates to arrive, since at the pace they had set they would be done up before the two ships met. His slaves completed their meal and sat under their oars, waiting for the gong and the ship. The pirate approached, rocking a little as the rowers lost their beat so that the mangonel mounted on the forecastle fired and missed the "Lion" three times. The overseer called out and the "Lion" dipped her own oars into the gentle waves and began to move head-on at the foe, and as the gong brought them up to speed and the collision was imminent, the seaman who stood in the bow hoisted the Temple banner to the forepeak so astonishing the pirate's steersman that he let his ship's head fall off, and the gallant "Lion", carried along at the pace of a fast walk by the sinews and straining hearts of a hundred and sixty men, with Beauséant flying out in a premonitory streamer of black and white over the heads of the suddenly confounded pirates, thrust her iron ram with all the weight of a treasury of gold behind it into the exposed side of the sea-robber.

The attack had begun with an outburst of sound when the great sweeps hit the water, and as the galley gathered speed the quickening stroke of the oars grew into a huge din which had for its in-breath the groan of wood on wood as the slaves threw themselves forward, all this accompanied by the mounting beat of the great gong, and all of it completed by the thunderous shake of noise with which the ships met. The massy horn of the "Lion" went full length into its prey. Jets of sea spouted up as the striking hull climbed the rolling side of the stricken, until the tearing iron lost its force and lay dark and horridly at rest in a litter of smashed timbers, flesh and bone.

Olivier, at the more fortunate end of this cataclysm, fell to the deck of the poop and lay there, not stunned but held by the instant of quiet. Even as he looked about him for the short axe which he had chosen for the coming mêlée, Diego spoke to Raspail, Raspail to the overseer and the overseer to the slaves. They, those of them that were only bruised or lightly injured by the shock, sorted themselves and the looms of their oars back into their places, and at the sound of the gong backed water and in one steady pull the Venetian galley withdrew her ram from the victim's flank.

"We could have boarded her," Olivier said. "Do you not want to fight?"

"No, that is it," Diego said to him with surprise in his voice. "I find that I do not want to fight." He looked at Olivier with perplexity written on his countenance, and Olivier was baffled: first, that Diego's face should so mirror his emotions, and secondly, that he should not want to fight. Olivier recalled their walk along the beach in Cyprus, when he had said that everything was splitting and taking new shapes. Diego too, perhaps; and himself, what of himself? Oliver found that he was suffocating and took this to mean that some fit of unprecedented perception was upon him, until he remembered to breath through his mouth. He had forgotten, in his sudden preoccupation with these questions of the working of change upon himself and Diego, that his nose was plugged with cotton to keep out the stench given off by the slave-deck.

A furlong distant, the pirate ship sank slowly and from the slaves in her chained where they sat, there began to issue a continuous low howl of lamentation as the sea, in which Olivier had taken so much pleasure and did so again now that he looked out upon it, began to wash over their feet. Apart from this melancholy clamour the scene was tranquil. The "Lion" lay almost still in the soft swell as her timbers settled with a mutter of creaks from their recent exertions; the carpenter came to Raspail and reported that the bow was sound, no more water having entered than was usual at the moment of impact; one slave who had been killed by the jumping loom of his oar was thrown over the side, and two of his fellows, one whose face had been broken in and one with a cracked arm, were despatched and thrown after him. The ship, in short, was ready to resume her voyage; only the fate of the pirates remained to be decided. These worthies, as their vessel wallowed lower and lower, and as the cries of the slaves in her changed from the unanimous moan to a succession of separate shrieks sounding, as it were, against a constant ground of fearful silence, had set about shedding such armour as they wore, and some of them could be seen working, with a listless lack of conviction, on putting bits of fragmented or loose wood together to compose a raft.

They did not seriously expect salvation, at least in this world, and even as the crew and crossbowmen on the "Lion" began to look to Raspail and Diego for orders, one or two of the pirates dropped into the sea and began to swim towards Rhodes.

Raspail, a man from the Dauphiné, with short black hair and humorous blue eyes in a round head, was pleased with the behaviour of his fine new ship. He laughed as he watched the swimmers. "It will be a rare man that swims that far," he said kindly. "Shall we leave them drown?"

Diego moved with a twitch that ran through his whole body and it seemed to Olivier that he had been in a trance. He spoke to the master with a smooth urbanity, perfectly foreign to him, which Olivier had seen only among the more cultivated of the Infidels or in smooth men of high place in Paris, where he had once served the Order.

"By no means," Diego said. "We must kill every man." It was as if he had looked at the refectory table and said, "I am extremely hungry, and shall leave not a crumb." He smiled too, in a most pleasant manner, so continuing his new style of showing with his face what was going on behind it instead of depicting, to which all who knew him were accustomed, the contrary. "Yes," he said. "We must kill them all. Let us row past the wreck and deal first with those swimming fellows, and then take care of the remainder." He bent his eyes upon Olivier, who flinched inside himself at the absence of disorder in his Commander's expression, and said that he would take a crossbow down to the bow, if Olivier would be kind enough to stay with the master. He set off down the gangway that ran along the centre of the ship, and as they passed the wrecked pirate Olivier heard the last slave shriek into the water that had come to bury him.

It was as he wound up his bow on the forecastle, that Diego first saw, not much more than the height of a man below him, the broken body lying on the bloodstained ram. It meant nothing to him then, or so he thought, save that he chose not to kill that one until he fell off into the sea. Over the next hour, however, it grew on him that he was being watched by that stranded, ebbing life below him, and afterwards that they had shared that hour together as much as any two men might share anything.

4

There were three pirates between the foundering ship and the blue-hazed island, and Diego shot them all himself. The first one the galley came up with he took in the back of the head and the man went down at once; the second he hit in the shoulder which did not sink him, and as the overseer, with pitiless acumen, held the stroke so that the injured man crawled slowly across the reddening sea exactly level with the forecastle, Diego wound up his bow again and sent the shaft through the side of his neck so that the swimmer turned slowly over in the water as the one churning arm hung in the air and dropped and fell with a little splash, the eyes closed in the sorrowing face and he fell slowly into the blood-clouded depths. The third man, however, was the best of all that day's slaughter. He was well ahead of the other two and swam strongly as if he had every confidence of ending his day drying his clothes and recovering his strength on some pretty beach. Diego watched the heavy shoulders and thick arms course him through the water. The gong quickened its beat and the fellow on the ram dipped in and out of the water as his iron bed rose and fell with the surge of the ship; and the hopeful swimmer turned his head and saw vengeance bear down upon him. Diego noticed that there was all the difference in the world between the passive creature riding the ram below him and the impotent fool who swam with frenzied kicking of his legs and whirling of his arms as if death could be outrun.

He felt something like friendship with the one and rage with the other. He leaned far out over the rail towards the fugitive and shouted after him. "Stop!" He filled his lungs and shouted again. "Stop!" Suddenly, and not at all to Diego's surprise, for his sense of mastery in today's events was now supreme, the ridiculous arms and legs stopped working and the big shoulders came up out of the water and turned to confront Diego with a bright red face, quite young, and a thatch of dark hair even in the wetness still springing into curls, and eyes which when the ship drew near showed themselves half-alive with hope, and last of all, as the pirate lifted in the water, a mighty chest bulging in and out to take great breaths after its terrific exertions. When Diego lifted the bow the eyes grew wider than you would have thought possible, expecting them to drop out into the sea, and as the quarrel sank with a thud deep into the expanded chest they filled with a passion of horror and—you could see it all clearly, as if you were yourself that newly dying man—turned squeamishly downward to confirm with vision what the body already knew, and then moved up again to look upon their executioner while the head they sat in turned slowly from side to side as if to say there had been a mistake, and then the chest collapsed with a loud whistle of air, like a bird calling once, and as the head fell forward blood poured from the mouth in a flood so that when the black hair went under it filled with blood, running in among the drowning curls, and so death took them all, legs, arms, chest, face, eyes and hair down into the empty spaces of the sea.

Diego put the bow on the deck and looked at the man on the ram. You are right not to struggle, he said. You are right to wait, to lie there and wait, or simply to lie there, if that is what you do. I also, he explained silently, have ceased to struggle, for I now see that there are two things to do in life: one is to kill, which you and I have done, pirate and soldier that we are and the other is to die, which you are doing. There is no third thing. This is why men struggle, to make a third thing. We have no need to struggle now, you and I. You are ending, there on that iron lump, and now the fight against the Infidel is lost, I shall begin to end. Here he lifted his silent voice to be sure the man heard: I shall profit by your example, he called out, and saw the high, pure tones with which the words rang clear in his head enter the head below him for the man's face moved in a spasm as he took to himself these truths of Diego's. I have struggled all my life against the heathen, Diego told the man who waited for death, and for Christ, be assured, for Christ. For this gold I shall not struggle; there is no virtue in struggling for the sake of this gold, which lies within a spit of your head, my friend; aye, within a spit for the root of that iron catafalque on which you lie rests against more gold than all the pirates in the world have seen.

It appeared to Diego just at this moment that he and the pirate had parted company into separate ways of thought, since, when he let the news of the treasure fall from his intensified gaze, the hitherto receptive eyes of the other man flinched off: for it was thus, down the passage from eye to eye, that Diego sent his words, and for such emphasis as this affair of the gold demanded he had leaned deep over the rail to fix into his stare the utmost force of silent eloquence that he could command. That the discharge of this cogent message should cause his companion so to bewray his upturned eyes made it dismally clear to Diego that the mere mention of untold wealth had turned the fellow's mind from the essential matter of their communion. He felt this apostasy to be mortifying in the extreme, and with a foot had already begun to feel about him on the deck where he had laid the crossbow, when he perceived that it was absurd to expect a professional pirate, even one who met the fact of riding towards inevitable death on that strange iron waterhorse with so much decorum, to show no sign of vexation at having missed by so narrow a margin as the fortune of war such store of gold. He therefore blamed himself, and bethought him also that the man might be glad of some time for private reflection on what had happened between them; so dismissing him for the time with a nod of his head, he lifted his eyes upon the sea through which they passed.

The ocean was now void of all trace of shipwreck. Diego had been slower to come into his new mind than the mere setting down appears to show, and indeed during much of this momentous colloquy the dying pirate had been carried through scenes which would have discomposed any fit man sitting the right way up. In addition, he had been under the strongest compulsion to seek what meaning he might find in the face of the remorseless executioner who leaned down from above, since to him who knows himself the next victim of the death-dealer, it is hard not to watch for those signals that herald the last moment of life. This had been the more difficult, that his feet lay towards the point of the ram and his head towards the stem of the ship, so that in all his viewing of Diego's face, as in Diego's of his, they had been in effect upside down to one another.

Almost at the moment that the marksman's visage had come to hover in the centre of the space above him, the pirate had found himself being carried sideways through the air, as the

galley revolved on her oars in her own length, at a rate which
would have turned, had there been enough of it left to turn,
his stomach. As it was, the movement threw the violated organs
within him into so dreadful a union of broken pieces that for a
space he fainted as much from horror as from pain. Returned
from that darkness he both saw the face still hanging overhead,
and heard the most dire cries from the water about him, and by
rolling his eyes this way and that was able to discover that on
either side of this damnable thing—what could it be?—on which
he lay, his shipmates were making practice for the crossbowmen
on the ship which cruised slowly and implacably after him. To
be thus poised between sea and sky, between ship and air,
between—if he was between them—life and death, and so to be
carried always through this watery lane bordered by the killings
of his friends; always to hear the bolts pound through their
bones, and tunnel into their flesh; always to catch glimpses of
their faces being torn off their skulls and feathered shafts springing from their eyes; always to wonder which of these shocks
brought to his ears or eyes he might realize the instant after to
have been done, at last, to him; and always to have above him
that stooping face and never to know its intent; and finally,
never to know—or to remember, since he ought to know—what
it was on which he journeyed, carrying his own pain and blood
and death eternally among the pain and blood and death of his
own kind: was this worse than Hell? Or had he reached Hell
already? If this was not Hell, then Hell could not be worse than
this. If he could but remember what it was on which he lay, he
would know that this was not Hell, and that therefore all he need
do was die, for better things to come.

And so for the two days of daylight hours the man looked up
at Diego and tried to remember what it was on which he lay in
the hope that Hell was somewhere else. During darkness the cries
and sights of carnage fell away until they were hardly there,
but with the return of that face hanging under the sun they came
back again. Sometimes he wondered what that face meant, upside
down above him, but chiefly until he died he listened to the
shrieks about him and held his mind to the one task: to remember
what it was on which he lay.

When, on that morning, Diego found the man was dead he held himself betrayed. Through two days of daylight hours he had belaboured the dying felon with the secrets of his spirit. He had not meant to go so far. At first he had tossed into the space between them mere glimpses of his distempered soul, had let whims of revelation jump from his ironic eyes towards the eyes of the doomed pirate as lightly (it now seemed to him) as blown kisses. How had he travelled from this simple pastime, this measured and self-mocking game to watching the sorrows of his broken faith emerge and marshal themselves before him, unsuspected and unbidden? Only for that man, Diego would not have known that his faith was broken. Only those inflexibly dying eyes, laid hour after hour upon Diego's own, could so have turned them against their master to draw out such ill tidings.

Each night after each of the two days of daylight hours, Diego had lain awake and looked into the darkness at the truth. All his life he had been good friends with the truth, but he reproached it now with lack of frankness, for had it not concealed from him that it had two faces, like a coin? One day before Shujai's army came up, he had walked out from Sidon to look at the walls with an attacker's eye. For no good reason he had counted a hundred paces before he stopped, and then he had not turned round at once but had stood with his face to the south and felt the chill touch of the darkness of Mahomet come up off the land at him. He had not wanted to leave Sidon but to fight on; the Grand Master had made him come away. Thibaud should have allowed him his heart's wish, to cry "Beauséant" and go down Christ's graceful paladin among the Infidel. Ah, Thibaud! When the Order of the Temple gave its last ground on that shore to Mahomet, everything that followed was imitation of what had been!

He had felt it at the time, but it was a thing you suspected without seeing it in words: There would always be men of Diego's mind, not to desert the thing that they had made their reason for being; and there would always be men of Thibaud's, to say that wherever they went, the reason journeyed with them. To each man the other was coward, cheat and traitor, but this too you did not see in words until later—perhaps never, for to how many in the aftermath of such predicaments was it given to stand two days of daylight hours in communion with a dying pirate?

"Not many, I'll be bound," Diego said to the waxy corpse, "and few of them Templars." Or imitations of Templars. "I was of one shape," he said to the corpse. "Thibaud should not have tried to bend me into another. A man wants to die in his own shape; as you did." He looked at the corpse and frowned. "I suppose? After all, you gave me no message." Yet the sense that by dying in the night, and sending from the threshold of death no news to Diego, the pirate had betrayed him, was gone.

Never mind that. It was one thing for Thibaud to try to change a man's shape; bad enough but not the worst. The worst was to set out to change the shape of the Order. "I have lived in it," Diego shouted across the sea, and everyone on the galley not yet roused by the risen sun, woke up. "I will not pretend to live in it still, now that it is gone."

Though he had gone two days and nights without sleep he found, suddenly, that his limbs were supple. His head was clear as if it had been sluiced out with spring water. That land off the bow must be Crete. He jumped down onto the ram and bent to push the carcase of his silent comrade into the sea. He patted him on the cheek. "You gave me no word," he said. "We had some fine shooting together, you and I, but you left me no word. Still, fare you well." What was this? He looked at his hand, and there was spittle on it; there was spittle on the dead face.

"Ah!" Diego said, and put the man gently into the sea.

When he stood up his eyes were on a level with Olivier's knees. "Your friend is dead," Olivier said.

"Yes, yes he is dead." Diego put up a hand and Olivier helped him onto the foredeck. "At least," he said to Olivier, "he spat, and that is something."

He became aware that all the men on the foredeck were looking at him, then he saw that even those slaves who had sight of him were staring also, and finally that on the poop, the master of the galley and those around him had each one so pitched his body that all its attention was upon Diego.

"I am much regarded," he said to Olivier.

"You have behaved oddly for two days now," Olivier said.

"No doubt," Diego said. "Now relieve me of these attentions." Olivier did not move and Diego brought his face round slowly, as if the air through which it passed was stiff, until it was exactly opposite Olivier's. He saw what he expected, that Olivier mistrusted him already, and was tasting the idea of taking command. Diego outmanœuvred him easily.

"Yonder is Crete. I would be moored in Candia by noon. Tell the master, for I do not feel well, and will rest."

He clapped Olivier on the shoulder and walked through after his arm, turning the other aside, and went below. Before sleep came he felt the oars tug movement into the ship, and smiled.

When it was dark he woke. He went on deck and found that they lay alongside the mole, and walked up into Candia carrying no weapon but his dagger and wearing the long white mantle of the Order. He entered the first church he came to and knelt there until some time had passed, and when he left the church began to stride uphill, a street no wider than three men, deep and dark, roofed by stars. He heard them come; three, he thought, and then the flat of the knife lay cold across his throat with the edge breaking the skin.

A voice whispered in his ear: "Beauséant," it said.

"What!"

Another point pricked the skin over his heart, and from the muffled sound of the voice he knew the face before him was wrapped in cloth.

"Beauséant," it said. "Do you come peacefully, or die?"

"Are you Thibaud's men? Olivier's?"

"No. We are a greater man's men. Do you come with us?"

"If you are of the Order, how can you be a greater man's men than Thibaud's?"

"Come and see!"

"Very well." He did not move, however. "I did not expect this. I had expected to be murdered, and by strangers. Still, I shall come."

The cloth-bound voice smiled. "You are obliging. I daresay there are murderers enough about; we were beforehand." The voice was silent for a moment. 'You say you will come peacefully?"

"Yes."

"You are Diego Maro?"

"Yes."

"I am surprised. I thought you would fight."

"We have surprised each other, then," Diego said.

"Life is full of interest," answered the man with the clothed face. "Now we must go. The Watch is out all night in Candia."

When the street had emptied Olivier's man fled back to the ship and told him of this strange ambush. The master and most of the sailors were ashore but the slaves slept chained in place under their awning, and Olivier sent his man to find Raspail, had the slaves wakened and set to their oars, and cast off. As the galley moved from the quay the master jumped on board.

"Where are you taking my beautiful ship?"

"Out," Olivier said. "Through that hole." He pointed to the harbour mouth.

"Good, good!" Raspail was sarcastic. "It is the best way. And after that?"

"Harbours have ears, Raspail, or so it seems. Let us just get out to sea."

Olivier went forward, and as the long galley slid out of the harbour of Candia, he looked down at the light breaking from the sea round the iron ram and wondered what had become of his friend Diego.

Chapter Thirteen

GEOFFREY'S MESSENGER

ST. HILARY'S voice was sarcastic and ill-tempered, and not at all what Beltran expected.

"Making friends with the world, I see. I had begun to hope for a better result."

I was tricked, Beltran said.

"He is not in his wits yet," St. Hilary said, no doubt to one of his colleagues.

"Och, he will be all right in a while," said the other saint. "I did not hit him that hard."

Holy intervention: a foul blow at that, struck from behind:

"All the same, this man is taking up a great amount of my time, and of my sense too, if it comes to that." St. Hilary sighed. "If I had not forgot my breeches I would have escaped this latest folly."

Beltran opened his eyes. Zazzara! Who then was his companion? That Catalan, that whatever-they-called-themselves, their leader. "Berenguer!" he said.

The Catalan was pleased. "You remember my name? You recall Signor Zazzara too? There, Signor, he knows who you are also. He will be right in no time. I had to hit you, and Corberan as well, or you would have killed each other." He made a quick, tentative smile. "I hit Corberan much harder; he is still out of his head."

"That is a lie," Corberan's voice said weakly, and far off.

At that moment Beltran perceived that there was a great ache in his leg over and above the beating pain in his head.

"It was a grand fight," Berenguer said to Zazzara, "and very funny. It is a pity you missed it."

"Be quiet," Zazzara said. "Here, make that dog over there drink all of this, every drop."

Beltran felt his fingers clasped briefly in a firm and gentle grip. Not Zazzara, surely! He lifted his head for a reckless moment, and saw Berenguer withdrawing his hand.

"I thought they had meant to kill me," he said to Zazzara. "Apparently not," the Venetian said. "Apparently, now that between them they have nearly killed you, you are their friend of friends. I who pay their wages and look after them munificently, am quite deposed and outranked. Perhaps you are not such a fool as you seem. Nevertheless, you have spoiled my evening as well as my day, so drink this stuff of the doctor's, and sleep."

Beltran dismounted, stiffly and not without a growl of vexation at a twinge from his wounded leg. "I rode for an hour," he said to Zazzara. "It will do."

"An hour is not a long ride," Zazzara said.

"From the harbour in Limassol to the commandery is not a long ride," Beltran said, "and that is all the riding I shall do."

"You must do it today?"

"Yes, Zazzara. I don't know why, but I must do it today. Here is Berenguer. Do you object to a council of war?"

Zazzara did not object, but he determined its location beside a fountain under a shady tree, and furnished for it fruit, wine, ass's milk and water from a cold well. A harsh high sound came intermittently to their ears round a corner of the house.

"What is that?" Zazzara asked Berenguer.

Berenguer laughed. "That is Corberan putting an edge on your sword, Beltran. He had the stone brought round in the pinnace. I asked him if working over the wheel did not make his head ring, and he said it was his amende. The kick was very funny," Berenguer explained, "but it was a dirty trick, even for Corberan."

"That is good news," Zazzara said.

"It is good news about the pinnace, too." Beltran was testy, both from his hurts and from the fact that most of the resources and all the arrangement of the day's ventures were contributed by the goodwill of these men. It would be pleasant if they could stick to the point, so that he would know how the resources and arrangings progressed. "How is the Grand Master?"

"As when you went out, dozing. The doctor goes with you. He is pleased with the pinnace, since it has an awning and Thibaud will have some shelter."

"Good, good," Beltran said. The three men sat and respected Zazzara's garden, and God's sky, and the conscientious rhythm of Corberan's useful penance. After a while Zazzara coughed, coughed again, and coughed three times together, when Berenguer got to his feet and with a meaningless but curiously ample elaboration of word and gesture set off into the orchards.

"He asked me," Zazzara said, "if you would take them on."

"He did, did he?" Beltran was amazed. "Quick loyalties, surely? Nervous work that. And steal from you?"

Zazzara's eyebrows lifted. "What a mood you are in! I have told them I can't take them to Egypt. Do you see them keeping their tempers in Cairo for six months while I haggle over fine points of trade?"

"No."

"And can you see them sit here for six months and do nothing?"

"No."

Beltran, whose whole military force stood in himself and one-handed Geoffrey, looked at these recruits in his mind's eye. He heard the hooves of a galloping horse come over the hill behind him.

"Yes," he said. "Tell Berenguer, yes."

The hoofbeats came down light and quick, one of the little Arabians that the Catalans rode. Zazzara stood up and looked at Beltran. "That is Siscar," he said.

"They will wear out their horses," Beltran said.

"No. They were to change mounts in Famagusta."

There had been a clatter of hooves on stone and then silence, and now the man came running to them from the house. He wore a tunic and gaiters. He stood before them panting, his skin heavy with sweat, and the black eyes that struck out from behind black thatch like a terrier's held fast to the splashing fountain. He took the jug of milk Zazzara gave him and drained it in three long swallows.

"Geoffrey is coming," he told them. "He said these things:

they are desperate to find Thibaud Gaudin; they put a spy in the house one night but Geoffrey killed him, and put the body in the street and it was gone in the morning; always between six and ten men are near the house, they have been watching it back and front and he thinks now they know he is alone there with the child."

"The child?" In his surprise Beltran had cut across the thread of the Catalan's rote-held message, and when the man flicked his fingers at him in irritation and said, "Later, lord!" Beltran waited meekly.

Siscar leaned his forehead into his clenched fist for some moments and set off again. "He has seen a Frenchman he once knew when they shared a house in Paris near St. Martin-des-Champs, so you may understand that you have a family quarrel on your hands; can you raise some money until your ship comes in; and the girl is with him because she swam ashore. That is all the message."

"It is well-remembered," Zazzara said. "Two of you went, one comes back?"

"Ramon stayed with Geoffrey; we thought there might be a little work to be done when they leave the house. I had a little work for myself." He half turned his head and bent his face at an angle to the ground; you knew it was the smile he wore to remember forbidden fruit.

"Yes?" This from Beltran, seeking to weigh what it was he had agreed to hire. "Did they try to stop you?" he asked Siscar.

"No," said Siscar. "They tried to follow me. It is what you would expect. After I left the town I got off my horse and listened to the ground and heard them coming."

"What then?"

Siscar laughed. "I could not help it," he said. "There were only two of them, and it seemed so funny I could not help it. Listen," he said, and touched Beltran on the chest with the tips of his fingers. "What I do is this. I have a good start on them you see. All right? What I do is this." He touched Beltran several times. "I wait until I have passed a good sharp corner, that amount of sharp, not too much, just that amount." He remembered the angle of the corner with his two hands. "I go past it, I turn in a circle and I put that horse back at the corner as fast as he will go and we arrive at just the right time."

He looked over Beltran's shoulder. "Hey, Berenguer! Are you hearing this?"

Berenguer answered. "I am hearing it, Siscar. What happens back at the corner?"

"What happens? Listen, when we reach the corner I am laughing so much—I hear them coming, you know?—that I just stick my head down with my eyes shut and hold my sword out in front of me." He shrugged.

They looked at him. "Finish," Berenguer said coldly.

"Finish?" said Siscar, master of his art, "I have finished. None of us ever turned that corner. There I am on the ground. There is one of them with a broken neck, and there is the other one with my sword in his side still sitting on his horse and looking down at me!"

"You lie!" Berenguer said.

"If I lie, how do I know what that one on the horse said to me, eh?" Siscar's day was full of triumphs.

"What did he say?" Berenguer asked.

"He said—he didn't know he was dead, you see; he was still dizzy, and he hadn't seen my sword stuck in him—he said, 'That'll teach you to look where you're going!' So then the blood came out of his mouth and he fell dead."

Only Siscar laughed at the end of his story. Zazzara looked out over the sea towards Cairo, Beltran looked at Berenguer, and while the laughter went on Berenguer looked at Siscar with his head nodding slowly up and down, a movement to which the exhilarated Catalan began to respond at the expense, as it seemed, of his merriment. Berenguer, and therefore Siscar, then stopped nodding.

"Siscar," Berenguer said, "you did not kill these men only for fun, but to stop them following you to this house; that is right?" He, and therefore Siscar, nodded to an almost imperceptible degree.

"That is right," Siscar said. He looked round the three faces. In the silence that flowed from Zazzara and Beltran he whispered, almost, his entreaty: "I did all right?" He had put it to Berenguer, but that excellent captain let it reflect from him to the others, until Beltran found himself saying that Siscar had done very well, and the two Catalans, captain and man, walked together towards the house.

Zazzara returned from his Egyptian speculations and he and Beltran looked at one another. Beltran nodded and Zazzara called to Berenguer, "Berenguer. Beltran says, the answer is yes."

Berenguer spread his arms wide, flung them in again so that they wrapped round his body, and bent forward his head. After this little mime, which somehow suggested at once delight, loyalty and gratitude, he turned again and caught up with Siscar.

"I like the sound of your Geoffrey," Zazzara said. "I like the idea of raising money until your ship comes in. You can raise it from me. Did you understand the rest of it?"

"No, not all. What do you suppose he means, he has seen a Frenchman he shared a house with in Paris?"

"He means a Frenchman who is one of you, a member of your Order. The house near St. Martin-des-Champs will be the commandery of the Temple; they are outside the city wall, not far apart from each other."

Beltran rubbed his head, remembering back to Geoffrey's message. "That's his family quarrel, then." Zazzara nodded, and Beltran laughed a little. "This is what you warned me about. You would tell me if I asked you, that this man Geoffrey saw is a spy sent here by the bankers of the Temple in Paris."

"I think he is," Zazzara said, "and it is only to be expected. I see too that you are getting ready to mock my worldly wisdom, so I'll answer no more questions. You are going to restore your incapacitated Grand Master to the bosom of his Order, and I am going to Egypt in the joyful expectation that all the problems I find there will be my own. Shall we pack?" He rose and Beltran was forced to do likewise.

In the courtyard he said to Beltran, "You would be wise not to put too much stock in my sort of wisdom."

Without being clear why, Beltran felt contrite. "Without you,

Zazzara," he said, "I should be in a fog, instead of only in a mist."

"That is very polite," Zazzara said. "I meant something serious: I meant that I have an understanding that helps me in the world, but you have your own way of going about things, and you have your instinct and your faith and your Rule." He stopped and looked in Beltran's face with something like shame. "What outcome do you see?" he asked. "What do you expect to come of this, with Thibaud gone witless and his treasure swimming about the ocean?"

"I don't know," Beltran said.

"Can you tell me, what would be a good outcome? What you would consider a good outcome for the Order?"

Beltran smiled with no trace of confidence. "Oh, no," he said. "I have noticed that. There is no good outcome for it. Whatever we do, or I do, it is only something that must be done."

They were reluctant to part, now, as if this thing they had brought into the open between them had thrown out a shadow, like the moment before a great battle.

"Well, then," Zazzara said. "It is an odd thing, that I should be off to Egypt, where all your troubles came from in the first place."

"Our enemies came from Egypt, the Order's enemies, but our troubles do not seem to spring from there." Beltran considered this. "No," he said, "our troubles seem to belong to us."

The sun lay over the courtyard and they stood perplexed in the heat and the light, among questions that would have better waited until they were apart. Zazzara feared he was in danger of knowing prophetic insights into another man's life; Beltran, that he was close to the ground where these recent enlightenments of his liked to walk, and that for such a visitation he was not ready.

"Come," the Templar said on impulse. "Will you visit Thibaud with me?"

The Grand Master was alone. He lay flung out on the floor with his head pressed to his clasped hands, and when they came in his body grew fixed and unnaturally stiff. They had not seen him like this before, and stayed in the first instant of it as rigid as the sufferer. When Beltran moved and spoke, the body on the floor flinched in search of an even greater intensity of stillness and so began to tremble.

"It is I, Beltran."

The trembling increased and tears began to run onto the clasped hands. The body loosened and settled down onto the floor, then came up on to its knees and drew in the hands, still clasped across the floor so that finally it knelt with the arms hanging in front of it.

"Well, then, where?"

The meaning of this, uttered in a voice at once fretful, hopeless and mixed with fear and sorrow, did not at first reach Beltran. When it did he went quickly to Thibaud, and whether he found it wrong that he should stand while the other knelt, he also went onto his knees and waited there, looking down at the crown of the bowed head.

"I am here, my lord Thibaud," he said.

The face that was then thrown up struck a pang into him that no hurt or loss of his own, he thought, would ever equal. It told of so monstrous a burden of complaint that you would not otherwise expect to see it save on a man being racked or burned. He had no more than a glimpse of it when the face hurled itself at him with such violence that he ended up sitting on his heels, while Thibaud's head rested on his lap and the clasped hands contrived to join one of Beltran's hands into their embrace. So, the Grand Master went to sleep.

Perhaps sleep would restore him to himself. Beltran sat there for hours, while the pity in his heart asked questions of God. When they came to rouse him at nightfall, Berenguer and his troop had ridden off according to the plan, and Zazzara had already departed on his own journey.

Chapter Fourteen

THE VOYAGE IN THE PINNACE

THE pinnace ran out of the bay under a glitter of stars. In the shelter of the awning Thibaud lay quiet. Roused from his sleep on Beltran's knee he had grown wild and pitiful but Abu'l Ibrahim had lulled him with opiates. The doctor handled the steering oar at the stern and Beltran sat amidships. He had his feet up on the thwart opposite and with his head back looked up at the long curve of the lateen yard moving across the starred sky. He was in a small boat being piloted towards Africa by an Arab doctor and looking up at the stars, and thinking about his Grand Master going mad. He found a black place among the stars and laughed into it. He laughed because when he had been admitted to the Order of the Temple he had felt that he had wrapped sureness round himself; he had felt as if he had been baked into a brick and lodged immovably into a wall that would last for ever.

Under his backbone the water slapped against the side of the boat. From the stern he heard a chanting sound that had for him no melody; Abu'l had warned Beltran that if he handled the steering he would begin to sing, songs of his boyhood on the delta. The doctor was an exile but his life seemed to be all of one piece, all of it suited him, there was no part of it he found mismatched with the rest. In any case, he had said to Beltran: It is written. Beltran had gone into smiles and frowns and neck-rubbings over that; It is written. Inside himself he felt the pieces that made up the tale of his life had come loose at the joints, and that therefore there was less of him than he had thought, than he had counted on. He had tried to put this to Abu'l, saying you are used to exile, I am embarking on it, does it make a man's life smaller? The doctor had said he did not know; that Beltran was older than he used to be; and that in any case: It was written.

Nevertheless, as he worshipped the Virgin and invoked the aid of St. Hilary to keep his courage up, he struggled hard to avoid the thought, that in a world where the parts of a man's life that had already been lived could cast themselves off from him, there was good comfort to be found in the words: It is written. From such evil fancies as this he sought comfort in the Rule. It was true that the Rule did not prescribe modes of conduct suitable to lurking and plotting in secular houses on deserted coasts, but let one day pass and he would be restored to a house of the Order, where the Rule would come into its own again. As much for this cause as any other, he had determined to lodge Thibaud in the commandery of the Temple at Limassol. He had not thought his way into what would happen once they were there.

"Does he sleep?" That was the doctor.

"Yes, he sleeps."

"I think we turn in now for Famagusta."

There was a group of islands off the town and their white beaches showed clear in the moonlight. Abu'l Ibrahim threaded the pinnace through them to the shore, and Beltran brought the sail down until the little vessel just had way on. The lateen yard dipped in the sea.

"Keep that thing out of the water. How can I steer?"

Beltran thought, back at Sidon, Abu'l Ibrahim was all salaams and courtesy, however ironic; perhaps it was because he had the helm.

"I see the pier," Beltran said.

"So do I," Abu'l Ibrahim said.

He ran the boat along the seaward side of the stone pier until Beltran found a ring newly driven into the wall, and they moored there. When Beltran stood up the top of the pier was four or five feet over his head. He had forgotten that on the outer side a wall rose up to give shelter to the top of the quay.

"I shall have to climb up," he said. "I want to look along the pier towards the town."

"Why?"

"What do you mean, why? I want to be ready when Geoffrey turns up."

"Geoffrey will climb down more easily than you will climb up."

Beltran tried to see the doctor's face but the high wall shadowed it from what light the moon gave.

"Abu'l Ibrahim," he said, "why are you behaving in this commonplace manner?"

There was a brief silence before the answer came. "The fact is," the Egyptian doctor said, "that the number of us about the person of the Grand Master has become smaller and smaller, and when I am all he has left, I shall feel he is inadequately attended."

Beltran thought about this. "You may be right," he said. "We call it tempting Providence."

"So do we," the doctor said. "They put the ring here for us to tie up to; they will hardly go astray."

Beltran settled himself in the prow of the boat. He hoped that Berenguer had stopped before dark and laid up for the night; he and his Catalans had the whole of tomorrow to complete their ride to Limassol, but they were stale from lack of action and might find it difficult not to hurry. The tops of the little waves had begun to turn over and the pinnace to dance up against the stonework; the wind was freshening; storms blew up round this island with no whisper of warning.

"Hold her off," he heard Abu'l Ibrahim say, and answered, "We cannot. Better to hold her on. She'll be driven on too hard for us to stop her." He held onto the ring and shortened up the line, and the doctor, finding nothing to make fast to astern, made a bundle of Beltran's mantle and lashed it over the gunwale where the boat had begun to beat against the pier. It had been like a pleasure cruise so far, Beltran reflected, and it was more to be expected that such an expedition should meet some obstacles. Still, if this wind kept rising and the sea with it, they would have to fetch off as well as they could and put down an anchor, and run in when Geoffrey appeared; it would depend on whether he was pursued—they might reach him too late. They could, of course, sail boldly into the shelter of the harbour, though how they would fare . . .

A voice spoke to him from the sea. "Geoffrey says, I am to

come into the boat." He looked down and saw a head of black hair dip under the water and then lift again; it was the infant blackamoor; she had swum ashore from Diego's ship and now she was swimming on board his. "The sides are too high," the infant said, and he put down his hand and hoisted her up.

"Where is Geoffrey?" Beltran asked the child.

She wrung the water out of her hair. She wore a tunic and trousers of cotton and began to shiver in the rising wind.

"Geoffrey and Ramon will be here in a moment. They will run along the wall and jump down. They are making some men quiet, the men who followed us from the house."

Ramon? Ramon? Siscar's friend, of course, who had stayed with Geoffrey in case there was a little work to do. He told the girl to go under the awning, and to find something to dry herself and to wrap herself in whatever she chose: "Thibaud is sick and sleeps in there, so try not to wake him."

"The Great One! Aiee! Who is that?" She pointed to the stern.

"The doctor."

She was delighted. "Abu'l Ibrahim! I will sit by him?"

It was high time the others turned up, for the boat was striking hard on the pier and in her position as a floating breakwater had begun to ship a good deal of sea. Through the wind Beltran heard the rustling sound of weapons in a small mêlée. There was a shout and with a hand cupping his ear he heard it a second time and recognized it: "Aur! Aur!" The noise of the fight drew closer but was muffled by the high wall and he could not make out just where it was. His patience vanished and he took his sword from its sheath and passing the leather thong over his head took it in his mouth so that the weapon hung down behind him and began to climb the wall.

"Back! Back!" Geoffrey's voice came from above. Beltran jumped back and swung his sword through the mooring line and held the boat fast by one hand. Geoffrey descended with great force and landed half on Beltran, so that his hand was knocked loose from the iron ring and the two men made a heap in the bow. Beltran saw the yard begin to climb the mast and the sail swell and quiver in the freakish wind that flurried under the pier. That was the child. As he watched she let the yard stop halfway up the mast, secured the sheet and began with a boat-hook to pole off from the stone wall, but with this wind the pinnace was too heavy for her and it kept sailing itself onto the stone as if determined to become a wreck.

"Get off!" Beltran said to Geoffrey, and pushed him so that he rolled suddenly into the bilge. "Are you all right?" He bent over him. "What of the Catalan?"

"Yes. All right," Geoffrey said. "Ramon's dead. They had a crossbow, of all things."

Beltran seized an oar from the floor boards shoving the child's head under the shelter of the gunwale, and began fighting to hold the pier at arm's length while the wind, which was partly off the land, worked the boat down towards the sea. He remembered the crossbow.

"Listen," he said to the child. "Did you see a shield inside that tent?"

"Yes," she said, "Do you want it?"

He glanced down into the blacker darkness of the scuppers and saw two eyes gleaming up at him. A considerable ally, he thought: failing a troop of Catalans, he would take an infant blackamoor any day. He pushed the oar into a good crack in the stones and pulled it out before it stuck.

"What's your name?"

"Shirin," she said. She stood up. "What about the shield?"

"Take it to Abu'l Ibrahim, get him to cover his back with it. These men have a crossbow and they'll find us when we clear the pierhead." As she set off he said, "Keep your own head down."

He put his whole being into fending off the pier. The oar had grown heavier than he had expected; he had known it would become too heavy, but not this much too heavy. His breath came into him like a door scraping over the floor and to pull it into his chest was as much work as wielding the big scull. He went at it all in great outthrows of strength and as passionately as if he would never do anything else again. He had no attention for the doctor in the stern or for Geoffrey.

Beside him a voice said, "Once more." As soon as the words were said a violent blow came through the wood and stung his hands, and would have taken the oar from his grip but that he seemed unable to let go, and having lost his balance he followed it down until half of him was out of the boat and his shoulder and the oar together, as if they had a common will, placed themselves between the pinnace and a very angular point of the pier while a strong haul at his belt kept him rooted inside the hull. He wished there might be a parley between the contending forces, and had begun to realize that he was not only being crushed and stretched, but also drowned, when the masonry of the pier vanished to be replaced entirely by sea, and almost at once he was dragged, along with the oar, fully into the boat. He felt hands at his neck and shoulder and something pricked into his skin.

"I will do that," he heard the infant's voice say, and there was some noise that he could not name close to his ear; there was a thud from elsewhere in the boat and the doctor gave a cry, sounding of rage and not of hurt; under him the pinnace bounced hardily and onto his face spray fell in gouts and his mouth was all salt; the infant's voice joined with Geoffrey's and at the very moment when it occurred to him that he was badly wounded, too badly to feel the pain, there was a dry snapping sound and he sprang to one side through no effort of his own.

He found that he was sitting upright on the floor of the boat with his back against the side, and nearby was the butt of the oar.

"See," the infant said, and pointed to it.

In the wood was sunk another piece of wood. He felt round the oar and touched a metal point. It was the head of a crossbow quarrel. He felt at his neck where they had been working, and found a hole in his leather jerkin.

"There is another hole in your sleeve," Geoffrey said. "The bolt tied you to the oar, arm and neck. Shirin had to cut well through before I could break it; her hands are too small and I've only got one."

They were going at a great pace and apparently running between the islands and the shore. Beltran looked aft and the doctor lifted a hand in greeting, but his eye was for sea and sail.

"Lift this shield off my back," he yelled, and the child went to help him.

Beltran sat there in the bottom of the boat and let the excitement pass out of him. It was good to be with Geoffrey again, and
he held him by the arm for a moment; it was good to have a
companion of the Order.

"What is that sound?" Geoffrey asked.

"Is there someone inside the tent? Listen!"

Beltran stooped under the awning. In there he could see
nothing but he heard Thibaud groan, and it was a sound unlike
those he had made during his torments of the day before; it was
the sound a wounded man would make. He ran his hands over
Thibaud. One of the sick man's arms was busy and he traced it
down to the hand. There was a feathered bolt in Thibaud's side
among the ribs, and Thibaud held the shaft in the curve of his
thumb and forefinger. Whether he was half-dead from the wound
or half-asleep from drugs, Beltran could not make out, but he
could get no word from the injured man.

The doctor would do nothing until daylight, and then, he
said, he would probably wait until they were on dry land. A
cockleshell like this among waves like these was not the place
for tending such wounds.

"But he will be in pain," Beltran said.

"Ease it," Abu'l Ibrahim said. "Contrive among you to keep
the arrow still. Try to have it descend no farther into the cavity."
There was a short silence while Abu'l Ibrahim hummed one of
his unmelodious chants. "You had better not do it. The child
has intelligent fingers, and it is likely that Geoffrey, now that he
has only five, has begun to notice them. Thibaud is as good as
dead now in any case. I must think about it."

"So you want me to steer then?"

"No. I like handling the boat. You will be as well to sleep."
He hummed again. "Your shield saved my life," he said.

Beltran looked at the strange suggestion, that he should sleep
while Thibaud, quite possibly, died. In the end he found nothing
wrong with it. So his shield had saved Abu'l Ibrahim's skin,
had it? On his way forward he passed through the tent where
Geoffrey and the infant were fussing over Thibaud, and took the
shield as he went. Settled in the forepart of the boat, he found the
stump of a crossbow quarrel lodged in the thick hide that faced

the shield. For occupation he took his knife to it and began to cut it out. It came to him suddenly that the man with the cross-bow was a rare marksman; their enemies, whoever they might be, were well served.

He should have had the shield put over Thibaud. A sweat came out on his body. Why had he not done that? Would he have been better to take Thibaud overland? No, he would not. It would have taken four times as long through the mountains with a sick man on a mule-litter. Well then, he would certainly have been wiser to sail to Limassol without stopping off for Geoffrey at Famagusta, but he could not have done that: their mysterious foes would have gone in after Geoffrey by now. Clearly, he had saved the lives of Geoffrey and Abu'l Ibrahim at grave cost to Thibaud. What sense did this make?

When he woke the morning was far on. He lay face down on a raffle of his own belongings and those of the boat, shield and dagger, anchor-stone and rope, the blade of an oar, an iron pot, and in particular a large conch-shell against which his cheek was squashed. As he lifted himself off this haphazard couch he felt the markings of the shell graven on his skin. The sun was hot on the back of his neck. The pinnace splashed pleasantly over a clear green sea that rocked slightly as if it, in turn, was thinking of going to sleep after its labours of the night before. He himself had slept for hours and hours.

He looked back along the boat. The doctor still had the helm. The yard was at the top of the mast now and Geoffrey was slumped at its foot. He made his way to the awning and put his head in. Thibaud was unattended and asleep with the arrow still in him; his breathing was deep and regular but the arrow hardly moved, for it was well up under the shoulder and indeed rested on the arm. Beltran felt quite cheerful about Thibaud for a moment and then remembered that, living or dying, the Grand Master was wandering in the head. He found the girl nestling between the doctor's feet and greeted him quietly so that she would not be disturbed. The doctor made no answer, and Beltran saw that he too slept.

Only the pinnace itself—for how long? since dawn perhaps—was awake and Beltran knew a relief such as he had not known for days, to be able to stand in that swift-sailing vessel and contemplate the next step in his little campaign against the unknown, without the need to speak to other people about it. It seemed to him that from each moment of this freedom he culled a fresh measure of restored vigour, and with this added to his long sleep he knew a great sense of well-being. His eye fell on the tent and again, yet again, he was aware that although Thibaud Gaudin's safety was the chief object of his plans and actions, the person of Thibaud himself, Thibaud in the flesh, had somehow come to take second place to the principle of Thibaud Gaudin, Grand Master of the Temple.

He took a swallow of water from his flask and nudged the doctor awake. The doctor's eyes opened straight at him and Beltran gave him the flask.

"We are near," he said to the doctor. "I will take the helm, Dr, you look at Thibaud."

The doctor under this brisk greeting shook his head as if he was falling back into sleep, drank from the flask, and made his way stiffly forward.

Chapter Fifteen

LIMASSOL

THE pinnace sped into the lagoon. It was a natural haven fringed with shallow beaches and Limassol boasted few harbour-works, only a wooden pier which ran from the customs house. A little cavalcade came into the shore from behind the customs house and down to the water's edge, and Beltran took the pinnace to them. There were seven ships in the lagoon, one of them a galley of the Hospital, the rest traders, and there was much activity between them and the warehouses that backed the bay. Beyond the customs house, to Beltran's right hand, the houses and churches of the town shone white in the sun; and beyond them on the crown of a hill stood the commandery of his Order.

Berenguer was doing his work well. On the sand stood a litter and its four hired bearers. Two of his men remained mounted further up the beach, working their horses on an imaginary line with much plunging and turning and kicking up of sand, to the effect that the area in which the pinnace disembarked its passengers was noisily asserted to be banned to the general run of passers-by. Beltran was determined that his Grand Master should not arrive incognito. Berenguer had also hired four men of the waterfront and as the pinnace came up the beach they ran into the water and pulled her high and dry onto the sand. The bearers put Thibaud into the litter under the guidance of Abu'l Ibrahim, who had made a pad between the arrow and the adjacent arm and then bound all three to the body, and who made a face to himself and shrugged as he mounted the horse that was led forward for him.

It was still not clear to Beltran why his instinct had told him to bring Thibaud into Limassol with as much announcement as possible, but the more they succeeded in this aim the more right it felt. Limassol was full of refugees from Acre, for it was an object with King Henry to separate them as far as possible from himself, and as Corberan went in front of this already noticeable procession demanding way for the Master of the Temple, it was to many of the people in the streets like a rumour of indefinable hope. That he was carried through the town with an arrow piercing his flesh for all to see—since the doctor had the curtains of the litter tied back so that he could see for himself—added to the pompous little procession a suggestion of martyrdom, so that by the time they had reached the commandery the fact that the Master of the Temple was in Limassol was the common talk of the town. It had not, however, preceded them; the gates were shut.

The commandery of the Temple at Limassol was not a redoubtable fortress. The short and arrogant lordship which the Order had held over the island a century ago, and which an indignant populace had forced them to resign in favour of King Henry's family of Lusignan, still lived in the common memory of the islanders. Since that time the Order had thought it tactful, both to the new proprietors and the former subjects to make their buildings on Cyprus as little warlike as possible, and the little castle which stood at the head of the winding road was probably as pretty a house as the Templars owned.

From the gateway at which it started, it completed its journey to the top of the hill in a pleasing jumble of one- and two-storey segments, until it arrived at what was no more than a large house with a fine view over the plain to the mountains on the one side, and over the sea on the other. The only aspect of all this which suggested fortification was that a tall watch-tower rose beside the gate across the road from the house which crowned the hilltop, the degree of ascent being so steep that in order to look the house in the eye, the tower had, so to speak, to stand while the other sat. Above the gate between them, the narrow space was spanned for a good way up by a screen of stone.

The houses lining the road had stopped some way back. On the far side of the wall trees had been planted for shade, but nothing grew at the roadside. Hardly a flower bloomed about Limassol, for it was the hottest place in Cyprus and it was near mid-summer. It was, also, approaching noon, and on the party before the gate the sun beat down with such a force that now that they were still, each of them unawares stooped his shoulders a little to hold up the heat, and the litter-bearers put their load down on the ground as if they had a single mind. The horses stamped a little and one whickered, complaining, and then their heads hung weightily at the stretch of their necks as if sleep might intervene between them and the heat. For a moment it seemed to Beltran as if the commandery were one of Zazzara's many houses, shut up and empty while the master was away. There was nothing at all to suggest that any human beings lay beyond that gate. The impossible idea came to him that the garrison had been slain by the Mamelukes, and to remind himself that he was in Cyprus, not in the Holy Land, that the war was over and lost, he said to Corberan, "Knock!"

Corberan hit the wooden door with the pommel of his short sword and the sound rattled and died off in the hot air. Beyond the gate nothing stirred. Corberan shouted once or twice in a dry voice and spat and shouted again.

"Stop that!" Beltran said. There was no one else in sight at this hottest hour of the day but it would not do for them to risk rousing the people lower down the hill, to let them see the Master of the Temple shut out of his own house.

"Look there," Berenguer had coaxed his horse up beside Beltran. "That window," he said. Beltran looked at that window. The main house had two floors and this window was in the centre of the upper floor. It was built out from the face of the house on a wooden balcony and had closed shutters made of slatted wood. Nothing, so far as Beltran could see, was moving at the window. He looked from the window to Berenguer.

"I have a feeling about that room," Berenguer said.

"The best chamber in the house, I suppose," Beltran said. "The commander's chamber, it will be."

"Yes," said Berenguer. "Yes."

From the litter came the sound of Thibaud coughing and Abu'l Ibrahim was down with him in a moment giving him water out of a little cup. The doctor turned his fist over sharply at Beltran as if to say, "Go through the gate!"

Beltran was stranded in his quandary. If he battered or burned the gate down the whole world would know about it in no time, how the Grand Master had been kept from his own commandery. What was in there anyway? Was it a garrison of the Order? Was it some of those mysterious enemies, from within or without the Order, and were they lying in ambush? His head cooked in the sun and he could make no use of it. He thought of returning down the hill and sailing away, so that the world would at least be baffled. Thibaud, however, would certainly die. They must get past that gate, and he could not.

"Corberan, can you aim through the shutters?" Berenguer had taken his friend a little to one side and the two of them squinted under the noon light at the slatted window.

"Yes," Corberan said, and without any pause drew the two javelins from behind his saddle, passed one to Berenguer, stood on the saddle with the other in his hand and threw; there was a sharp crack and the missile vanished through the decorated wood-work of the window, Berenguer held out the second javelin and there was another crack, and then passed to the thrower the two missiles from his own saddle. The first of them thudded into the sill but the second smacked through the same shutter as its predecessors. After that everything was held in a long silent moment without movement, until the wounded shutter turned outward with a rusty growl to clatter on the wall, and inside the room a woman squealed.

Beltran looked at Berenguer. The Catalan nodded. "What I thought," he said, and drawing his horse aside from the look in the Templar's face he quickly embraced the newly re-seated Corberan, and smothered the imminent display of vainglory.

"So," Geoffrey said. "Whose voice was that?"

"I do not know," Beltran said, "but I suspect luxury."

Geoffrey turned his face hard down into his shoulder and then decided to speak plain. "There is no merit," he said, "in being diffident to spy vice when it is staring you in the face."

"No, there is not," Beltran said. "Look! Here it comes.

It came in the guise of an elderly man who put his head and shoulders out of the window. The distance was too great to decipher what emotions his face showed in answer to this sudden interruption of his day, but from the way he carried himself there was nothing in him but bewilderment. The upper half of his body was bare. He leaned it out of the window and looked first of all straight down and saw nothing strange. He turned away then, almost going from sight, as if he thought he might have fancied that three javelins had fallen into his room; as he did so, however, his hand bumped the lance that had stuck in the window-still. He gave it a little tug, but it was fixed there firmly. Whereupon, and Geoffrey began to find it touching to watch him, he gave it a little pat: it was plain to Geoffrey that the old man was thinking, there's one of them, what do they like to eat? Then, however, the old man's gaze turned and came over the gate, and he saw them waiting.

He looked long. Do not be a knight of the Order, Geoffrey implored him. As if in answer the old man went from the window for a full minute, and when he returned he was wearing the same white mantle that Geoffrey and Beltran wore. Geoffrey put his face to the sky and nodded it a few times, and Beltran sighed and looked down at the dust.

"Who are you?" The voice from the balcony spoke a strange Norman French coloured with the Levantine intonation.

"An Englishman," Beltran said to Geoffrey. "We," he shouted, "are of the household of the Grand Master of the Order of the Temple." Then suddenly he threw both his arms forward in a great rage and bellowed, "Open the door!"

"No," the old man made it not a refusal but a comment. "The Master was killed at Acre."

"The new Master was elected at Sidon." Beltran passed the words across the gate like diamonds going over a table to be assessed one by one.

"Well, I'd heard of that." The Englishman looked down where his hands gripped the window-ledge. "So it is true." He looked straight out in front of him. "It is all too late," he said. The brief turn of his head towards them showed the tears running down his face, and then he knelt with his face leaning on the hands that grasped the sill. A woman's head appeared and bent over him and without looking at them vanished. Later they heard footsteps on the far side of the gates and then the scrape of wood on wood. A leaf of the gates opened and a woman stepped out. She was middle-aged, by her clothes a Cypriot, and to those of them who were in the way of considering these things, she was ripe with beauty. Her hair was dark and her eyes, which were also dark, were strong.

Beltran found that she and he were alone on the road. The others had passed through the gateway and he was sitting on his horse looking into her eyes, and she was standing with her back to the wall of the tower looking into his eyes. She was calm and serious, and she gave him a little shake of the head and set off down the hill.

Chapter Sixteen

THE DEATH OF THIBAUD

ABU'L IBRAHIM and the child cared for Thibaud, admitting no one to that balconied room. Old John Fairchild, the English knight, imparted only his name and retired to the chapel where he spent three days in penitential silence. The Catalans were variously employed, on watch, guarding the pinnace and proving the country round about. Geoffrey rummaged in Limassol for news.

On the second day he told Beltran what he had heard: that the commandery and its dependent houses had been more or less emptied to reinforce Acre, leaving behind only the very old, like Sir John Fairchild. On the third day Geoffrey rode through the town and out to Kolossi where the Hospitallers had their commandery. "A great affair," he said to Beltran, "more like what one is used to." What they had told him there puzzled the two Templars. According to the story, a galley from France had touched at Limassol two weeks ago and from it had stepped the new commander of the Temple for this all but empty commandery in which they stood; the man had with him another knight, two sergeants and two grooms. "Where are they?"

"Where are they indeed?" Beltran repeated it.

On the fourth day Sir John keeled over and when Beltran went to tell the doctor about this they met on the stairs: Thibaud was, it seemed, going to live for at least a little while. "What is more," Abu'l Ibrahim said, "he has not spoken yet, and is very weak, but I think he is back in his senses." Told about the English knight he said he had no interest in the old fool, and if Beltran wanted to care for him the best thing would be a little water and some egg-white to be going on with.

While the doctor and the girl slept, and old Sir John digested his first nourishment for three days, Beltran sat in Thibaud's sickroom. He spent a long time looking at the face. There had

5

been many meetings with that thin head since he first saw it against the white wall at Sidon: almost every time there was change in it. So little flesh lay over its narrow bones you would not think of it as a face with much room for change, but what happened to it was as if its sculptor came back to it now and then with a pressing need for an ounce or two of clay, and set himself to winnow it out of the whole head so that Thibaud's face, when you next saw it, had not only shrunk but had exchanged part of what it had been for something else.

With this last illness the face had once again grown less. It was in slumber so deep that Beltran felt safe to lean over and search there for what was lost. The skin was grey like the smoked wax of candle-ends and from Thibaud's countenance the character had all but perished. He felt like a spy and turned away. He walked to the window where the javelins had entered and at sight of the sea and a galley making up the lagoon he thought of the gold. It seemed to him that he had been close to marking what Thibaud's face had lost, and he went back to the bedside.

Most of what told you whose face it was lay in the mouth, the eyes and the forehead. The eyes were hidden. The long and sparse-lipped mouth cut across in its straight line and the brow, that calm frontlet still held its promise of unyielding force. The character was not quite perished, since these landmarks stood. For the rest, however, Beltran had never seen a visage so wasted on this side of dying. The changes that had doctored Thibaud's face in the past month were as profound as the changes that followed death. Mouth and brow—and perhaps the eyes—had kept their natures, but this they could not much longer continue while the rest of the face went down in havoc.

Beltran stood to his height and looked down at the frail thing on the bed. He saw that it was fighting beyond its powers to put off its own end: it was not what the face had lost that spoke to him, but what it had kept. It was as if Thibaud had exacted from some unknown source the assurance of a little inroad into mortality, a little extra hold on life, and was clinging to the very last extremity of this pledge. But from what source and to what end? Then he saw that they were the same: the gold, Thibaud's stewardship of the gold, his friendship with the gold.

It was blasphemy. Beltran stood while the spell touched his spirit. His skin moved against him, shrinking from evil, and his scalp grew chill. He turned the sinful thought out of him and looked at it. It made no sense. No amount of gold would keep Thibaud's soul on earth when it was commanded to Heaven.

"A man cannot feed on gold," Beltran said. "If he wrapped himself in gold or made his bed of it he would not live longer."

The pale eyes opened and they were not changed; like mouth and brow they were not changed. Beltran did not shirk that lucent gaze. It thrust at him the same earnest of constancy that his own eyes had met across the sandy courtyard at Sidon, the constancy that would outlast all calamities, and even to the extinction of faith.

"The gold is not Caesar's," Thibaud said. His voice was vastly diminished and far off, but very clear. "I have promised it to God." His eyes closed again and he seemed swallowed by sleep.

*   *   *

Beltran grew aware of noise. There was a knocking on the door and hubbub below the window. He opened the door to Geoffrey and went to look outside. He heard a clatter of horses and stopped short of the window.

"What is it?" he asked Geoffrey.

"It is two knights of the Order," Geoffrey said.

"The new commander for Limassol?"

"I think so." Geoffrey looked at the bed. "How is the Master?"

"When he wakes he is sensible." Beltran chewed on the knuckle of his forefinger. "The doctor says he will live for a while."

"For a while; I see." Geoffrey's face was pulled hard in at the lips. The bright blue eyes stared at Beltran. "Afterwards, what then?"

Voices rang out in the courtyard.

"Come on," Beltran said.

Geoffrey stooped over the couch and his hand rested, hardly touching, against that of Thibaud where it hung almost off the bed.

"I am with you," he said.

It was time, for the sound of strife had begun to come through the window. The two men went quickly to the floor below and to the door of the house, where they stood looking down from the top of the steps at the comedy before them.

With his back to the steps Berenguer confronted two knights of the Order and would not, clearly, let them pass. They had most likely just come to this alignment for all three of them were in a continuous motion that was, to those watching, like a dance. The two knights were trying to pass one on either side of the Catalan and against these attempts he did not give ground but, like an animal at bay, turned from side to side at such a rate that neither of his opponents went unconfronted for anything so measurable as a moment. Berenguer's short sword was out and did not turn with him but led unpredictable courses of its own, so that the outflanking efforts of the two knights had about them the particular lightness that fighting men show in front of cold steel.

In Beltran's ear Geoffrey said, "The dark one is the man who watched our house in Famagusta." Was he indeed? He was too, in that case, the man whose archer had put a crossbow quarrel into Thibaud.

The knights had caught sight of them and now withdrew from their engagement with Berenguer, who turned and, seeing his employer, took himself to the side of the steps and leaned on the wall of the house. He folded his arms so that they held the naked sword against his breast like a man who carried a spare garment against a change in the weather.

"Welcome, brother knights," Beltran said and started down the stair. He heard Geoffrey pull in his breath with a hiss, but what else was there to say to them?

"Welcome? Welcome!" The speaker was a good hand's-breath shorter than Beltran, a sturdy man turning stout, red in the face from the heat and vexation, with a ring of fair hair round his head like the tonsured orders. He kept his chin high as if there were a flame under it, and pushed it far forward when he spoke in this little rage so that Beltran had all he could do not to walk backward before him.

"Welcome, sir? Do you know, brother knight, who I am, sir?"

"No, brother, I do not," Beltran said.

"I am Renan La Hune, brother, and I am the commander of this commandery, and I desire you to step to the side that I may enter to my chamber."

"I am Beltran . . ."

"I shall enquire of you later, sir, brother, who you may be, but in the meantime, brother, I desire you to step to the side so that I may enter to my chamber."

The man had a vehemence which served him like a physical activity, and his words came from him in spurts between quickly snatched breaths. Beltran realized that he was snared in a kind of combat he had not met before, for the first effect on him of this highly charged delivery was to leave him at a loss what to say.

Geoffrey's voice came past his ear. "Your chamber, Brother Renan, is occupied and cannot be vacated."

Two deep folds of flesh appeared along the length of the new commander's forehead with the effect of all but closing his eyes, and at the same time the tilted chin leaned even further upwards. When he spoke it was still to Beltran.

"Who is this?"

"I am Brother Geoffrey, Brother Renan."

The dark man came beside Renan. He said nothing but after nodding shortly but with a kind of polite gravity once at Beltran and once at Geoffrey he looked at the ground and stirred the dust a little with his foot.

Renan spoke again to Beltran. "Who has my chamber, brother?"

"Thibaud Gaudin." Beltran watched the other man and caught his darting look.

"Thibaud Gaudin! The Treasurer of the Order!" Then, brother sir, I will pay him my respects." Renan plied his face with unction.

"The Grand Master of the Order," Beltran said shortly. He had recovered his stroke. "He was elected at Sidon after the fall of Acre. I take it you are new come from Europe."

Renan was playing out his game, whatever it was, to the last.

"Grand Master!" There was a singing note in his voice.

"Yes, Grand Master," Beltran said. "He has been ill; he is still ill."

"What a responsibility!" Renan said simply, "The Grand Master—we had not heard—and ill! I shall rejoice to oversee his welfare."

The breath fell out of Beltran's mouth almost in a laugh. "That you will not," he said. The dark man's head lifted; what a graceful, silent figure he made beside the other. "Hear me," Beltran said. "I do not accept you, Renan La Hune, as commander of this commandery, for Europe does not appoint commanders in Cyprus. I accept you as a knight of the Order and you will be given room with your companion."

Suddenly he was finished with them. Rage and hate rushed through him and filled his throat. "Geoffrey," was all he said.

"I will dispose them," Geoffrey said.

Beltran climbed the steps into the house and crossed the stone floor to the staircase in the corner. It was cool and dark. By and by the temper went from him and he felt the strings of his body loosen. He eased and stretched himself into a yawn and snugged his head into the crook of his arm, and went to sleep.

His first waking thought was to wonder where, in this dried-up hilltop, the crickets found grass enough to make their homes: the din of their nightly chorus pressed on his ears.

"Beltran! Beltran! Oh, waken lord!"

That was not the voice of crickets. Behind it beat the tattoo they made with their hind legs, but the voice was not theirs. All at once he came awake. For a moment he was exhausted as if he had run many miles, then for another moment he was himself again, and then, ah, his head was deep with pain, and pounded. No, the pain was in his head but the pounding, which caused it, was elsewhere. Beside all these confusions, where he lay it was pitch dark. Through the doorway he could see moonlight, and in the lighter darkness between him and the door he saw a small figure jump up and down and heard its voice again. It was the infant.

"He will not waken. He is dead too. He will not waken."

Slowly he sat up. The leather on him creaked and at the sound the child was still. The beating had stopped.

"I am not dead," he said. "Who is dead?"

The child was mute. He sat on the stair in the darkness and looked down at the black patch she made there.

"What was that noise outside?"

The patch moved. "Oh, what do you think?" she said. "Olivier is at the gate, Olivier from the ship. I cannot take off the bar. He would not stop beating to hear me."

"Who is dead?"

The black patch thinned and drifted towards the moonlit night.

"You must let in your friend Olivier. Well, who do you think is dead?"

When he came to the doorway she was sitting at the top of the steps and was very small. He could see that her head was pressed to her knees, Thibaud was dead, or Geoffrey, or both. He would not ask her more, only a child. He went down the steps slowly. "I feel older than old men feel," he said to himself. He crossed to the gate and took the bar off it and outside on the road, even in the little light there was, he knew Olivier.

"Olivier," he said. "I was asleep you know." He looked at the moon-shadow of the man he spoke to. "Olivier, Thibaud is perhaps dead, and it is you that must find out." He tugged on the leaf of the gate and let its weight walk him back till he leaned against the wall. As he looked up at the black window-space over the door Olivier led his horse into the yard and Beltran heard him go up the steps to the door. After a long space a glimmer of light appeared in the house, brightened and grew dim, and then came bright again within that upstairs room. Beltran put down his head and walked to the foot of the steps, where Olivier's horse nibbled his shoulder.

Olivier's voice came down from the window. "Thibaud is dead," he said. "I think he has been poisoned."

Thibaud was dead and his face had turned black. Berenguer was dead too, of a sword-wound that cut through the shoulder to the heart; the great bleeding had pasted him to the refectory floor. Sir John and the doctor they had bound together and gagged them, and thrown them down the well. Of them the doctor was alive and the old knight dead.

Geoffrey lay senseless in the dormitory. By the dim and flaring light of a cresset they thought that even in his swoon he was clutching his ankle, until they saw the knife. It ran through his hand into the bone of the leg.

"It was a neat stroke," Geoffrey said afterwards. It was too soon for the bone-cut to show poison and he was talkative after having his wounds dressed. The doctor had built a blaze in the kitchen to cook the chill of the well out of himself and the flames gave them comfort. "I took them to the dormitory," Geoffrey said, "and sat on a bed to be hail-fellow-well-met and let them give a bit of their game away. I sat on the edge, this ankle on that knee and my hand holding it. His knife came down like a thunderbolt. He meant to pin me up like that. 'There,' he says. 'Now I will have your knife. Fair exchange.' No more words and out they went. Every time I tried to move I fainted."

It was the dark one that did that, Geoffrey had said; the dark and silent one. It was the dark one who killed Berenguer with the sword-cut and the child had seen him do it, for she had been at the olives in the pantry. He had come noiseless into the refectory with his sword out and halfway down the room began the stroke. Berenguer heard something and stood up into the blade which came through him like cheese but with the crunching sound you make eating nuts. Then Berenguer fell and there was blood all over him. The dark man took bread from the table to clean his sword. After that the child hid, and followed.

Had they come at us with sword-strokes from the first, Beltran thought, we might have beaten them. At least I should not have gone to sleep. There was a trick in the way the talking man had come at him. There must have been a trick in it to send him to sleep. He had not followed Olivier to Thibaud's room. He would not go to it again. He would not look at Thibaud again. It was Beltran who had brought Thibaud here, and when Thibaud's assassins came, Beltran had slept so that they had but to kick him on the ear to make more sure of him. Then they had gone past him up the stairs. The child followed.

They had waked Thibaud, the child said, as if they had been his doctors, but first they had prepared his medicine.

Here is his bowl, said one, and had by the sound emptied it

out of the window. Then they had been quiet for a time until one said, I must wash this out well before I use it again. You fool, the other said, throw it away, or you will kill yourself. Something had rattled on the floor. Now then, Seigneur, they had said. Wake up there, Seigneur! That's right. The doctor is resting Seigneur, and you must drink. Where? They are all resting Seigneur, now that we have come. It is tiring work they have, caring for you. Now drink, Seigneur! Drink! Good, drink! Good! Lay down the bowl, La Hune! Put off that glove, for your sake. Here he goes. Come. Yes, there he goes. Time to leave. They had gone down the stairs and she had not gone into the room until the noises of Thibaud's dying had ended. She stood on the balcony and saw their shapes below her in the dusk as they climbed on their horses.

She stopped speaking and after a little while the doctor asked, "What then, child?"

Olivier was indignant. "What then? Why, then the poor lass came down to succour Beltran. For my part, she has said as much as she need, I am sure."

Beltran nodded to himself. "Ah," he said. "But when she came to rouse me, it was because the gate was barred, and you were there, and she could not move the bar."

Geoffrey eased himself where he lay. "If you know more, infant," he said, "tell it. It is a dismal tale but my leg hurts less while you tell it."

The doctor threw some pine logs on the fire and the bark flared up so that each of them saw the smile move onto the girl's face.

*   *   *

Once in their saddles, the two knights had listened to be sure there was no more noise from Thibaud. The child drew her foot across the floor of the balcony and at the sound they looked up, and she dropped the poisoned bowl onto their faces.

Geoffrey looked at his only hand in its bandage, and smiled. "Oh, to have seen that!" he said.

"It was rare," she agreed. The dark knight stayed on his horse and cursed, and she thought tasted, and cursed again whoever it was on the balcony, and went off at a gallop through the gate and down the hill. The other one fell off; after listening for a little to the noises he made, she decided he had damaged himself. When she came at him cautiously she found that he had broken or twisted a knee. She feared lest the dark knight should come back, so she told the injured man he must shut and bar the gate; she told him that the doctor had an antidote for all poisons and that if he would bar the gate she would give him some. He said that when he moved, his knee hurt a great deal, and she told him that was because it was injured. He could crawl to the gate, she said, and get onto one leg, and lift the bar that way. He had best be quick, she said, because though he had taken but little of the poison, and it would take longer to work than Thibaud's dose, yet it was a good poison and would do for him soon rather than late. Had he seen Thibaud's face? Black, it was, and so far as she could see, most of his insides spewed out before him on the bedclothes.

The knight began to crawl towards the gate. When he stopped and cried out at the pain in his knee she described Thibaud's corpse to him, and he moved on again. She asked him where they had come across the poison and if he had used it before, and in no time he was at the gate. She pushed the gate shut herself, careful to avoid his reach, and showed him how the bar lay inside the wall and need only to be drawn across to the socket on the other side of the gateway, and how it was above her head. He called her a she-devil as he pushed his way upright against the wall, and he fell down twice as he pulled the bar across the gate.

When he had done his part she led him back past the house to a place where the ground dropped steeply some six feet. He landed on something soft, by the sound, but complained. She waited there above him, in silence, and listened to him be afraid before his Maker, and then when it was black dark she heard him make the terrible noises that had come from Thibaud, and she left him.

She thought they were all dead, she said. She thought she was shut in with nothing but dead men, and then Olivier came and beat upon the gate and Beltran woke up.

Chapter Seventeen

THE BURIAL OF THIBAUD

WHEN she had ended they sat on in their silence. The girl's look caught Beltran's and he thought how clear her eye was, the white of her eye, after a night of so much killing. She had been quick with vengeance. In the boat she had been a handy recruit, nimble and fearless. Now she had a clear eye and a cheek that gleamed in the firelight. Vengeance was not provided for in the Rule of the Order. Why was he thinking these addled thoughts? She was an infidel child, not a knight of the Temple. Had he been so startled by the clarity of an eye? Bah! I am not young, he told himself, and made a joke of Olivier's which in more settled times he had disapproved; I am not young, and I am old in innocence. He disapproved it still. His mouth hardened and he looked into the silence.

On the stone stair that led down into the kitchen a sound scraped. In the dark cavern that the stairway had made showed the first paleness of day, but nothing else. Olivier was up the stair and gone. Well if daylight was coming, then it was yesterday that Thibaud died, and time to put off silence.

"Nothing, unless perhaps a rat," Olivier said, coming down the staircase. "Nothing except morning."

Beltran crossed to the wall and pulled open the heavy wooden shutters that closed the window. He leaned out into the light and looked over the countryside, the plain blackened by carob trees and the vineyards rising on the mountains, and thought he would like to go up into Mount Troodos. High in that mountain lay the Order's vineyard of Engadi, of which it was said in the Song of Songs, "my beloved is unto me as a cluster in the vineyard of Engadi." Its grapes were famous. Why, Beltran could do worse than seek the government of Engadi; had he not earned it, so humble a living? Perhaps he had, but there were a thousand dead at Acre who had earned as much. Besides, to whom could he take this wish, and the Grand Master dead upstairs? For was not he, and were not Geoffrey and Olivier and Diego, at war with the Order: or at least, was not the Order at war with them?

"Not Diego," Olivier said. "We three, but not Diego." The thought of being in conflict with the Order had matured in Beltran since it had been revealed to him with the dawn, and now, sharing it with Olivier, he heard for the first time of Diego's strange disappearance on Crete. It was noon, with the sun over their heads where they stood in the churchyard of Saint Nicholas.

The little church was on the edge of the town, its burial ground a walled terrace patched onto the hillside with room for few more tenants, but the parish priest had been pleased to inter the Master of the Temple. Less pleased, but at least willing, to lay Berenguer next to him.

"There will be no fee," he said. "You know your Order has the privilege to consecrate its own burial grounds, and had they done so here we should have been quite out of business. I shall tend the grave myself." A Mass would be sung at midnight. The grave-diggers had smoothed over the grave, taken their gift and gone.

Beltran looked down at the dusty earth. "Two months ago I did not know Thibaud Gaudin," he said. "Now I feel we have buried the Order."

Olivier was looking up to the road that ran to the commandery. The grave-diggers' cart was passing down it, taking the bodies of the old English knight and Renan La Hune to be buried in the town. "I do not feel we have buried the Order," he said. "One buries dead men, not sick ones. And you, Beltran, unless you break faith, for one thing, you will not live to see the Order buried. For another . . . You have been my friend, so listen: Diego's spirit was overturned by that gold. For a while he seemed to go mad, and what he is now, who knows?"

Beltran worked away at the earth on the grave with his boot.

"I have thought about how he behaved," Olivier went on, "and about how he left with these men. He was not the Diego we knew at Sidon, he became something else. It was as if the gold had done it. You know how angry he was to us about all the secrecies and night meetings? I think it was the gold made him angry." He stopped. "I am not being clear."

"No," Beltran said. "You are not being clear, but do not stop on that account, or perhaps for the rest of the world no one will speak at all."

They smiled at each other, at last, and Olivier pounded his fist into the palm of the other hand. "Oh!" he said. "Beltran! We must not feel, because of the gold, that we have been saddled with a burden!"

Beltran gazed at him, and could not forbear to exclaim, "Not been saddled with a burden! What would you call it?"

"Diego counted it a burden because he took the charge of it to be a business between him and God. He was wrong, because there was no business between him and God that had not been there before."

"You have had charge of the gold from Crete to Cyprus," Beltran said. "You have not felt it made more business between you and God than was there before?"

"No," Olivier said. "Truly. I can truly say, no."

"Poor Diego," Beltran said. "He has taken all the businesses between him and God with him. What now," he asked Olivier, "Are we to do with the gold?"

"You know that you must decide that. You are the most senior of us."

"A choice of this kind," Beltran said. "I would have us agree on it. I would leave Limassol at once. We do not know who is against us, all or part of the Order. Until we know we have our duty to the Order in the Holy Land, the Order that fights the Infidel. We have no duty to the Order, or that part of it, that murders its Grand Master. Our duty lies in seeing safe the gold, and so I would have it out of here. What do you say?"

"I say the same. Get our gear, and go."

They went into the priest's house beside the church, and paid him for the Mass they would not hear, and set off up the road to the commandery. As they walked Beltran said, "We must take the child and the doctor. They are not safe here."

What he was thinking was, where is Corberan, and why were not Corberan and his troop here last night?

Olivier was speaking. "After all, we can work out what to do once we are at sea."

"Yes," Beltran said. "Yes, we can do that. I wonder what became of Corberan."

"Corberan? Who is that?"

"I forgot, you would not know him. One of the Catalans."

Olivier stopped and mopped his brow. "You know, Beltran, it serves us ill, it serves the Order ill, that its members should have such different experience of the world outside it."

Beltran thought he understood this and that it made sense. "We must do our best to share what knowledge is proper to think of, and put away the rest." They walked on and into the gate of the commandery.

Chapter Eighteen

CORBERAN

TRY as he would, Corberan had got himself no wound, and those of his men who lived had in the morning called on him to run. Even his horse, alone of beasts as he alone of the men he had led into this ambush, was unscathed. They had been trapped in the winding gorge at the first cooling of the afternoon, shot down with arrows and faced with mailed men at each end of the little space. The last onfall had been made by Corberan and Siscar. They had made some attempt on the besiegers in the early night, but soon left that: the others knew the ground, even in the dark it seemed, and took two Catalan lives for no loss of their own.

With the daylight the Catalans had hardly stirred on their first sortie when arrows from men invisible among the trees dropped two more; a third man was killed outright and only Corberan and Siscar came back. At noon Siscar died.

When that happened, Corberan and his horse were all that lived of the troop of Catalans sworn to guard Thibaud. The man led the beast to the middle of the road where the trap had been sprung on them, and mounted in full view of the dead and the living. He took his short sword once more into his hand and, shouting his warcry, "Iron awake!" he put the tired horse into a canter and ran at the grim place where his friends had taken their deaths. The horse ran over and past the killing-ground without a check and slowed to a walk, and stopped. Corberan's hands had left the reins and he sat with the sword laid flat across the saddle before him and his face turned up to the sky, to the shady leaves and the sky above.

A voice spoke from behind him. "Ride, Catalan," it said. "We have no more work with you."

"Then I will bury my dead," Corberan said, looking down the winding road in front of him.

"No. Ride on."

A small wind stirred the leaves that dappled him and the horse and the roadway, and the horse stepped forward gently as if trying out its rider, to see if he would pull on the rein. As the curtain of leaves blew aside a face showed through, mottled in grey and black like old armour. Corberan went through the long alley, out of the green shade of the wood. The horse came to the road that wound away down the mountainside, and followed it, and carried him across the parched coastal plain until the evening brought them to the sea.

PART II. 1303–1314

Chapter Nineteen

ANAGNI

DIEGO'S face had quickened. It was not that it had grown younger but that it moved more easily. Those lines of rigour that put coherent grip onto a countenance had slipped away— those rigours of conscience, duty or suffering, or whatever else— leaving his face smoother than it had once been. It would fly from pleasure to alarm, from thought to feeling, from comfort to activity as fast as a swallow turns in the air. He was almost old, and the face told you this, yet he showed himself on its expressions as plain as a boy of five. Despite this outward play of frankness he did not seek to be trusted, but rather the reverse, and in this he was successful. It had been noticed that the tale told by his seeming would not always survive as a true history of what passed within him. For eleven years now men had doubted Diego and few, therefore, could claim to have been deceived by him.

He had ridden a week with this cantankerous platoon of assassins. They had met on the border between Florence and Siena, passed east to the mountains and come by highland bandit tracks down the spine of Italy. Yesterday they had turned to cross the valleys and made west again all day, and now, bright and early in the morning, they had put their horses up the little road that led to Anagni. Anagni was their journey's end, for there, a long day's ride from Rome, the old Pope holidayed in the late summer airs.

Diego and his companions numbered two score. Some were hired men, but most of them had been chosen for being enemies of the Holy Father, which is to say his victims, having been deprived by him of their possessions, despoiled of their lands, and exiled from the Papal dominions. They were men of sour temper who lived in hope of the Pope's dying, and who anticipated in his death the key to their restored fortune. Diego found little mettle in them. They were querulous and complaining, which made them anathema to Diego, for he had come to the view of life that a man must take the reverses which befall him as no more to be remarked then the growing of his finger-nails.

The chief of these wretches was of another stamp. Sciarra was a prince of the Colonna, and he and his had seen the Pope's family of the Gaetani endowed with stolen Colonna lands, castles, towns and palaces. They had seen their stronghold of Palestrina destroyed and the country about it ploughed, a thing that hitherto one had only read about in history, with salt. The offence of the salt lay heavy on Sciarra. He held it to be the worst of the Pope's crimes, and whereas the body of the exiles in this troop were bent on no more than retrieving their lost estates, the Colonna was too full of rage for such trifles. He would have jumped off the edge of the world if he could have taken Pope Boniface with him. Towards vengeance alone, he had confided to Diego, he made his journey. Diego found this admirable and esteemed also his bearing, which was unfailingly stark and sombre. Sciarra had eyes as hard as stones, dead to all expression until you witnessed a miraculous occurrence which happened at most once a day, when a wide smile sloped across the bitter carvings that cut down his face, and his eyes would soften and grow warm with malice.

The purpose of this enterprise was not, however, to tip the Holy Father off the edge of the world. The Italian exiles led by Sciarra Colonna had been simply the tools most convenient to a Power with designs more elaborate than theirs, so the true leader of the expedition had attached to it half a dozen cool heads like Diego. This leader was Guillaume de Nogaret, counsellor to the French King Philip, called the Fair, and his mission was to kidnap the Pope and carry him to France. So had they come to Anagni.

*   *   *

"Here we are then," Nogaret said to Diego. "We shall let the Italians find him. They can nose him out like dogs, and we shall follow them like huntsmen and whip them off before they tear out his throat." He smiled with mischief. "You can whip off Sciarra."

Diego's long face was amazed. "I shall try. I am flattered you expect so much."

"Don't be," Nogaret said, all the time scanning the streets of the village as they opened before them. "I don't expect to succeed, but that is the plan, and I am dedicated to carrying out plans." They came to the square and still no one stirred in the waking day. Across the gleaming cobbles was the cathedral church and beyond that the Pope's palace. The buildings were all white in the sunshine.

"They had better dismount," Nogaret said. From the top of the campanile a bell sounded the alarm and two men-at-arms came one after the other from the door at the foot of the tower, turning from sleepiness to activity as they moved. They ran along the lower steps of the cathedral and stared at the menace that faced them out of nowhere.

Sciarra ran his horse straight across the square and put it at the flight of steps. The beast went over one man and he cut the other with his sword, stretching suddenly wide and low and taking him in the thigh. The man fell in a fountain of blood. Sciarra went on up the steps and found the door there opening as he reached it. He vanished inside and the sound of his horse's feet rang away into the darkness. The bell had stopped and there was no sound but the sorrowful cries of the man who saw his life depart in the blood that rushed out of his leg. His comrade crawled off to the side of the steps.

Nogaret looked at Diego and made a grimace that quirked his mouth and tossed up his eyebrows. "What would you?" He turned to Sciarra's lieutenant. "Musciatto," he said. "Your leader has shown you the way." Musciatto sighed and calling to his men crossed the square. At the foot of the steps they left their horses and tramped up into the open door of the cathedral. Soon there was a noise of shouting and the clash of arms, and a light flared dimly within. Nogaret looked nonplussed.

"It is fire," Diego said.

Nogaret nodded and set off round the sides of the square followed by his six cool heads. He did not go to the church but turned off down a shady street which ran on into the countryside, and then a high wall rose beside it and a gate with a porter's lodge. Behind the wall cypresses and cedars grew far into the sky.

"He lives here," Nogaret explained. He made them stay close under the wall away from the gate, all save Diego. They two got down and Nogaret knocked on the gate. They heard the door of the porter's house and at almost the same moment some noises of the events in the church came to their ears.

From behind the gate a voice spoke. "Who is that? What is happening?"

"Let us in," Nogaret said, full of fright. "I have brought the Holy Father's spring water from Fiuggi. There are bandits in the square." He looked at Diego and shrugged. "It is true," he said, "he has water sent up every day from Fiuggi." The door opened and the porter stood there looking nervous and suspicious. Nogaret moved a little forward as if to speak confidentially and as the man lifted his head for converse, the Frenchman slipped a knife into his throat and in the same movement took himself and his horse sideways so that they got no blood on them. The door of the porter's lodge closed gently. They ignored it.

"Why does he have water sent from Fiuggi?" They entered the Pope's garden, and the other five followed.

"He thinks it is good for his health," Nogaret said.

"Something is," Diego said. "He has lived a mighty long time."

Nogaret grinned. "If he is to live any longer," he said, "we had best hurry a little."

They brought their horses to a canter and crossed the great garden to the palace, from which there now came the sounds that had earlier issued from the cathedral, and to which the fire that had started in the wake of the Italian exiles had now spread.

*   *   *

Sciarra Colonna burst out of the burning passage that joined the palace to the cathedral and found himself with the Pope. He saw the Pontiff on a golden throne with the two-crowned tiara on his head and in his hands the keys of St. Peter and a golden cross. Beside him stood a servant who had neglected to flee. The chamber was grand but Sciarra had owned grander, and he moved onto the floor with its half-moons of tesselated marble, between the walls tapestried with ancient myths, as if he had come into a sheepfold after a wolf. He was on foot now: his horse lay on the floor of the great church kicking its entrails out of its belly. Four paces from the golden throne the floor lifted a step and he stood there and looked. The smile sloped onto his face and he knelt on one knee with his hands grasping the hilt of his sword and his chin lying on the crosspiece, and looked still at his enemy. Blood ran down the channel of his blade and made a little pool. He saw a man too old to have done all the wrongs accounted to him in the past nine years. He saw an old man whose hour had come but who trembled from age not fear, and whose face woke into life at the mockery of respect displayed in Sciarra's pose.

Boniface laid the keys beside him in the chair and let fall the crucifix which hung by a chain from his neck, and then lifted the tiara from his head and laid it on the floor beside his feet. He ruffled his hair where the weight had rested, and hooked a forefinger at the servant. This was a gaunt man of middle years who seemed to regard today as if it were any other day in his life. He approached his master and held out the plate that was in his left hand and the cup that was in his right. Boniface took a honey-cake from the plate, and accepted the cup. He broke his fast and waited for the Colonna to start hacking at his ancient flesh. He thought of something. He gestured with the little cake in his hand.

"Your bees make good honey," he said.

So it was that when Nogaret's little band entered the room by the doorway from the garden, Boniface lay on the floor before his throne with Sciarra's hands squeezing his skinny throat. At the same moment there was a rush of flame from the door which had brought in the Colonna and through the smoke stumbled a pack of the Italian exiles. The smoke ran round the room like a sudden mist. The flames crackled briskly and in front of them the Italians looked like imps dancing out of Hell. In the cathedral a horse began to scream and the bell began to ring out again from the tower.

Nogaret pointed to the two on the floor and hit Diego on the arm. "See to that," he said. "I'll keep these Italians quiet." He jumped down the three steps into the room and ran into the smoke with his men behind him.

Diego walked over to the throne. As he reached it Sciarra made the discovery that his hands were too big to strangle so small a windpipe, and leaving one hand there to secure his victim he put the other to his belt and pulled his dagger from its scabbard. The Pope's eyes flashed at Diego through the haze. Sciarra's right arm lifted and Diego put his left foot on it near the elbow and took it by the wrist with both hands, and broke it. The knife fell onto the floor. Sciarra gave out a howl. There was no pain in it and no anger, nothing but vengeance frustrated. He took the Pope with his good hand and shouted surprisingly, "The salt! The salt!" Diego cast about for something with which to club Sciarra, since to let his blood out in front of his native allies might provoke them to any folly. A man came up to him through the smoke. He had a napkin over one arm and the other he held out to Diego, the hand grasping some solid object. Diego took it and it hefted weightily in his fist. He smote Sciarra on the side of the head, and the Colonna fell limp onto his side. Diego peered at the weapon in his hand, and found it to be a statue of dark green stone.

With the help of the servant Diego carried Boniface into the arcade that made a cool terrace between the house and the garden. He left them there; he left the Italians to Nogaret, the palace to the fire, and the Pope to his servant, and walked off down the steps.

He went through a garden of flowers and into a garden of herbs and sniffed the sweet perfumes that rose from them. From the trees a heavier scent drifted down. He crossed a canal by a little bridge and passing through orchards came to the vegetable gardens, dry and dusty in the September sun. He could no longer see the palace or smell the smoke or hear any of the turmoil. He sat against a hedge of laurel and closed his eyes, and listened to the insects buzzing about in the air and to the birds singing as they crossed the garden. The sun shone at him over a wall and was warm on his face.

He heard a scuffling noise and as he opened his eyes a voice said, "Ah!" There was a man on top of the wall in front of him, a young man with the fair northern hair who sat with his legs swinging and his heels kicking on the stones. His eyes were blue and less careless than the rest of him seemed. He smiled down at Diego and Diego looked up at him. The man on the wall spoke first.

"Who are you, Sir?"

"I am Diego Maro," Diego said. "A Brother of the Temple."

The man on the wall lifted his eyes towards the palace and frowned. "The Temple would hardly lay hands on the Holy Father," he said.

"Certainly not," Diego said. "I have just saved the Holy Father from the knife of the Colonna."

The young man smiled a second time and said, "The Colonna. Yes."

"Yes," Diego said. "And who, sir, are you?"

"A gentleman of Anagni," said the young man. "We have taken the horses which these Colonna left outside our cathedral, and we have put out the fire which was roasting the one they left inside. It is not like the Colonna to plan so ill."

Diego did not remember when he had spent so pleasing a morning. Sitting among the leeks and onions he nodded at the man on the wall. "You may be right," he said. "I know little of them. One Colonna, and some fellow-exiles. The thing is, though, that the whole foray seems to be under the conduct of the French."

The young man took this in and despite his best efforts the temper showed in his face. He gazed over Diego's head once more towards the palace and then vanished in the twinkling of an eye, down on the other side of the wall. There was a stir of horses and then for a little the sound of hooves running on grass. Diego rose and went back through the gardens. As he went he kept his eyes everywhere and his ears open, and noticed no scent of flowers.

The room where Sciarra Colonna had failed of his vengeance was still hung with smoke but the burning in the passage had stopped. At its mouth a group of the exiles stood in argument, and by the door where Diego entered from the gardens were two more of them, minding Sciarra. They had pulled a tapestry down from its hooks and made a bundle of it as a couch for him; his broken arm was bound to his body. His eyes were shut and his face was still, but the motion of his chest told of his breathing.

Across the room a man of Nogaret's came out from behind an arras and lifted his chin at Diego. Diego passed the arras and went down a long corridor without doors or windows towards the light at the far end. There another corridor ran across and facing him was an open doorway.

"You would as soon Colonna had killed me," Diego heard Boniface say.

"Yes," Nogaret said. He graced the admission with a touch of quaint politeness. "Yes, Your Holiness," he said, "I would as soon Colonna had killed you."

Diego advanced to the doorway and saw he had come there unnoticed. He leaned under the arch, with his arms folded and his chin on his chest, as if he had been there all the time and forgotten by the two speakers. The room was small and plain after the fashion used by some princes of the Church, but the narrow bed was curtained in white silk brocaded with gold, and there the Holy Father rested. Head and shoulders were hidden from Diego by the curtains but he saw the old man's feet move, rubbing against each other under the eiderdown as if to express what his voice did not. Nogaret stood with his back to the room and gazed out of a window that looked far eastwards over woods and valleys to the mountains.

"That would not have served your king," said the voice from behind the curtains. "He wants me in France, to see me publicly denounced by his patriotic French prelates. He summoned me to him. Me! Did you know that?"

When Nogaret answered it sounded as if he was chewing on

his thumb. "Yes, I knew. I knew that." The Pope's feet thumped on the bed and Nogaret stirred as if he would turn round, but he stayed looking out upon the distant hills.

"Yes," the old man said. "Everyone in Europe knew it. It makes good sense, too, if the dog is to throw off my lordship: that's why you come to kidnap me. Everyone knows a priest can be murdered, but to drag a Pope to trial in your own country makes a picture the world had not yet thought of painting. You serve a political dog, Nogaret. Why then would you have let Sciarra kill me?"

The servant came out of a cupboard and took honey in a golden bowl past Diego's nose and went to feed it to his master with a spoon. He looked Diego in the face as he went by. Nogaret leaned hard on the sill of his window and gave his answer.

"I have a weakness," he said. "I hate the Church. I love my master because he too hates the Church. Sometimes I lose sight of the greater harm I hope to do the Church in favour of what is to hand." He turned from the window and looked across at the bed. As if he saw a question in the Pope's face he said, "The Church burned my grandfather for heresy."

When he turned round Nogaret had seen Diego but made nothing of it, his mind was all on the dialogue with the Pope. The servant at the bedside would dip the spoon in the honey and pass the spoonful within the curtains and after a moment withdraw the spoon and wait, and then fill it again with honey and pass it again within the curtains. The servant did this now and after a hesitation withdrew it to hover over the bowl, still untasted. From Nogaret's expression you would suppose that he, as also perhaps the servant, was waiting for Boniface to speak; then, that he saw Boniface was not going to speak, or had not heard him.

"My grandfather," Nogaret spoke his words very clear. "The Church burned him."

The feet at the end of the narrow bed had become quite still. There was a slight dry sound as if Boniface were clearing his throat, and then he spoke, "Grandfathers," he said. "The Church burned your grandfather." His feet began to rub quickly against each other, "For heresy," he said, "Ha-ha." The Pope laughed.

Then he laughed in triplets, "Ha-ha-ha, ha-ha-ha, ha-ha-ha!" The Pontifical feet beat up and down on the bed.

The laughter stopped. Diego saw that Nogaret's eyes were wide and staring. "Oh," said the voice from the bed, run out of breath. "Oh do we remember our grandfathers, these days?" The air came gaspingly from his mangled windpipe. "Because your grandfather was roasted at the stake, the Church must be brought to ruin?" He seemed about to laugh again but instead he said, "I, the Supreme Pontiff of the Church, born Benedetto Gaetani, become Boniface the Eighth, God's Vicar on Earth, and so on, and so on, and so on," he pursued, suddenly sweeping himself into a rage, "am to be murdered by ruffians of the Colonna because some Frenchman's grandfather burned! How senseless to die so! I had rather be murdered by the Turk!"

He spat this jibe across the room as if he had good hope the venom in it might be mortal. It seemed too from some sounds that followed as if it promised to set the old man laughing again, but the servant, a man of indecipherable motives, had resolved his master must take in some more honey, and the two expectations collided in a flurry of uncouth sounds and clumsy movement behind the curtains. Even as this little turmoil broke out Nogaret, whose appearance had grown more and more wild as the Pope's address continued, advanced upon the bed with his eyes so concentrated with hatred upon the choking creature lying there that Diego was able to take him, one hand by the beard and the other by the belt, and pluck him out of the room all in a movement.

"Do not," Diego said, "start swearing oaths and drawing daggers, but listen to me. The jig is up. They have taken the horses of your Italians. They have sent for help. You will be pursued and can make no speed with so old and ill-used a man in your party. The scheme was a botch from the start. I might yet make something of it, but you must leave."

Nogaret had some of his wits in order by now, and hearing this last he looked askance at Diego, "You will stay, but I must go?"

"Do not trust me, then. What does that matter, to you or me? Eh? If you stay, there will be French corpses or French prisoners here and that is all your king will win from the business: mockery and odium, and the loss of his most trusted counsellor, Guillaume de Nogaret. Well?"

The sounds from the bedchamber had sorted themselves out into an old man coughing, and a servant making those soothing but wordless noises that settle children, horses and doctors' patients back into tranquillity of temper.

"Why do you stay?" Nogaret could not manage to be puzzled without also being suspicious.

"Why not? I keep saving His Holiness from harm, do I not?"

The man who had been minding the arras came in to them, and as he did so they heard a scream and much shouting from the great room at the end of the corridor, and then the sound of steel thrashing on steel as not enough men encountered a determined assault. Though the words could not be heard, the desperate cries of doomed man rang unmistakably in their ears. The man who had joined them was one of the cool heads but he had no time left for politeness.

"We have the horses under that room." He meant the room where the Pope lay. "Sciarra is bound fast onto one, but we are a horse short and can cut him off in a trice if you wish it." He managed a sardonic smile as he jerked his head behind him. "Your Italians are holding your rear, though they don't know it. They are fighting like brother against brother in there; I doubt there'll be prisoners taken." He prevented himself from putting a hand on Nogaret's arm. "What are we to do then?"

Nogaret looked at Diego and lifted his eyebrows into the same question, "Do?" Diego took them to the doorway and pointed out the window. "There. Go there. Get into your saddle, ride for these blue mountains there. Throw the reins on your horse's neck and stop for nothing." He shoved Nogaret into the room and saw him out of the window. "You!" He held the man for a moment. "Take my horse, but first cut off my saddlebags and throw them in the window, in here to the back of the room."

The sound of weapons from up the corridor grew less and among the noises from men's throats, the killing and the killed, rose the cry for quarter. "Will you do that? Here, to the back of the room?" The skin on the man's face was tight and he seemed to have lost his voice but his eyes glowed and he nodded once, deeply, as if he were saying a word, and walked across the room to step, rather than jump, from the window. The Pope was silent behind his curtains, and the servant was silent beside the Pope. To Diego waiting at the door came flying and landed solidly against the wall his saddlebags. The man had found his voice again for lightly through the air came an ironic laugh and a single cry of farewell.

Diego opened one of his bags and took from it his white mantle with the cross upon the breast and shook it out from its folds. He found in the corner of his eye that the servant was close and his hand, since he was stooped, went to the knife in his boot, but the man took the mantle with one hand and straightened him up with the other, and dressed him. The Pope, whose last and only sight of him had been when he broke Sciarra Colonna's arm, found it natural to associate the return of the Templar (as he now saw him to be) with the departure of Nogaret.

"The French are dogs," Boniface said, "Why do you not pursue them?"

"The dogs have taken my horse," Diego said.

After that the Pope would not have Diego from his side.

Chapter Twenty

DIEGO AND THE POPE

BONIFACE was some years past the four score, but the terrors and stimulants of the day had fired him with vivacity. He was further cheered to find that in the person of Diego he had a Knight of the Temple for the companion of his journey. He touched lightly the snow-white mantle of the Order.

"The warriors of Christ," he said, "the soldiers of the Church!" With an ironic spasm of regret he added, "Would I had made them mine! I dare say, though, I have the best of them at my side."

The complicated look with which he uttered this trivial flattery announced him to be largely restored to himself, and all that afternoon Diego found the eyes gleamed as lively as they had when they first lit on him over Sciarra's shoulder. To this lustre was added that of the declining sun, for most of the day between noon and dusk was spent travelling westwards to Sermonetta. Thanks to the Pope's sense of family this place had now become a hold of his cousins of the Gaetani, and a messenger had gone forward to warn them of his coming. Sermonetta was, besides, on a roundabout road to Rome, and unlikely to be under ambush by any vexed and bleeding survivors of the slaughtered exiles. They rode tranquil, therefore, with a small escort.

The vines were heavy and the olives were being picked. They had descended to the plain and it was a country thick with vegetation and the heavy green of sun-enduring trees. The heat of the day, the richly swollen countryside, and this business of being carried on, rather than making, a journey, all joined to bring Diego to a state where he felt like a man painted on a wall, a figure in a fresco among others; a man most of whose nature was asleep or in a dream, and only the fringe of him awake.

In the picture the Pope's eyes shone with rays of gold and an out-fingered hand showed the smile of his talking mouth. He was full of pleasure to be out riding, and rode a pretty white mule. In the distance was the blue of the sea, although on their real journey there were hills to be crossed before they saw that blue. They rode on and on through the green day and Boniface confided greatly in Diego, Diego was sure of it.

They slept easy at Sermonetta, but in the morning there was no light in the Pope's eyes. "We have been rescued," he said gloomily to Diego, and pointed to the window of his room. Diego looked first across the low flat land to the sea and then directly below. A camp had gone up in the night. He reckoned a good four hundred men and looked close at the pavilion that housed the leadership of this force. He saw the emblem of the bear and the coats of arms of two cardinals.

"It is the Orsini," Boniface said. "When these fools at Anagni sent for help they sent for the Orsini, they being enemies to the Colonna. I have no more expectation of joy at being surrounded by the care of the former than by the hatred of the latter." The servant waited on the Pope with a cup of warm spiced wine, and the face of this enigma wore so grave an aspect that it was plain the Pope spoke not from peevishness but in earnest. The room was still cold, the sun not entering it so early in the day, and a disheartened tremor played in the air among the three men. Diego for all he had thought it was now a principle with him to bend to every wind at once, felt the sinews within him gather to meet earthquakes.

The Pope drank from the cup. "I am a man of little merit," he announced, with a smack of the confessional. "I have sins I wish to forget. I have sins for which I see no remission." Diego had gone as stiff as a dog among rabbits that suddenly scents bear, but the servant had philosophy enough for both of them, and apart from the gravity that unusually beset his countenance he heard as if he did not hear these franknesses of the Pope. He took his cup from his master and tasted the dregs. He pursed his lips doubtfully. At a buffet by the wall he ground some herb in a mortar and added it to the hot wine.

"That French dog!" Boniface shouted loud and Diego, from the window, saw men in the waking encampment lift their faces towards the castle. "Oh," Boniface cried again, "that French

dog!" He accepted the cup from his servant, sniffed it and drank
and then nodded, so that his man came within a hair of smiling.
"You see," the Pope said to Diego, "Philip of France denies my
suzerainty, disavows me as his sovereign, refuses me the taxings
of my Church in France, conciliates himself with his clergy,
which is to say my clergy in his country, and seeks to have for
himself, in that small space that is his France, as much power of
as many kinds as that France can contain." He finished with the
cup and the servant had him sit, and began to complete his
travelling toilet by exchanging his slippers for soft riding boots.
A trumpet sang from the slope below the castle.

"Aye," Boniface said, and there in the chair went off into a
long and gloomy silence. There was a knock on the door, and
Diego forestalled the servant, though he let the man open but
himself filled the space. He saw the gentleman from the garden
wall at Anagni.

"Sir," the man said, and bowed a little, "Their eminences and
the princes are ready to escort His Holiness to Rome."

"Good, good!" Diego said, "Why do you camp in the shade
of the fortress? The sun will scarce be on your tents until noon,
this time of year." He signalled to the servant, who closed the door.
They waited, and at the first knock opened the door again.

"I failed to say," and the gentleman from Anagni was pink,
"that their eminences and highnesses had thought His Holiness
would be early on the road."

The servant let the door fall further open, and peered at the
pink gentleman as if astounded by what he had heard, and Diego
looked as if he had not heard it at all, and then the servant closed
the door gently and ran up the bolt.

Into Boniface's eye had come far back a dull gleam like the
shine of lead, like a wet sky with the sun hidden at its back. He
gave them both impartially an arid smile, that closed almost as
soon as it had opened.

"When men feel free to sound trumpets outside my window,"
he said, "well then, I had rather have Colonna spitting on my
face with his hands at my throat." He stood up and waited for the
servant to lay his riding cloak upon his shoulders.

"The King of France," the Pope said to Diego, "has brought

me to this pass. When either the Orsini or the Colonna fears that the others have designs upon the Pope, they keep him captive, and call it a bodyguard. I am today the prisoner of the Orsini. I have failed the Church, since I have let the King of France humble my estate. I had expected to fail God, but had expected to do better by His Church." He looked surprised. "I begin to think," he said, "that only a godly and a pious Pope could stand up to Philip. Come on."

He went to the door and the servant loosed the bolt and swung it open. A lord of the Orsini stood where the winding stair finished its spiral, backed by a group of lesser lords in armour, and a herald beside him in a tabard of colours shiningly embroidered.

"Going campaigning, Giacomo?" Boniface said. "Why do you people always think a herald will legitimize a kidnapping? You sir," this to the herald, "why don't you get out of my way and read your summons to me as we travel? It is too cold for old men to loiter save before their betters." He smiled like a meteor descending from the sky and the group fell apart, leaves before a puff of wind. Boniface turned his mouth wryly at Diego as if the images had occurred to him also, and so entered captivity with his little retinue.

They went down to the flat land into the morning mist that flowed off the marshes, and at length rode along the Appian Way to Rome. It was a different day from yesterday, and Diego felt that he was nothing but awake: the frescoed wall with himself painted onto a dream no more than brushed his memory. Today he would have broken mountains to sustain this evil Vicar of God against his enemies; but no mountain came within his reach. The Pope's escort came into Rome and pushed among the first questionings of the people. Ever proprietorial about the Holy Father, the Romans grew hot as they recognized that Boniface was not his own master. When it was clear he was being taken to the Castle of Saint Angelo the crowd rashly blocked the bridge, and two or three of them lay bleeding in the gutter before the Orsini could get by.

Boniface would not let Diego be the companion of his prison. "They would poison you, and that would be a waste."

Diego stood at the Pope's stirrup in the gateway and wished him well and asked for his blessing.

"You can have mine," Boniface said. "It may not be God's."

Diego looked into his eyes and saw the third light he had seen there: the first had been of yesterday, the second of this morning, and at this one he shuddered. Then he knelt, and the Pope blessed him, and went into the castle with his servant.

Diego took himself to the House of the Temple. In thirty days the servant came to him, bringing the news that in the night Boniface had run head first against the stone wall, and knocked his brains out upon the floor. Diego took the servant with him, and they came over the Alps into Savoy under the first snow of winter.

Chapter Twenty-one

RUAD

FROM north and west the sea surged onto the rock. It came in great waves that leaned on the rock and then drew off, to flow by on either side like river water polishing a stone. The waves were broad and deep but no foam broke on their rounding crests. To Beltran, who stood at the edge of the rock and looked down on the untroubled passing of the sea, its disregard of this island where he lived came as a vexation. So much power came within the waves that for them to divide upon his rock, meekly and with no stir, called to him of mockery. Some little attention, some ineffectual pounding, say, from which the sea might fall back broken into bursts of white spray, seemed to Beltran to be due to twelve years of life spent as warden of this desolate outpost.

Ruad was a cramped tower in a walled bailey with outbuildings and lean-tos stuck here and there. The island ran to little more than two acres, and the tower and bailey covered less than half of this. In the old days Infidel princes had used the rock as a prison, and to dwell there was to Beltran the essence of imprisonment. Across the two miles of sea to the east was the land from which he and his Order had been driven. For twelve winters he had watched the new snow refresh the mountain tops across that water, and in twelve summers he had watched it melt while his own throat parched.

It was a curiosity about the fortress of Ruad that it was supplied with no water but what rained from the sky. From periodic drought as much as from other causes their number was now less than ten. Often they fell ill, and each of them had shown some madness in the years on Ruad. They knew by now that this desolation of theirs had made different cares for each man, and that each bore his cares in his own ways, and with strange signs and habits of behaviour that his fellows must let pass. In a

Christendom of two acres there was not room to order life's bodies and souls as neatly as in the world at large.

"In a Heaven this size," Beltran told Saint Hilary, "you would be in much the same boat." He spoke to his saint with freedom, but the irreverence had no zest: in the same way that it was modulated not quite to challenge Heaven—which might, after all, have had some worship in it—so also the speaker never lifted his eyes. They looked always at the sea.

It had become Beltran's custom to stand here, near nightfall on the edge of the rock, and look at the sea. At first he would look across the gulf towards the Holy Land, but now he looked out into the sea. There was some fear in this, for to make such traffic with an ocean put out the balance of a man's dealings both with other men and with God. He had spoken of it to Olivier, who had referred to Neptune and sea nymphs, and to Venus. Beltran had not been rattled by any of these pagan names. The exchange he made with the sea was not one in which the sea was a spirit, or inhabited by spirits, but one where he looked as a man might look at time, or at a mirror, or at the skin growing on his hands, or at those sins whose shape, bend them how he may, had not yet come to a form that seemed likely to win God's mercy.

He heard the thin clang of the iron postern that stood in the bailey wall, rusted to a skeleton. It was that time then: they had sent Honfroi to call him. No man looked up at the sea. Well, no man that was not drowned, looked up at the sea for long. He heard Honfroi slip and stumble past the place where there was no handhold. It was a contrivance, either of Honfroi or of his soul, to be nightly taken unawares by features of this baby island that were to all the others as familiar as the taste on their own tongues.

Why look into the sea, instead of up at Heaven? He would prostrate himself before Heaven in the chapel. In the chapel, from where he could not see the sky, and hardly the light, so dingily was it built and windowed, he would kneel to God and Christ and the Virgin, and to Saint Hilary. Out here, upon the edge of the rock, he did not do this. Yet he had done so once. He had spent much of his life out of doors, and was used—or had been used—to worship there, alone or with his fellows. It was a part of his life that he had lost, to stand in the light and look up at Heaven, from where light came.

As all this went through his head he remembered how they had buried the gold. At first and for a long time after they had settled at Ruad there had been nothing remarkable about the gold; it had been much as it had been on board ship, the cargo they carried. It had sat among the stores, in its boxes and barrels, until the year of the plague of rats. They had supposed the rats came from some of those cities of the coast which the Infidel had emptied and cast down. Anyhow they had come up out of the sea in their thousands, and as the Infidels in the Holy Land had been too much for the soldiers of Christ, so these creatures were too many for the thirty or so Templars then on Ruad. In those days they still had the old galley that had brought Thibaud up from Acre to Sidon and they had drawn off in her pulling the oars themselves, having now no slaves. They left two men dead or dying.

"Beltran! Hey, Beltran!" Honfroi had three stations along the short path from the postern to Beltran's pitch on the edge of the rock, and there he would stop to shout, "Beltran!". It was not Beltran's way to acknowledge these shouts, since it might have put an end to them, and have cut short Honfroi's nightly expedition to fetch Beltran.

When they had come back to the island they were prepared, and they pelted the castle and the rock with Greek fire until the whole place flamed and smoked and the rats singed and sizzled. A small party armed and vizored landed with clubs and so the invaders were routed, and the island was reclaimed by the Order. It took them days to rid the island of the last wreckage and the last corpse, and weeks to make good the castle again. During those weeks men would look sometimes at the gold, since it was naked now, the rats having eaten away all the boxes and barrels it had sat in. Men would look at the gold and smile; there was something friendly about it shining away there in the cellar. Then they had everything put to rights and life became what it had been before. Beltran remembered that. It was what life was now but still he remembered that time of it, being then what it was now; being then what it had been before. He remembered it, living on this island, doing nothing for his faith, in no way serving Christ, in no way serving man or honouring the image in which he was made, being neither engaged with nor retired from the world, until his soul grew numb as if it had been a limb paralysed by a blow.

One day he was asked at a chapter meeting that the gold should be laid out of sight. Men had stopped smiling at it. It shone still but the light with which it did this was no longer a light that moved you to smile. The gold had lost its innocence in the eyes of these men, these servants of the Temple's island and God's, these guardians of a treasure house on the edge of nowhere. The gold that they were keeping for God had become lively in a way they did not like, and they asked Beltran to put it away. So it was lowered into the pit that the Infidel governors had used as their deepest dungeon, and the same rock was rolled over the top of it that the Infidel had used to cork in his prisoners.

He heard Honfroi's feet rambling not far away at the level of his ear, and was reminded that Honfroi, at that meeting of the chapter, had first put the question to him, that the gold might be laid away out of sight, for it had become to some of them, and in ways they could not explain, disgusting. Another had said, that either in itself or of its effects, the gold was impious. "Beltran," Honfroi called. "We are ready, Beltran!"

After they had put the gold away Beltran found that he did not stand and look up to God in the daytime or the night, neither at the blue sky nor the black sky of stars, but only in the dim custom of the chapel or here as now, downward at the sea. The others too no longer showed worship out in the air under the sky, and their eyes were all at the level of each other's eyes, or downward, as if indeed the whole of what was overhead had been lowered so that life had shrunk by that space. In this less life than there had been before, more years went on.

"Beltran," Honfroi said. It was the time when rock and castle made their shadows on the sea, and as Beltran turned he and the younger man stood in the dark image thrown down by the tower. There was something in Honfroi's look that turned the heart in Beltran's body. Part of it he had heard in the voice saying his name, as if for Honfroi simply to speak the name sounded like

a promise: with Beltran here, nothing could be wholly wrong.
Then there was the smile, which he should not have, since he
was so ruined, man and monk and knight, for Honfroi was turned
to sodomy and drunkenness: yet with that smile his face could
still tell some echoes of its own morning. Lastly there was the
invisible pall in which he wrapped himself, for Honfroi had in
despair grown dedicated to his death, and some of his smile—
that smile illumined by errant rays of the early light that had
bathed his blithe novitiate—drew strength from the renouncing
of life, hope and Heaven.

"Honfroi," Beltran said, and spoke with too much pity in his
voice, so that Honfroi withdrew and smiled across at him, and
then they went back up to their companions in the tower. Even
as they walked along the stone path above the sea, the bow of a
boat came into Beltran's view just beyond his left foot and drew
forward past him, and then he felt a touch on his shoulder as
the light yard of the lateen sail brushed him. He caught his balance
and stopped as the boat glided on below him. "Oh," he said, and
again, "oh!"

He tossed up his arms and shouted at the sky, as if it had a
right to know. "Zazzara! Zazzara! Zazzara!"

Chapter Twenty-two

DEPARTURE FROM RUAD

"MEAGRE fare," Zazzara said. "Meagre fare!"

The Templars, whose guest he was, realized that he was right. The bread steeped in wine, which they had come to regard as their evening treat, was meagre fare. It was this slight meal to which Honfroi went out nightly to summon Beltran, and it was Beltran who had some months past recalled from his knowledge of the Rule that the Brothers of the Order might, before compline, be served with bread soaked in wine.

"You still keep to your strict Rule, Beltran." Zazzara helped some more of the dunked bread into his mouth.

"It is what we have," Beltran told him. "If we had more light here, you would see we are less pampered than the Rule allows." This rejoinder made, Beltran looked at it and said silently: I am still myself then? Some of myself, at any rate.

For the sake of the last daylight they ate on the roof of the tower and not in the refectory, and at such a snack speech was allowed. A good way off the shape of Zazzara's galley loomed before the rising moon. The Venetian peered inquisitively at the little group with whom he sat but could hardly make out the features of men he did not know. He had seen that Beltran was a sparsely fleshed fellow of the man he had known the long years ago in Cyprus, and he could suppose the others were the same. He had been able, also, to make his reading of the young man who had been with Beltran when the boat ran up to the mooring, and from these things and other marks that men carry in their speech and movement, he had drawn an inkling of what this garrison had been.

"The old Pope being dead," Zazzara said briskly, "and the new Pope likely to die, then the French king will be ready to make his own."

"His own what?" The voice was old and dry and brought the

words out short and with spaces between, so that its speech
was like one of those classical ruins you found left behind by the
Romans, clear but aerated.

"His own Pope," Zazzara said. "King Philip will make his
own Pope."

"My dear sir," and the voice was now as haughty as you
would find, "we do not make gossip of Popes here. Beltran,
you will excuse it to my years if I retire before compline."
The old knight Alonso went down the winding stair into the
tower.

"He pretends to be in a huff," explained Pico the Florentine,
"so that he can get early to bed."

Opposite Zazzara a movement by one man was checked by
another, who said, "Be still, Honfroi. Alonso will do better
without your help."

This was more cruel than if the speaker had said outright that
Honfroi was drunk, and the victim whimpered like a dog. The
Venetian knew also that by these words the speaker was remembering himself to Zazzara and declaring himself vicious,
corrupt and callous. The voice was Olivier's.

"Best to be off with the old love," Olivier now said, in a
miraculous marriage between private coarseness and public
profanity, "before we are on with the new. In other words, how
did the old Pope die? I have had dreams."

Zazzara told them the tale of Anagni, an event but three
months past.

"I have had dreams of Diego Maro," Olivier said, "who went
mad or bad, I know not which, on that ship of yours. Was
Diego there? At Anagni?"

"I did hear, just before I sailed," Zazzara replied, "that besides
Nogaret and Colonna and their crew, there were some mercen-
aries at Anagni provided by one called Raynaldo de Supino at a
figure of 10,000 florins." He looked into the night as if he could
make out the face opposite. "That is the sort of thing I hear,
Olivier. Of your dreams what should I know? You might have
had word of Diego. There has been word out of Ruad lately,
there might be word into it."

Olivier's laugh was an imitation of joy. "I am a speechless

poet these three years," he said. "There has been no word out of me that long."

Beltran heard this complaint with half an ear. It was part of Olivier's disease to win as evil a reputation as he might, and there was no forgetting Zazzara's habit of being ever on the scent of something. Beltran had not thought of spies on Ruad. They were now but seven men, so stilled by their thousands of sea-surrounded days that the idea of one of them lifting a hand to such a business came as hardly serious. On what, for example, would such a spy do his spying? Beltran put in his oar.

"We spoke a Genoaman three weeks ago," he said. "We gave them our news, which is none, for theirs." He found himself frowning now. "So, that would be word out of Ruad."

"This word was," Zazzara said, "that the gold was still here, but that it could not be so for long, your company being reduced to seven."

A sound passed through the group of men, and Beltran felt it to say more of leaving the island than of spying. Why did Zazzara, indeed, make all this talk of spies and dwindling garrisons, and now of leaving Ruad? Beltran eased himself to his feet, for in his close attention to these things his muscles had gone stiff.

He was about to speak when Olivier's voice came jeering through the night. "I am much abused, it seems. Our Venetian visitor calls me spy and you, Beltran my commander, do not defend my honour."

"Well, Olivier," Beltran said, and chewed his lip seeking for some words to put him off. "Well. Men who tell their dreams to men who think of spies may expect sudden shriving." He touched Zazzara on the shoulder. "As to your honour, Olivier," he went on, "I account only for my own."

Zazzara stood up. "If it is a matter of honour between us," he said to Olivier, "I am a Patrician of Venice."

"Pah!" Olivier said. "All Venetians are descended from fishermen. Patricians forsooth!"

"Forsooth indeed," Zazzara said. "He is quite right, quite right. I bid you good-night gentlemen, and thanks for your meagre fare."

In Beltran's room when Beltran had lit the lantern, Zazzara gave him the packet he had brought and said, "I think your time is up. I think you are leaving."

The lamplight rose and brought Beltran's face out of the darkness, hagged and puckered into age by torments surpassing anything Zazzara wished to imagine. "You are still there," he cried idiotically. "My dear Beltran, how have you survived?"

Beltran's head stretched out on its neck like a bird about to fly off. It was like a round stone strangely patched with tufts of grey hair from a disease of the scalp. His face was tilted forward and the nose with its straight edge jutted at Zazzara. The mouth had struck into a harsh curve. Before the impassioned attention of all these parts of Beltran's face Zazzara was hard put to it to stand fast.

"Is it true?" The mouth whistled breath into it as if the lungs were bursting. "Is that true?"

"Why," Zazzara said. "You will find it in the letter."

"No," Beltran said. "Not that. Is it true," and he pushed his face at Zazzara, "that I am still here?" He had raised his eyebrows in an anxiety of doubt and was pointing a forefinger at his face, and this finger had begun to jump in a series of jerks so that it seemed ludicrously as if he was trying to eat it and could not catch it in his teeth.

Zazzara went to the door and shut and bolted it and returned to the lost figure in the middle of the room. He took Beltran's shoulders between his hands and said the one thing over and over. "Yes," he said. "Yes! Yes! Yes!" He shook the other man a little with each uttering of the word and stopped at length when he saw the silly smile begin and the tears open from the eyes. He sat Beltran down and put himself beside him and patted his knee.

"I don't know how," he said, "but you are still there. There is something in you," he added, "that has made it so. You had it when we dealt together in Cyprus. I have no name for it, but I recognize it."

The packet had dropped to the floor and he picked it up and gave it into Beltran's hand, and put the lamp just so for him to read the message.

"There you are," Beltran said. "We are to leave Ruad."

Zazzara leaned at him. "Nothing more? The treasure, what of that?"

Beltran rose and stretched. He pushed away the stiffness which the first emotions of this meeting had left in his limbs and smacked his hands together. "Jacques de Molay has written to me three times, 'Stay', and now he says I may leave, and that is all the dealings I have had with him. He has never mentioned the Treasure to me, or asked for any accounting of it."

"Well, he could not acknowledge it without putting it back into the hands of the bankers," Zazzara said. "He is not the Grand Master that Thibaud would have been, but he wants the Holy Land back. He is all for a Crusade. As you know, he has raided Egypt even to the interference of trade," Zazzara's eyebrows rose comically, "simply to assert that Christendom is not at peace with the Infidel."

Beltran remembered. "When he was mounting his expedition against Damiette I had forty men here, and I sent to ask if we should join him. That was the first time he said, 'Stay'." He passed a hand down his face, "That was the first time you called here."

"This seems like to be the last."

At these words Beltran's head passed through the air in an arc and it was as if he was about to dance, and had caught the first notes of music. His mouth opened in a smile, but he made no sound. When these movements had been made none came to follow them and he stood with his head leaning over and his mouth ajar. A moment ago he had been running with life in a way not known since boyhood, and now he was faint. He sat down again.

"When we were up there on the roof, Zazzara, what were you saying about Philip of France, and about the next Pope?"

"Yes," Zazzara said. "You think the same thing I do." Beltran held fast to the edge of the table and let his head swim while Zazzara pranced by on his hobby-horse. It was plain to the Venetian that the next Pope would be Philip's man, and after that it would be all up with the Temple. "He wants your treasure," Zazzara said. "We knew he wanted it as soon as Acre fell. He is a man who can bide his time, Beltran." A thought came to him. "He is a man who can bide his time, almost as well as you."

Beltran's head had cleared. "Zazzara," he said. "De Molay sends me no ship to carry the treasure. If it is to pass through the world in secret, yet it needs a bottom to carry it over the sea. What can you do?"

"Oho," Zazzara said, like a man with something up his sleeve. "Let me see. How would this do? I have a decent little galley fitting out in Corycus; stranded she was, beached by the Order of the Temple on Cilicia long ago. They say there, she was a treasure ship once. I have a man in Seleucia now, buying slaves for her oars. A good man, a certain Catalan, one Corberan."

Beltran could not speak or laugh, nothing but the smile opened on his face, and the Venetian fell into convulsions enough for two, spluttering and whacking on the table top. Beltran let him have his fit out, and after a moment or two of exhausted silence, he came to the great question.

"Zazzara," he said, "If I am to leave Ruad, and Philip the Fair seeks my Order's Treasure, where shall I hide it?"

Zazzara looked ill with excitement; he spoke the words as if they might escape before he delivered them.

"Where else but under his nose?" He let his mouth twitch a couple of times before he went on. "After all, Geoffrey is expecting you. He has risen in the Order. He has charge of a commandery now, near the border between France and Provence. It is called Richerenches."

Chapter Twenty-three

THE COUNTING HOUSE

THE king was in his counting house. It was practically new, its age being not much more than the king's 40 years: A donjon, for such it was, may celebrate its prime at an age when kings feel old. This donjon climbed two hundred feet into the air and presided over an impressive array of lesser buildings, among them a hall almost as high as itself, a chapel as big as a cathedral, and handsome dwellings of three stories graced with gardens and orchards, all these securely enclosed within a rampart, buttressed, crenellated and towered at the angles, and as high as three men along its length.

The king was taking his departure, jolting down the donjon stairs four at a time and crossing its great floors as if driven by whips. He made mighty strides, Philip the Fair, for he was a large and active man; besides, he was in a rage. He hated to come here, for it was not his. Since his grandfather's day the Order of the Temple had been bankers to the kings of France and now, the biggest bank in the world, it acted as his Treasurer. When he visited his own Treasury, therefore, he was forced to visit the Bourg of the Temple: it was not proper. It was not proper, but since he had no money, and had exhausted the Jews and the Lombards with his borrowings, it must be borne until he saw his way round it.

Outside the keep in the Enclosure of the Temple he repelled his waiting gentlemen. He rose into the saddle of his horse with no break in his progress, and as if the energy of his anger had flowed into its legs the beast began at once to walk. The king gave himself up to pique and refused to go home down the street of the Temple, instead riding over the fields of Saint Martin and down the main road over the bridge to the gate of his Palace on the island. He dismounted there and walked between his new towers to get a feeling of their size. He told a servant to follow him with wine and climbed the shallow stairs to the chancellery, where Guillaume de Nogaret was working among his clerks. Nogaret rose and bent and the clerks began bobbing and startling each other with their eyes, and Nogaret sent them away. In the window Philip looked down on the streets that ran out from the city.

"How many streets outside the walls now?"

"Fifty-one, Sire."

Philip walked up and down.

"All roads lead to Paris, now, Nogaret. It used to be Lyon, but now it is Paris. How many are there of us, we Parisians?"

Philip was so volatile of mood that he had early trained his face to be as motionless as stone, but he could not quell the movement of his body. When such springs of energy rose as that now welling up in him, all his limbs must move, all joints and knuckles turn in their sockets, and still so much life left over started out of him into the air that Nogaret already felt the first pricklings on his own skin that told him by tonight he would be headached, liverish and sleepless: for this, this was to be one of Philip's days for kinging it.

"We of Paris, Sire, number seventy thousand and on top of that, we have in the colleges ten thousand students."

Philip laughed noisily and liked the sound of it so well that he let open his throat and heard the laughter burst far within himself. Through all this, his face showed no expression and his eyes were like ice. Nogaret, in a peeve, put a term to these joys.

"Only Venice and Milan," he said, "are bigger."

The king stopped laughing as soon as he could, and in the meantime kept his head back and looked along his nose at the disgruntled counsellor.

"Well," he said. "Italy. Italy cheats, Guillaume, her cities make states of themselves." He hummed a little and walked here and there about the room. "Still, you are right to bring us down to earth." He sat on his counsellor's table and said, "Sit down, and tell me what I want."

"You want France, Sire, to have four straight edges like this table. England must lose Guyenne, Naples must lose Provence, and Flanders must lose everything on this side of the Rhine. Straight edges," he said grumpily.

Philip had been swinging a leg and now stopped with the foot out before him, and remained so, studying his toe with an appearance of interest.

Nogaret sighed ostentatiously and picked up the lesson. "All of which," Nogaret said, "must be ruled by the Royal government securely based in Paris." He smiled. "Although," he went on, "can we talk, Sire, about the Royal government being securely based in Paris when last year, Sire, only last year, you were yourself forced to take refuge in the Temple from the mob?"

Philip swung round and turned upon his secretary of state with eyes that shone like the winter sea. "Precisely," he said.

Nogaret thought furiously. Precisely, the king had said at once; no sooner had Nogaret referred to the incident of the mob and the Temple than, Precisely, had said the king. Either the mob or the Temple was in the front of the king's head this afternoon. It was the mob that had threatened the king's person, but it was a curious habit of the king not to take the mob personally; when the mob rose in the streets he took it to be the only form of expression they could use to him. On that occasion Philip had been about to tinker with the money supply. Money. The Temple! Today the king had been to the Temple.

"You wish, Sire," Nogaret said, and the complete intuition of it broke in a flush over all his body, "to be done with the Order of the Temple."

"Nogaret," Philip said, "yes."

"Your Majesty wishes to dissolve, for the safety of your realm, this Order which is so precious to itself that it must build fortresses more powerful than your own."

"Nogaret," the king said, and over the frozen surface of those eyes ran a movement of light.

Nogaret had not felt so well since they had set out upon the affair at Anagni. "What you want, Sire, is to see the Order extirpated; not cast down, nor weakened, nor lessened, but utterly destroyed."

The king came out of his dream. "You have taken my meaning, my good Guillaume. No doubt some device will occur to you?"

"Device?"

"Device, Guillaume. Device, contrivance, scheme. Some snare that we shall set into which the Temple will put its neck."

Nogaret looked anxious, and the king, had he been a cat, would have purred: the day was bringing its little successes after all. He smiled towards his secretary. "The fact is, Nogaret, that we must begin not to irritate the Pope."

Nogaret found he had thrown up his hands, there they were in front of him. Ever since he had joined the king's service, it had been his mandate to combat Papal pretension. The affair at Anagni was the end of a road along which Nogaret and his king had hounded Boniface VIII to his death. After him Benedict XI had died, almost as soon as he had begun: and this very day Nogaret had received a letter bound from Clement V to King Philip of such sarcastic temper that it was plain the feud between Paris and the Papacy was in good heart; and now, it seemed, that feud must be cruelly put down. And yet was there not a flaw in the royal design?

"Surely, Sire, since the Temple is under the direct protection of the Pope, it will be impossible to exterminate the one without vexing the other?"

"Precisely!" The king had said it again! "Precisely, Nogaret," he said. The royal head rolled from side to side on its shoulders like a diabolo running back and forth on its string. What a merry monarch, Nogaret thought dourly, and sat on his hands.

"That," said King Philip, "is your dilemma, Nogaret. You must stop twisting the Pope's tail, and start at the other end."

Nogaret tucked his hands firmly under his buttocks and waited grimly for the resolution of this riddle. The other end? Tweak his nose? Pinch his cheek?

"Pull the wool over his eyes," Philip said, and stood.

Nogaret rose also, therefore.

"Sire," he said. "May I ask Your Majesty why, having kept the Pope sour for so long, we now seek to make him sweet?"

Philip's face was pulling on its expressionless character so that it might be perfect when he left Nogaret's room. It looked at him now as flat as a painting.

"I hear from my brother of Naples, who is also Count of

Provence and a vassal of the Holy See, that His Holiness thinks of becoming our neighbour, and moving the Capital of Christendom from Rome to Avignon." He shifted his head an inch and Nogaret, interpreting, opened the door. "Anything we can do," Philip said, "to promote a proximity in the Vatican so beneficial to France, we must do."

On these excellent periods Philip the Fair went off down the stairs. Behind him Nogaret stood blind at the open door. He had thought the affair at Anagni must be the summit of his hopes for insulting the Church, but what peaks rose before him now! A mandate to destroy the Order of the Temple! As to pulling the wool over the Pope's eyes, he who had seen off Boniface need not fear to outwit one so green on the Pontifical stalk as Clement the Gascon.

Chapter Twenty-four

CLEMENT IN HIS GARDEN

"CLEMENT," His Holiness dictated, "servant of the servants of God, to the most excellent prince and devout son of the Church, Philip, by the grace of God king, no, illustrious king, of France." The Pope looked down at his feet after this aberration and fell into a brown study. The secretary, who had pushed his knees up the hill to work only an hour ago, let the warmth of the sun swing him back and forward.

On top of the rock at Malaucene they had built for the Pope a little castle with its garden, hardly more than a summer-house. Up into the September airs of this tiny paradise the perfumes of Provence rose from the valley floor. They laid themselves to Clement's temper like a balm on troubled skin and he came to himself with a smile turning his lips: he would make his journey now. There was still heat in the late summer but with the light wind off Mont Ventoux he could look forward to the ride. He would take the big gelding, no clerkly mule, and would send no more letters today. Let Philip of France be busy by himself for a while.

Clement woke his secretary and sent him on before, then walked slowly down the hill to the stables. The road made one circuit of the rock like the turn in a corkscrew, and was dressed with full-grown cypress trees, for the place had been built on before. The breeze blew into the dark leafage of the trees so that he walked down a lane walled with music. The lavender was past now, but he would travel to Richerenches over thyme and sweet basil, and in the evening pick the ripe olives of Tricastin from the trees as he came to his journey's end.

Chapter Twenty-five

RICHERENCHES

HUGUES PERRAUD stood on the gate tower of Riche-renches and slapped at the flies. He faced the north-west, glowering at the memory of a week spent in travelling from Paris to this far-flung property of the Temple. Perraud was the Visitor of the Order in France and would have been elected Grand Master had the chapter not chosen Jacques de Molay instead, and since de Molay spent all his time in Cyprus, Perraud felt himself to sustain the burdens of responsibility without the dignity of office. In Paris Perraud directed the French Treasury business in the Temple's bank, and to him this simple piece of the world's business held the vitality of a keystone and the magnitude of a pyramid. No wonder that so great a man felt irked, to be summoned down to the country for audience of the Pope.

Had he not been so steadfast a dignitary Perraud would have noticed that he was standing on wealth. The rampart round Richerenches walled an area as big as a town; indeed, you would find smaller cities. The wall was thirty feet high and joined at its corners by massive towers, and where he stood above the gate were two more mighty towers. From the high plain where it lay tribute poured in to the great commandery, for all that fertile land was in fee to it. Perraud saw below him fields fresh-stubbled from the harvest and yet made no reckoning of what this meant; he looked at the long-backed cows passing under the walls and thought them ugly; he looked at the vineyards and olive groves and at the forests on the far hills and thought nothing at all. Yet had you sought an exemplar of the rich estate of the Temple that made the king in Paris so fidgety, you could not have done better than pick Richerenches.

"Consider myself," Clement encouraged after dinner. The partridges had been reared on thyme and marjoram, and the Pope found it only proper that after so excessive a pleasure he must do the penance of discoursing with this Perraud. "Consider myself," he suggested once more. "It is true that Philip may kidnap me as he did my predecessor, but for the time being he thinks I am in his pocket, since he conspired for my election against the Italians."

Perraud plainly found these honesties rather seedy, and the more Clement prepared the ground that lay between them by setting forth this or that instance of the French king's fondness for the violent act as an instrument of policy, the more confused and questioning grew the countenance that faced him. At last the Pope reached the point where he must go on or draw back altogether.

"The king writes to me," he said, "that he has causes to seek the dissolution of the Order of the Temple."

Perraud nodded gravely, and in a response which took the Pope quite by surprise, his face cleared of doubt. "Well he may," he said. "Well he may."

When Clement had been Archbishop of Bordeaux he had used to fancy himself as a gargoyle with three faces, one for the lord of Bordeaux, the cantankerous Edward of England; one for the French king who held suzerainty over the lordship of Bordeaux; and one for the Head of the Church. With some rapid sculpting, therefore, he was able to shape his expressions into a pomposity as inscrutable as the other's was habitual.

"What I mean to say," he offered, "is that Philip means to exterminate the Order and seize its French properties."

The Visitor smiled with understanding. "The king is impetuous. I am in his counsels every other day—what matter of affairs or policy does not come down to money in the end?—and I know how much he overswears and overstates, he is full of threat and promise, that one." He ran the fingers of his hand down his face as if it was a thing that sages, particularly any with financial acumen, might do. "When the king talks of extermination and appropriation, he means that he is vexed with some of my colleagues at the New Temple. We do our weighty business at the New Temple," he educated the overlord of his Order, "and lesser things are done at the old building."

The Pope tried to laugh lightly, but though he opened his mouth pleasantly he made no sound. "What do you mean," he asked the Visitor, "by saying that Philip is vexed with some of your colleagues?"

"They question his security against further borrowing," Perraud exclaimed; it was a proclamation, not simply a statement. "What do they want—a lien on the kingdom?" He leant himself forward over a sizeable stomach to be closer to Clement. "It must be remembered that a king is in a strong position to turn nasty with his bank."

Clement, whose only purpose here was to explain just this one fact of life to the other, made his face as much of stone as he might, and nodded it stiffly up and down, and waited.

"If you make restrictions on a king, if you refuse his offer to borrow your money, he can put you out of business overnight." The bench he sat on threatened to topple as he pitched himself closer and closer to the Pope's ear. "Philip has reneged on the Jews and the Lombards. We must be wary lest he do the same to us!"

Perraud slowly drew himself back and upwards. His eyes held fast to those of the Pope, so that it was only by retiring behind the gaze of a basilisk that Clement was able to consult with himself on this curious question: how to explain to this man that when kings proposed to levy disasters then the result must be seen as a phenomenon of nature?

"Philip not only cheated the Jews and the Lombards," he said slowly as if calling on memory, "he expelled them from France." Perraud seemed about to speak and the Pope held up a finger. "The Lombards, no doubt, went back to Lombardy, but where did the Jews go? They cannot," he said neatly just as Perraud was ready to speak again, "have gone to England, because they had already been cheated and expelled by Edward."

Perraud's mind was held for the moment by the predicament of the exiled, the twice-exiled, and at last by that of the ever-exiled Jew. "They have no country," Perraud said, and it was plain to be read in his face that this new thought was the first to meet him for some time.

The Pope rose and walked into the room's shadows. The other

man sat staring in front of him as if he had gone into a dream, but Clement had no real hope that the small fear that had begun to stir in the banker could be brought to rise through the thick ice of his practical understanding. Yet it must be put to the trial. He moved forward to the edge of the firelight.

"You are right, Perraud. The Jews have no home and no country." He did not know what to put into his tone now, and he heard it come out oddly boisterous. "No country," he repeated, "any more than you or I have."

"What!" Perraud was at least startled. "No country? I? I am of the same country as King Philip. I am a Frenchman. I, landless as a Jew? Why, was I not my father's heir, and my mother's?" He had come up to his feet like a child slowly learning to stand, and was turning away from the suspicion of knowledge inside him into the echo of a child's rage, home-made but determined. "Have I not country in Artois, and castle and houses besides, that would grace a viscountcy?"

He looked at the Pope in a brief passion of filial hatred, and then his face sprouted doubts and questions and he sat as slowly down.

"At least," he said, "had I not them all before I came into the Order?"

Clement felt irresistibly, and paused within himself to notice that he must later consider the impiety of the notion, or otherwise —as if he embodied the wrath of God shaken out over the head of the baffled and astonished Perraud. "I mean," he said crisply out of his thin-lipped politician's mouth, "that just as you once had an estate, and just as the Jews once had an estate, so the Temple once had an estate, but now is exiled. Even," he added, "as I am. From Rome," he elucidated, suddenly small with irritation at this need for so arduous an explanation. It was like trying to explain to one side of a coin what its other side looked like.

Perraud stood up to his height with a spontaneity that barely kept the top of his head from taking the Pope under the jaw.

"I am to take the meaning, Your Holiness, that the Order of the Temple is a broken reed, merely because it has left the Holy Land? It was never the business of the Order, Your Holiness, to defend the Holy Land on its own. We were the last to fight and the last to leave."

Clement had sat down to receive the onslaught that he knew awaited him. "Questionless," he said. The cause was lost, but he would play it out.

Perraud was recovering from the shameful and nameless fear that the Pope had managed to raise in him, and having besides room to wave his arms about, now did so.

"As to the Order being exiled from its native land, Your Holiness, we have possessions, great possessions, possessions that kings might envy, in France, England, Aragon, Castile, Italy, Germany—"

The Pope interrupted. "And so forth, and so forth, and kings do envy them, Perraud, I believe you."

"We are bankers to Europe—"

"Be silent, Perraud, and listen to me. My assurance to your Order is this, that Philip Capet, your client and France's king, means to bring your Order to destruction. The strength of your Order in France he sees as a weakness in the fabric of his state, and its wealth he needs and covets." He was suddenly stilled of breath, for he could see, with what horrors of violence Philip might seek his ends.

When he spoke again it was in a whisper, being all the voice he had. "I shall at first defend the Temple against Philip of France, but in the end I shall collaborate with him."

He looked long at Perraud until he saw the inquiry begin to rise in his eyes. "You see, Philip has already weakened the Papacy and the Church beyond compare. His whole public reign and private temperament join in this, and the symbol of it was his attack on Pope Boniface at Anagni." He shrugged his shoulders in despair.

"Your Holiness," Perraud said. "I can believe none of this. I heard of Anagni as a rumour put abroad by the king's enemies." His face looked straight at the Pope in a candid puzzle that made it, rather late in Clement's day, perfectly likeable. "I heard it was the Colonna took him, or the Orsini, the same that drove you from Rome."

"Never mind, Perraud, tell them in Paris what I say, whether I

convince you or not. Now, the reason I shall eventually collaborate with the king in extinguishing your Order is this, that if I
do not he will do such harm to the Papacy, and through the
Papacy to the Church, as will cost the Church the worth of many
Orders of the Temple."

Perraud looked and looked, and Clement, having pronounced
this wretched but politic doctrine, bit his lip and dropped his
eyes. Then he put weakness by as a carpenter knocks sawdust off
the cut in the wood.

"There is only one Pope, Templar, so that when he is a refugee
from his own city, he knows he is a refugee. I, Clement, am God's
Vicar on Earth and I am a vagabond. I live by my wits. Like you
I may have palaces and castles for my abode, but all the world
knows that a Pope was once set on in his palace by a king's man,
and died of it. You know it, whatever you tell yourself. Most
of all, though, I know it, Templar, and when I am gone my
successor will know it."

Perraud was waiting now only for leave to go. Clement could
see that the picture of the unspeakable that he had tried to
paint was already turned invisible by the blind eye of practical
politics.

"Your Order has not noticed that it is a refugee, Templar,
for it is as rich and busy and has as many houses as an ant hill.
A rock can crush an anthill, and Philip has the rock before him,
if he can lift it."

"What rock is that, my lord?"

"The rock of heresy, Perraud. He will charge heresy against
your Order."

The disbelief in Perraud's eyes went through an alteration.
Contempt for rhetoric replaced mere incomprehension. He,
Perraud, began to smile.

"No, no, Your Holiness. Philip has some joke with you. To
charge us with heresy, like some cranky mountain sect, like the
Cathars! With the rack and the Inquisition, my lord? The
Temple! The Order of the Temple! The Temple is a bank, my
lord, and in banking, only the client can be the heretic."

Since Perraud was the man he was and believed as he did,
Clement supposed he was entitled, after holding himself in so

long, to end the business with quips and puns, so he sent him to bed.

He found the chapel in the darkness and made his prayer. Afterwards, he sat by a window for a chilly hour and listened to the crickets ringing through the dewing grass, and now and then a beetle knock against the stones of the window-ledges, and fell asleep like the vagabond he was not knowing in what room he had laid his head.

Chapter Twenty-six

NOGARET'S MEN

PIERRE DUBOIS, whose pamphlets had so blackened the reputation of the late Pope Boniface that the sky darkened when he went abroad, showed Nogaret what he had written.

"Moses," Nogaret read, "the friend of God, shows us how we should behave towards the Templars when he says; 'Let each man take his sword and kill his nearest neighbour!' "

Nogaret tossed it onto the table. "Yes," he said. "Keep it. The scribes will not start copying for a fortnight yet. You have much against the Temple: sodomy, witchcraft, the sacrifice and eating of babes, blasphemy and so forth. It is well done. Now write me something against Pope Clement."

Enguerrand de Marigny had just lifted his cup and the wine spilled over his hand. "The king said not, Nogaret."

Nogaret ran his finger through the wine on Marigny's fist and took it in his mouth. "Nogaret says so, Marigny."

Dubois looked from one to the other. "I could write it now anyway," he said, "and if the king needs it later, we shall have it ready."

Nogaret smiled at him. "You will write it anyway indeed, Pierre, and you will not bother your head about anything else." He looked from one man to the other and sighed, and slapped his hands onto his knees. "The fact is," he said, "that if the king wants to make an end of the Temple, he'll need to have Pope Clement submissive to his will unless he puts the fear of God into him at the start."

He gave a little heave, to show that this was a joke, and the two contrived a laugh at the notion.

"This process against the Temple," Nogaret went on more sharply, "must be prepared as thoroughly as if it were the plan of a cathedral, and it must be carried through as if it were the conduct of a war, and from the publishing of the first of Pierre's libels to the summoning of the first witness and on, on, on to the burning of the last Templar, from the lowest to the very highest, no one must leave this work to which we set our hands, or I will have his blood, and I will make it," he lifted his hands from their tight clasp on his knees and clapped and then clutched each of the others on the shoulder, and laughed cheerily, "into gravy, and feed it to wife and children." He shook them both as if he had appointed himself best friend to each, and leaned on their shoulders and stood up.

"You have done for one Pope," he said to Dubois. "Who knows, you may be the death of another."

"I did nothing in that," Dubois said. "It was you, Guillaume. I am merely a writer of pamphlets."

"You are a historian, my boy, that's what you are. As to Pope Boniface, well, when a Pope runs his brains out against the wall, it may as well be at what has been written about him as anything else."

Marigny stood up, ready to leave. "What about that man who was with him, and with you beforehand, wasn't he? Once a Templar, now I think of it. Yes, once a Templar surely. Spanish?"

"What about him, Marigny?"

Marigny frowned at Nogaret. "I irritate you easily today, don't I? It is a clear question, since the man is one of yours, and is or was a Templar, does he help you in this?"

Nogaret being accosted so straightforwardly his face clenched like a fist. Dubois pulled his head down between his shoulders, but Marigny met his temper head on.

"Where he is, I don't know," Nogaret said. "My own thought, once, was that he talked the old Pope to death, but maybe that's an idea I picked up somewhere, from some dirty pamphleteer like Pierre."

"Not from me, not from me," Dubois said. "I never wrote that."

"I think he serves the king," Marigny said. "I remember his name, it is Diego Maro."

Nogaret's eyes on him turned thoughtful.

"Whose man are you, Marigny, mine or the king's?"

Marigny said, "I am the same man's that you are, Guillaume. Good-night."

The door quietly shut behind him, but one of the cressets had blown out in the draught that ran up the staircase, bringing darkness further into the room.

"Dubois," Nogaret said, while he looked at the panels of the door and Dubois looked down at the floor, "write me an accusation of witchcraft against Marigny. Write it to be useful in the future, a year or so. Write it soon. Let me have it tomorrow."

Dubois tried to stand up, but the bench he sat on stuck behind his knees. He sat down again and tugged at it in a curiously mortifying operation, jumping his bottom off the seat and jerking it backwards with both hands at the same time, and then falling back onto the seat again. By the time he had fetched it clear of the raised stone that was holding it he was as sweaty as if the trap had been man-made. At last, when he stood up, he knocked the bench over with the backs of his knees, and at the noise all his nerves leaped within him, and he was hard put to it not simply to fold over and weep, and let the worst—whatever that was—happen.

Then, to his terror, he found that he had spoken. What he had said, and he knew that Nogaret had hypnotized him into saying it was, "Since you will not be using it for a year or so, why do you ask me to bring Marigny's accusation tomorrow?"

He could not bring himself, in the silence that followed, to lift his eyes towards Nogaret. When he did look up he saw nothing but a mask of exhaustion and two eyes that gazed at something beyond the room they stood in. At the movement of Dubois's head the face turned itself at the doorway like a signal, and Dubois began to steal from the room. He had the door open, and his hand turned round its edge to pull it to after him, when the voice came at him from behind.

"Who knows where you might be, in a year or two, Pierre Dubois?" There was then a dry cough. "Your work might live after you, Pierre, it is what all men dream of." Perhaps it had not been a cough; perhaps it was a laugh. Dubois shut the door behind him and went away down the long, winding stair, and he knew that the other cresset had blown out, and that Nogaret would stand for long in the darkness.

Chapter Twenty-seven

REFITTING

THEY came down the inland sea with a fair wind. Three weeks from Ruad they were through the Strait of Messina and beached the old galley on an islet north of Sicily. They had entered and cleared the strait in the dark and met no one on the island but a herd minding goats, a boy of a dozen years. They had seen a town on fire and heard war as they came by the edge of Sicily, but they could make little of the boy's speech beyond that there was always fighting there.

To strengthen the slaves after the voyage, Beltran let them free of their shackles, half of them at a time, which made a score, and he put them into two parties of ten at either end of the island, and let them run or swim or fish as they liked. He had the goats slaughtered and fed the slaves meat for five days, so that with the fish caught by them and the sailors, they were in good fettle by the end of a week. They killed the dog as well, for when the boy protested at the first throat-cutting of his goats the dog went for Andras, the tall Magyar, and though the lad was quickly subdued the dog fought to the death. There were other islands nearby, but though the islanders had clearly seen the galley they made no move to help the boy, having perhaps as little care for him as he, dry-eyed, had for his dog.

Beltran kept going over the plan in his head. Sometimes he talked about it with Olivier, whose idea it was, and sometimes he thought about it on his own. Trying to reckon the chances of a design which Julius Caesar, Olivier said, would have approved, but which to Beltran was as novel as the land for which he was bound, he fell into a persistent headache. The more the ache beat into his head the more he felt that if he could but abandon the enterprise, and throw slaves, sailors and his fellows of the Order back into the galley and sail on and on for ever, then not only would no harm be done to anyone, but he would never have a headache again.

Olivier must take some of the blame for these headaches. Beltran could not see back past the voyage. He could not see to Ruad, to the place where he had not been Olivier's friend; he could not see back to the place where he had been Olivier's enemy, and their friendship had dwindled to a small thing, merely remembered. In all their time in the Order they had been friends, until Ruad, and now it seemed that as soon as they had gone to sea again the time of long friendship had resumed, almost not been broken, and therefore not, in truth, broken at all. Olivier might not be God's friend, or Honfroi's friend, or anyone else's friend, but between him and Beltran the friendship was as fast as ever.

A truce to these questions. Never mind Olivier—what of Olivier's plan? How fast flows that river, which I have not seen? He looked at the slaves on the shingle beach below him. They had been rested and fed for a week, and would grow no stronger than they were now. It was an odd thing that Julius Caesar had seen that river and Beltran had not. I think I am old, Beltran said inside, it is well for an old man to have a friend. He said it aloud. "It is well for an old man to have a friend."

Early the next day, when the galley was riding in four feet of water with the slaves chained at their oars, and all was ready to take up the voyage again, Beltran had the astonished shipmaster and his seven sailors put over the side where they could walk ashore. He put a barrel, well weighted and floating one end up, into the sea beside them.

"You will find money in that to console these fellows for their goats, though I've left weapons on the beach in case they prove nasty. Money besides to honour our contract and something over. God be with you."

They were still standing in the water and staring when the ship pulled out of the bay and turned before the wind so that the big lateen sail, its yard already up the mast, filled with a kettle-drumming of smacks and cracks. Olivier had the helm and Beltran's eyes passed over the upper works of the galley so that he counted, without meaning to, the roll-call of his remaining army. Besides Olivier they were Pico, the Florentine; Andras, his face and throat in bandages from the dog's teeth; Honfroi, thirty days' sober, mute, passive, obedient, grave and solitary; Alonso da Luna, much refreshed by their westward passage and with his face held always to the horizon before him, for he was sailing homeward. Lastly, he who had brought the ship, slaves, and crew down from Cilicia as Zazzara had promised, Corberan y Lluch.

His hair had turned white and he had more flesh on his bones than the scarecrow Beltran remembered. He had lived a new kind of life since they parted. "I am a factor for the great Venetian Signor. Listen, in the old days, when people who laughed at me got killed, they laughed and got killed; now, when they go out of business instead, no one laughs at me." Thereat he laughed himself, merry enough, to the ear, but if you looked you saw nothing in his face to go with the sound. "Since I became a merchant I kill almost no one, but I have kept myself a little in practice." He smiled widely, for a moment Beltran expected to see the old grin split across his face, and wondered if he saw a flicker of real humour in the cold eyes. "Hey, you want to fight with me?" Beltran had shaken his head, not turning down an offer, but saying yes, he remembered, he remembered Corberan. The Catalan thanked him with a confidence. "This," he touched his hair, "came in a night."

With these men, and the forty slaves at the oars, Beltran meant to take the gold to Geoffrey's commandery at Richerenches. To pack it on mules would have made a train so long that the treasure must become the wonder of the countryside. To this conundrum Olivier had said that they could take the galley up the Rhône, so long as the river was not in flood. If his memory was right, there was a lesser stream into which they could turn the ship up by Richerenches, and they could surely, he thought, berth her within a league or so of the commandery. There, at any rate, they would be on Geoffrey's ground, and should contrive to lodge the gold.

Corberan completed the muster of Beltran's warriors, but it was the galley-slaves who were the backbone of his enterprise.

"How am I to take this hoard in secret over Provence,

your Provence?" Beltran had laid his problem on the doorstep of Olivier's nativity. "In night-marches with an army of mules?"

This presented itself to Olivier with such force that he laughed. "No," he said. "Anything but that. Even up the river."

"Is that possible? What river?"

Olivier looked askance out over the sea, his face stopped between expressions by the sudden flowering of this little seed of an idea.

"It is possible," he said.

"Very well, it is possible. What river?"

"The Rhône."

"It goes far enough? It is wide enough?" Beltran's regard ran about Olivier's face to weigh what he saw there against the doubt in his friend's voice.

Olivier laughed. "It goes far enough," the Provençal answered. "It goes to Lyon. If we get as far up as Richerenches, well, the commandery is two to three hours' ride from the river." His head was poised as if it listened for messages private to him. "Two or three hours' hard riding. We could lay up somewhere, no, the ship is too big to hide; we empty out the treasure and send the ship downstream again, or kill the slaves and sink her." The slaves were Infidels, but Beltran had been so long from bloodshed that he blinked.

"Then what is against it, Olivier?"

"Flood, spate," Olivier had said. "There is heavy rain, this time of the year, among the mountains. The hill streams grow into rivers and swell the Rhône until it pours down to the sea as fast as the wind, like a waterfall, one long waterfall."

"A waterfall?"

"Well, a torrent," Olivier said, "Still," he said, "What else is there to do?"

"Nothing else," Beltran said, "that I can think of."

"No, nothing else," Olivier said. "But when the spate comes, there is no warning. We might be hard put to it. We might lose all."

Beltran laughed, and cheerfully, because the path had been pointed out to him. "We might lose all," he said, "this minute.

We are a prey for pirates or anyone else, nothing but slaves and a handful of armed men."

It was now ten days since that council. The galley floated on black creek water, among a desolation of salt-marsh and lagoons that were the false mouths of the Rhône, while they waited for the moon to rise. Olivier was gloomy for the season had turned cold. A fresh wind had struck up from the south-east, and the weather would come down against it from the north, he said: if they went up the Rhône now, and it rained tomorrow morning, they would be sunk by nightfall.

Standing beside Beltran and looking with him over the night-covered delta he saw Port St. Louis begin to trace its shape upon the darkness, the little harbour built by that crusader king for his fleet. Beltran had seen it too, and stood straight.

"It is not your conscience in that gold," Olivier said. "Even your conscience is not so heavy."

"We can go," Beltran said. "We'll see our way by the time we reach the river." He took Olivier by the arm. "You are right," he said. "But whose conscience is it?"

"Thibaud's," Olivier said. "Thibaud Gaudin's. Other dead men's of the Order, dead in the Holy Land. His, even." He pointed to King Louis's harbour. "His heart was in the right place, his soul was in the right place, and is now, doubtless, but he crusaded the Holy Land towards its ruin. Is he not a warning to you, Beltran? That when one man sets out to put all right, he will put all wrong?"

Beltran gripped tighter on the arm he held. "I am not out to put things right, Olivier. All I am doing is carry the gold. Eh? Eh?" He shook the arm. "What harm is there?"

"It is obsolete gold," Olivier said. "It is left over, from another country."

Beltran let go his arm. "That means nothing," he answered. "That says nothing to me."

Beside them Corberan grew out of the darkness as the sky lightened. The galley rocked and the water slapped against the hull; Pico was waking the slaves.

Olivier spoke to Corberan. "You heard us," he said. "What do you think about this treasure we carry?"

"No," the Catalan said. "We don't carry it, Olivier. Beltran carries it. He carries the gold he started with, that's what he does."

The slaves pulled the galley out of its hiding-place and rowed west towards the river mouth so that the whitening moon chased the ship's wake with silver.

Chapter Twenty-eight

THE RHÔNE

THE two corpses were nailed to the raft. The raft itself had fallen out of the current into the lee of one rock and snagged, not quite aground, on another. Its voyage was not over, for it half swam on the smoothly glossed but deeply roiling pool and half walked, as it were, on the submerged rock that could not make sure of holding it, of holding anything on that pouring stream.

They made no interruption to their progress against the constant tide, but craned down with twisted necks to make sense of the grim spectacle. A message painted on hide was fixed to one man's breast with an iron-hilted dagger, and though they could see there was writing no one could make out what it said.

"They look like merchants," Pico the Florentine said. Corberan thought the same.

"Fresh killed," Olivier said. "Killed today." He bent over to read the placard but could not, and as the ship passed on he bent his head round a bit more, so that he nearly fell off the poop, and was giddy when he stood up again. "Avignon," he said. "I read 'Avignon' but there's more than that on it."

In the prow of the galley Alonso de Luna stared with ancient rage on ahead to northward, which was not where his homeland lay. Up and down the catwalk Honfroi kept an unbroken promenade, having found a perfect solitariness for himself in the function of overseer. Andras the Magyar, who could do tricks on horseback, had been accounted agile enough to climb the mast and from there kept a survey over the countryside. Pico returned to the foot of the mast, where he played spokesman to the look-out, for the Magyar's voice was husky since his dog-fight and Pico could roar like a bull at need.

They now had, besides, a pilot on board, who held the steering-oar on that side of the poop away from the raft, so that while

Beltran at the other oar could see the two bodies jump and bounce and revolve full circle as their vessel floated, grounded, lay becalmed and again fell to spinning round with many knocks against the rim of the illusory pond in which it was briefly trapped; while Beltran could see all this, the pilot could not: until the galley passing the spot, a view of it opened to him over the stern.

This man, in a two-oared skiff, had run foul of them off Avignon that morning. Passing through the islands there in the mist that rose before morning, they had backed water in fear of grounding and the skiff had come up past the stern to run under the raised sweeps. He was all but drowned and trapped as well when the sweeps came down, and they hauled him on board and lashed his battered skiff on behind. He was close to being knifed and sunk for a spy when he offered to pilot them up-river; they could pay him in steel or silver afterwards, he said, when they had made up their minds.

Now, as he caught sight of the raft with its miserable cargo, and heard also Olivier pronounce the name "Avignon," his face went as white, Corberan said after, as the snow on Mount Lebanon. For all that, he moved like lightning ("like a hero in a dream," Olivier said unusefully): snatched Beltran's dagger from his belt, cut the rope that lashed him to the pillar of the steering-oar, sprang from the poop-deck to the water and came up in time to catch hold of the skiff, cut the painter and was swept off in the rush of the stream, still in the water with an arm over the gunwale of his boat.

He shouted up at them as he went, and seeing perhaps that no one was minded, or sufficiently awake, to put an arrow in him, he scrambled into his skiff at the same moment that the two dead men and their floating bier shot out again into the flood. The last they saw of him and them, he had unshipped his oars and was pulling his boat as hard as he could out of the main stream, no doubt wishing to voyage separately from the strange ferry with its passengers nailed to its deck, and which seemed, as skiff and raft passed from sight on the bend of the river, to press straight across the rush of the current, as if Charon stood invisible plying an invisible oar, in pursuit of the fleeing oarsman in his little boat.

"What did he say?" Beltran asked. "Did anyone hear?"

"Something about Orange," Olivier said. "Orange is some hours ahead of us." He had been invigorated by the episode and took it lightly.

Corberan, on the other hand, bore on his face signs that would have done credit to his patron Zazzara, of seeking in his head for wisdom. "I heard it," he said. "I know what he said.

He said, 'They take toll at Orange!' "

Beltran stared at him. 'Then why look so amiss? Who will take the other oar? We can pay toll, Corberan. Can we not pay toll?"

Olivier took the oar and jerked his head downstream. "I believe Corberan takes him to mean, and I think he's right, I think he takes him to mean that these two fellows on the raft were being sent down to Avignon, where our friend came from, or at least where we met up with him, as what you might call, a receipt." He looked across at Beltran with an expression in which real and whimsical alarm jostled with each other for space. "What you might call, an acknowledgement of a debt settled."

"You saw how he was astonished," Corberan said.

Beltran meant to put a stop to this. Running the gauntlet of the Rhône, with the risks attendant on that presaged for him by Olivier, was bad enough. Joined to it, also, was the question of what form their first real encounter with Europeans in Europe would take; what should be said and done that such a meeting might pass by without harm to his purpose, he could only leave to the event itself. Certainly, he found this nonsense, with which Corberan and Olivier were playing, had a very jangling effect on him.

"That's enough," Beltran said. "You cannot mean me to believe that at Orange they take lives to let ships pass. What profit would there be in that?" No one answered, and their faces did not unbend from their perplexities. "We came by Arles and Avignon without hindrance. They have no reason to watch the river. It will be the same at Orange. You heard him wrong, Corberan."

"No, that's just it. I don't know what he meant but I heard him right."

Olivier, grown unwontedly serious and instructive, began to speak, watching the river as if it became him to be at particular pains to steer the ship exactly. "Try this," he said. "Orange is independent. It is a principality or a city-state or whatever you choose to call it. It is no fief of France or Provence or Burgundy or Toulouse, it stands on its own. At least it used to, in my time. If it does so still, well then, might it not levy toll?"

"It might levy toll," Corberan said, "but hardly of men's lives."

Beltran said nothing, and listened.

"No," Olivier agreed. "Not of men's lives. It is a place to start, though, trying to see what our pilot meant, that took him off into the water so sudden. He seemed to want not to go to Orange, perhaps."

"Bah!" Beltran spoke out despite himself. "He saw we were all eyes on that raft, and took his chance!"

Together Corberan and Olivier refused this simple view, the one citing the snowlike pallor and the other the miraculous speed and certainty of his flight, which, Olivier said, only ecstatic fear could produce "It is an experience I have known myself," he said, "at least once. It is like being a hare or a deer on the run; your limbs go in all the right places and there you are, out of it."

Beltran wished he could escape from all this, and shouted. "There is no sense in it, what you say. Make sense of it."

There followed a silence in which the galley moved steadily on, riding slow but sure the broad stream. The river banks had drawn apart so that the force of the brown water was less, making lighter work for both slaves and steersmen. On the lofty poop they passed along higher than the countryside, so that magpies, flying low and wending homeward before evening came, looked them in the eye and whipped faster on their way. Behind and to their left the sun rolled its clear yellow warmth towards the mountains.

"I can make sense of it," Corberan said. "I can make a merchant's sense of it, anyway."

"Very well," said Beltran, vexed to have lost his temper. "Thank you."

"Avignon is growing into an entrepôt, trade has begun to come there from Italy, Spain, England, everywhere, China; and then Orange levies toll on Avignon's own river to the northern markets."

Beltran looked at it. "You mean the two cities are quarrelling."

"Why not?" Olivier said. "Avignon aspires, Orange is jealous, or greedy, or dog-in-the-manger. A quarrel of merchants, then."

At this Beltran began to chew his lip. "That would be bad," he said, "a quarrel of merchants. We have seen it back at home." He smiled at himself. "I mean in the East. When merchants take to blood to settle their disputes, they become very terrible."

He saw in his memory merchants from every trading city of the Mediterranean, bearing civil war against each other in this or that combination of alliances. He saw street-battles, massacres, and even sea-fights up and down the coast of the Holy Land, all in the name of trade. He saw too the Orders of knights drawn in on either side. Foremost in his memory was the ferocity with which merchants fought.

"They take to blood," Olivier said, "like ducks to water."

A bellow came from the foot of the mast. "Ohé," Pico shouted, and they saw him waving and Andras, up above him, pointing ahead. The ship was pulling round a bend in the stream.

"What does he see?" Beltran shouted.

There was some passage of words up and down the mast before Pico turned again towards the poop, and then he shrugged and when his voice came along the ship it carried little confidence in what he was saying. "He says there is a wooden tower in the water." He looked up at Andras and finished the message. "A wooden tower like a siege tower."

There was a place not far down-river where the water had cut an extra channel for itself and meandered off on a round of the countryside. They put the galley into it a good way, and leaving Olivier in command Beltran took Corberan and Honfroi and set off on foot. They had not far to go, for when they climbed the hill that had turned the course of the river they saw what Andras had seen. The sun had but just gone from sight below the western mountains, and the pale light put a winter glow on the river. The air above, in the little time it had taken them to reach the hilltop, had already grown half-roofed with clouds; to the north the sky was thick with them and laid them on the distant hills.

This evil weather was spreading out so fast that the tower before them made a ladder into the storm-cloud. It was built heavily of timber. Thick baulks of wood made a massive strength of its base, from which it rose to a height that overtopped any ship's mast, and at which a sloping roof housed the fighting-platform: for it was a war tower, no question, though how it was used they could not say.

"Look at that, on the other side!" Corberan was pointing.

"Something like a raft," Honfroi said. His voice was low, as if the tower had awed him.

"Yes, that," Corberan said. "It is a boom waiting to be floated out."

The day had been crisp with autumn cold, but now the chill of damp air touched the skin. Mist flew into their faces and the tower went from sight.

"Good for us," Beltran said. "A thick night. They have nothing against us, for we are not merchants, and not of Avignon. But it would be no pity to slip by these people."

"There is not much chance of that, Beltran!" The voice was Honfroi's and it shuddered with the cold that had swallowed them up.

"It is a chance," Corberan said. "Let us go down now, before we rust in this confounded wetness."

They picked their way down the hill with care, for it was marvellously tussocked and holed by animals, and they could see nothing below their kness.

"The water is rising," Olivier said. "At this place, it will soon be over the top."

"We shall not be here that long," Beltran said.

"No," Olivier agreed. "It is as well," he set off again. "Over the bank here the ground falls away, a gully, full of trees." He had taken a stance by the rail of the poop and kept looking down, or turning an ear down, to the flow of water licking along the hull. "We must move soon, we must get the ship to a landing-place, quickly, before the river floods. What did you see from the hill?"

Beltran kicked down on the deck with the heel of his boot, as if to test that it was still sound. "It little matters what I saw from the hill, for we will go on up the river. I saw the tower that Andras saw." He looked into the gloom to make out Olivier still canted over the water. "In the north I saw clouds all over the mountains. What's up with you, Olivier?"

"The matter!" His face suddenly appeared before Beltran's, round still and still almost smooth, but close-to the lines showed, harrowed there on Ruad and softened on the voyage since, and here and now working deep again. "The matter is, that if you put this ship to the water beyond a half-hour, the slaves will not be able to stem the current. That is the matter, and that if there is anyone up ahead who wants bodies to stick onto rafts, we are in no case to prevent them; and that this old hulk has done marvels for us in coming this far, and to engage her against the risk of war and the certainty of the river-flood—at any moment, Beltran; at any moment—is to throw the gold, your treasure, into the river."

Beltran took a breath and answered. "So it seems to you, I know. We will go on, though, because if we go back, now, or stop now, too much heart will be lost. Lost by me, the slaves, the rest of us, even the ship."

Olivier's voice came eager and mocking. "That is it, where you stop: 'even the ship,' you say. Even the ship will lose heart, you say. You mean the gold. What you mean is the gold. You think the gold will lose heart, and stop shining!"

"Lose heart," Beltran said, looking at Olivier, "and never recover." He prisoned the bleak eyes between his hands and tried to strike life in them from his own. "What sense is there, what is the point of trying to bring sense into this. It is all out of faith."

Olivier shook his head loose. "You have a duty to think, also," he said. "You can't make faith a moonbeam, and slide down it all your life."

This description of Beltran's career so little resembled the fact that they looked at and around each other until they began to laugh. A gust of wind flew about them and Olivier said, "There will be rain behind that."

"Light a fire," Beltran said. "No one will see it in all this mist. Light a fire and we'll make a porridge." He looked about him in the fog. "Honfroi!" he bellowed, and, "Here," a voice said in his ear.

"Good. We will light a fire. If we put your fellows round it, to warm themselves, will they run?"

"Where would they run to, branded?"

"Where indeed? We'll have them round the fire and fill them with porridge. Where's the fire, Olivier? Corberan, you're a porridge-cook. I'll want porridge for fifty men in an hour. We'll put some heat in these men before they pull this tide."

Their heads gathered suddenly round him in the grey darkness, joined again by his little whirl of energy into one army, a brotherhood; they surrounded him haphazard, even old Alonso had been drawn down from his station in the prow. Some were helmed, some not. Their faces leaned in at him on different angles, and were smeared featureless by the drizzle, but their eyes ringed him like spears.

Chapter Twenty-nine

THE WOODEN TOWER

THE slaves pulled mightily at the sweeps. The galley came from the backwater into the river with speed enough to turn her bows to the current, and was swept hardly any way downstream before she had a grip of the water and was moving up, despite the wilder strength of the flood, towards the mysterious tower.

Olivier and Corberan kept the tillers, and the rest were strung out along the ship's length to the foredeck to pass guidance back to the steersmen.

They had piled fresh wood on their fire before they left, to make a telltale that would show whether their oarsmen had mastered the force of the stream. While they were passing it, the fire glowed through the mist like a window, as cheerfully as if it expected them back to make more porridge. When it was gone, they were held all about by mist and behind it the dark, for now it was full night.

The ship and the river joined in continuous din and movement. Behind all other sound, just as the night was background to the mist, the river poured its thunder on their ears. Soon its other voices grew clear: wave-splash alongside, the rush of eddies slanting across their course, and the great and steady hiss with which the river raced past its confining banks. In-board the vessel, old and hard-pressed as she was, the sounds were legion. There was little rolling, and they had even hauled down the mast to make the ship more handy for the oarsmen: yet Beltran, used as he was to the groan and creak of the timbers, was disconcerted by the outcry that seemed to him to spring from the whole frame and planking of the galley as the slaves, at the pitch of each stroke, threw themselves onto their benches. He felt the wooden world beneath him shake and tremble, leap and fall, and was so awestruck that he dared not stand still to receive the messages that came to him through the soles of his feet.

He left the rest of them to it and went below. To do this he had to jump from the poop onto the catwalk and make his way forward, where a trap in the deck led down to the hold. He worked past each of the human chain that was calling instruction from bow to stern, and clambered over mast and boom, for they lay athwartships at an angle, from one side of the ship at the foredeck to the other side at the break of the poop. We are not in much case to fight, he said to himself, with all this lumber on deck; but they could not fight the ship anyway, only seven of them. He went through the trap and stood on the ladder for a moment with his head in the opening. It was on a level with the heads of the slaves, and the surge of their breath as they jolted the ship on its way dismayed Beltran: they could not do this for much longer.

He stepped off the ladder onto the gold, and went forward in the darkness. The ship was floored with gold, which crunched under his feet like gravel; no barrels or boxes had survived on Ruad, so they had thrown it in with shovels. The gold did not help him, for it was more slippery to walk on than gravel, and he stumbled blind and slow until he felt the planks close in on the stem of the boat. The noise had all the time been beating gigantically on his head, for above him the oars creaked, and beside him they thrashed the water; above him again the rowers slammed down on their benches, and here next to him the timbers scraped against each other with a sound that rang down his spine; and the river flew past his ears with a shout like the Sultan's army rushing to the attack.

He heard and felt the water spurting in between the planks as the ship kept up its progress, and all the time as the hull worked between the opposite forces of the oars and the river, the seams leaked a steady flow that ran down the walls.

The treasure, Beltran said to himself, is going to drown. The planks will draw wider and wider apart and the ship will break up, and the gold will fall down to the bed of the river, it will be rolled up in the mud and never seen again. The ship bounced sideways and he fell. The gold was awash, it was a shoal of sliding pebbles where water tumbled, and he wished he could see the clear water and bright gold mixed with light. He failed to get to his feet and lay there for a space to arrange himself. Gold does not tarnish or corrupt: look, he told his hands in the darkness, and they let the round unrusting ducats run among their fingers.

Then Beltran noticed that his fingers had gone still, and after them his arms and then he himself, the whole of him gone as still as stone. Though the hoard where he was bedded did not cease for a moment changing its shape, now falling here from under him and now heaving up there, while the bow of the boat in which all of them lay, the coins, the water and he together, jumped and dived, shook and pitched, so that no more tranquillity was to be had down in the forefoot of that leaping galley than you would offer a child by hoisting its cradle up a tree in a storm; yet notwithstanding that he partook fully of this turmoil even so to Beltran stillness entered when the image of Christ, struck in its hard edges on each innumerable coin, told his fingertips to remember where they were.

The turbulence went away and the world where he was housed turned calm. The golden shoal beneath had come to rest. He closed his eyes. One hand held his face, the other rested in the lapping water and he did not breathe, for voices called his name.

"Beltran," the thin voices cried, and he listened hard. With a hand in the water, a hand on his face, and his breathing stopped, he waited for the manifestation.

As if an angel's sword had cut the sky in two there was a swift and tearing sound. The shock put a tremble into wood and water, bone and flesh. Over Beltran's face swept a draught of air, past his closed eyes light flared and high and far above a soul howled, seeing that its road home had brought it to the gates of Hell. The lost soul, might it after all be his? Beltran sat up and opened his eyes.

The soul was not his, though the scene he entered was a vision of the Devil's gateway. Heat blew in his face and light swept his eyes shut. An outcry of dying men broke on his ears. He took sulphur into his nose and stood to his height; burnt sulphur racked his throat. His feet staggered on the shifting gold and he pushed out an arm; the deck was gone. The deck had been arm's length above his chin where he lay in that cubbyhole and now by standing he had risen through it, so it was gone. The human sound he recognized: it was the shout of men joined in common cause of being killed, from which solitary cries issued, falling off at last in fear for ever. He bent his head from the wild light and coughed the fume from his throat and wiped the blear from his eyes. The lost soul bayed again from its high perch. Beltran made a careful opening of his eyes, downward, onto fast water running deep with fires. He licked glances about him, and saw the fore-deck was gone and all its upperworks so that here in the bow, where he stood, the sides of the ship came up only to his knees, edges of cracked wood. The shouting from behind him began at last to bring him towards a sense of what was happening. It had climbed and splintered into a clamour of those shrieks and yelps with which men try to refuse, disguise, and hasten an appalling end. Like an old warhorse at the sound of the trumpet Beltran lifted his head and, crunching his feet on the treasure beneath them, turned to look down the boat. He knew where he was now, and had come out of his dreams, for this was battle: chained to their benches, the slaves were on fire.

As he passed back along the remains of the galley Beltran saw that the slaves had been hedgehogged with arrows before the Greek fire burst over them: stuck in shoulders, heads and thighs, the last of the bolts were burning to smoke while he went by. Half of the slaves were dead, smothered in oil and sulphur though flesh and bone burned on; most of the others were still in torment. Fire and arrows had come from above. For the first time Beltran thought of the tower and looked up. They had built a giant for destroying ships. He could see it plain, for not only had the mist betrayed them to a full moon and flown away (and were there not also human candles burning at his side?) but these determined engineers, his enemies, had driven piles into the river bed and from them ran out iron baskets filled with flaring pine. By these lights Beltran saw crossbowmen single on perches and grouped on platforms, and a windlass of great size and as if they had seen the white of his upturned eye the men winding at its handles jumped away and he heard the familiar buzz as the huge bow sprang free. He saw also something else, that he dared not believe, and laid from him like a sin too hard to think of. He stumbled and fell on hands and knees and saw the missile from the great engine on the tower shoot across in front of him into the side of the galley.

For a moment it was strange to him that the thing had done no damage, then it began to move. It jerked once or twice and then leapt at him, but got stuck in the catwalk, a spitting distance from his face. He stared at it. It was a stout wooden shaft, as you would expect, but its head was an iron grapnel.

A voice yelled, "Cut!"

He looked along the gangway and saw Corberan shouting at him. "The rope! Cut the rope!"

He answered by instinct, and had his sword in his hand before he saw the rope that ran from the shank of the grapnel. The rope drew taut and he felt the ship lift. The catwalk shivered under him like a horse and he saw the iron bite into it; this was how they were pulling his old ship to pieces. He cut through the rope and it sprang apart like a split bowstring. The grapnel still hung in the wood and he put a finger over one of its points. He thought it was as sharp as a spear. The lost soul in the sky cried again, and this time Beltran shuddered. He went on and jumped to the poop, where were Corberan and Olivier.

Olivier's face was turned upwards. His eyes were wild as if their sight had just been stolen. He stood stiff but had some fit on him that clutched at his body. On a thought Beltran looked back to where he had fallen on his knees: Yes, that was Pico, for he remembered clambering over the stout corpse. There was little sound from the slaves now: they were all but burnt out. He blinked and turned again. Olivier had no sign for him and he went on to Corberan who was looking down over the stern. Beltran went off to one side and when he looked down into the water gouts of vomit poured from him.

Corberan turned an eye up at him sideways.

There was the humming sound and the crash made by the discharge of the engine on the tower. Corberan turned his neck a bit more and they watched the grapnel jump across the charred shambles that lay in the hull. It failed to make a lodgment and retreated up into the night carrying awful remnants from the cindered bodies it had tumbled about in its passage.

"See," Corberan said, and Beltran put his head over the side again. "We are snagged on that boom, not much more than a cable; they pulled it up when we had passed over." He faced about and pointed forward. "The current holds the bow against that piling." The ship was bows-in to the bank with her stern shoving the boom. The lights in the iron baskets had lost much of their brightness. Corberan turned Beltran again to look over the outward side of the galley.

"What is it?" Something floated in the water. Like the galley, it was hard up against the boom.

"It is the forecastle," Corberan said. "It lifted off in one piece. Old Alonso is on it, alive or dead. The Magyar was knocked overside by one of those flying hooks." Corberan's head was bowed and his eye looked on Beltran again with that odd sideways turn. "Now," he said, while irony stroked his voice, "you must look up, Lord Beltran."

Bird-flight whirred in the air and Beltran was flung on his back. He lifted on his elbow and saw that the middle of the ship had caught fire. Bolts pelted into the deck about him and he was knocked flat again. He heard Corberan's voice close to his ear.

"Do you live?"

"Yes," Beltran said.

"I have fallen down," Corberan said, "and they will think I am hit." He sighed a huge breath into Beltran's ear. "Olivier was filled with arrows. He went into the river."

Beltran's eyes, which had been dizzy since he struck the deck, began to see clearly. The picture that had beaten off his appalled gaze, when last he looked upward, he now beheld since it was all that came within his vision, as if it were a part of his own fate. Dangling, from the top of the wooden tower like a fish on a hook a man's body hung. The body leaned towards the tower at a pitch that gave it a false appearance of vivacity, like a puppet.

Beltran said, "How was that done to him?"

Corberan answered at once. "He stooped to cut the rope and the grapnel took him under the ribs. I would not wish a better end on my worst enemy."

The moon had come out large and bright and shone down as if she herself had cleared the mist from the sky. The body on the hook moved. The knees and hands lifted together then fell slowly apart. When the body was again still and Beltran hoped, the soul sped from it, there dropped the same dismal shriek that spoke of seeing into the Devil's eyes.

"Honfroi," Beltran said.

"Yes," Corberan said. "Up he went, kicking and struggling. He made no sound going up. Olivier went into a statue and watched him all the way, right until just now."

Beltran spoke it aloud. "He sounds as if he is being dragged into Hell."

"Look below," Corberan said. "Look below him a little way. Look where his face is looking."

Beltran could not do this for a few moments, and was half of a mind to wave his unwounded leg in the air, and his arms, to tell the crossbows he was still alive; rather than to see, whatever it was that made a man howl as if the Devil had hold of him.

"How am I wounded?" he asked Corberan.

"In the thigh the first time, the bolt passing right through."

Beltran was pleased. "Right through, I would like to have seen that."

"And to the side of the belly, the bolt now tying you to the deck. Let us see if we can move you. They won't leave us be for long."

There was the sound of Corberan crawling over the deck. "There is less light now. Look or you will not see him! Look!"

This was very insistent, and since he was skewered to this place, and it was probably, therefore, the place where he would die; since it would be hiding from his end to lie here and refuse, in his last moments, to open his eyes upon the scene in which the object of his life was withering on the bough; since this was the place where the trust laid with him by one Master of the Order and left with him by another, was to reach its dissolution at the same time as he; then it would be a poor thing to shut his eyes to so grand a misfortune and die like a child going to sleep on a broken toy.

He opened his eyes and looked up where the tower rose into the bright moonlight, and where Honfroi hung on his gibbet.

Then he looked lower down, as Corberan directed him. There was a platform there and a figure standing on it, seeming to stare Honfroi in the face.

"Corberan," he said.

"Yes," Corberan said.

"Corberan," he said again. "Free me off this deck."

Corberan came round in the gathering shadow to his side. He had a knife in his fist. "Take hold," he said. "If you make a noise we are done."

Whereupon at once such hurt thrust into Beltran's inside and back and belly that he felt it pull from his neck to his ankles, to the back of his feet, and then to his neck again and at that blackness filled his head.

The first thing, he tasted vinegar on his tongue. He took water and drank it. He felt puffed up like a bagful of wind. Now that his side was doing its worst his leg sought to surpass it. He felt cold and began to shiver. Something ran across his mind.

"Diego," he said. "That was Diego. Diego up there on the tower." He looked up, but did not see Diego. He saw Honfroi lying across his hook, all of a sudden like a dead fish. He did not see Diego on his platform. Truly it was growing dark, but there was no one on the platform. "I think Honfroi has died," he said.

"I think so," Corberan said. "I tied a cloth round each of your hurts, one tie and one knot, no time for more. Come on, we must swim for it. Your friend Diego is on his way down."

The wind was pushing steadily now. Honfroi was out of this world's torment. Diego was coming down the tower. The moon was not having it all her own way, and out of the velvety black sky there came dark clouds across her face. He let Corberan's arm sit him up against the rail of the poop. In front of him fire burned, at the far end of the galley.

"If Diego is coming for us," he said. "He'd better hurry."

"For us? He is after the gold," Corberan said.

"My head is pickled," Beltran said. "The gold." The gold, then. "Stand me up, friend Corberan. The gold is not his to take."

On that moment, as Beltran came trickily to his feet, cheating

his wounds as well as he could, Diego appeared before him at the
foot of the great tower, with his henchmen crowding the platform
about him. The fire burning in the ship threw itself into the air,
making a gust of flame that died down leaving sparks dying and
falling against the night. The renegade came to the edge of the
platform and looked down into the ship. Gold and fire played
on the dark armour that he wore. The gold was open to the light
of the fire and gilded the air above it, so that far beyond the
flames the darkness glittered, a black curtain stabbed with golden
knives.

For one interminable moment Beltran saw clear into Diego's
face. There was no marvellously wicked mark on it. Nothing
there spoke of malevolence. Looking him eye to eye across twelve
feet what Beltran found uncanny was that worse than not being
recognized, he was half-remembered. Then from that calm
expression of the enigmatic conqueror Beltran received a glance
which said to him, as plain as speech: This is Diego's soul, as
lonely as God before he made earth and heaven; this is I, so much
more alone than you have been, you thinking yourself isolated
among men, that compared with you I have been opposite.

It was all Beltran could do not to reply.

"If you will not swim," Corberan said. "I have a question to
ask your friend." He propped Beltran against a steering oar and
bent over a bundle on the deck. When he stood up he was holding
a pair of javelins. "Hey, Beltran," he said. "Remember how we
woke that old man in Cyprus?"

Beltran's ears filled with a wild yell. His eyes were on the score
or so of those stark fellows who had killed the most of a shipload
of men, and he was pleased to see how the surprise took them.

"Aur! Aur! Desperte ferra!"

The warcry of the Almugavars had the effect on Beltran that
he thought, I shall pray to Saint Hilary. His prayer was short
and devout only in the certainty that it was being heard. "Hilary,
Saint of the Order, do not let them have this your treasure."

He saw the faces turn towards them. As Corberan made to lift
the first javelin he called out his own battlecry.

"Beauséant," he croaked. Again he whispered. "Beauséant!"

Corberan gave him the profile of a smile and whipped his

javelin straight, it seemed, at Diego. At the instant that he threw, however, beside Diego there appeared a man with a face that shone, even in that rarely gleaming firelight, no other colour than grey. It was the face that Corberan had seen among the leaves in Cyprus when he left the corpses of his men. It was the face of the dark and nameless knight who had helped to murder Thibaud at Limassol. The javelin went askew and took one of the crossbowmen in the throat.

"Saint Hilary," Beltran said. "Guard your treasure. Mother of God, shelter us. Christ, destroy our enemies."

The wind flew up from the river over the side of the ship and shook Beltran's shoulders.

"God aid," Beltran said.

There was a noise like mountains falling and the ship trembled. Beltran thought the top of the tower had moved. It moved again, and like a horse the burning ship shook itself in the water and dipped its golden head.

"Oh, God, aid," he said in wonder.

"Hold on," Corberan cried, "it is the river." The whole tower shook.

The noise of mountains falling came again and burst all about them like a storm made of sound. Beltran went down and gripped the steering-post. He saw a wave curl over the prow and run half-way up the boat so that when the hull miraculously lifted after it the fire was out, only a few flames flickered here and there. By their light he saw the men on the tower fighting each other to climb above the water.

Corberan had joined him down on the floor of the poop, and was holding them to Beltran's steering-post. When the river came down in its fury, the tower rocked and swung and men fell off. Then there was no more to see, for the ship was moving, poured over the boom like a twig in a stream, and then coursing down the flood, going round and round by the feel of it, with Beltran emptied of faith, hope, excitement and fear, and wishing that if Corberan must hold him so tight, so tight round his wounded belly . . . always taking care for him truly he was a good man, but his belly was wounded, and would that Corberan would not laugh.

Whereupon Corberan released him, and Beltran took some breath in. He recalled that this flood belonged to the treasure and contrived to sit, to flop over and so to kneel with an arm on the rail of the poop. There was enough light on the water from moon and stars to see that Corberan had abandoned despair and taken to the steering-oar. Beltran had no activity left in him. About him, and no great way below, this solid mass of moving thunder gleamed on its rushing way.

The galley, flying along at its tremendous pace, leaned far down into the water as Corberan turned her across the flood. He would be wiser to go down to the sea, Beltran told himself. The ship, however, settled firmly to the business of cutting across the current while drawing from it the impetus of its speed. Unless the flood had covered the land, they would soon come to somewhere. Corberan began to shout at him, and he inched his way over the deck towards him. When he got there he found the Catalan was babbling and had taken to laughing again.

"See!" Corberan shouted. "See the fire! The fire!"

Beltran grabbed him by the belt and stood up. There was a fire, burning brightly across the flood. It was coming towards them like wildfire, it was running towards them. It is the fire where we made the soup, Beltran told himself, and the galley went straight through it and fell into the air.

Chapter Thirty

THE KEEPER OF THE SEALS

"I AM not of that temperament," said the king, "that will abide to be thwarted by the Pope." He got down from his horse. "Why," he said peevishly, "if I am king of this country, must I go through this rigmarole every time that I come here?"

Guillaume de Nogaret passed from the royal stirrup to the door, opened it, held it, bowed, and answered as he followed his master up the steps. "This little passage usually wins your admiration, Sire."

This little passage was a covered bridge that spanned a wide country lane, walled on both sides. It provided the gateway of the Abbey of Maubuisson. The abbey was a favourite resort of the king, but the bridge and its steps obliged him to enter the abbey grounds on foot. It had been raining heavily for an hour.

The king stepped out of the covered way and was met by a little cloud of moist nuns.

"Mother Abbess, I need your blessing!" The king spoke as if he had knelt to her and walked on without pause. "You cannot answer me, Nogaret? Are you an attorney or aren't you?"

Nogaret, who had much evil to do before night, was not going to have his day spoiled by this kind of thing. "The land on either side of the lane belongs, Sire, to the abbey. The lane is a right of way belonging to the town of Pontoise. I believe the rain is less."

The king looked at the sky, by which he announced that he was out of his bad temper. He took Nogaret down an avenue of chestnut trees, past a small chapel standing on its own, and along a flagged path that led to a huge barn. Suddenly he gripped him by the arm and said, "Listen!"

Beneath them, but so far beneath that a vertigo began to stir in Nogaret's stomach, a dim rumbling beat upwards through the earth. "Is it not fine?" The king laughed. "It is a river, deep below the ground. It must flow under the Oise, eh? Is that not fine?"

"It is very fine, Sire." The rain, if it had lessened, had now repented of its weakness and had begun to fall with the determination of English arrows in a battle. Nogaret wished the king would stop teasing him, and let them go inside, and be about their conference.

"The river has not been wasted, Nogaret." What was to follow under the colour of that smile? "One of these flagstones is an oubliette. To prepare it you put your hand down a grating and turn an iron lever, and then, beware of the stone walk!"

The king laughed like anything and laid a familiar hand on the jurist's shoulder. "Come," he said, "you are keeping me out in the rain." He began to walk very fast towards the abbey, his riding boots swishing in the long grass and Nogaret, perforce under the royal hand, keeping pace with him along the dreadful path.

The ground was strewn with autumn leaves and on a pile of them Nogaret's heel came down; oiled by the wet they skidded under him. Before the vigour of his forward stride, and with the skidded foot throwing itself into the air, Nogaret fell back as sudden as if the ground had vanished. The skin chilled on his body.

Then he felt an arm catch him round the shoulder and he and the king, a rare privilege with this autocratic monarch, fell together. The king came down mostly on grass and Nogaret on stone, but the royal arm saved Nogaret's head from being split open. The king was laughing still: there were days when he was his own favourite.

"Oh, Nogaret!"

The king sat up and worked his arm, which was bruised or twisted by its defence of Nogaret's skull. He looked at the lawyer, who was still trembling.

"You thought you were down the man-trap, hey! You are as white as old soup bones. I wonder if it still works; rusty, no doubt." He stood up and struck leaves and grass off his clothes. "Come on, man. It was only a fall. Go in and make them have my hot wine ready, ready in two minutes, spiced, and some sugar handy. Up you get!"

He hoisted the aching Nogaret to his feet and packed him off with the day's share of humiliation already under his belt. The lawyer knew he would soon be out of the rain, in the warm, and on with his business. The king's following laugh left no further marks on his spirits.

"Too much sugar," the king said as he sat in front of the fire: pine for quick and jolly heat. Later, he would become gloomy, and have elm burned, slow and flameless. "Too much sugar," he said again.

"I have come on a way to prosecute the Templars despite the Pope's objections," the lawyer told his master.

"Have you then?" Philip was greatly pleased. "Have some wine. Perfect." He poured it himself.

Nogaret drank and warmed. "We will charge them each as individuals, I should say each as an individual. Each and every jack-knight of the bestial Order of the Temple, he will be charged as an individual with his bestialities."

The king digested this proposition. He frowned. "What then?"

"We do not proceed against the Order of the Temple. The Order is answerable only to the Pope, who protects it. I shall have each of its members charged with heresy, and that must put them beyond the special regard of His Holiness."

"What of the Pope?"

"His Holiness will be outraged, and will end by endorsing what you have done."

"Why?"

"Because of the charges, the evidence, and the constant noise and clouds of words I shall proclaim and publish about the iniquities of the Temple. The Pope does not even live in Rome, now. He will find a persistent stand on the side of the Temple will leave him too much alone."

The king's face was impenetrable. "The Grand Master—what is his name?—has come from Cyprus to see His Holiness. You cannot drag him from the feet of the Pope. Whatever is his name?"

"De Molay, Sire. Jacques de Molay. Him I shall arrest in Paris."

The king stood to stretch himself. "You will never coax him to Paris, Nogaret."

Nogaret's feet moved in something like a dance, so agitated was he to explain to the king why it would all work marvellously well, and why de Molay would indeed come to Paris.

"Sire! Sire! The charges are so appalling—heresy, bestiality, sodomy, worshipping heathen idols, eating new-born babes before the altar—that de Molay, the whole Order, does not believe they emanate from here!"

The king interrupted. "All that! I had no idea." He sat down again. His face was still unmoved, unfathomable, but a lustre as of pearls had risen on it.

"Oh, yes, Sire!"

"Eating new-born babes?"

"Yes, Sire. Well witnessed."

"It is appalling, Nogaret. Go on."

"Well, Sire, they, the Master and the Order, do not believe that you would dare bring forward such charges."

The king went into a long silence. He gestured to the fire and Nogaret laid on it some pine logs to bring the blaze up again, and some elm to accompany the king's changing mood.

"Sire!" Nogaret's voice was rarely diffident.

The king, affronted by this interruption to his brooding, shot him a venomous look. Nogaret maintained his position, however, vaguely supplicant, since he had but three-quarters risen from tending the fire and his back was stiff about the hips from his fall, and with his eyes only just lifted enough to see the royal face. The king gave a nod.

"The Archbishop of Narbonne, Sire, will not seal the orders for the arrests."

The king eased his vexation a little. "Be easy, Nogaret. He needs but urging. I have spoken to him, on the principle. He wants only a little wheedling, and will do it."

"He is the Keeper of the Seals, Sire. Without his sealing them, the arrests will be much weakened. The orders must go out all over your Majesty's kingdom. Only the Seal will carry your authority to your officers."

The king knew these things and was impatient. "Why have you put elm wood on the fire, Nogaret, in the middle of the day? Look how dull it has gone! Archbishop Aycelin will certainly seal the orders, take my word for it." He banged his fists on his knees to signal that he had come to the next stage in his day's routine. "Very well, Nogaret. Good."

Nogaret had turned hangdog again, but maintained his irritating presence in the room. He now went so far as to kneel, and the king found that Nogaret was presenting him with a box.

"What's that?"

"The Archbishop has laid down the Seals. He resigns his office, Sire, since he will not sustain your Majesty in the process against the Temple."

"Where is he?"

"In the anteroom, Sire."

"Get him." Nogaret turned to go. "Wait! Wait! Put the box on that table. I have not yet accepted the Seals. Now go. Send him, do not bring him."

Gilles Aycelin and the king exchanged no word. The king rose from the fire, which he had been roofing with elm, and came face to face with the Archbishop. The heat of the flames still flushed his skin. Aycelin had been at the king's hand through each great enterprise, every triumph and upset of the reign, and now he was in a hurry to be gone. He came in booted and spurred, and as a complete sign to the king that he had quit the honour along with the duty of office, he had emptied his sword from its sheath.

The king was stung by this last to accept the finality of Aycelin's resolve; it provoked in him also the rare sense of being rebuffed by a subject, and he found he was too overset by Aycelin's defection to retaliate. Nothing had occurred to him to say, so he continued in the recourse of silence. He put his enigmatic gaze on the candid eyes across the table, and laid his hand on the box as a token that he took the return of the Seals. He had lifted it again, and had already gestured with it that the interview was over, when his eye fell on his own sword where it stood in a corner. The Archbishop was into the room beyond when Philip called him back.

"You go to your archdiocese, Aycelin?"

"Yes, Sire."

"To Narbonne it is three hundred leagues, my friend." The

king made the three paces to the corner and back again. "Three hundred leagues of cut-throats, bandits and wild beasts. Here, you will need a sword!"

With his own hands Philip unhooked the empty scabbard from Aycelin's belt and replaced it with his own, sword and all. "It is a stout blade," he said. "I have fought with it in two battles. Fare well!"

"It is too much honour, Sire!"

The king noticed, with pleasure, two things: that touching the hilt as an accompaniment to his words, Aycelin did not then let go; also, that the candour of his expression had grown confused. Now that the balance was redressed, Philip was impatient to be alone.

"No, no," he said. "Now off with you; October makes short days for travellers."

So these two, one set on the destruction of the Temple and the other determined not to abet it, and both deeply antagonized by their disagreement, shared at parting one of those luxurious moments in which great men feel that they have uniquely detected a touching weakness in the other's armour.

Nogaret wisely gave his master an hour before returning to the presence. His earlier expectation of the day's merits was borne out to the full.

"Nogaret," the king asked him. "The orders for arrest are ready? The messengers are ready? Their horses are ready?"

"Yes, Sire."

"Take the box, Nogaret. You are the Keeper of the Seals. Use them tonight. Your messengers off tonight, and the arrests in a fortnight."

"Tonight, Sire." Nogaret picked up the box and held it between the palms of his hands. "It is too much honour, Sire."

The king let down his mask and looked atrociously sardonic. "Yes, yes," he said, not quite echoing his farewell to Aycelin. "Yes, yes. Now be off with you; October makes short days for travellers."

Chapter Thirty-one

THE CAVE

BELTRAN lay in the dark. He saw a patch of grey, like day-light, but all about him it was dark. The daylight, if it was that, stood on some perch in the blackness, down beyond his feet: or up beyond his feet, or along, or some other thing. It was much what you would expect to find, on your first moments in Purgatory. In case, now that he was awake, he ought to speak, he put two words into the air in front of him.

"Saint Hilary," he said, at little more than a whisper.

That ought to do. It must be wrong to say something idle, as men did to each other, for example about the state of the seasons. It might equally be out of place to offer a prayer, or to ask a question; or to present, should one arise, an idea. He had spoken, therefore, Saint Hilary's name, and was at once pleased, for the amount of sound he made with it was discreet and yet enough to be heard. Saint Hilary would no doubt be his sponsor here, so far as he had one; to call the name of any of the Holy Family, while natural in life, could only be presumptuous when you stood, or lay, or whatever it was he was now doing, in the purlieu of Divine justice.

This question, in what sort of place and position he was lodged, now came at him again. He remembered flying through that cascade of moonlit gold and nothing afterwards, but guessed that he had continued in that way and arrived here like a bird in flight, headfirst. Every circumstance but one made it likely that he was now at the bottom of an empty cistern, a dry well. He could move none of his limbs, since the narrow space he was in fixed them close to his body, and the patch of grey on the other side of his feet was very like what you would see from the bottom of a well in which you lay head down. It was indeed his head which told against the probability that he had been so confined, for it gave no sensation of being put to the effort of sustaining his

weight, or of being disordered by being upside-down. Insofar as
it was disordered (and in the very passage of the thought he was
surprised to find himself so definite) the disorder was not that of
being inverted, but of being exposed to foul stench. The fact
was, that though he did not complain of it, the air of Purgatory
had a stink more vile than his nose had ever known.

The next time he woke Beltran found that the darkness had
gone. The grey patch which he had seen as daylight now shone
blue and clear, and he could make out most of his surroundings.
He was not lying on his head but on his back; what was plainly
the blue sky was in front of him; and he was not in a well, but
in a cave. What held his arms to his sides and fettered his legs
was a huge animal hide. This was copiously haired, a pelt long
and thick, blackish brown. Above everything, it smelled. He
wondered what gigantic beast had walked in it. It had been
killed a good few days back, for its skin was far gone in ripeness.
It swathed him to the neck, and both pillowed and helmeted his
head, in a shroud of greasy, hairy, stinking heat.

It was odd he had not sooner thought of it as a shroud, since
he was so confined into its discipline that he had plainly been
sewn or knotted there. Maybe it seemed too palpable a thing to
belong in Purgatory, the more so now he knew it to be the origin
of the stench. Further, his head was free, and in a shroud would
have been wrapped like the rest of him. The difference between
this waking and the one before bemused Beltran, and being
unsure on which side of the grave he was to account himself, he
lifted his head up and looked round about.

His cave was roomy enough, but it was no vast cavern. He
was lying close up to the back wall and where he lay the cave
was at its largest, for it narrowed like a bottle towards the
entrance. The sun must be not far out of his vision, for the
inside of the cave was now well lit. There was pain in his side
and he laid his head back to rest, but he was smiling, for he had
seen a small row of his possessions ranged along the back of the
wall near him. He remembered the arrow-wound under his ribs
and as he shifted for comfort he was reminded of the one in his
leg. He stayed quiet for a space to let them settle.

When he lifted his head again he contrived it without rousing the pain in his side. The objects he saw on the floor of the cave were few, but they were what he would himself have chosen to save from a shipwreck. There were his sword, a dagger and his boot-knife. There were the contents of his cooking-bag: the little cauldron; the bowl for measuring corn and the cloth for sifting it; the iron grate; the hatchet; the two goblets called hanaps; the two flasks on a strap; the ladle, spoon and eating-knife; and the towel and the napkin. There was also his great white mantle, which looked sodden. That was the roll of his familiar belongings, but to them had been added the wooden box that carried Alexander's heart.

When he saw the box it seemed to Beltran that it might have been Saint Hilary who put these objects by him. To fetch into the cave the weapons and the cooking gear was an act you might expect of the Saint of the Order, and to add old Alexander's heart showed an understanding of comradely ties quite in accord with Beltran's view of Saint Hilary. He must have been at some trouble to find it, because the box had been stowed in Beltran's linen-bag, not among these cooking utensils that were its present companions. Beltran decided that if he were to lie here for a while, and it seemed likely, then he might give some thought to old Alexander's heart. The heart had, up to now, been simply part of his baggage, for his first charge was the Treasure: but now the Treasure was drowned.

Was he not also drowned? Where would that leave him, between the Temple's drowned Treasure and Alexander's dead heart?

"What use am I to Alexander's heart, if I am drowned?" He said this aloud, and daring, added, "Saint Hilary, why do you bring me the old Scotsman's heart, if I am drowned?"

He had moved carelessly and the pain burst out in his leg. "I am not drowned at all," he said, and there was nothing in his voice but irritation. Soon he fell asleep again.

When Beltran woke the third time what he saw out of the cave-mouth was black night lit with stars. Though he was warm inside the smelly skin the air on his face was cold. The leg-wound came suddenly to life, pouring gusts of pain through him, flesh and bone, leaving his mouth open and the sweat chilling on his brow. He heard a sound outside the cave.

"Beltran?"

He said nothing. Whose voice was it? Well, whosever voice it was, he was in no case to deny that he was there. Whoever it was, had come because he was there.

"Beltran?" The voice was soft and had a familiar song in it, like some voices in the Holy Land. It was right at the end of the cave. His head lifted and he saw that most of the stars were blocked from light by the newcomer.

"Be careful for my leg," he said. "It hurts me sorely."

The voice laughed. "You are still here, that is the main thing." It was like a woman's voice. There was a scraping sound that irked his leg, but it had stopped by the time he found his tongue. Yellow light shone in the cave-mouth and he smelled oil, perfumed oil from Syria: his memory had told him this without stopping to take breath. The visitor came into the cave and kneeled beside Beltran.

He looked into the face that stooped over him; it was the face of a Saracen. The Saracen produced a little knife with a leaf-shaped blade. Beltran laughed at the knife.

"I am dead already," he said.

"You think we are in Paradise, and I am a houri?" The Saracen nose wrinkled. "What a stink!" This knife began to open the skin in which Beltran was packed. "I am Shirin, the girl from Sidon. Remember how I helped you in the boat at Cyprus." She moved toward his feet, and cut away more of the hide. "Do you remember Limassol? I took some of your revenge for you at Limassol."

He felt the cold come at his body as she pulled the hide off his injured leg. "Shirin," he said. "Shirin. What are you doing here?"

"I am come to tend your wounds. You remember Abu'l Ibrahim the physician? He who steered your boat for you at Cyprus? Well, he is dead now two years, but he taught me doctoring."

She withdrew and there was some unpacking and laying out of this surprising physician's tools and potions. Beltran tried to see what his uncovered leg looked like but could make nothing of it in the half-lit gloom. He sought a question whose answer would explain the Saracen woman's presence.

"How have you come here?"

"Corberan came to Richerenches."

"Richerenches?"

"Yes," she said, with a sudden loss of patience. "To Riche-renches. There he told Geoffrey, Beltran is wounded in a cave." She lifted his head on her arm and made him drink from a small horn cup. The blackness outside the lamplight began to join itself to him through his own skin, making him warm and well-feeling. She began to work on his leg and his ears hummed, and he vanished.

Chapter Thirty-two

THE OUBLIETTE

THE king came after the appointed hour, and waited at a distance from the avenue of chestnut trees until the moon shone out. He peered warily around before he spoke.

"I am here," he said.

There was at first no answer, but Philip the Fair did not announce himself again. He had been much to the wars and knew when other souls were in the night with him. He pulled his sword a little from its sheath, a handspan of steel, to be sure it moved easily.

The little chapel showed pale in the moonlight. What had been a shadow moved and became a man.

"I have come," Diego said.

The king walked eagerly towards him. "Tell me," he said, "Do we wax rich?"

Diego laughed. "Sire, no: we wane."

The king stayed where he was, still some way off. "There was no treasure?"

"I saw it," Diego said. "It was all the gold of former ages lying in the one vessel. You would have been pleased with it, Sire. It gleamed in the light of our torches like sunflowers at noonday."

"Maro!" the king said. "Do not play with me! Where is the gold?"

He stepped forward and the sword drew further out. Behind Diego another shadow became a man and moved a little along the chapel wall,

"What, treason!" the king exclaimed.

"Bah!" Diego said. "It is my horse-holder."

"I see no horses."

"Sire!" Diego was deprecating.

The king gave up being circumspect. He let his sword back

into its sheath and walked five steps to put himself face to face with Diego. He stared at him close in the bright frosty night, first sparing a glance for the other: it was the man with grey skin like a mask. Both were armed head to foot. The king could not see into Diego's eye, for it flashed in the light of the moon and was dark within.

Diego gave him his news. "It was heart-breaking, my lord. We had the boat fast. The crew were more or less dead. The treasure was ours, the gold was yours. Then the flood came down the river. It whipped the boat away and sank it. The galley was all broken and besides weighted with metal. It must have gone down in no time at all."

The king felt his eyes stretch in his head. His hands and arms went into a palsy and shook. He had gone cold, not from the wintry night, but from the picture that had jumped out of his imagination: he saw, he continued to see, the treasure ship before his eyes, and he with his foot poised to step on board; he saw the mighty wave rush past higher than his head and whisk the coveted loot from under his hand. He heard himself make a sound like a moan. A fiery liquid burnt his lips and dropped hotly into his stomach. He was being poisoned, and fought himself free of the dreadful picture to discover that he was being, in fact, consoled. Diego put away his flask.

"I know Sire," he said. "It is hard to bear. Since that day, the hair has rotted on my scalp."

He swept off his mailed coif and the hood beneath and bent his head. The king saw a patchwork of bared skin and hairy tufts. He withdrew a little.

"Cover your head," he ordered. "You will catch cold." He communed with himself. Alas! Alas, alas! Yet it was done. The thing was done: whatever it might have been, now it was spilt milk, and no use to cry over it. His own little plot too; Nogaret had been given no part in it.

In snatches the wind came and then blew steadily. Sheep pastured nearby began to bleat, waking each other so that the chorus grew. The great branches of the chestnut trees thrashed about and filled the air with sound. The king wanted his bed. He remembered something else, and spoke his thought aloud.

"It is Nogaret who will be catching cold," he said.

"Sire?"

"Nothing," the king said. "It is a pity you failed," he went on, "now you must go. Best go from France: a trap is set for others that might catch you." He walked towards the stone path that led past the great barn.

"Ah, Sire!" Diego was by his side.

"Well, sir?"

"Sire, I have not had my fee."

The king walked on. "The gold is lost, and you want your fee?"

"I need it for my journey, Sire."

"Where will you go?"

"To the Baltic, to hunt bison," Diego said.

The king stopped short and looked at him with a sudden rage; it must have carried through the night.

"The Teutonic Knights," Diego explained. "They crusade up there. It wins them land, for everything that moves is heathen and to be killed: Balt, bison and Slav."

"God knows," the king said, "you are a profane heart. Take care how you choose allies."

They were at the place where the path of stone flags began. Philip cried out, and at the far end of the path a lantern showed.

"Your money is there," the king said, and pointed along the path.

Diego sighed and made a gesture of his own which sent his companion down the path. The wind had drawn clouds across the moon and the man's shape vanished into the darkness. There came a thud, and a single shout, and some noise of scraping and bumping; then nothing more.

"Here comes my fee," Diego said, for the lantern had picked itself up and begun to travel towards them. "You need not regret that fellow," he said pleasantly to the king, "he poisoned the Master of my Order."

The lantern was in earshot. The figure behind it called out. "It worked," Nogaret proclaimed. "The oubliette worked."

The king felt steel pierce his side. "Be still," Diego said softly in his ear, "or I will cut away your kidneys." The knife drew out and the king felt the warm blood run down his body. There was some straining at his sword belt and it parted and was gone. The knife-point returned, this time to his throat. A quick rogue, it was a shame to lose him.

The lantern had stopped its advance and presented itself at head height in a series of inquiring movements. "Sire?" it said.

Diego answered it, "Stay where you are, or I shall kill the king."

"What!" Nogaret's voice was of a man thunderstruck. "Devils in hell!" he said. "Rubbish!" he said, and came on.

Diego pushed in the knife. "Ah!" the king said gasping. "Nogaret! Nogaret! Oblige me, Nogaret! Stand off!"

The lantern came no closer and was lowered slowly to the ground.

"You have money," Diego said. "Shake it." There was a clinking sound. "Put it on the ground." The sound followed. "Shine the lantern on the money, and then take the lantern with you, and walk as far as the oubliette."

"Sire?" came hopelessly from Nogaret.

"Do it!" said the king.

"Now then," Diego said, when it had been done as he wished. "Farewell, Sire! Farewell!"

His hands left the king, who waited until he heard the money go off chinking towards the chestnut avenue. Then Philip went up to the lantern.

Nogaret had words bubbling at his throat but the king stopped him. "Nogaret: say nothing to vex me, as you value your skin."

A dreadful groan came out of the pit, echoing the dismal noise of the underground stream.

"You are not hurt?" Nogaret dared.

"Less than that creature," Philip said, looking into the hole. "He didn't fall far enough. Put the stone back in place."

The lantern flickered and went out.

"The other one, where has he gone?"

"Where do you think, you fool? He has gone to the Baltic to hunt bison." The king left Nogaret to replace the lid on the oubliette and its victim, as well as he might in the darkness.

The man in the pit groaned once more and fell into the river with a splash, Nogaret scuffed his knuckles and swore, and the king's laughter came again through the cold and windy night. Along the road to Pontoise a horse clipped by on frozen ground.

Chapter Thirty-three

NIGHTRIDE TO RICHERENCHES

ON a windless day there was still heat in the October sun. Beltran sat outside the cave couched on the bearskin, for such it was: Corberan had found the cave with the bear in garrison of it.

"Asleep," was Corberan's telling of it. "I put my iron in his neck and he died dreaming."

Corberan and the mule were walking up the gorge side by side. As they passed from cold shadow into sunlight the mule stopped and so did the Catalan. They went twice a day to the miraculously preserved wreck, and the animal had imposed on its companion the habit of resting at several places on the return journey. Events that were to Beltran curious marvels won no surprise from Corberan. His marriage of cut-throat youth to mature merchant had produced a nature not cynical, not credulous but sanguine. "Consider," he said to Beltran and Shirin one suppertime, "that a contract may bind men, but never binds the sky, the sea, the beasts of the forest or God in his Heaven. Once you notice that, you may look for unpredictable things to happen at any time." The galley, he said, had been taken by the river on a new course it carved for itself in the flood, and dropped into the bottom of a wooded ravine. The river had then chosen another path and when the water went down no one could see the wreck from outside the wood.

It was to and from the wreck that Corberan and the mule, and sometimes Shirin, had travelled twice a day for over a week now. The mule returned laden with leather bags filled with ducats, which were emptied into the back of the cave. He had come by the mule, he said, when he saw it swimming manfully down the flood at the very moment that he needed it, for he had just pulled the unconscious Beltran to safety. The mule had difficulty in making the bank, for its head was held towards the middle of the river by a hand on its bridle, and the owner of the hand trailed in the stream as one dead.

"Thereby the animal was much imperilled," Corberan said, "but I was able to urge it towards me by shouting, and then to jump in and cut the bridle so that the poor beast was relieved of its burden."

He had put Beltran on the mule and travelled part of the night and part of the day, and on finding this excellent hiding-hole, had made an end of his journey.

It was not, in some senses, a pleasant place, but Beltran liked it greatly. The world here was made mostly of black rock, with now and again a tree or a shrub. On the far side of the gorge Beltran looked at pine trees climbing their way up a mountain slope, but on this side, they had told him, the land ran away to the north in a high plain: and to Geoffrey's commandery of Riche-renches. Soon he would see Geoffrey, the first time since Cyprus, for the Saracen woman had gone to guide him here. He looked up the gorge; if they were not here soon they would miss the daylight. He looked the other way, and Corberan came on again up the gorge to the cave.

"Well, then!" Corberan threw the bags of gold onto the floor of the cave. "How is this fine soup we have made?"

The fine soup was simmering on a corner of the stone hearth that framed the fire. It had neither cooked itself into nothing nor left off boiling, and was now a rich broth. Beltran had tended it honestly, with his whole care and conscience, for since he had been an invalid the great affair of the Treasure had taken its weight off him. He had woken from Shirin's opiates to a time of pleasant ease, and while he watched the gold accrue each day by the exertions of the mule, he watched the sky more. Or, as in today's case, the sky and the soup; and likewise the fire, to be sure it put as little smoke into the air as need be. The brilliant blue of the sky had begun to turn thin, and its lower edge was a glowing fall of purple, rich but pale. Beltran huddled down into the bearskin and pulled it round his shoulders, and ventured out a hand to turn the soup three times in its pot.

"The soup is in good heart," he said.

"I am not," Corberan said. "I grow as thin as a bandit."

He was rubbing down the mule, which pretended to eat him, for it too was hungry. "Wait," he said to it. "Wait until your betters are ready."

A little wind came down the gorge. The fire burned up and the steam over the soup blew every way.

"Look," Corberan said. "Geoffrey and the girl."

They feasted off the soup, bread and onions, cold mutton and strong wine. The fire was put out when dusk came down, and they made their banquet inside the cave. The horse led here for Beltran to ride on the morrow had carried a pile of deerskin cloaks, and they had been able to throw away the untanned bearskin. With two of the cloaks they curtained the wind out of the cave and with the others they wrapped themselves against the cold.

The next day, dawn was still clearing the stars out of the sky when they left the gorge and rode north. Corberan and the mule stayed behind to continue their work with the gold. Shirin rode a bowshot ahead, and Geoffrey filled Beltran's ear with the affairs of the Order. They agreed that Diego seemed to be in service with the French king. They could not see how the king meant to accomplish the destruction of the Order, though with so methodical a man, Geoffrey said, the beginning should give a clue to the ending, and the king had begun by accusing the Templars of a hundred or so heresies and abominations.

"It goes down quite well in the countryside," Geoffrey said. "We are passing rich, and the French are dreadfully exacted upon by their impoverished monarch."

"Then is that not unjust?" Beltran made it more an exclamation than a question.

Geoffrey laughed at him. "I see you had little time for politics on Ruad."

Beltran told him about Ruad, even about Olivier and Honfroi, since it had been no secret there.

"A pity," Geoffrey said. "That is the sort of thing Philip's lawyers bring against us."

Beltran felt suddenly that he had been a bad Commander of Ruad, to let this evil between the two knights take place, and grew disordered in his temper so that his horse fretted and began to jump.

"Let us run a little," Geoffrey said, and they galloped the horses over the plain, catching up with Shirin and taking her into their stride.

When they were walking their horses again Geoffrey said to Beltran, "Your business has been with the treasure. Ruad was only a stop on the way. Besides, no man could command such a place in such a predicament, a dozen years on a bare rock in the sea, no relief, no change in the faces about you except when someone died, no expectation of leaving it ever, for anyone." He looked at Beltran and away, and spoke over his horse's ears. "No one else would have brought the gold this far," he said.

Beltran was cheered by these remarks, and at this last one he laughed out loud. "I tell you, Geoffrey, it was Saint Hilary that did it. There have been so many amazements on the way that only by his intervention can we have reached here." He looked across Geoffrey's face into the sun and screwed up his eyes to meet it. "While I have been living in that cave and even today, talking about it, the treasure has been less weight on my head than ever before, than ever since Thibaud died."

Geoffrey looked across the plain to the east. "I must tell you: though I hope it does not bring the weight onto your head, Olivier is a league or so over there"—he nodded into the sun—"at our house of Mormoiron. Time enough to see him tomorrow, if you are fit after this ride today. He is much scathed."

"He was shot into the water."

"No. Not only that. His tongue is cut out."

Beltran pulled up his horse. Geoffrey's either would not stop or was being fidgeted by its rider. "Come on, Beltran, come on. We must be on to Richerenches. I dare not be long away from it in these days." He had the wisdom not to take Beltran's bridle and the other man soon put heels to his horse and their journey went on.

It was a full hour later Beltran spoke.

"That was because he was a poet. That was Diego."

"He has gone mad, then," Geoffrey said. "I had rather lose a hand than my tongue." He waved his iron hook at Beltran. "Or my wits."

Beltran began to wonder what he himself had lost, or was in

store for him to lose. His friends had lost hands, tongues, lives and wits. He had lost the Holy Land, his native earth. He had lost the Order in the Holy Land. Perhaps they were to lose the Order here as well. He pulled up beside Geoffrey.

"What do you do about the king of France? What is the Order doing?"

Geoffrey's response was strange. He settled himself in the saddle and felt his sword and stared quickly all about him, ending with his eyes on Shirin down the road ahead. "What the Order does," he said "what the Order does, is to petition the Pope. The Order seeks also help within the Church, from the Bishops, when the Order has not one of its many privileges, that is not held at some expense or other loss to the Church." He was scowling. "The Order, in fact, does not believe the king means mischief, or that God will let him do mischief. They think that because it is unthinkable to contemplate destroying the Order, he will not dare."

"You think he will dare."

"No. I know he will dare."

Geoffrey had not told Beltran the story of the Pope's visit to Richerenches. He knew that he could not tell it without divulging the place of Shirin in his house, and no one could be eager to put such a thing before Beltran. He told the tale now, however, and at the end said baldly, "Shirin is my leman."

"I know," Beltran said. "What am I to do," he went on at once, "with the Treasure of the Order if the king of France, like the Sultan in Cairo, tears the Order to pieces?

"Once in five years," he said, "I have a message from the Grand Master by way of Zazzara. The Master is careful as I am for the gold, so that it will not fall into the wrong clutches inside the Order." Beltran's voice had gone so low in his throat that Geoffrey expected him to choke. "The fact is," Beltran pursued, "that the carefulness of the Grand Master occupies him one hour every five years, but mine continues lifelong. Now it seems I must seek him out."

"You must seek him in Paris then," Geoffrey said. "For this week he is a pallbearer at the funeral of Catherine of Valois."

"Of Valois? The king's—?"

"Sister-in-law. Wife to Charles the Count."

Beltran sat up straighter in the saddle. "If the Grand Master is so honoured at the obsequies of the king's sister, you would hardly think the king was on the point of laying hands on the Order!"

"You would hardly think so," Geoffrey said.

Shirin was coming back to meet them, making signals with her hands. She began to draw her beast off the road and pointed to an oakwood that lay about a furlong off. Beltran and Geoffrey met her there and the three of them dismounted and led their horses among the trees until they were sheltered by the yellowed leaves.

"Spearpoints," Shirin said. "Crossing the bridge, as if they had come from Vaison, going our way, going north." She looked at Beltran. "How are your wounds, Beltran?"

"Well," he said. "Well–doctored," he added, with a courtesy he remarked as rare in himself.

"Wait here," Geoffrey said. "I will look closer." Geoffrey went off through the wood and everything was still, save that now and then an oakleaf fell or a bird moved to its roost, for the day was darkening. A chill passed through Beltran like a faintness. It is your wounds, he told himself. Then he knew it was not the wounds, and by knowing it he nearly fell where he stood, yet he kept a hand on the saddle bow. The Order will end, he said to himself, there will be no more Order at all, the King of France will eat it up. The King of France became the Devil and he saw him feeding the Brothers of the Temple into his mouth, but the king's eyes hunted for the gold. What wrong have I done, he asked the dark woman, that the Order will be destroyed and I am to live my life out with the gold? When I die, his thought had become stiff and awkward, when I die, God will ask of me: Why have you left My gold?

He had not spoken aloud. He looked across a space at her, into the deep gaze that still in this dusk-filled wood gleamed from her brown eyes out of whites as clear as silver.

"My troubles are too deep for me," he said.

Geoffrey came back through the wood.

"They have crossed the bridge," he said, "fifty of them. They are three hours from Richerenches. We must pass them in the hills; for they show no mark, but are men of the king's."

A part of the column marched on foot while the others, mounted crossbowmen, carried their heavy spears for them. Geoffrey, Shirin and Beltran followed them for an hour. The road climbed into the hills and a river ran beside it. They mounted a crest, and after that the river flowed wide and quiet and the hillside drew away from them. Geoffrey turned off through the water and across an upland meadow. They put their horses in a gentle run up the far side of the meadow screened by dusk and the patches of alder and willow on the riverbank, and the mist rising from the valley floor, and the small oaks and wild olive trees that rimmed the valley. When they crossed the river and came back to the road they had made a wide loop round the king's men.

Soon the road pitched downwards and brought them out of the hills. They crossed stubble fields crisp with the cold and came to a high-walled house. Shirin whispered a word, Geoffrey beat on a heavy gate and when the bolts scraped back and she passed into the enclosure, he smacked Beltran's horse and they took away over the fields again. They came in the moonrise to Richerenches.

Chapter Thirty-four

A QUIET FARM

THE young knight's red crown recalled to Beltran that day at Athlit, when Aimard's golden head splashed open like a melon under twenty scimitars. Nothing else about him, however, rang echoes of the long-dead voice. At Richerenches each knight had his servant, so this boy in his fine-laundered mantle came out with a groom to ride behind him and carry half his armour like a squire. Yet all this was according to the Rule. There was nothing in it to make Beltran favour the dead recruit over the living.

Indeed, a true balance would weigh otherwise, for Aimard had died from an outrush of childish enthusiasm, but this fellow was self-possessed beyond his years. Seeing for the first time this newcomer to whom he had been appointed guide, and who still bore the arms and armour that had survived the fight on the river besides the dozen odd years on Ruad, the youth had given a kindly smile, not to Beltran himself but to his scarred, burnt and patched harness, and said to it as if to a deserving horse, "You have been in the wars." In saying so he suggested nothing else: neither that Beltran's gear looked shameful beside his own; nor that his own showed up sadly unwarriorlike in comparison; nor that he had any interest in these wars of Beltran's.

An hour after noon they had made two leagues from Richerenches and the young knight, by name Amaury, took them on a climb through scrubby woods to a hilltop of short grass. The groom took care of the horses a little way down the slope, and the two knights found a place in the trees that let them look down over the far side.

"That smoke," Amaury said, and pointed. "That is the place."

It was a good way across the plain. A column of smoke going up into the sky came from a fortified farmhouse, as big as some

castles Beltran had known. Geoffrey had mounted a watch all
night at the commandery but there had been no sign of the soldiers
they had passed on the road; and no word of them in the morning.
Now, therefore, he had considered where a command of fifty men
might lie in the neighbourhood and sent out scouts to a few
likely places. Amaury took in the time of day and said his orders
gave them till dusk and if they had seen nothing by then they
must go back.

They sat in a litter of fallen chestnuts looking down over the
plain, over harvested fields, stripped vines and orchards emptied
of their fruit. The big house they watched presided over its
kingdom as if it was resting from the work of gathering the
year's tribute into its barns and cellars. Its expression, Beltran
thought idly, is not that of a house that lodges soldiers. He
pictured the commandery.

"You have been long at Richerenches?" he asked Amaury.

"Two years. It is where I entered the Order."

"It must be as fine a commandery as we have."

Amaury laughed. "It is a perfection of plan and design,
certainly, and rich beyond anything. It is like that great farm in
front there, only more so: Richerenches makes me think of a
Roman city, sitting behind its safe high walls in the middle of its
province."

Beltran was a little shocked and could say nothing. He was
already put out by the aimless peace in which this land spent its
days, and in the midst of which such affairs as Crusades came to
seem like chapters of history.

Amaury spoke again. "The big well, however, needs some
attention. I think," he said, "that at least twelve courses of stone
should be replaced. I have been down to see, and for some
reason the stones have rotted."

Beltran told him that wells in the Holy Land were scarce, and
rain infrequent, and how the rainwater was caught and stored in
cisterns. "Underground, where can be," he said, "for else the heat
drinks up the water."

Amaury was, it transpired, interested above all things in ways
of keeping and supplying water. There was much guidance in
this field offered by the Order to the managers of its estates, but

it was now time, he said, to bring a new eye to these familiar ways and seek how they might be developed. At first Beltran fell into a warm harmony of feeling with this view of the Templar's mode of life, as foreseen by Amaury for himself, for it called to mind recollections of his more tranquil years, when he had been so well disposed to the business of husbandry. A revulsion suddenly overcame him, however; for the thousands of Templars whose bones were in the Holy Land had not, surely, died in order to establish a heritage of miniature provinces where future generations might practise the art of rustic government.

He interrupted Amaury's recital of a scheme to resuscitate the system of aqueducts.

"What do you know of the Temple in Paris?"

"That it is the leading bank in Europe," Amaury said. "It is a distinction, I admit, but I am no banker. In any case, there is more true profit for the Order in seeing to the good ordering of its estates."

Beltran lapsed into a long silence. He tried to still within himself every faculty that understood what he was being told: he strove to deafen the ear of his spirit and close his mind's eye. He sought that the reach of time he was in might stretch itself out and hold him in a space between this hour and the next, between earth and sky, to hang meaningless like a fish dozing on the current of a stream.

None of these benefits came to him, and the day moved forward. A cold air rose from the fields. Two or three of the late chestnuts fell from the tree above. The sky broke into a sunset of blue and red and began to darken.

Here at the far edge of his life, Beltran had been told at last that the Holy Land was gone forever. He had heard it in the words of the young knight, dedicating himself to build waterworks across such countryside as this they sat in, this earthly paradise. The way the boy spoke of picking a career, within what was already a vocation, rang inside Beltran's head like a bell. It said as plain as anything that the Order of the Temple had too much a life of its own, here in Europe, to feel on its shoulder any shadow of Christ's lost Kingdom stretching out of the past. This was the revelation that crushed Beltran: that by the past, the Order understood events which were still forming the chief part of his own life. His vision of the Holy Land redeemed fell like a mirage from the high hope of his soul. He felt the stark rock crack in him on which his being stood, and what had been adamant crumble into sand. Weakness flew about in him like a bird loose in a room.

He thought of his life in the Order and this boy's design for his own life, and by how much they did not meet; and of how the new life would discredit the old: how the boy's life would mock his, Beltran's. He remembered suddenly, that the lives of all of them were about to be re-ordered by the King of France, and came out again from his thoughts. It was like a man breaking from a forest floored with brushwood and thicket. He gasped for air as if he had been holding his breath. Simple in its cave, the gold called to him.

"What have you seen down there?" he asked Amaury.

"A quiet farm," the young knight said. "No soldiers." He looked at Beltran and smiled. "I do believe Geoffrey overdoes the menace offered by the king."

"I was with Geoffrey. We did see soldiers," Beltran said.

"One does," Amaury said, "going from here to there."

"Where might they be going, then, if not to Richerenches?"

"Which they have not yet reached?" Amaury smiled again. "They might be going to Lyon. The king is to buy it. He would put some garrison there."

Beltran had grown ancient. He could stay there among the chestnuts and they would become part of the earth together. "Where these soldiers are bound, I do not know," he said. "But today, they are down there in that farmhouse."

He knew that Amaury was perplexing himself to find a decent way to express doubt, one that would not insult Beltran's years and station. He stood up. "Come on," he said, "I am not guessing. I have seen them. My eyes are used to this."

They rode back while the night made itself round them. Beltran had questions within that he wished to ask himself, but he could not find what they were, and so asked others of Amaury instead.

"Why do you fear King Philip less than Geoffrey does?"

"Because I do not see the king's need to bring such damage upon the Temple, such damage as Geoffrey talks of. Geoffrey talks of the Order being destroyed. If the king wants more money than he can win by borrowing from us, there are many things he can do. He can work on the Pope to have our exemptions whittled down, to levy tax on us, to make us yield up these riches or those, to exact fines for some of these evils he alleges against us."

"These evils he alleges, they are as if the Order was in the power of the Devil. He tells the world, apparently, that we worship Mahomet, are sodomites, defile the Sacraments, consume new-born babes. You think he would go so far and mean only to trim our wings?"

"Oh, yes. That is politics in France, under Philip the Fair. He keeps a stable of men to write abuse of his opponents. The viler the things they say, the more rashly the opponent behaves, or else comes to heel."

"You see us coming to heel?"

"I do not see us making war on France."

"War? Your thought a moment ago was, that Philip does not aim near so far."

"However far he aims, we are in touch with him daily in Paris, and he and we are skilled negotiators. It will be settled there and in a peaceful form."

Here Beltran made no response, and in a moment Amaury went on. "He would not dare! We are the Order of the Temple we are two hundred years old, we are under the direct protection of the Pope, are we not the richest bankers in Europe?"

Beltran thought about these things and answered, "Well, my friend, listen: we are the Order of the Temple, and where is the Temple? We are two hundred years old, and in the fifteen years since Acre fell, have forgotten the reason for our founding, your two hundred years ago; one Pope is no shield against the king who has kidnapped and killed another: before us the Lombards and the Jews were the richest bankers in Europe, and King Philip the Fair did not stay to negotiate before he threw them out of France with one hand and kept their purse-strings in the other."

The moon walked with them, bright and full in unclouded sky.

Sometimes now under the horses' feet the earth crunched where frost settled.

"I do not know," Amaury said. "I do not know." Something came to his mind and he said, "You are much informed."

Beltran, resting more easily, for this moment, on the rubble into which his spirit had collapsed, had a memory and laughed. "I was taught by a Venetian," he said.

He thought, I am better alone. I could talk like this forever to my comrades, or to anyone, until the thing sought by the French king happens, whatever that may be; and then I could talk about it after, and all the time do nothing. I will do better to be alone, and live beside the gold in its cave, and Corberan and Saint Hilary will visit me from time to time.

They crossed the hunting-ground of a screeching owl and it flew low above their heads. Chained dogs began to bark and they had come to Richerenches. I have forgotten Alexander's heart, Beltran said to himself; there is Alexander's heart to be taken to Scotland.

Chapter Thirty-five

THE BREAK-OUT

A T midnight, waking from a little sleep, Beltran rose to the matins bell. He had been all day on patrol and might, by the Rule, have stayed in bed and said his Paternosters, but it was half his lifetime since he had been in a commandery of such size, and with chaplains to sing the Office. Besides, he said to himself, although after tonight everything may be as it has always been, perhaps it will not. The chapel was as big as a church. It was all darkness save the two great candles on the altar. Five chaplains sang.

Beltran stood until his head bent of itself, and a hand between his shoulders pushed him down on his knees. This always happened when he had been long prevented from the true worship of Christ. Here in the chapel it seemed to him that he should no longer seek to represent the Order that had been extinguished in the Holy Land, but must reconcile himself with the Order as it was. Knelt in the dark, between the stone under his knees and God over his head, he found his knowing of this simple thing had become intense and pulled him towards an ecstasy. He had no strength for this. What had already overtaken him that day had left him featherlight, as if he had been purged empty and bled to the last ounce. He rocked his knees into pain on the floor and so threw off the tempting warmth, the hopeful excitement, that had begun to work into him.

My Latin is rusty, he told God as he began reciting the office. My Latin is rusty, and so am I. If Saint Hilary can show You a rustier knight than I in his Order of the Temple, I should like to see him too. There would be a comrade in that. Better not to be my comrade, he thought, better not. He wondered what was left of Olivier. He put his eyes into the darkness of the vaulting roof and thought of Honfroi, who had begun his Purgatory while still on earth. Beltran's resignation of himself into the arms of what he had, in conscious error, come to think of as the new Order, brought another spring of exultation to him. He thought his eyes would pierce the roof and spy out Heaven, and brought them down instead to the altar.

Below the candle-flames he saw Geoffrey's face of a renounced prince. Shadows passed over it in the drifting light, but grief and anger were marked plain there. Beltran was startled from his new comfort. Geoffrey wore armour and leaned on his sword. They had left more space round him than respect needed, but some knights were under the fall of candlelight and none of them showed mail. What this betokened Beltran did not know. The solace he had taken to himself since he entered the chapel began to steal away: a false and shortlived friendship. When he went out again into the now clouded night he felt himself to be an object very spare, meagre in his body's force and holding the winnowed faith to him with a frail clutch of his will, hiding its shape from his own eyes.

The wind flew. It came from the east and brought the cold of the mountains. The men who had been to matins hunched their backs to it. It was already strong and you could hear it lifting into a storm. A trumpet sang. All the knights became still, and their heads leaned for the horn to sound again, and round their stiffened bones the white mantles flung and whipped.

Beltran stood on the chapel steps and Geoffrey spoke in his ear. "If that trumpet is the king's I ride against it. No other will come with me. I had the chapter meet and let them choose: You who trust the king's justice surrender to it; you who fear his mischief stay with me, and Richerenches will defy him."

The moon's light came and went. Beltran stood beside Geoffrey and looked down at the innocents in the cobbled square. The clouds that had poured across the sky were followed by an army that blotted out the stars. The moon showed the billowing cloud-rack and was gone.

"Geoffrey," Beltran said. "Geoffrey, are you there?"

"I am here," Geoffrey said.

"Why will you ride against them, instead of holding this place?"

Far back in the chapel the faint light glowed. Geoffrey loomed over Beltran. "Ah, well," he said. "They think I am deluded, and if the king hales them to his court on whatever dire inventions of his own, they will go and answer his prosecutors and expect, being blithe of soul and since the world is not a naughty place, to smooth from Philip's troubled heart the misconceptions he has about our Order." Geoffrey collected himself and became practical. "I speak of each single one of my men. I am alone, and I cannot defend this place on my own, so I shall go out instead. I am armed and my horse is ready."

Beltran said, "Let me arm."

The trumpet beyond the gate howled again through the wind.

"Axe and sword," Geoffrey said. "It is no night for breaking lances." He was on the move now, his voice at the foot of the steps. "We cut a way through. We do not stay to win honour."

Beltran laughed. "Agreed."

"I shall have sconces and watchfires lit, so that we can see what we may."

On his way to the dormitory Beltran took the first cold flakes on his face. The wind had brought snow. He had campaigned in snow in Syria. When he was armed he went to the harness-room and took from it one of the thick and wide-spreading blankets which the Order issued to cover horse or man. He took provision from the kitchen. When he had what he needed and had packed it on his horse, he wrapped himself into a deerskin cloak. He threw away the scabbard of his sword as a handhold to pull him down, and hung the weapon by the leather thong from his saddle.

All this while, during which he passed among such brother knights of the commandery as were not at the gate to see what might befall, it was as if he and they were made of different clay. He did not speak with the same voice as they, and kept silent. In the stable the young Amaury came and petted a horse and looked and looked at him, but Beltran saw him no more than if he had been tack on a peg. After a day of vicissitude, Beltran had got his state simple, and meant it to rest there for the next while.

The ground was white. The snow fell thick and in the yard

at the gate it tossed in the wild air. The wind soared. It cracked into the trees with the jump of a harpist slapping the strings. Baskets of fire flared on the gate towers and inside the walls cressets waved their red streamers of flame. The flying light thrown by these torches into the whirling snow made an uncanny union of earth and sky. On the floor of the yard the knights in their white mantles tilted against the gale as it bounced this way and that among the walls and buildings.

Geoffrey too had a deerhide cloak on him, and he called to Beltran, "We look like two Tartars. Are you ready?"

"Yes. Who is at the gate?"

"Them. The king's men. The secular arm, they assure us. Each of us is summonsed in his own name. They won't have your name."

"No. Not now or later. Go as we are, since you are now left-handed. The fires out."

Geoffrey rode out from his place, axe in hand, to order the fires thrown down and the cressets quenched. When he came back he said, "We shall ride west until they stop chasing. We'll stop every two furlongs or so and fight and draw off until they run out of heart."

Knights tugged open the gates and Geoffrey said, "Come on." They set their horses to the gateway at a walk until their eyes settled to the dark.

Black as was the night, the fallen snow cast up a faint glow and they could see the shapes of their enemies.

"Their pikes are not planted," Geoffrey said at once. "Go!"

They jumped their horses to the gallop. The roadway was unpaved and they had good grip on the new snow. As the horse sprang out of the shelter of the walls and into the blizzard the wind beat Beltran's eyes into tears. He struck into a head and cursed but the blade came free. He hacked into a face and took off an arm that tried for his bridle. He had heard no voice. The hooves were quiet on the padded earth, and all the sound was in the wind. There was nothing to see save snowflakes, and at the very moment of striking, the object and the blood. He was through. He whisked his sword up and down and galloped on. Geoffrey's horse shouldered his and they rode knee to knee for a few bounds of the blood-crazed beasts, before they could pull them in to stand and listen. They heard nothing but the gale and the trees thrashing above them, and rode westwards along the skirt of the forest.

Chapter Thirty-six

MASTER OF THE TEMPLE

JACQUES DE MOLAY, Master of the Temple, on the windy Thursday at the grave of the king's sister-in-law Catherine, Countess of Valois, stood pall-bearer among the princes of the Blood of France. By so distinguishing de Molay the Royal protocol assured the Templars that, blackguarded though they be by the king's servants, the king himself respected the vaunted sovereignty of their Order, and the princely rank in which the Holy See held their Master.

The princes of the Blood were not, therefore, more serene of countenance that day than Jacques de Molay. Yet when a drift of snow came from nowhere onto the mourners and then ran on into the west, leaving men no more frozen than they had been before, that corner of the canopy which was in his grasp shook and jumped so that all the lilies on it danced.

De Molay rode home at a canter to keep his thin old blood awake against the chill. His little following conformed in number to the Rule of the Order, one knight-companion and two grooms. The sun set in front of them as they went, throwing a pale radiance into the sky's edge: it shone with cold, a mirror of winter. When they rode through the gate in the Temple wall it was black night, but the spies knew by all their senses that it was the Grand Master come home, and one stayed and shivered while the other ran.

In the darkest hour Nogaret came. He remembered the parley in which he had tangled with Pope Boniface and resolved to eschew courtesies. He tossed himself off his horse to the ground like a bundle. He would walk in. It was one of those mornings of early winter when the frost arrives with the dawn; and today Nogaret as well.

The gate opened in the king's name and the king's men went about their business. Nogaret walked with no eye to left or right, directly to the great keep, climbed to the first floor and pointed to the Grand Master's chamber. Two men pulled the Master out of bed in his shirt and brought him to Nogaret, and as soon as the old man began to protest Nogaret beat him with mailed fists. Afterwards he leaned on a window-sill to watch the moon fade on a light sky. When he had recovered his breath he rode back to Paris, towards the rising day.

The twenty-third Grand Master of the Most Sovereign Order of the Temple had gone on before, strapped belly-down on a bare horse as if he were already a carcase.

Chapter Thirty-seven

THE BANKERS

"KING! King!"

Philip did not believe he had heard so impious a sound, and sat his horse this fine frosty morning between the two new towers, his mighty, vaulted, round five-storey towers of the Palace of the King.

The horse caracoled for its master with pretty enthusiasm and the two of them revolved. When the horse stood foursquare again the royal eye was caught by a movement, a little above its own level, at a window in the tower opposite. The movement spoke.

"King!" it said, and, "Help! Help, king!"

Philip did not converse upwards, but to end this involuntary audience without precisely turning tail, he spoke down his horse's nose. He had not seen the man for a week, but the voice behind the red and white mask sprang an echo in his memory. What the devil was Nogaret about, to lodge him here?

"You have fallen, Templar," he said. "Hush!"

He put a forefinger to his lips and set off on the old fishmongers' road through the city. As he went, he made his face enigmatic for the day.

The king had waited a week. After burying his sister-in-law he had spent the night, and the nights that followed, at his darling abbey of Maubuisson. During this retreat there was a great rime, and each day he woke to find the trees and meadows covered in white. There was an oak tree still full of leaf as if it had been summer, but the frost ended that. Through the whole daylight of the third day the oak leaves fell. Frozen stiff, they pattered their way down with the sound of rain, and had by nightfall covered thick the ground beneath the tree. The next day the tree was bare. Nogaret sent to him, unseasonal and arduously secret, that the "sheaves had been gathered," and he went back to his capital.

The king, then, had waited a week. Now he was off to inspect the Treasury from which hitherto he had been able only to borrow, and the grubby episode with old de Molay at the Palace gate had quite clouded his morning. He let his horse up the road at a gallop and then, unpredictable, he turned east to the cemetery of the Innocents. He jumped from the saddle and put out a hand in the same movement, but the secretary was ready for him, and slapped the Pope's letter of outrage into his palm. While the king's troop walked the horses Philip strolled among the tombs with Clement's bad temper.

"You, my very dear son, and We say this with sorrow, in contempt of all Order, while We were distant from you, have put out your hand on the persons and goods of the Templars, have gone to the length of putting them in prison—"

One of them is in my Palace, the king said to a headstone, but the sky was bright and rooks cawed in the beech tops, and he saw that his vexation was diminished. He went back to the letter: ". . . . you have committed this assault on the persons and possessions of men who are the immediate subjects of Ourself and of the Church of Rome, etcetera etcetera, an outrageous contempt of Ourself and the Church of Rome."

A covey of short-sighted jackdaws had flown among the rooks. From the trees above the king a commotion of squawks, feathers and cracking twigs overwhelmed the Pope's prose and Clement's letter went into the clerk's bag again. The horses ran all the way to the abbey of Saint Martin, where Saint Benedict's monks were in the fields having hard work of late tilling. The king curbed his horses, dissembled his haste, and trotted decorously round the Benedictine farmland to the Temple.

The Dominicans were in, known as the Black Friars, and the Hounds of God. They were the Inquisition and they had set up house in the Temple, since the State lawyers had arrested the whole occupants of the place. Where else could so many miscreants be contained? Mahomet being, as it were, too unwieldy to go to the mountain, the mountain had come thither. The friars had brought with them their clerks to set down what was said and their torturers to elicit speech, and each of these trades had brought its equipments, so that here was the whole business being conducted to the common advantage.

The king dismounted in the wide space beside the church. He walked the length of this building and looked round the end of it at the old keep. From the cellars of this stark and unembellished tower, though muted by earth and thick foundation walls, carried the sound of two men in torture. One howled as if he howled forever. His howl spoke not only of present pain but of the interminable, eternal pain that he had not yet been dealt. The other screamed so high that the king's eyes lifted in his head, then the scream fell away, and then started again at its height till it seemed the head it came from must split. Perhaps it did, for the scream broke suddenly like a bit of stick, leaving behind it the suggestion that it had meant to say more.

Philip turned his back to the old keep and walked across to the new one. The church stood between them, and as he came near the massive tower which the Order had built to store its bankers' wealth, and which, unlike the gaunt affair so aptly tenanted now by the Dominicans, was decorated with tourelles, the noise of the Inquisition at work went away.

The silence in the new building was profound. Philip knew when he entered that it was not simply the silence of absence of noise, but a silence that was being kept: it was the silence that is kept, so that it may rest easy, round money.

He found the Italians simply by following the train of servitors they had left to stand at stairheads and doorways: each man next ahead on his road bowed when the king reached the predecessor, so that he made his way by these silent guides without thought. The tranquillity of this passage was such that Philip wished it might go on, say, for an hour. Never had a king felt so assured of respect. Never had he been so sensible, for that matter, of esteem so confidently given. He stood and thought of this. Not far ahead, down a spiral of wide steps, he heard the movement of voices: he was arriving.

The king walked on and for experiment, with a gesture lifted the last man from his bow and smiled on him. The smile that he won in return had a curious gravity in it, as if worship was being offered at the same time that valuation was being made. So the king awoke from his daydream and peered into the depth of the lackey's intelligent gaze. What he saw there was that the man and his fellows were adoring Philip, not for anything at all to do with majesty, but because he owned a bank. With the irony of this he consoled himself, and ran down the stairs to meet his wealth.

When he entered the vault the king kept inflexible the muscles of that schooled countenance, but to the three Italian brothers who managed his money, the rhythm of the feet betrayed his jubilation. It was a blithe pace that took him to the objects of his new treasure. He carried in him the wish to present his own embodiment to those of the untold riches he had won; to show off their new ruler to these boxes, barrels and coffers where gold and silver lay in wait. Among the palpable edges and corners, lengths and heights, strapped oak and beech, copper and iron, sheets and staves hammered and steamed, he stepped with the certain grace of a welcomed family man into a gathering of kindred. Exhilaration swung the muscles and sprang the sinews of his legs, and unswerving instinct bore him towards the centre of the room.

The instinct began to falter. He glanced about him to provide it reassurance, and found none: the room was not lit bright at all points but it was adequately illumined for the work that was going on in it, and even so the king could not spy out the limits of this mighty chamber. Its size was all unexpected, and it was with a palsy of incertitude, as if he had come to the wrong place, that he stared down the ever-stretching lanes of caged and cradled gold: lanes that ended not in walls but in horizons. So his instinct failed and, indeed, swerved: and his feet unsteered got clumsy; and he was at a stand. He was like a man who besieges, breaches, takes and spoils a great city and then at last, going for a stroll, becomes lost in the streets and knows his first dismay. He was, however, the king and he sat down and waited until they came to find him.

Muschiato Guidi said to Biccio his brother, "It frightens any of them, emperors and popes and kings, it frightens them all." He let his toe scratch at the iron chest beside his feet and left the high desk where he stood to go to his master.

"It makes a man philosophise," the king said.

"Not I, Sire," Muschiato gave back.

"Not you, then, being a banker; but ordinary mortals, grown rich, will become reflective."

To Muschiato this was so much sentimental hogwash and he set out to scotch it. In any case, now that the Templars were out of the reckoning, he hoped to become the Royal Treasurer in both name and fact, and to this end, his Florentine mind recommended an outlay of pessimism.

"Rich, Sire?" he said.

"Is that not, then, the apt word?" The king was sitting half in the gloom, half in the light from the desks.

"I will put it to you, Sire."

The king stood. "No, Muschiato. Not yet."

A little tentative, perhaps, but certainly no longer timid, he tapped the box he had sat on with a fingertip. "This box, what is in it?"

Muschiato hardly looked at the box. He lifted a hand and said to Biccio, "Ask Nicolo what is in Naples IV, something July last year."

It was plain to the king that Muschiato was dealing with him in some way. He could not, today, outwit a team of three brothers on their own ground, so he resolved to abide the issue.

Biccio came back, and said, "Plate."

Muschiato asked him, "To what value?"

Biccio said, "In detail? It is inventoried against borrowing."

"In sum," Muschiato said, and was told, thirty-five thousand florins, the which he repeated to the king.

"My cousin of Naples?"

"No doubt, Sire."

"Ha, very well then! My cousin of Naples owes me thirty-five thousand florins."

"No, no Sire. He may not have borrowed that far. In any case Sire, it is most likely an arrangement to borrow money for merchant venturing. He need not, by this time, owe the bank anything."

The king blew on his fingers as if they had been burned. He scowled into the distance that the gigantic room offered to his eye. The place was full of man-traps. He eyed the way back to the stairs. He became crafty, and when Muschiato was about to advance his argument, or campaign, or whatever it was, to its next stage, Philip held up a finger to prevent him.

"Biccio," he said. The younger Guidi came forward. "Biccio, you have been here a week, with your brothers. How would you report to me on the conditions of things as you find them?"

Biccio had no hesitation. "Excellent, Sire."

"How excellent?"

"Very well, Sire, the bank is solvent, Sire, certainly solvent. It does a very large business, Sire, over many countries, a very complex business, Sire, but"—the king's eyebrows, at this word, shot up and then down a good deal lower than they had been before—"at a cursory glance the bank appears to be in as good a state as a bank may be in these awkward times."

"Excellent, in short," the king said coldly.

"Excellent, Sire."

The king dismissed Biccio and resumed Muschiato. "Now, Signor Muschiato, I understand that whichever of these boxes I choose, you will say that it represents no advantage to me. Why you will do this is your affair and so does not interest me. Tell me, however, this one thing: am I not richer than I was?"

Ever since the king had interrupted him, Muschiato had been breathing in and out like a man suffocating, and now the words rushed out of him. "Richer, Sire? If you want to be a banker, Sire, yes, richer perhaps, but perhaps not. Much of the bank's business is with crowned heads, Sire, and independent cities, and states of this or that size, Sire, and has come here because of the bank's impartial, international standing, and that has now been cancelled, Sire, so it is probable that the crowned heads and sovereign states and even the trading cities will mostly withdraw their deposits where they are in credit, Sire, and where they owe, Sire, where they owe, will be hard to satisfy as to your Majesty's credentials to receive monies owed to the Temple, Sire, so no, Sire, I would not advise your Majesty to go into banking.

"Indeed, Sire, by and large, so far as the banking side of things goes, you may say that France is now less rich than she was in the sense that she loses the seat of the biggest bank in Europe, and to that extent, Sire, the answer to your question is, that you are not richer, but are poorer, than you were before you toppled these Templars."

The king had sat down again on the box belonging to his cousin of Naples, with his face bent towards the floor. The Italian looked down on the top of the royal head with pleasure. "I speak only of the bank, Sire, there are also the countless castles, manors, towns and villages, but the Knights of Saint John, Sire, of the Hospital, Sire, do seem well assured that they will fall heir, so you might say, to many of these, such castles, lands, towns and so forth having come to the Temple as donations for the assistance of the donor's soul, and not reasonably expected to resume secular possession when the Hospital is available to receive them."

From between the king's face and the floor, from clenched jaws came the words, "You are cool enough about all these little misfortunes, Muschiato." The king looked up at him.

"Misfortunes, Sire? I do not perceive any! It is indifferent to kings and bankers, Sire, whether they are rich or poor. One funds oneself from those creatures who feel themselves to be rich or poor, and for one's own part stands aloof from such unserviceable feeling."

Philip went on looking up at him and to Muschiato, watching, it seemed that gradually the king became more definite in his mind, though how this showed simply in the way the man sat would be hard to determine. Philip stood up and became extremely definite. He departed.

The king went out by the same stairs, and corridors, and landings, but the human signposts had gone; perhaps because he was only a king, after all. At the steps leading down to the yard outside he found Nogaret looking up at him. The guards on the staircase saluted the king.

"They do not let me come up, Sire," Nogaret called to him.

"You would not enjoy it," Philip said, and went down to the yard. "Come to Paris," he said. He took Nogaret with him like a musty old cloak, for the familiar odour of his company. "It has been a week," the king said. "You have the evidence you need?" The king got onto his horse. "You have enough to persuade His Holiness that our zeal for the Church has not outrun itself?" By the time they reached the gate Nogaret had still not answered him. The king looked down. Nogaret was walking at his stirrup with his face straight to the front. The king bent forward and peered into it; it was bitter and tight-mouthed. He kicked his minister on the shoulder. "Do you have evidence?" he repeated.

Nogaret crept a little distance out from the comfort of his chagrin. "Yes," he said tamely, and nodded a good deal. "No," he amended, "not exactly. No." He had come to the man holding his horse and he took the rein and walked on at the side of the mounted king. "Sire," he said, and swung into the saddle. "Sire, these Dominicans had killed twenty men before I found out that they had elicited nothing from their victims."

"Victims, Nogaret! These are souls in care."

"Souls, Sire."

"Why did the souls not cleanse themselves with confession, being in extremis?"

"Because, Sire, it was not made plain to them what they were wanted to confess."

The king reined in his horse. "And now?"

Nogaret's horse had to walk round in a circle to bring him back to the king. "Now, Sire, I have the list of crimes and heresies with which they are charged read to them constantly in their prison. In this way, Sire, their heads are filled with these dreadful things and will leap to mind to relieve their sufferings. They have the right to be fully aware of what is alleged against them."

The king slapped his horse and it started into a walk. "I have a letter from the Pope," he said, "and letters also from my bishops." His horse began to clip along at a trot. "They have heard that none of the Templars has confessed despite the Inquisition and its torture." He checked his horse a little.

"How do they torture them?"

"They burn off their feet in fires." Nogaret replied. "They are not subtle," he said crossly. "They hang weights from the genitals."

The king put his horse along again. "Meanwhile," he said, "if the Pope has my French bishops on his side, why should he not

9

vindicate the Temple? Then where shall I be?" The king pulled jerkily on the reins with his evil temper. He cut his fine horse's mouth and yet had his spur in its flank. The horse bounded one way and its head knocked Nogaret from the saddle. It bounded the other way and spun about and stood into the air. The king jumped off and the horse fell backwards but Philip had shifted nimbly out of the way. The horse came to its feet and stood. There was blood on its side and its mouth and in its eye, and it shook its head while the legs gathered themselves firm again. Nogaret, who had come up as far as his knees, envied the expression with which the beast looked at the king from out of its blood-filled eyes. The horse turned its head far round to one side and followed after it, and made off at a solid run towards Flanders.

The king waved back those of his attendants, trailing always in his wake, who set off after. "Leave him," he said. "He is going home, and quite right."

He sat on the road beside Nogaret. "What the Devil, Nogaret?" he said. "What the Devil shall we do?" The sky had lost all its light and over their heads, behind their shoulders, all was grey and dismal. "We must quell Pope Clement, Nogaret. Shall we kidnap him?"

Nogaret stayed knelt: if he stood he would look down on the king, to sit might be over-familiar, and the mud was being kind to his knees. "Not kidnap," he said. "You want the Pope to abolish the Temple: it must be called anathema and be abolished. It will serve nothing if he pronounces interdiction from a prison. What we shall do, Sire," and he smiled at his master with the unholy, lifeless gaze that meant he was mining the most abysmal veins of his spirit, "what we shall do is be patient!"

The king, although sitting, jumped as if he had been struck. "Curse it, Nogaret!" he said. "No games with me, play no games with me!" He scrabbled in the mud and threw a dollop of it at the Keeper of his Seals. "Tell me what has come to you."

Nogaret wiped the dirt from his face. "Sire, we shall so work on the Pope that he will call a Council of the Church and at this Council will extinguish the Order. We shall have the Council near at hand, Sire, so that your own bishops are there in plenty. It will take time, Sire, so we must arrange for the Inquisition to send more slowly to Hell these souls they care for back there."

The king's face was now as muddied as his minister's, for he had been rubbing these thoughts into his head as they were expounded. "How," he asked, "will we achieve this?"

"By calumny, Sire. We shall defame the Pope, calumniate the Pope, denounce, blackguard, libel and slander the Pope throughout Europe." He picked a piece of mud off the ground and looked ambitiously at the king. "We shall throw mud at him, Sire. Some mud always sticks. Sooner or later, he will conform to your will." He squeezed the mud out of his fingers. "Then, Sire, he will ask you to call off your dogs." He flicked a sly finger but the speck from it met the king's look and fell.

The king waited until Nogaret was brushing his hands against each other. "You are right, Nogaret. Apart from yourself, Nogaret, yourself the leader of the pack; apart from you, who will the dogs in this case be?"

"Pierre Dubois, Sire, and Enguerrand de Marigny. No one on whose behalf they have taken up their pens, Sire, has ever complained of being insufficiently maligned."

At this last phrase Nogaret turned his head on his neck like a hen listening to grubs working in the ground. He began, in the dry scrape of a dead leaf over stones, to laugh. It was not permitted, without the king's leave, to make so merry, but were it treason he could not have held it back. "Forgive me, Sire," he said, and laughed. "It was they who published the infamies about the Temple!" He laughed like anything. "It was because of them, Sire," and he heaved in and sighed out air as if he would choke, "because of Dubois and Marigny, that the Templars were paralysed when we went to arrest them." He suffocated and grew crimson in neck and face. The king smote him on the back five great smacks. "Oh, Sire!" He recovered and was calm, more than calm, deeply serious. "The fact is, that if you go at it hard to defame a man, and malign him; to say all evil of him and above all to lie—for to take off his reputation leaves him alone before others, but to lie while you do it, that leaves his will paralysed. It bewilders him; it astonishes him; he is dumbfounded; hamstrung; then the fact is, Sire, he is then as much at your mercy as if you had put out his eyes, cut out his tongue, and taken off his hands and feet."

The king regarded Nogaret with something like friendliness, and was quite moved by the man's excitement: he remembered why he hated the Church, that the grandfather had been burned as a heretic in the south, "Did they lie about your grandfather, my Nogaret?"

The question had an extraordinary effect. Nogaret went as stiff as ice. His two fists clenched and lifted a little into the air and fell onto the earth as if they would break it in two. "He was heretic, to the Church, so they did not lie. Yet he was as my parent, and they burned him dead." He smiled widely. "The Dominicans, my today's allies, they burned him." He became solemn and simple. "They hardly tortured then, you know, there was not much torture of the Cathars. My—he was a Cathar, my . . . anyway, he was a Cathar. It was the Church who burned him, though, I am indifferent who of the Church I harm, save as I may harm them, I thank Your Worship's Royal Grace. Oh, Sire, I would I might burn the Pope! One day to burn the Pope!"

"Well, well, Nogaret," the king said kindly. "You are a conscientious and faithful servant for a king, and you have pointed out, that such a thing would not be politic at present. You may, however," said he remembering, "you may live to see that old Grand Master of theirs burn, but only if you will be kind enough in the meantime to remove him from my new tower at my palace."

The king had been so gentle to him that Nogaret's eyes, already pent with the complication of his feelings, were moist. "You will see, Sire," he said. "You shall have your Council of the Church. The Pope may stand stiff enough now, but we shall bring His Holiness down to earth."

They looked at the mud from which they had risen, which stuck on their clothes and which they were engaged in brushing off with the cuffs of their besmirched gauntlets.

Chapter Thirty-eight

SHIRIN

"BELTRAN! Beltran!" she said weeping. He had seen her far off, making her way down the rocky glen. Twice as he watched she had fallen. She had tripped over a stone and then pitched down a steep drop in the path where she lay at full length, but for only a moment before she was up and moving again towards him. It was as if the ground where she walked or fell was not real to her: as if only the space between her and where she was going had strength to sustain or hurt. So he had gone running to meet her. When they met, then her journey was done, and she flung an arm up across her eyes and turned aside and stood weeping and said only his name. She had got herself tangled in a bush of thorns and he set her free of it, and carried her to the cave.

On the first moment of seeing her he had known her spirit was dead. In the cave she had slept out the half-a-day that remained and all the night. After that she was no more of the Shirin that had once been, than a butterfly with the miraculous dust knocked from its wings. Geoffrey, she said, had put himself into the hands of the Inquisition.

Beltran was a hermit now. He had made a cell of the cave and he kept the days as if he were still in the Holy Land, under the Rule of the Order. He had filled the back of the cave with rocks, once all the gold was in, and lived in front of it. He was a solitary monk, and kept his sword on the wall. He had not seen Geoffrey since they parted that night in the snow, the night they broke out from Richerenches. When she told him about Geoffrey, he wished she had not come here.

"Geoffrey would do that," was what he said to her. "Because of his men? He would do it because of his men."

"Ah! They were all dead, long ago." The eyes she lifted to him, that had shone like grapes in the bloom, were ransacked and dull. "They were tortured and burnt at the stake long ago," she said. "But that is why he went, because of them."

Colour sprang in the new grass where the wild flowers urged out their buds. They would bloom again in their myriads and he would not see them.

"It would be the more worth doing, to the mind of Geoffrey," he said, "if they were all dead. I don't understand it, but it is true."

"Yes," she said, "it is true."

"What do you want." he asked her crossly. "I have lived away from all these things. These things are nothing but tales of foolish men failing. Except when they deal with madmen like Geoffrey. What do you want?"

She would drag him away. He would have to take down his sword and go off into the world. He would have to leave this place where the clean rock lifted from the sweet grass, in which grew the many-scented herbs, and where the flowers grew and danced all through the summer, higher and higher.

"You are old. You have grown very old," she said.

"I do not deny it," he said to her. He looked at her, less than half his years. "Yet I may be younger now than you."

She touched the back of her neck with the flat of her palm and sniffed up tears. "Yes," she said. The black hair drifted and swung round her head. "Well," she said. "What I want is your youth. I have mislaid mine and would lean on yours."

His eyes were harsh and kept her off. "You keep your pretty ways," he said. "Old woman; dead woman. You still use your pretty ways. Without knowing it?" He took that from her widening eyes. "Without knowing it, and on me. Twice wasted, dead old woman." He was amazed to have said these words. "I have been alone too long," he said. "I have been alone, well, years. If I was ever gentle, I am no longer."

For the first time since she had come, she smiled, and it was as if she had never meant to smile again; but there, had done so, was doing so. His cruelty had eased her pain. People were absurd, and she would make him go among them again. What to do?

"What is there for us to do, Shirin? We can do nothing."

She turned her lip at him. "Go where he is, till he dies. Then take my vengeance."

On the mountain slope the oak and the wild olive, the beech and the chestnut, waited for the time to flourish their leaves. The life ready to burst from them met the sun and went into a haze of budded twigs. This year he would not see the leaves grown in to colour and fall on the mountainside.

"Vengeance," Beltran said. "You heathen! Vengeance." All the same, he had begun to remember Geoffrey. "Where will you make vengeance?"

Something flashed in the grass. A green shimmer darted across the ground before them. "See the green lizard," she said. "On the king of France, is that not right? His Vizier also, Geoffrey called him: Nogaret." The lizards were swift and shy. On this one the skin shone like a hundred emeralds as it flickered past. "I am not a heathen," she said. "I was baptised a Christian. We Christians are in the habit of revenge."

She called the lizard to her hand and before Beltran's astonished eyes it came. She touched its collar with the back of a fingernail and it ducked and lifted under the feel like a stroked cat. She told it to go and it skimmed into the grass.

"Beware," Beltran said. "Its bite is dirty."

Shirin looked into the ground, "Oh, Beltran," she said. "It can be made dirtier." She looked like a witch.

He asked where she and Geoffrey had spent the years since the escape from Richerenches. In a tower of Geoffrey's mother in Portugal, he was told, where King Denys was deaf to Philip the Fair's urgings to prosecute the Temple.

It was four days before he was ready to leave. It was not that he had much to put together. He took nothing that would mark him as a Templar save his sword, for he would not forsake it: he wound it in cloth and carried it hid. He had no mind to walk into any prison, to take a stranger's justice, or to fall on his back and die for the king like a dog. Beltran called forth again into the world meant to go hiding and furtive, disguised. Therefore, although he took his Templar's sword, he stowed it in the long pack on his shoulders. The wrapped hilt came handily behind his neck where he could draw it over the collarbone.

It was small gear, then, that he mustered for the journey, and it was not the packing of it which needed four days: he had the gold to see to. He did not expect the road he now took to bring him back. For one thing, old age was on him: and for another, he saw this coming of Shirin, drawing him at last from his den, as a sign that it was time to take Alexander's heart to Scotland. So the gold must be sealed in its tomb.

Beltran had understood for long enough that this was to be the treasure's ending-place. He had his provision made, the store of stone and the mounds of earth beside the cave-mouth, turfed now with time. The gold was already beyond a wall, but to make it safe until God chose to draw on it he had to build a second wall at the cave-mouth and make that invisible behind a pile of earth.

It was a strange thing to do, like performing a pagan burial rite, for in the outer chamber between the walls he left behind, as if for the service of the treasure, most of the equipment that had been rescued by Corberan and him from the galley, when the gold was all out and before they put the wreck and the wood it lay in to the torch. There was even another sword, though there was no way to tell whose it was. Besides two daggers of like pattern, there were sundry small knives, again all in the same style. There was one of the curved shields of the Order, with the wood in a good state but the hide that had covered it long stripped off; there were the pots and grates for cooking; the barley bowls and the flasks and ladles and goblets. Over all these and what other small effects he resigned to the cave, Beltran spread first the great woollen blanket which he had from the commandery of Richerenches, and over that two of the white mantles, red-crossed, of the Order. One of them was his own, but for the other, who could say?

Each of these objects he left in as good a state as it could be won to: washed, secured, oiled, whatever became it best. When it was time he withdrew from the cell and began to build the wall. It was a dry-stone wall. He had practised the skill when he raised the first one. Shirin had taken a leather bag and gone, so she said, hunting. While the wall was still lower than his knees he began to feel, and did not at first believe it, bereaved of the objects that lay under the two white mantles. When he believed it, he saw the reason: he had made a little Order for himself from these weapons and clothes and utensils. From the wreck of the arms of the Order; from the remains of the East after the massacre at Acre, and from the remains of the West after its surrender, en masse, to the French King, Beltran had preserved enough to let himself continue housed in the Temple.

The morning of the third day the almost-relics, as he thought them, were walled-up behind an arm's length of stone and he cut into his earth mound and began piling it up against the wall. Shirin came to help him.

"What have you been hunting?" Beltran asked her.

"Lizards," she said. "See."

She pointed to the leather bag that she had rescued from his store. It moved now and again when the prisoners within dashed across its confining space. On the fourth day the existence of the cave was wholly blotted out by the heap of earth, and this was once more covered with the turf that had crowned the original mound.

First light saw Beltran on his knees outside the hidden cave. He knelt there long, while the damp ground soaked his breeches and the cold seeped into him, and he grew chill, and trembled. He waited in vain. No sign was given him. He did not hear again the crack with which Thibaud's galley, that galley he had brought to ashes beside the great river, struck against the harbour wall at Sidon. Christ did not come as a vision to him and speak from a golden cloud. No gulf opened in him wherein he might plunge to meet his soul.

He looked through the earth and the arrow-deep wall into the cell where he had lived five years. He did not know, now that he was leaving, if he had done his duty. The thought which had begun four days ago was troubling him: that from the weapons, clothes and cooking-irons now entombed in their cell, he had made an image of the Order and dwelt there. It was as if, from the collapse of the Temple, he had gathered shards and made himself a hutch. Should he not have done that? He did not see what else to have done. He did not know where the thought had come from, or why it brought unease.

9*

"Saint Hilary," he said. "The Order is yours, was yours. I have followed the Rule as best I might, since the Order fell about our ears." He vented a sigh, and said, "My ears." He had a great and pointless longing to return here and see this bank of earth when its turf had bound together again, and it was all splashed with flowers. He had no feeling that Saint Hilary was listening to him.

He fidgeted his knees, on the point of heaving to his feet, and remembered the gold. It had hardly been in his mind these four days. He had been all on this business of walling-up the cell, when it was no more than an ante-chamber to the treasure room. He put his spirit at the gold, but it would not: it refused, like a horse at a leap. Therefore he let his spirit stand, and waited for the gold to issue as much refulgence as it chose. Nothing: there was such an absence of life between him and that cave in there that he stared with panic at the new-hacked turf. For God, the Order and Saint Hilary, he had of that gold in there been the guardian, and now when he took his hand from it, all that he heard from Heaven was silence.

The chill in which he knelt touched his soul. He commended the gold to God and the gifts of gear to Saint Hilary. He did know how he stood with Heaven at all, and made his commendation brief. He was upset and sulking. When he stood his eyes went wide at the stiffness in his legs. He saw that Shirin was awake and watching him with her knees under her chin and the bag of green lizards at her feet. He grunted at her and made some nods of the head, and waited for her to rise in her turn, and they went up out of the gorge before the sun was yet warm.

In her hand she carried her revenge, and in his he carried the box with Alexander's heart. Quite soon he felt relieved of weight, and the spring came into his step.

Chapter Thirty-nine

THE PAPAL BULL

CLEMENT sat in the bishop's seat at the head of the cathedral in Vienne. It was six months since he had first seated himself there, and he knew every runnel and edge of its complex theology. The triple tiara crushed his head. The weasel Philip Capet, oddly known as the Fair, King of France, affronted his eyes. The assembled dignitaries of the Church sat and resented him, and his stomach turned at what he was about to do. He was going to extinguish, finally and formally, the Order of the Temple.

The council had declined to endorse the extinction of the Temple, and what was more, had given safe-conduct to nine Templars who had turned up out of nowhere to defend their Order. Clement, accordingly, postponed the hearing of these nine champions and drew the affair into his Pontifical hands: today he was going to finish the Order's business for it by decree.

It seemed to Clement a misfortune of the Supreme Pontiff that he must sit at the wrong end of the Church. Lesser folk could walk about and esteem such constructions as this from a delightful variety of positions. The Bull rustled in his hand. He lifted it. This church of Saint Maurice was cold. The Bishop of Valencia, who had been complaining about it all winter, sneezed again. The vaulted roof was enormously high.

"Without doubt," Clement read, "the proceedings so far conducted against the Order do not enable us to condemn it canonically as heretical by a definitive sentence."

At least, sitting in the episcopal throne built into the rounded end of the church, one was safe from being stabbed in the back by Philip's minions. Not that they would shirk coming at the Holy Father from the front. "As, however, the heresies attributed to it have cast a slur on its reputation, as an almost infinite number of its members have confessed, as all this sort of thing makes it very suspect, as no one would wish it to continue, and for the weal of the Holy Land; then between those on the one hand who would wish for condemnation and those on the other who wish that judgement be suspended, We take the course of issuing an edict, and We suppress the Order by Our irreversible sanction."

Old Valencia sneezed but by convulsion only, without sound. There was no sound. The king turned his face to the Pope and said nothing. Clement had not seen before how round it was, and it was as bland now as the moon, as meaningless and cold and calm. Yet the mask, because it was so experienced, no longer presented the image of silence, but the visage of quelled secrets: it was as a gargoyle that had been too strong for the chisel.

The hubbub came from the far end of the long church. At first it fell into the awful stillness after Clement's reading of the Bull like a light pebble falling into a pond, but it continued into a commotion. Clement was pleased to find that he had guessed the cause before Philip did. It was that the nine Templars had seen in the feebleness of the Council a fatal flaw in their safe-conduct, and were making a path for themselves out of the church. Light came in at the doorway and gleamed a little on iron-shod heads and the door closed again. Soon they heard horses at the gallop.

Philip understood. "The Templars," he said to Clement.

"Of course," the Pope said. "They do not trust your honour, nor mine," he added, pleasantly intercepting the king's retort.

A captain of the king's came up the church and confirmed to them that the Templars had ridden off.

"They must not be pursued," the Pope said. "They have safe-conduct."

The captain looked at them both. "There was one stayed inside," he said, "to hold the door. He has put up his sword and we have not laid hands on him so far." He looked back up the church and they saw dimly a man standing with his arms folded. "He has but one hand." the officer said. It sounded hopeful, as if he wanted to give the man at the door a passport to join his fellows. The Bishop of Valencia sneezed just as Clement opened his mouth, and the king got in first.

"Give him to the care of the Dominicans," Philip said.

Chapter Forty

THE BURNING

THE clouds were black. A glow of silver lay on the sky and the black clouds, as black as soot, flew towards it like forerunners of the night. Black images swam deep below them in the river.

When they stood Geoffrey against the post his voice climbed in the sound of a man laughing that became like the bleat of a lamb. Words passed through the huddle of people.

"His feet are burnt off," they said. "He has no feet."

Shirin shouted. Beltran grasped her by each arm. Corberan took a knife of blue steel from her hand. His eyes had a mist on them and were flown up under their lids like a madman's. The Catalan ran into the little crowd. He ran across the open ground among the soldiers and up to the place where the executioners were tying Geoffrey to the post. Some of the soldiers had started after him. In all this there was no voice uttered. Corberan ran through the crowd and the soldiers in a silence. He jumped onto the pile of wood and set the dagger twice in Geoffrey's heart.

The people began to cry out and exclaim and noise returned to Beltran's ears. He heard the scraps and cracking of wood when Corberan fell off the woodpile in a tangle with one of the executioners. A soldier thrust at them with a spear. There was a scream and then Corberan got up, a little crouched over like a toad from some hurt. The soldier had his spearpoint stuck fast in the executioner and did not know what to do, so he stood holding the spear where it was. Corberan ran off to the far side of the island. At the very edge of the water another soldier stroked at him with a sword and made a cut. The Catalan jumped and fell away into the river. Beltran heard the splash and saw its foam in the air. The soldier peered long, turning his head downstream, before he came away from the bank. Perhaps Corberan would save himself.

The sun flashed as it set and the clouds were red and blue and green. On the Isle of Jews the people settled down again. The spearman at length tugged his point from the executioner's ribs with a foot on the man's breast and a rending of bone and muscle. Beltran and the girl sat on the ground. The dark skin of her face had paled and she began to shudder, and Beltran, for it was both fitting and wise, covered her in the cloak he carried. He watched the men at the stake finish tying the now peaceful Geoffrey as upright as they could. There was one other stake.

Tonight the last Grand Master of the Temple was to burn, and with him another Geoffrey, son of the Dauphin of Auvergne and the Order's Commander in Aquitaine. The old man, the Master, is the last shadow of my refuge, Beltran said to himself. His ashes will be the last ashes of my Order. When he is gone even that fancied shelter where my spirit flies for comfort, even that dreamed fragment of the Temple, will go from me.

I shall not die in the Order, then. The old man will die in the Order. Geoffrey has died in the Order, but when the poor old man has burned my dying will be after the Order and out of it. My living also. I am not far younger than the Master, the old man, I call him; but he has spent seven years in dungeons with torture and starving along the way.

The Order can disappear as much as it likes, he cried out in his silence. It can fail in the East, and the West, and tonight it can show me even its last shadow fly in smoke to the air, yet I will not be separated from it, for I have it caught alive inside me.

Perhaps it was a lie, to say that. He stood on the island across from the rag of Geoffrey's corpse, and felt himself as empty as a blown egg. The Order keeps pretending to die, he said, and I keep pretending that it has not. Truly my Order died at Acre; and truly for me it died when Thibaud died.

Save for the gold which has not died; to which I clung like a hawk to the wrist of its dead master; which was the hump on my back but I adored it. It kissed me with its blessing the one time that I had kindness of it, there in the galley's darkness. We made a sacrament, the gold and I.

He stood and listened to what he had just said, and shivered away from himself. All the knights had died for what he had done. For blasphemous worship of a golden idol they had been torn up and burned and sent to Hell.

"We made a sacrament, the gold and I," he had said the words bravely and aloud, though they came in dry scrapings from his mouth. I do not believe it, he said. This is what comes of too much in-dwelling. All that I did was fall down among the golden coins when the boat heaved in the river.

He hungered for the gold in its cave. He turned to the river's edge behind him and ran down the bank to a solitude among bushes. He hunched his face in his hands and his limbs flicked like minnows, and the hot liquid poured from his eyes and from everywhere, from his mouth and his skin and from his groin into his breeches. He lay still. He huddled like a child knowing it was to be born, but nothing happened: in a while he decided that nothing would happen. Later he smelled sweet flesh burning and got to his feet, but then he could not move.

Shirin came and said they were burning Geoffrey's body and the Grand Master, and the third man.

"I will not come," he said. "I have not been sufficient."

She hit him about the face with the flats of her hands. "I have left Geoffrey up there," she said. "You have journeyed all your life to here, but so has each of us. Come back with me."

Flames tore at the black sky and began now to weaken, just as Shirin restored Beltran to his place. He made sure of his pack. It sat on the ground as he had left it, nothing gone from it. He felt for the box in which Alexander's heart travelled, and it was safe. He leaned his knuckles on the box gently and kept them there. His eyes blinked. He looked at the wrapping over his sword and did not touch it and let his eyes pass on to nothing. He pressed the backs of his fingers against the casket and his breath puffed in little sighs. He stood up and looked towards the fires.

This is the way Olivier died, he said to himself, at the great burning in the south. Olivier knew me to the marrow, and to my soul's marrow. Perhaps I went corrupt before Olivier did. Perhaps he knew me corrupt and turned to evil for reproach, or to share sin. Perhaps this and perhaps that. I must determine not to think about them. Geoffrey has quite vanished. The

Master has become a cinder. His hands hold up where he prayed with them, the bones must have got locked together. Well Shirin, I have seen it. It is over, all but over.

The fire glared suddenly and threw its light up like a torch. A group of figures showed, standing on a height behind a wall. The men in the flames turned to nothing.

Shirin said. "The king is in his garden."

The crowd pelted the king with whatever came to hand and he went away. By their burning the Templars had become the precious ones of the people, who borrowed pikes from the soldiers and began to spread out the remains of the fires.

"What are they doing?" Beltran asked of the man beside him and saw that he was a Dominican, a friar of the Inquisition.

"They are cooling the embers, my dear son." The monk had calm eyes of grey and a wise face full of strength. "They are deluded, for tonight at least, and think these are the ashes of martyrs."

Beltran turned to Shirin and she was gone. He looked all about and saw nothing of her. "There was a girl," he said to the Dominican, "did you see her go?"

The Dominican looked at him. "You have a strange accent, but I have heard it somewhere," he said.

"I expect you have," Beltran said. "The Syrian girl, did you see her go?"

"Towards Our Lady's church," the Dominican said. The round windows of the church were touched with colour from the light within.

The fires were as good as out now and had been spread on the cobbles in a glow of hot coals. The people rummaged among these, knocking chosen fragments clear of the heat with knives or sticks or other makeshift tools. They blew on their garnerings and tossed them from hand to hand. They had not made a large crowd, and they seemed content with what they won, as if there were enough for all.

"What do they take?" Beltran asked.

"Relics, the poor fools think them: bits of bone. They believe they have seen the souls of saints fly to Heaven." All his face drew together in a spasm of emotion, compounded as it seemed to

Beltran of grief, rage and other elements. "Man is a heretical animal." His eyes opened suddenly very wide at Beltran. "Where are you from with that voice?"

Beltran gripped him by the ears. They were unseen of any in that crowd of relic-gatherers, and he gripped the Dominican by the ears and said to him. "My home is the Holy Land. We are all of us saints and heretics out there." He let go of the ears. The man's eyes were thin with pain.

Beltran took up his pack and crossed over Saint Michael's Bridge. He set off to the northward.

Chapter Forty-one

THE GREEN LIZARD

"YOU do not belong here," King Philip said to the green lizard. It did not look at him. "It is not your season," the king said, "nor your country." It was the king's country, his own all to himself, the king's garden. A yokel had been at work but the king sent him off, to be alone. The man had been cutting chamomile to dry and it lay in bundles of paled yellow flowers, which cast their scent about the king's head like perfumed scarves.

Long beams of sunlight came patiently through the treetops. They made the garden an arcade of brightness. The king stood in a quiet, and moved not even a finger. The lizard rustled and was hid, behind it a flash of green melted to nothing on the sight. A clouding sky dimmed the sun and coldness entered the day. The king looked up and saw magpies that lived north of the river skim down over the roofs of the great church on their way home. They ruffled the pigeons on the church roof and passed through a flock of sparrows who were flying down river. The sparrows flew like specks of dust, leaping and falling up and down, and darting from side to side, to cheat the hawks that glided the low hills.

The king's feet shuffled on the path as he began to walk on, disliking the chilled air. He climbed to the raised walk and when the sun struck its way through the clouds again, filling them with a mystery of colours that spoke to Philip of ancient metals and forgotten flowers, he sat on the wall and partook of a little more of his kingdom. From the other side of the wall sang out a chirping sound, such as he had heard used to a pet monkey. He bent his head from the sky to look down the wall and a shaft of green light shot up at him and sank into his neck. He put a hand to it and touched nothing there but the stinging pain. The chirrup sounded again and his friend the lizard stood before him for a heartbeat and then sped over the wall as quick as a whiplash. The king touched his neck again to be sure it had not been a daydream, and found blood on the palm of his hand.

He said aloud. "Then what is this?"

Almost he did not move to look over the wall again. There was a woman passing below it about to turn the corner out of sight.

The king called to her. "Wait!"

The woman turned and came towards him. She wore dark clothes and was dark, of face and hair and eye. A leather bag hung from her wrist with live things in it.

"Was that your dragon bit my neck?" He pointed to the place and let her see what mark there was. The life in the bag kicked and jumped.

"Yes," she said. She had looked well at the bite. "Hush," she said to the bag, and it was still.

"You are a witch," he said. "You shall be burned."

Her face looked full at his face and he watched amazement go into it. She walked off along the wall.

He said quickly. "You shall not be burned."

She stopped and stayed. He moved along the walk to the place above her.

He stood and looked down more than his height at her, and asked her. "Am I killed?"

"Yes," she said. "By Christmas."

"Why?"

"Ask Nogaret."

"Nogaret has died; this very summer."

Her face looked up at him and the light went from the day so that he no longer saw her eyes. Coldness was all about him now. She said nothing. His head shook with the anxiety to know why he was killed.

"Why am I killed?"

"Ask Pope Clement."

He fought as close as he could win to anger but it passed from him in a sigh. "Why do you riddle at me, woman? The Pope died in the spring. Clement died in the south. We have no Pope."

She nodded. "They are both dead," she said. Soon she would

go. That she had killed him and would go seemed to him terrible: he had a right to her company, since she had killed him.

He would have spoken then, but she said to him by way of farewell, "You must ask them at Christmas." When she would not speak again he jumped down from the wall and found nothing but darkness in the place where she had been.

Chapter Forty-two

ALEXANDER'S HEART

BETWEEN the snow plain and the moon silence hung and waited. Towards the west cowered a clutch of desperate trees where a man listened for what had woken him. With a thud the gale fell on the trees and passed on through the stillness. Into the quiet, which the sudden gust left deeper than before, a wolf called from the long hills where the moor ended. On his feet now Beltran looked there. He could see far in the moonlight in this white land. To the south was that rampart of low mountain and to the north the dark edge of forest; before and behind the moor ran into the starry night. He had travelled eastwards from the sea and when he had passed the moor would come at the place Balantrodoch, and lay there Alexander's heart. The night was still again, as if it were an ambush not yet sprung. What had waked him?

Birds that made a sad and piping song fled past him. From the way they had come, from the sea far at his back, out from the starred darkness rushed the wind. In the moment that it reached Beltran its voice leaped from a whisper to a howl, and over that night and its dawn the howling of the wind cast a roof of perpetual noise. It was to this wind that the trees, leaning to the west and reaching along instead of upwards, had made their growth submissive. Now when it struck them moans sounded from their trunks and in front of the greater outcry of the storm broke out a steady cracking and snapping, and Beltran found that fragments of twig and bark and moss were falling to his chest and shoulders. Besides the great noise in the sky and the little frenzy in the wood he saw that the wind was lifting the snow into the air, and driving it on like spume carried across the sea. Clouds had come in behind the storm and rode forward to obscure the stars. About Beltran, the night that had been part of an eternity of quiet had changed into a turmoil of noise and movement. Only he was still.

Beltran, therefore, bowed himself under his pack and put off into the chaos. More cold washed about in him than his old age might hope to carry long, but he would have died lying on under the frozen wind: now, at least, the wind pushed him on his way. Also, the sudden breaking of the night's bright peace into these thousand sounds, into the flowing of the snow and the pouring of the clouds, and the beating of the storm as it rained its blows on him: all this outbreak of excited noise, this wild movement of sky and land, had no less than its equal in the disordered world that had roiled within Beltran from the hour of his self-revelation on the Isle of Jews. Beset equally within and without, therefore, and perhaps upheld by this demented balance, his ancient flesh plunged on through the night's storm.

When dawn came Beltran was in fever. He was tired with the fatigue of all his life but a smile kept lifting on his mouth. The breaking of the day at his back threw a gloomy light to the horizon before him. He trudged towards it.

"I will not live beyond you," he said to the light.

At the crown of Beltran's head clouds spanned the earth. There was no sun. The world beneath the low sky was lit by the whiteness of the snow and scoured by the wind.

He felt sick as if his insides had been drawn up through his mouth. He felt himself emptied. His whole life had emptied itself out behind him where he passed and here, none the less, he was: lifting forward one sopping leather boot after another, leaning back on the gale and stepping his knees high over the heavy snow; here he was, whirling his arms like a dervish not to be overset by the storm, with his clothes soaked to his skinny frame, he and they as much matter of this winter-stricken land as any stunted thorn, or starved hare, or any of the moaning birds that laid sad voices to the sky. Here then, he was, decrepit, fevered, clad more or less in wet and wind, with only the sword on his back and the dead man's heart in a box to assure him that his journey went from a beginning to an end: but moving onward still.

There was a house in front of Beltran. It lifted the tip of a grey roof where the moor dipped at last into broken ground. He stood looking there too long and found himself on the snow.

His cheek was on the snow and his old eye, sighting so much purity, showed for a moment the bitter appetite of the hawk. He sat himself up and in a while undid the pack of his belongings. There was ice on the wrappings. He picked ice from his hair. He had fasted since he woke and fasted still. When he stood up again he carried only his sword and the heart in its casket.

"You are nearly home," he said to the heart.

He felt the smile shake on his lips. He walked with the prancing gait and his feet stamping down on the snow, and his head leaning back past his heels onto the push of the wind. The march out of the night had done for him. He had complained of it to himself and been answered, this will be the last exertion of my life.

Now each one of the high-lifting footsteps was the last effort that would be demanded of each leg. When the step was made and he was on two feet again he stood to rest. After every step he rested, one foot forward from the other. He kept from falling, in the wind and on the ice his weight made? of the packed snow, by the same actions he had seen in tightrope walkers. The house was near. He stepped and took his balance. He could see much of the roof now, and past that a mass of treetops that spoke of a deep valley dropping away below the house. At the bottom would be Balantrodoch, where Alexander's heart had been set, and would be again.

Beltran stepped once more and poised himself in his footsteps to rest, with his arms flailing for handholds in the air, and through the snow on which he stood and which in these few days had come to seem to him the very flooring of the world, he fell among three black cattle in a byre, standing warm in their own dung and steaming generously into the cold morning. Two of the beasts danced but soon calmed down to see who had come, and he lay there happy in the warmth, looking up into six brown eyes and a hole in a straw roof, and went to sleep.

He dreamed of firelight and a woman feeding him thin porridge, and a boy with foolish wits standing behind her. When he woke he lay at a fire of wood and true coal, blown to a fierce heat by the wind up the chimney.

"A good chimney," he said.

"Aye," the woman's voice said. "Your friends made it."

She was the same woman of the dream. She was twenty years his junior and full of trouble and fear. He sought the boy and found him on the hearth just behind his head. He was leaning forward, propped on Beltran's sword, his hands on the hilt at a level with his foolish face.

"My friends?" Beltran turned his face to the fire again.

She knelt by him and took his bony arm in both hands. He did not want to see her eyes. He carried his own woe, and kept it deep to wait for his dying; that might well hold off to the evening if the fire went on burning, and while he lived his only care was Alexander's heart.

"There was a box," he said. "A casket." He still looked into the fire. He would not look into her eyes and see grief in them.

There was a moment of waiting and then she laid it on his breast and put his hand on it. "There you are," she said. "That's your wee box, quite safe."

She was no longer holding his arm but he knew she was by his side. He stared at the fire a space longer and turned his head at last. Her eyes were fouled with misery and they were mildly offering that bargain he had sensed of her; we are two people in straits, and we will help each other. I have helped you and you will help me, her pale blue eyes said to him. As if she had said it aloud, he answered her.

"I will be dead tonight," he said. "I am an old man dying. This fire is a great blessing to me, but I got too cold on the plain out there; on the snow. I will be dead tonight, do you see? I can be no help to you. I will be dead tonight."

"Tonight!" she said finely. "Never mind tonight! They will be coming today!"

"Today!" The boy's voice had no meaning in it.

"You are a Templar," she said. She spoke a strange French.

"Yes," he said. "Speak slow. How did you know?"

The boy's hand stroked his face. It was a big hand. Only the silly face said he was a boy; he was her son and might be thirty. For all that they did him no harm, Beltran flinched from the stroking fingers.

"Don't shy off," she said. "It is because he was right about you. He saw that your sword was the same as theirs."

It came to him that she spoke as if the Templars still flourished.

"Madame," he said, "I have been one, but there are no Templars any more."

She met this with a smile so marvellous, of wistfulness soured at birth into despair, that Beltran shuddered.

"There are still Templars at Balantrodoch," she said, "which is at the foot of this glen."

She came to her feet and stood whistling at the fire, a tall woman stiff in the back from sustaining ill fortune. Beltran clutched at the casket, now so near, and confirmed by her words, to its resting place.

"Johnnie," the woman said. "Get milk."

She took the sword from him as he passed and put it up in a corner. "When I talk about it the lad gets in a state," she said. "You'll have wondered we have no dog. They've killed the dog, as an earnest. This noon they will be up to turn me from my house. I am a widow and my son is half-witted, so we will die soon, one or both of us, when they put us out. This time of year," she said, and left it, jerking her head to let the buffets of the gale speak for her.

The boy might take the casket down the steep valley and bury it there. If he could be got to know that it should be buried in the chapel yard, then Alexander would have been well done by. Then the lad could come back and take and bury me, Beltran thought to himself. It would be a burial ground of the Order, he thought, with the Order still here, she says. I will be buried in the Order after all.

"What is it?" the woman said.

Beltran turned his face to the sound but he hardly saw or heard. There is no Order now, he told himself, the Church has ended it. He fought to quell the excitement that surged like heat inside him, inside this failing union of soul and body. Yet if there are Templars here, then the ending of the Order has not reached here, and Beltran may in the meantime die and be buried in the Order; since Beltran is here.

The boy came in with milk in a bowl and she laid the bowl on the hearth. She put fresh wood on the fire and sang a few lines of a song at it.

"Johnnie," she said. "Will you see to feeding the beasts."

The young man went out again.

The woman went on with her story. "The house is my own," she said, "and was my father's. My husband made a lease of it for his own lifetime, to the knights at Balantrodoch. It was a life rent and ended when he died. When my man died, the house was all mine again."

The wind began to move round the house, so that its blows struck upon the stout building of stone from a new quarter. The fire took to fits of flaring up and then by turns cowering under the draught; but there was still little smoke put into the room. It was a good chimney. The Order made good stonework. He had known castles of the Order that might stand forever.

"Do you hear me?" The woman kneeled beside him as she had at first. Smoke came out of the fire and he coughed on it. To cough was a terrible endeavour and suddenly he was filled with weakness and threw his hands in the air. They lifted as far as you would toss a feather.

"Well," the woman said.

The Order's stonework would last forever. The Order's gold would last forever, and not change. The Order would last forever.

The boy came in and piled wood against the wall and the woman put some more on the fire. "The land as well," she said. "The land is mine, my very own. They were quiet enough when I first came back, two years ago but a few months; mighty quiet for such proud folk."

She stood looking into the fire and whistled again, and then sang and again whistled. Then she heaved out a great sigh and looked a bit sideways at her son and, without dismissing him this time, on some errand, went on with her story.

No, Beltran contrived to tell himself, the Order will not last forever, and it has already not lasted forever. As to the stone and the gold, they are no longer the Order's, they are only stone and gold, and there will become of them what will.

"They say they will have my house again," she said, and the boy came into Beltran's sight, bending over and listening to his mother's tale. "The land too," she said. "They say they have their own courts."

"That is your impiety," Beltran adjured Beltran. "That gold trapped you in itself. That is why you worshipped it, because it was sure, and outside the gold was no safety."

The boy was now leaning forward into the firelit space above Beltran's recumbent body, moving like someone in a dance, but slow and stiffly. He lifted one foot widely to the side and laid it gently down, and then lifted and brought down the other, and while he did this he held his hands with the fingers spread wide stretched before him over Beltran's face, and waggled them at the wrist. It was a child's game, or a witch's spell, but neither could touch Beltran now.

"You may bury me out on the moor," Beltran said to him. "The casket, of course, should go in the churchyard of the Order." He thought that he would be fortunate to die now that he had found a clear view of his sin, so that he could take it with him and not leave it hidden back here on the earth. He felt better. The boy, at Beltran's words, had stopped dancing at him. Beltran lay there looking up at the boy. The boy stooped over him, looking down. The woman looked at both of them, and the fire blazed handsomely again as if the wind had returned to a side more favourable to the chimney.

"I think I might get up from here," Beltran said.

When they had him sat on a wooden chest and wrapped him with woollen blankets and were all three taking broth out of bowls a thought came into his head.

"Who is it that comes tonight to put you out of the house?"

She threw her bowl of soup across the room and put her head in her hands and began to weep. It became a storm of weeping. Beltran went on with his broth but the boy hid his eyes until she was finished. She lifted her face and wiped at her eyes with each hand and looked towards Beltran with her lips pulled together and twisted. She would have wished to shout at him, he could tell, but when she said the words she would have shouted, it was almost a whisper.

"The knights, you fool! The Templars, you old fool! Your friends!"

She got up and took more soup and sat again.

"That's rubbish," Beltran said. "They would not steal your house." He remembered. "Besides," he said. "I told you: the Order of the Temple is ended.

This time she laid the soup beside her and nearly brought out a shout. "I know that," she shrieked. "That's what I'm telling you. I mean you told me that, and I'm telling you, if you bide here till they come, you can say to them the Order's ended, and they'll maybe go away again. When the snow's done I could fetch out the king's officer from Edinburgh. If you could get them out of the road tonight their courage might shrink a bit, do you see? I daresay if you did that, there would be a thaw almost at once. That is how things happen. One piece of good fortune will turn up other pieces, and so on. Do you see?"

The boy smiled and laid his head from side to side. The woman looked at Beltran and waited. The fire blossomed, and outside the walls the gale whooped.

Beltran shook his head, but he smiled, and said, "I will do what I can. Whoever they are, they will hardly listen to me. You might be wiser to take garments and provision and hide in the storm."

The woman's face, that had been a little plumped out by expectation, drew gauntly in. "No," she said. "That is my sorrow, that I must stay here, and the boy with me, and face them in my house." She swallowed another of her great sighs and put a hand out to stroke the lad's hair. "Johnnie," she said. "You're a sight after feeding the beasts. You'd best be out of here, and mend the byre roof where our friend came in."

The boy leaned over Beltran and brought his face close to the old man's face, and stroked it again with his fingers, and went out.

It was long before dark that the knights came. In the house, they heard the bellowing of the cattle and a long scream, a scream that howled on and on, from the byre. The woman sat like a statue till the scream stopped.

"Oh Johnnie," she said, and looked at Beltran. "I should just have gone." She looked at Beltran again. "I will not go now," she said.

There was a clank of steel and loud talk and the door came

open as if it had been taken off the latch and lightly pushed. Under the wooden lintel were three faces to be seen, and they were coifed in the mail hood of the Order, and all the rest of them armed according to the Rule, and against the storm and cold were wrapped in the deerskin cloaks of the Order. The wind whisked suddenly into the room and the fire roared and threw ash and smoke into the air. Beltran made himself acquainted with the three faces and with the certainty of intuition he rose from the chest, placed Alexander's heart in its box right in the heart of the fire, and went to the corner where the woman had laid his sword.

"I think you will be pleased enough with that," he said to Alexander. "The ashes will settle hereabouts."

He wondered if he could lift the sword. He must get outside where there was room to swing it. He hoped they would come in and open up the doorway.

The woman pointed a shaking finger at the three knights, and said in a wailing voice that mourned the little hope she had made for herself, "My Johnnie."

One of the knights came stepping into the room with no weapon in his hand. He took her pointing finger in his mailed glove and stood still a moment, and with the same movement that took it from his belt, drew his dagger through the finger so that it came away into his own hand, and then threw it out the door. "Follow it," he said. The woman stood rocking in her pain and would not move. The knight put a hand to her throat and lifting her by the neck hefted her to the door and passed her on to his friends.

He turned to the old man hiding in the corner and looked down the long blade of Beltran's sword. The stroke was good and went in the mouth and out through the back of the head so that the man was quickly dead and let the sword out as he fell.

"I can lift the sword," Beltran said aloud.

He shouted at the men in the door, who were staring at him. "Beauséant," he shouted, and remembering Corberan, he shouted as he went towards the door, "Iron awake."

He did not try to run, simply to get where he wanted. The men were still amazed as he came towards them but one of them fell back from the door to clear his own sword from its scabbard, and Beltran took himself clear through the space and out into the snow.

The woman leaped away over the snow as he came out. He turned and lifted the sword to the height of his breastbone, and hoped it would not fall before the men reached him. They advanced from the firelight like two giants. Beltran looked up into the snowfall and the dark.

"Now," he said.